I0831752

THE MENDELSSOHN MALICE

Also by Alessandra Comini from Sunstone Press

Schiele in Prison
Egon Schiele's Portraits (nominated for the National Book Award)
Gustav Klimt
Egon Schiele
The Changing Image of Beethoven: A Study in Mythmaking
In Passionate Pursuit: A Memoir

The Megan Crespi Mystery Series

Killing for Klimt
The Schiele Slaughter
The Kokoschka Capers
The Munch Murders
The Kollwitz Calamities
The Kandinsky Conundrum
The Mahler Mayhem
The Beethoven Boomerang
The Brahms Bust
The Schumann Shaming

THE MENDELSSOHN MALICE

A Megan Crespi Mystery Series Novel

ALESSANDRA COMINI

SANTA FE

This book is a work of fiction except for historical facts about the lives of Moses, Fanny, and Felix Mendelssohn. Names, places, characters, and incidents are either products of the author's imagination or used fictionally. Any resemblance to actual events or persons, living or dead, is entirely coincidental.

Sunstone books may be purchased for educational, business, or sales promotional use.
For information please write: Special Markets Department, Sunstone Press,
P.O. Box 2321, Santa Fe, New Mexico 87504-2321.
Printed on acid-free paper
♾

Library of Congress Cataloging-in-Publication Data

Names: Comini, Alessandra, author.
Title: The Mendelssohn malice / Alessandra Comini.
Description: Santa Fe, NM : Sunstone Press, [2023] | Series: Megan Crespi mystery series novel ; 11 | Summary: "Researching in Germany and Italy for her biography on 19th century composer Fanny Mendelssohn, Megan Crespi is confronted by modern-day neo-Nazis and neo-Fascists"-- Provided by publisher.
Identifiers: LCCN 2023039858 | ISBN 9781632935410 (paperback)
Subjects: LCSH: Hensel, Fanny Mendelssohn, 1805-1847--Fiction. | Women art historians--Fiction. | Lost works of art--Fiction. | Neo-Nazis--Fiction. | LCGFT: Detective and mystery fiction. | Novels.
Classification: LCC PS3603.O477 M46 2023 | DDC 813.6--dc3/eng/20230905
LC record available at https://lccn.loc.gov/2023039858

WWW.SUNSTONEPRESS.COM
SUNSTONE PRESS / POST OFFICE BOX 2321 / SANTA FE, NM 87504-2321 /USA
(505) 988-4418

DEDICATION

To my "little Sis," indomitable Adriana Comini, unstinting caretaker of animals and their humans

and

To the memory of Simon Sargon, 1938–2022, esteemed colleague, extraordinary composer, and dear friend who joyfully read the manuscript for this book

Wilhelm Hensel, Portrait of his wife, Fanny Mendelssohn Hensel, pencil, 1847 (year of her death), Mendelssohn-Haus, Leipzig.

Left: Wilhelm Hensel, Portrait of Fanny Mendelssohn Hensel, pencil, 1847; Right, Portrait of Felix Mendelssohn, oil,1847.

Caricature of the philosopher Moses Mendelssohn (1729–1786), grandfather of Fanny and Felix Mendelssohn, seeking admittance into Berlin through the City Gate for Jews and Cattle, etching, c. 1765. Jewish Museum, Berlin.

Island of Ponza off the coast of Southern Italy, photograph by Gian Paolo Comini, 1983.

LIST OF MAJOR CHARACTERS

Megan Crespi: retired professor of art history, author, musicologist, and international art crimes investigator

Mary Russell: collaborative pianist and vocal coach in the fields of opera and recital in an international career covering forty years and twenty-five countries

Richard Sire: retired international investment banker, now active world traveler, photographer, and amateur violinist

Jared Oppenheim: basso and composer; founder of the new Mendelssohn Complex in New York City

Michael Bormann: mesmerizing leader of Hamburg's neo-Nazi organization

Rachael Skylar: multi-talented, discerning director of Hamburg's new Fanny and Felix Mendelssohn Museum

Salomon Mendelssohn: direct descendant of Fanny and Felix Mendelssohn's sister Rebecka; lives in Hamburg

Johannes von Bandtrop: meticulous leader of Berlin's neo-Nazi organization

Barbara Badubrecht: Hamburg-born lieutenant of Bandtrop, assigned to Hamburg

Simon Saragn: renowned composer based in America

Nathaniel Darenborne: world famous conductor born in Argentina

Helmut von Bandtrop: impulsive teenage son of Johannes von Bandtrop

Homer Wesselmann: icy-eyed "independent" member of Hamburg's neo-Nazi organization

Tina Crespi: younger sister of Megan Crespi with two overriding interests: creating fiber and glass art and the ethical treatment of animals

Nathan Bartholdy: direct descendant of Fanny Mendelssohn; lives in Rome and claims he has discovered an unknown oil portrait of her

Giorgio Complice: professional painter working for Nathan Bartholdy

Alessandro Divitore: served with pride under Italy's dazzling prime minister Mario Draghi until the recent successful revolt of the 5 Star Movement

Ursula Ladro: observant, ambitious cleaning lady for Nathan Bartholdy and wife of Carlo Ladro

Carlo Ladro: hearse driver for Rome's *Obitorio Scaduti e Figli* and husband of Ursula Ladro

Cesari Cacciatore: Rome's Chief of Police and friend of Alessandro Divitore

Amadeo Seguire: respected private detective in Rome

Vittorio (Vitto) Trovato: young detective, works for Amadeo Seguire in Rome

Homer Capo: proprietor of Rome's historic Caffè Greco

Tullio Guido: Colosseum guide knowledgeable about Rome's Lazio region

Arlotto Zitto: dedicated Roman neo-Fascist assigned to surveillance work

Devora Rossi Finzi: owner of Grand Hotel Palace in Terracina and wife of Medad Finzi

Medad Finzi: director of Grand Hotel Palace in Terracina and husband of Devora Rossi Finzi

1

"*Because that is simply not the way it works!*"

"But..."

"I can only authenticate the portrait after I've seen it in person, not via photographs, no matter how high the quality. However, I will be in Rome next week. You can contact and show it to me then if you wish."

This was the way retired professor of art history, musicologist, author, and occasional international art crimes investigator Megan Crespi had ended the urgent phone call initiated by a garrulous man who identified himself as Nathan Bartholdy calling from Rome. He claimed that he had discovered an unknown oil portrait of the granddaughter of famed eighteenth-century German philosopher Moses Mendelssohn. Her name was Fanny Mendelssohn Bartholdy Hensel. But Megan Crespi was at that very moment boarding a plane in Dallas and she had quickly terminated the peculiar if somewhat intriguing conversation with the stranger who had managed to call her from Rome. Was the man contacting her in her capacity of solving art and music crimes, or had he read her most recent publication?

After the success of her book *Reverence and Disrespect: Clara Schumann Across the Centuries,* Megan, a sprightly woman in her eighties with sparkling brown eyes and renewable brown hair, was taking a flight from Dallas, via a plane change in London, to Hamburg in order to beam her scholarly, some might say feminist, flashlight upon one of virtuoso pianist Clara Schumann's most impressive musical contemporaries. This time it was composer/pianist Fanny Mendelssohn, older-by-four-years sister of composer/pianist/

conductor Felix Mendelssohn. The two musicians' careers were both sadly short: Fanny died in 1847 at the age of forty-one, Felix died six months later the same year at the age of thirty-seven; both of fatal strokes. To indicate their respective places in the musical world of nineteenth-century early Romanticism, some wags referred to them as "Felix F major" and "Fanny F minor"—"*F dur und F moll.*" One of Megan's aims for her as yet untitled new book was to illuminate what recent scholarship had revealed considering the surprising span and weight of Fanny's musical legacy.

Megan's travel companion on the trip was Mary Russell, who had recently earned her Ph.D. in music history, thus capping her profession as collaborative pianist and vocal coach in the fields of opera and recitals. In a career covering forty years, her profession had taken her far afield: Canada, England, Ireland, Latvia, Lithuania, Germany, Switzerland, Italy, Japan, and China. For thirty-one of those years she had lived and taught in Paris.

Megan and Mary had three things in common: both had been born in Minnesota, both had attended the National Music Camp in Interlochen, Michigan, and both were world travelers who had ended up residing happily in Dallas. Hard for some people to come to terms with. Megan occasionally recalled with amusement how, during the opening of an exhibition of works by the Austrian Expressionist artist Egon Schiele which she had curated for New York's Neue Galerie Museum, a visitor had asked where she lived. When she answered "Dallas" the man reacted in shock, sneering "Dallas? *Why?*" Her immediate, gut answer had been "Why *not*?" For Megan the city provided genial temperatures, green neighborhoods, and friendly faces. After many years of apartment living in New York, Vienna, and San Francisco, having an actual house for herself, her books, her musical instruments, her art collection, and her Maltese dog Button was ideal.

Mary, a generation younger than Megan and also once a dog owner, had offered to do the driving for their research in Germany and Italy. She was distinctive looking, with merry blue eyes and auburn hair covered by an unusual natural topping of white.

The two convivial colleagues had planned their itinerary to begin in the old Hanseatic port city of Hamburg, birthplace of both Fanny and Felix Mendelssohn as well as Johannes Brahms. In the

"Composers Quarter" at Hamburg-Neustadt, the three composers plus Gustav Mahler, honored for his years of conducting in Hamburg during the eighteen nineties, all had museums dedicated to them. Recently, in twenty eighteen, the city had created a Fanny and Felix Mendelssohn Museum.

Then it would be on to historically liberal Berlin where Fanny and Felix's banker uncle Joseph and their banker father Abraham moved their families in 1811. The change in location was due to two things. First, beneficial societal factors in Berlin had recently lifted prominent Jews out of the ghetto and accorded them the privileged status of a new term: German Jews. The prime example was Moses Mendelssohn. Second, was the Mendelssohn family bank's role in breaking Napoleon's Continental System blockade. Fear of French reprisal had actually forced the family to leave Hamburg, then occupied by French troops, in the dark of night and in disguise according to family legend. The J. & A. Mendelssohn bank was successfully reestablished in Berlin and would remain at its Jägerstrasse fifty one address until the Nazis closed it down in 1938.

Megan and Mary's stay in Berlin would coincide with the opening of an unusual exhibition of historic photographs taken by Mary's British partner Richard Sire—known simply as Sire—who had also chosen Dallas as his home. Tall, slim, with short-clipped wavy white hair and hazel eyes, he was a retired international investment banker and a still-active world traveler, persistent photographer, and amateur violinist. His Berlin exhibition would feature haunting images of the beauty of Afghanistan he had taken some thirty years earlier and, more up to date, some he had taken after the recent American withdrawal from the country.

Then, after attending the premiere of a contemporary requiem by a friend and colleague of Megan's, the reunited trio would fly to Italy, using Rome as their base, with a specific mission. They wished to search out the places and remember in situ the historic persons Fanny and her husband, court painter Wilhelm Hensel, had visited during the happiest period of their lives—a productive year's sojourn in Italy from August 1839 to September 1840, of which six glorious months had been spent in Rome.

Also upon arrival in Rome Megan would be joined by her younger sister Tina, dedicated animal lover who was attending an international conference of PETA—People for the Ethical Treatment of Animals. Active in Dallas on behalf of animal rights, genial, persuasive, and tireless Tina had been the productive president of the local PETA organization for several terms. Her stay in Rome coincided with a two-week class on glass and fiber-working, a course that fit in handsomely with her own interest in glass art and fiber art. Although the two sisters couldn't be more different in their interests, they were supportive, appreciative friends and frequently traveled together. And they shared a love of dogs. Megan's canine companion was an adorable Maltese named Button who responded to commands in three languages—English, Italian, and German. And he was learning French. Four Japanese Chins vied for Tina's attention, and when she was out of town they enthusiastically stayed with Bill Frait, a genial neighbor who owned two Chins himself. Presently, with both sisters out of town, Button had joined Tina's vacationing canines. And thanks to Ring Security Europe, the two traveling sisters were able to observe and hail their beloved canines whenever time permitted.

But right now Hamburg was first on the agenda for Megan and Mary. And there, the afternoon of their arrival on Monday morning, they had scheduled a visit to Salomon Mendelssohn, a direct descendant of Fanny and Felix's sister Rebecka.

Now ninety-seven years old, he was one of the few survivors amongst some eleven thousand Jews sent to the Nazi concentration camp at Dachau. What fascinating topics might their discussion cover, Megan wondered with anticipation, and what a remarkable man he must be.

2

Everyone Jared Oppenheim knew in New York told him what a fabulous idea he had to create a Mendelssohn Complex in The Big Apple. It would be an archive for the hundreds of newly discovered family letters, portrait drawings, and music autographs by Fanny and Felix in the collection of the late Herschel Hirschstein of Riverdale, New York. Bachelor Hirschstein had willed the extraordinary trove of Mendelssohniana to his esteemed bachelor "son," voice teacher Jared. They had long discussed how such a musical legacy could also serve as an active salon for musical performances, just as Fanny Mendelssohn's Berlin salon had been in the nineteenth century. What a combination that would make: previously unknown music by Fanny and Felix premiered at the Complex. This live music aspect was especially dear to the talented, forty-year-old Jared. Tall, brown-eyed, with closely trimmed facial hair, he was an especially deep-voiced basso, able pianist, and innovative chamber-opera composer—all of which linked him closely to the world of music.

Publicity for the project was supportive, and to help raise funds Jared set a televised example by making a splashy first donation of one hundred thousand dollars. As the son of a local Jewish real estate tycoon, he was able to do so comfortably. Yes, he had wealth but no stable, satisfying profession. Establishment of a Mendelssohn Complex could give Jared a greater purpose in life. His financial gift was instantly used to secure choice space in one of the tall buildings on West 56th Street to the right of Lincoln Center. This inspired others, and copy-cat donations flowed in and within a month the Complex was open, complete with a board of directors.

Imagine, then, Jared Oppenheim's stunned disbelief when that board named a retired professor of musicology at Hunter College, Dr. Monica Sallinger, as its director.

To gain perspective and regain calm, Oppenheim decided to quit New York for a while and visit a new Fanny and Felix Mendelssohn Museum in Germany. He'd not been to Hamburg before and so it should be doubly interesting since he had discovered the museum was in an area called "Composers Quarter" which housed other museums devoted to musicians in an impressive span of periods dating from the eighteenth to the twentieth century.

His transatlantic flight departed the States one day after Megan and Mary's.

3

With an outstanding arrest warrant hanging over his head, enthusiastic neo-Nazi, Hamburg-based Michael Bormann had come to a decision. The tall, blond, fifty-something-year-old mesmerizing orator would urge his large, like-minded group of followers *not* to join the demonstrations planned to take place at tomorrow evening's performance of the all-Black ballet company *Noir* inside the city's innovative Kampnagel. No, they needed a new kind of target for their racial superiority message and he had something quite different in mind.

For several years now, a disgusted Bormann had avoided even driving by a new entity the misguided city of Hamburg had recently forced upon its citizens. It occupied quarters at Peterstrasse 29 in the so-called Composers Quarter of the city's old Altstadt district and its rebarbative name was Fanny and Felix Mendelssohn Museum. Its director, Rachael Skylar, would have to cope with a shockingly undesirable publicity. Taking a page from Russian president Vladimir Putin's accusatory Ukrainian playbook, he and his followers would stage a demonstration outside the building in which the museum was housed. They would be carrying signs that read "Support neo-Nazi director Rachael Skylar!" Of course as a Jew she wasn't one, but television and press coverage would lap up the surprise accusation and havoc would reign. It would result in public discussion of the pros and cons of neo-Nazism. Not a bad consequence for his party. Amazing he hadn't thought of this before! He would set the date for this coming Wednesday morning.

4

Director Rachael Sklyar knew immediately she had been born for the position. A pianist of considerable talent, an excellent sight reader, and a respected musicologist, she had been fascinated since she was a teenager by the Mendelssohn siblings and their achievements. The beauty and energy of Felix's overture *A Midsummer Night's Dream*—composed at the age of seventeen and a half—won her admiration and love when she herself was a teenager and led her to Felix's *Incidental Music to A Midsummer Night's Dream* of 1842 for the eponymous Shakespeare play. On the way, thanks to Felix's instrumentation, she learned that the ophicleide he called for is a conical-bore, keyed brass instrument similar to a tuba and just right for comical emphasis. She adored its donkey heehaws in the music score. In fact, she had impishly directed that an ophicleide be hung over a new exhibition case featuring the prize of the Fanny and Felix Mendelssohn Museum. It was the recently discovered original score to the overture which, after twenty-year-old Felix had conducted the piece in London, had been entrusted to a fellow composer who had inadvertently left it in a carriage at the after-concert festivities. An undaunted Felix had rewritten the score from memory. To have such a stellar Mendelssohn object in her museum was a triumph. One that outshone by far the holdings of a new Mendelssohn collection in America called the Mendelssohn Complex located in New York City.

The day after tomorrow, Wednesday, was slated to be an interesting day for Skylar. Two American scholars from Dallas were meeting with her at eleven in the morning to discuss and see the various holdings her museum possessed. The publicity over the original score to Felix's *A Midsummer's Night Dream Overture* had reached as far as Texas. And then another American scholar, from New York City, one connected with the Mendelssohn Complex, had booked an appointment to see her at two o'clock the same day.

5

After Megan and Mary had taken their seats on the second lap of their flight to Hamburg, both were wide awake that Monday morning, having slept well on the overnight flight from Dallas to London. They began to discuss Fanny Mendelssohn Bartholdy Hensel in regard to Clara Wieck Schumann, the subject of Megan's last book.

"Of course I've played a few Lieder by Clara for my singers—the gorgeous song '*Am Strande*'—'At the Beach,' for example—but I've never performed a Fanny song. Strange, huh?" asked Mary.

"Not really. Neither Fanny's father nor even brother Felix encouraged her to publish. They shared the nineteenth-century position that a woman's place is in the home. You know of course the embarrassing story about Felix, when performing privately for Queen Victoria and Prince Albert at Buckingham Palace."

"Oh yes, I remember!" Mary exclaimed, laughing. "How Victoria requested that he play her favorite song by him—'*Italien*'—and he had to admit with chagrin that it actually wasn't composed by him but by his sister Fanny. He had published it and a few other of her songs in with his own so that at least they'd be sung."

"Nice, but duplicitous," murmured Megan.

"So tell me, how many of Fanny's pieces were included in the new treasure trove of unknown works that was given to the Mendelssohn Complex in New York recently?"

"Well, one source I trust says she composed...hold on, I've got it on my iPhone...okay, here it is: exactly four hundred and sixty-six pieces of music!"

"Wow, that's impressive for any composer, I'd say." Megan nodded and continued.

"That number includes two hundred and fifty songs and a hundred and twenty-five piano works. And in addition she composed quite a bit of chamber music, including a frequently performed Trio in D Minor for piano, violin, and cello. I've watched and listened to it on YouTube several times and it's very powerful. Just imagine how exciting those Sunday performances were at her Berlin salon!"

"Ah, to have been at one of them. To have *seen* and *heard* her play!" moaned Mary rolling her eyes heavenward. "Perhaps they'll make a movie about her and we can 'watch' her play."

"Which actress do you think should be Fanny?"

"Hmm," pondered Mary. "She was a small woman so it can't be anyone tall. I'd go for a young Judi Dench."

"Maybe. But can you think, more suitably, of a *Jewish* actress in her young years?"

"Not offhand. Umm. Whom do you have in mind, Megan?"

"How about a young Barbra Streisand?"

"Yes!" Mary exclaimed. "Could have been perfect. And wouldn't she have loved to play such a role."

"Don't put it in the past tense. She's alive and thriving with all her political and philanthropic causes."

"True. Great. Now let's get back to Fanny. You were telling me about her four hundred and sixty-six compositions."

"Right. In addition to the kinds of genres I've already mentioned, she also composed an orchestral overture—her only known orchestral work—concert arias, and three sacred a capella cantatas."

"She even wrote cantatas?"

"You bet. And the most famous of them was one she composed in support of victims of the plague that took hold of Berlin, as well as other parts of Germany and Europe in eighteen thirty-one and thirty-two."

"Goodness! A plague. How history repeats itself! What did she call her cantata?"

"She originally titled it *Oratorio on Words from the Bible*, but it became known as the *Cholera Cantata—Musik für die Toten der Cholera Epidemie—Music for the Dead of the Cholera Epidemic*."

"How suitable for our own times!"

"That's what I hope my book on Fanny will demonstrate: that her music is still viable, suitable, still worthy of posterity. After all, in hindsight she turns out to be the nineteenth-century's most important woman composer in all of Europe."

"I'm beginning to see why. And your book, Megan. Do you have a title for it yet?"

"Not yet. Any ideas?"

"*The Other Mendelssohn*?"

"I'm afraid that one's already taken."

"Okay. I'll keep working on it. Your description of her work is *fanny*ing the flames."

"Mary, that pun is beneath you."

Before Mary could answer, a man's voice sounded over the speaker: "Ladies and gentlemen, we are about to land in Hamburg. Please close your trays and fasten your seatbelts."

As both women traveled only with roller bags, they were among the first to claim a taxi after passing through customs. Megan had made the hotel reservations for the trip and her instructions to the smiling woman driver were simple and precise.

"Please take us to the hotel Scandic Hamburg Emporio in Neustadt—Dammtorwall nineteen." Mary smiled with pleasure.

"Neustadt? Oh, how wonderfully convenient! We'll be near the Fanny and Felix Mendelssohn Museum."

"Exactly. And it took some research to find the hotel, but I think we'll like it. And just for you, my friend, it has a gym."

"Perfect! Will you use it too?"

"No. I'll be using the pool that's there. My snorkel and swimsuit are in the bottom of my bag."

"I don't use a snorkel but, ha, ha, there's a swimsuit in my bag, too."

"You win! The hotel is all very modern and, as they advertise, 'eco-friendly,' whatever that actually means. The rooms are quiet, have huge ceiling-to-floor windows, nice double beds, wooden furnishings, tea and coffee makings, and great bathrooms. At least so the reviews and photos indicate."

Twenty-five minutes later they had checked in, located their double room on the fifth floor, opened their bags, washed up, and were back downstairs devouring a delicious breakfast. The only down part was that the breakfast was not included in the hotel price. But no matter. It was now ten o'clock and they were ready to book an Uber to take them to the assisted living facility where ninety-seven-year-old Salomon Mendelssohn awaited them.

6

Why not have a *double* demonstration while he was at it?

Michael Bormann nodded vigorous agreement with himself at the inspired thought. Both institutions were in the same part of Hamburg's Altstadt, the Composers Quarter, after all. His primary target was the Fanny and Felix Mendelssohn Museum and its Jewish director, some woman named Rachael Skylar. But an equally offensive museum was also in the district: the Gustav Mahler Museum. And that Jew composer wasn't even from Hamburg! In fact he wasn't even German! He was Austrian. Mahler himself used to say that he was three times homeless: "as a native of Bohemia in Austria, as an Austrian among Germans, and as a Jew throughout the world." Well, Bormann had no argument with that.

Another irritating factor about the Composers Quarter area was that crybaby city officials had allowed small brass memorial plaques, *Stolpersteine—stumbling stones*, to be set into certain city streets and sidewalks listing the names of the local Jewish inhabitants who had been deported and killed during the Holocaust. Will they never let it go, Bormann asked the air angrily.

He had also noted an interesting fact: while the Brahms and composer Georg Philipp Telemann Museums had been opened back in 1971, the two museums devoted to Jewish Mahler and the Mendelssohn siblings, weren't established until 2018. This was a frightening indicator of the growth of Jew sympathy in his beloved Hamburg: a phenomenon that he articulated repeatedly in speeches at his antisemitic rallies. He would harp on this again tomorrow at the demonstrations in front of the Mahler Museum and the Mendelssohn Museum. The latter one really irked him: why feature two composers of the past when most people nowadays don't even know who they were? And especially the sister. A *woman* composer? Come on now. Time to apply the brakes and stop circulating feminist claims! Even in his own private sphere, how many times did he have to tell his wife to stop aspiring to finish her university studies when it was their twins, Adolf and Eva, who needed her, their home who needed her, *he* who needed her!

But now there was work to be done before Wednesday. Two lieutenants were already rounding up the 500-plus member organization. Their Berlin counterpart, with many more adherents, had agreed to join the demonstration. And Bormann needed to compose the chants and update his own message as he aimed at a new public disgrace. The first demo would be at ten tomorrow morning in front of the Mahler Museum. An hour later, as media interest grew, it would be in front of the Mendelssohn Museum. And at noon the demonstration would chant in front of the nearby Hamburg Museum which hypocritically maintained a permanent exhibition about the history of Jews in Hamburg. That evening's news would be full of gratis publicity and perhaps the citizens of Hamburg might finally be getting tired of all this crazy new Jew love their city was paying lip service to.

One more thing brought a rare expression to Bormann's face. It was a smile. A genius idea concerning the image for tomorrow's demonstration posters had just come to him. It would wow onlookers, to say nothing of attracting press and TV coverage.

7

Salomon Mendelssohn's Hamburg assisted living facility, called *Zweite Jugend*—Second Youth, was in the green Blankenese district, west of the city and overlooking the Elbe River. Winding brick paths punctuated the greenery of the steep hills rising from the riverbank. Although the morning was overcast an abundance of wild flowers lit up the landscape through which their Uber was traveling.

"What a beautiful site for a retirement home," commented Megan, gazing around. Mary nodded in appreciative agreement.

As they rode, Mary tried again to reach Sire in Berlin on her cellphone. And again there was no answer; not even a recorded message asking the caller to leave a message.

"I wonder what's the matter with his phone?" she asked Megan.

"Probably organization of his exhibition is taking all of his time," Megan suggested.

"Yes, but if he's too busy to answer, the recording of his voice asking callers to please leave messages and he'll call back—that message doesn't play. Strange."

Eventually their Uber driver pulled into a gravel parking lot surrounded by young juniper trees framing a modern, rectangular, two-story building with stone fronting.

Minutes later they were walking into the *Zweite Jugend* lobby and before they could reach the reception desk a man's voice called out to them.

"Professor Megan Crespi?" he asked in English.

Megan turned and saw a slender, elderly man with long white hair and flowing beard who looked to be in his seventies, not nineties, sitting across from them in the seat of a rollator walker.

"Yes. And you have to be Herr Mendelssohn!"

"Indeed I am. How nice to meet you. And your friend is...?"

"This is my dear colleague Doctor Mary Russell. She is a vocal coach who has traveled the world as collaborative pianist for recitals and operas."

"But! So also was I in my middle years! Worked at our Hamburg State Opera in the late 'sixties through the early 'nineties. It was during my time there that we became the first company to broadcast its operas in color on television."

"Goodness! And what was the first opera you broadcast in full color?" asked Mary in happy surprise.

"What else but *Le Nozze di Figaro*? Mozart is my great love."

"This is a dimension of you we certainly didn't know about, Herr Mendelssohn," Megan smiled, then continued. "But can we be sure you are Salomon Mendelssohn? We're supposed to be meeting a ninety-seven-year-old man here, not one who by his looks is only in his seventies."

"Ha! Thank you. It is just the luck of good hormones and decades of daily exercise. There are wonderful hiking trails here in Blankenese. That's why I decided to 'retire' here some twenty years ago rather than remain in the crowded heart of Hamburg with all its hustle and bustle. And now I am the oldest resident of this elder home." Salomon's voice lowered and took on a bitter tone.

"Unfortunately, I can no longer hike, scarcely even walk!"

Mary and Megan nodded with respect and expressed admiration for how he was dealing with his handicap.

"No, no. Thank you, but there is nothing to congratulate me on. I am spiritually and psychologically ready to go. It is only my permanently aching body that is stubbornly clinging to life on this planet."

Not knowing quite what to say, Mary asked a question.

"And what do you think of the new Fanny and Felix Mendelssohn Museum? That is why we've come. Megan here, having written a well-received book on Clara Schumann, is researching for a book she now wants to write on Fanny."

"Ah ha! Shall we go outside and sit on the terrace to talk?"

Herr Mendelssohn slowly stood up and began with the help of his walker laboriously moving toward a door opposite the entrance.

With Mary going ahead of him to open it, they passed through into a beautifully maintained patio lined with rising rows of lilies, daisies, roses, and chrysanthemums.

"Here, let's sit at this table," suggested their fragile host. "It has the best panorama of the hillside above us. I used to love mounting the steep path you can see winding up there."

The next hour was filled with talk about the extensive Mendelssohn dynasty over four centuries, beginning with Fanny's renowned grandfather, Moses Mendelssohn, who died in 1786 at the age of fifty-six. Discussion ranged across several countries of family migrations, including a third cousin, Nathan, whose great-great-grandmother was Fanny herself. Nathan's Italian opera-loving grandparents migrated to Rome and joined the local Jewish community there of about 15,000—a number which has grown to double that in the twenty-first century.

The fascinating if complicated conversation returned to family founder Moses Mendelssohn, who tried to reconcile life as a traditional Jew with the idea of being integrated into modern secular society, something he did with success in his own life. His bold ideas questioned traditional authority and championed rational change.

Salomon gave his rapt audience-of-two some background on the man including one particular fact neither one of them had known about. He touched upon his famous ancestor's roots as penniless child of the Jewish ghetto in Dessau, his self-taught knowledge of languages including German, which brought him out of the world of Yiddish and Hebrew and gave him cause to be the first to call himself a "German Jew." Salomon characterized Moses's move to the liberal Berlin of King Friedrich II and the growing circle of contacts that lifted him out of poverty and placed him as intellectual equal and close friend of the famous playwright and writer of aesthetics and philosophy, Gotthold Ephraim Lessing. And finally Salomon touched upon a personal aspect of the great philosopher.

"Moses was diagnosed with a mild form of familial dysautonomia, which is a hereditary disease of Ashkenazi Jews. What it often manifests is a disparity in shoulder heights and curvature of the spine which can be pronounced, leading to the term 'hunchback.'"

Neither Megan nor Mary were aware of this affliction in

connection with the great philosopher. Nor were they prepared for what Salomon said next.

"And some descendants of Moses also unfortunately manifested the disease, including the Mendelssohn you are interested in, Fanny." Megan's jaw dropped.

"*What*! I have not come across that. Are you certain?"

"Of course I am certain. And there is a subtle allusion to its presence in the four-year-old child in a letter Fanny's mother wrote to a cousin in Vienna about the birth of her next child, Felix. She referred obliquely to the family situation by mentioning that the newborn son promises to be 'more pretty'—implying that his sister was not. The curvature of her spine as she grew older was by no means deforming, yet inescapably noticeable. And one shoulder was noticeably higher than the other."

"But what about the many pencil *portraits* of Fanny drawn by her artist husband Wilhelm Hensel?" Megan asked, still stunned. "You don't see curvature of the spine or shoulders out of joint in any of them."

"And you don't ever see her from the side, do you? Hensel adored her. His sketches are always made from the front. And petite Fanny had early on developed a way of sitting, with her arms folded in front of her, thus raising her shoulders to almost the same height and minimizing the curve in her back. You've seen the formal portrait sketches of her. They are mostly made by Hensel who knew and sketched her as a very young girl and then at various stages of their happy marriage. He certainly did not want to draw attention to her uneven shoulders."

"Of course. It's been heartening to learn that he also supported her as a performer and a composer. And he didn't burden her with a bevy of little ones, as did Robert Schumann his wife Clara," said Mary, joining the conversation.

Megan added a comment. "Both were content with their one son, Sebastian, named in honor of Fanny's favorite composer, Johann Sebastian Bach. Fanny did suffer two miscarriages, and Sebastian was the only child the couple had and he grew up, as you well know, Sir, to be his parents' invaluable biographer."

The modern-day Mendelssohn looked at his two visitors silently for a few seconds.

"Just so you both know, and you're sure to come across a reproduction of it in your studies eventually, there does exist a drawing of a petite, somewhat older Fanny seen full length from the side as she plays the piano, seated on a pillow in an armchair and only if one knows about it, one can perceive the slightest of humps. The drawing was executed from memory in Rome in eighteen forty-five—sadly just two years before her early death—by one of Hensel's adoring students, August Kaselowsky. Five years earlier Kaselowsky, during the family's stay in Rome, had painted a half-length portrait of Fanny's then nine-year-old son, Sebastian."

"Thank you, Herr Mendelssohn. I'll certainly hunt down that drawing and that painting," Megan said gratefully, entering the artist's name into her phone.

"Herr Mendelssohn," asked Mary, "considering that photography was introduced into the world in eighteen thirty-nine, eight years before Fanny's death, have you ever wondered if there might be photographs of her and Felix somewhere?"

"Actually I have thoroughly researched that, so hoping the answer would be yes. But to my knowledge there are none. I learned that portrait photography only came into fashion in the late eighteen forties and fifties. That's why, for example, we do have photographs of the younger Robert and Clara Schumann."

"Well, then, which portraits of Fanny do you like?" Mary pressed, smiling. Salomon's answer was immediate.

"I like the ones that record rather than minimize her beautiful Jewish looks: black hair, thick eyebrows, large dark eyes, long nose, and full lips. A three hundred Deutsche Pfennig stamp honoring her came out here in Germany in nineteen eighty-nine before we went euro and it was a good thing her name was on it because she had acquired a twentieth century Aryan look." Salomon laughed heartily along with his guests. He took up the subject again.

"And one more thing while we're talking about postage stamps. The Republic of Liberia is crazy about pictorial stamps and seeks out cultural figures to honor. They have produced not one but two in regard to Fanny. One shows her with Felix with their names and dates; the other, value of fifty Liberian dollars, shows just Fanny alone and reproduces the, in my opinion, best image ever made of her."

"Ah. That has to be the eighteen forty-two oil portrait by the

Jewish painter Moritz Daniel Oppenheim," pronounced Megan, smiling with certainty.

"Exactly!" Salomon was delighted with his visitor's answer. "He was just five years older than Fanny and they got along splendidly. Later he became the official Rothschild family portraitist."

"I love his portrait of her," said Megan. "To me it is the essential Fanny Mendelssohn Bartholdy Hensel: courageous, bright, creative, knowledgeable, and loving, yet somehow with a hint of inner Weltschmerz."

"This is extraordinary. You have summed up my feelings about Fanny's portrait exactly." Elatedly, Salomon grasped Megan's hand in his. Then he thought for a moment and asked both visitors a question.

"How is it that you two knew about my familial relationship in the first place and how to contact me in Hamburg?" Megan answered.

"Oh, it was Director Rachael Skylar of your Fanny and Felix Mendelssohn Museum. She kindly answered my letter, in which I wrote I was coming to Hamburg and would like to meet her and see her museum. She wrote me about you and your direct descent from Fanny Mendelssohn Bartholdy Hensel's sister Rebecka, to use Fanny's two maiden surnames and her married name in that order. Now how could I pass up such an opportunity to speak with a third cousin of Fanny's through her sister Rebecka?"

"I see. And did she tell you there is another Mendelssohn who is also still here on planet Earth and is a direct descendant of Fanny herself through her son Sebastian?"

"No. Not yet. We meet with her on Wednesday morning."

"Well, by all means ask her about my third cousin, Nathan Bartholdy, when you talk with her. As for Director Skylar, I have not met her in person, but from our many phone conversations she seems to be a most convivial spirit."

"You've not met her in person?" Mary asked in surprise.

"No. She's been too occupied to visit me here and I have not wanted to chance a visit to her museum without someone to help me overcome the obstacles this goddamn vise I'm in presents me." Salomon hit his wheelchair dramatically with the knuckles of his left hand.

"But surely you have friends who could accompany you, help you?"

"No. Not anymore. They're all dead." Megan was alarmed at the man's somber tone.

"But this situation, the fact that you've not been to your famous relatives' museum nor met its director in person can be remedied. Consider *us* your friends and allow us to bring you with us when we visit Skylar at her museum on Wednesday morning. Please! Let us swing by and pick you up."

"Mobility is not a problem," added Mary reassuringly.

"You think not? In my case it is. I simply cannot *move* my body anymore. Only with the greatest of pain. And then there's my balance, my fear of falling." There was a brief silence, then the elderly man spoke again.

"But with two of you accompanying me perhaps . . ."

"No perhaps. Prepare to be picked up and packed into a car at precisely nine-thirty in the morning, day after tomorrow, Wednesday." Megan was not to be answered in the negative. After a moment of silence Salomon's gloomy expression turned into a sparkling smile.

"All right. Yes. I will be ready. And thank you, *meine Damen*, thank you! You have brought me sunshine."

8

Jared Oppenheim's eight-hour flight from New York to Hamburg deposited him in the busy city a few minutes before nine that early Tuesday morning. He immediately took a taxi to the city's westernmost borough Altona, on the right bank of the River Elbe. Even though physically far from the center, Altona supposedly got its name from merchants who complained that the big city was "*all zu nah*—all too near" their shops.

Jared had chosen to stay in Altona because it contained a major testament related to the history of Jews in the Hamburg area: the two-acre Jewish Cemetery of Altona Königstrasse, laid out in 1611. Better put, Jared thought, it was two large contiguous Jewish cemeteries, both going back to the seventeenth century. One was the Ashkenazi part, with some 6,500 tombstones honoring those Jews whose ancestors were from central and eastern Europe, and the other was the Sephardic section of 1,600 ornamented and inscribed tombstones as decorated by descendants of those Portuguese Jews who were baptized against their will and forced to emigrate in the late fifteenth century. The Sephardic gravestones were lying slabs or tent-shaped stones; the Ashkenazi ones stood upright. The variety and beauty of the inscriptions and decorations was something to behold, even though so many of the gravestones remained in fragments due to Nazi vandals during World War II.

Although he was not particularly religious, Jared felt an inexplicable obligation to spend some hours at the hallowed grounds. He would first check into the Altona designer lodgings of Boston Hotel Hamburg, noted for its enormous bathrooms—something he always luxuriated in when traveling.

Then it would be on to the poignant lessons awaiting him at Altona's Jewish Cemetery.

9

It was a problem Rachael Skylar was grappling with that had nothing to do with her museum. She needed to find a way to explain to her five-year-old son Davyd why his father—his Táto—had suddenly left them to return to the land of his birth, Ukraine. Nazar Skylar's parents still lived there in Kyiv and while Rachael understood and fully sympathized with her husband's need to return to his devastated country, explaining such a thing to their anxious little boy was daunting. She did not want to scare him with descriptive information about what was going on in his Táto's country, but she wanted to explain his sudden absence as having to do with visiting his faraway parents.

And so she played and sang a little song to him instead. The words she wrote were:

We miss Táto, we miss Táto very much
Where is Táto? Where is Táto? He is out of touch
Táto is with his Mama. She misses him very much
Táto is with his Táto who misses him very much
And your Táto loves you and he loves his own Táto too
So soon they will come and be all together with you

The words seemed to comfort little Davyd and the melody, of course, was one of Fanny Mendelssohn's songs, a spirited march composed in 1843 titled "When We Move Through the Villages," Opus 398.

10

Tuesday for Megan and Mary was without appointments but with plenty to do. Both wanted to see as much as they could at Hamburg's abundant museums. The choice was overwhelming, but they had narrowed their list down to three: the city's main art museum—*Hamburger Kunsthalle*, the museum for art and industry—*Museum für Kunst und Gewerbe*, and, opened in 2007 and new to them both, the International Maritime Museum. All three museums were near the city's main train station and from there could be reached by bus or on foot. They decided to take on the Maritime first while energy was at top level. But before that they would prepare themselves with a bit of splurging at the delicious buffet breakfast their hotel did not include in its price.

By opening time at ten, thanks to their preordered Uber, they were in front of Warehouse B, an ancient ten-story, red brick quayside building in the port city's historic Speicherstadt, the largest warehouse district in the world. A plaque by the entrance informed them that the building stood on a timber-pile foundation of oak logs.

"Are we sure we want to go inside?" Mary whispered, only half in jest.

What they were about to enter was a vast building devoted to the world's largest private collection of maritime treasures and trinkets from three thousand years of naval history. Ingeniously laid out on the ten "decks" were items and subjects ranging from 2600 ship models, including one of the Queen Mary 2 constructed from 780,000 Logo bricks, to five thousand sea panoramic paintings and graphics, to 50,000 ship construction plans, to a history of piracy. In addition, the museum's ten decks contained historic uniforms, nautical devices and maritime objects, as well as 1.5 million photographs, and more than 2,000 films.

All this was explained on plaques and information screens. One could either take a guided tour or wander independently. The duo from Dallas chose the latter and soon chanced upon what would win the prize as the most ghoulish object in the museum: the skull of notorious fourteenth-century pirate Klaus Störtebeker, hunted down and beheaded in Hamburg.

After careful study and Megan's predictable photographic recording on her "iCamera" of intriguing objects and exhibitions on all ten decks, the two tourists from Dallas exited the atmospheric building, almost staggering from the standing they had been engaged in for, it turned out, an unnoticed three and a half hours. What a spellbinding museum!

"Well, we're certainly ready for lunch," Megan said, "so I wonder, just to save time, how about eating at the Japanese café inside the *Museum für Kunst und Gewerbe*?" She knew that this huge museum would be next on Mary's list because of its notable collection of keyboard instruments.

"Great idea and suddenly I'm hungry," responded Mary.

They caught a bus heading toward Hamburg's main train station and soon dismounted in front of the capacious three=story beige museum building on Steintorplatz. The Japanese café was still almost full but they found a quiet table and their food choice—in both cases identical—was one soup and three sides paired with rice. Mary, whose opera work had deposited her in Japan several times, explained to Megan how important the "rules of five" were for the country's cuisine. Balance and variety were achieved by the application of five colors: black, white, red, yellow, and green; five flavors: sweet, spicy, salty, sour, and bitter; and five cooking techniques: raw food, steaming, boiling, grilling, and frying. As Megan listened and ate, the food tasted five times better. At the end of lunch Mary tried once again, and unsuccessfully to reach Sire.

And then on past what the enormous museum boasted were approximately 500,000 objects from 4,000 years of human history, past the beautiful display of art nouveau and art deco graphics, past pottery from all over the world, and fashion design, to what was Mary's goal. It was the museum's collection of keyboard instruments featuring harpsichords, spinets, square pianos, clavichords, including laptop claviers, and modern-day concert grands, both acoustic and digital. The display was everything she had hoped for.

Next and last, it was on to another bus headed for the main train station and off at Glockengiesserwall for the great Kunsthalle, one of Germany's richest museums and twice expanded architecturally. Here they knew exactly what to head for and each, by agreement, initially went her own way—Megan, to international modern art; Mary, to Rembrandt and other seventeenth-century Dutch artists. In thirty minutes they would meet in front of what Megan was sure her friend would like as much as she did: Caspar David Friedrich's *A Wanderer above the Sea of Fog* of 1818—German Romanticism's most mesmerizing painting. And Mary did.

"Why do I feel as though I'm right there with the man on top of that cliff overlooking that vast fog?" she murmured. Mary was referring to the only figure in the painting—a red-haired man dressed in black with a narrow alpenstock standing atop a jagged black cliff and looking out over the mist blanketing other cliff peaks. Megan smiled. She was well acquainted with the optical device used so effectively by the great artist.

"Because his back is to us. We are seeing what he sees."

"Ah! Of course. Now I understand. The viewer *is* the figure in the painting."

"You've got it, Mary," Megan smiled at her musician friend fondly.

They had picked a perfect trio of museums and now the next thing on their agenda was returning to their hotel in Neustadt and grabbing a nap. Even though Mary was seventeen years younger than Megan, she was ready to take a rest. And then would come the fun of selecting a restaurant and relaxing over a meal as they reviewed their busy first full day in Hamburg.

Tomorrow they would be meeting with Fanny and Felix Mendelssohn at the new museum dedicated to them.

11

Poster designs, scripts, and images for Michael Bormann's three antisemitic demonstrations had been finalized and were ready to be printed. So many members of Hamburg and Berlin neo-Nazi organizations had answered the call to join the protests on Wednesday morning that double the usual number of signs had been ordered. Bormann was particularly proud of using Gustav Mahler's words about being "three times homeless" against him. The banners would read: "Don't let Hamburg provide a home for wandering Jew Mahler!" And the composer's image Bormann found to accompany the text had been culled from Vienna's leading newspaper's vicious 1907 cartoon portrayal of the controversial Opera House conductor.

Concerning the Double Jew Museum, as Bormann called it to himself, he had discovered an extraordinary "Jewish" image related to the siblings while researching their grandfather and founder of the huge family clan, Moses, for his banner for his demonstration in front of the museum! If Fanny and Felix had such ancestry, how could they amount to anything?

And what a brilliant idea he, Michael Bormann, whose surname he shared with Hitler's private secretary Martin Bormann, had come up with to conclude his triple-antisemitic protest in front of the nearby Hamburg History Museum at the Holstenwall. A museum devoted to presenting the one thousand, two hundred-year history of Hamburg that opened in 1922, it had, in order to attract visitors and get good press, created a permanent exhibition documenting the history of Jewish life in Hamburg. The sycophantic ploy had worked, much to Bormann's disgust. What his posters would say about that would be eye-stopping.

One thing was certain: Wednesday was going to keep the local and probably the German and perhaps even the international press very busy.

12

Visiting Hamburg's almost deserted Jewish Cemetery had affected Jared Oppenheim far more than he had anticipated. And for a very different reason from the heartrending one of paying tribute to the dead. After a slow tour of the two adjacent cemeteries—the Sephardic and the Ashkenazic—with stops at different intriguing grave markers, he was just about to leave the grounds when he heard loud voices shouting and laughing. How improper for a cemetery, he thought, turning to see from where the noise was coming.

What he saw gave him the shivers. Four athletic young men all wearing brown shirts were attempting to lift a large, flat Sephardic gravestone t its characteristic highly decorated standing tombstones. A few they had just dug up. Guffawing, they encouraged each other, and once the slab was off the ground they raised it onto their shoulders and began marching toward the Ashkenazi section of the cemetery. Jared was horrified. Keeping out of sight he followed the vandals across the lengthy crowded terrain of gravestones to what was indeed Ashkenazic ground with feet inside this part of the graveyard the ruffians came to a halt in front of a beautifully inscribed erect slab and positioned their slightly smaller load with its front up against the slab's front so that both inscriptions were completely obstructed. When their work was done the men took turns photographing each other next to the double tombstones. The one who seemed to be their leader pretended to be drinking a toast to the two damaged slabs.

To the two Jews who cancel each other
When Sephardic meets Ashkenazi brother!

And then it was over. The ruffians quickly dispersed, one of them shouting in farewell: “Good practice for tomorrow!” And Jared, frozen in place behind a tree, sobbed aloud, unable to stop. Why had he not had the courage to confront the vandals? Neo-Nazis who had desecrated the tombs of his people, his ancestors. He hurled the answer at himself: COWARD, you are a spoiled American coward. Afraid even to be a Jew.

13

Museum hopping could also have its drawbacks. When Mary and Megan returned to their hotel a little after five they were both more than ready for a brief lie-down before doing anything further. They were due to be picked up at six-thirty by Megan's friend of many decades, Tönnies Helfer, a retired ophthalmologist who lived in Hamburg. Megan had last stayed with him when she was in the city recently to give a lecture on "The Visual Brahms." Tönnies had tucked into her short stay that time a performance of the Brahms Requiem at the magnificent new building for the city's orchestra, the 360-foot-high Elbphilharmonie concert hall in the harbor section of the city. No chance for a repeat visit this time, however, as Megan and Mary would be flying on to Berlin tomorrow afternoon. Their meeting this time was for talk and catching up. Plus, Megan thought her two friends would thoroughly enjoy each other's company.

The brief nap had reenergized them both, and they were already standing outside their hotel when a snazzy white Audi A3 convertible with top down pulled up to the curb in front of them. A grinning Tönnies was waving at them.

Introductions made, Megan climbed into the back seat before Mary could say a word and off they roared in the direction of Altona, the wind blowing through their hair.

"What restaurant have you chosen for us?" Megan half yelled.

"And could you slow down a little, please," added Mary.

"The restaurant is called *Casa Mia* and it's at Klopstockterrasse number two," Tönnies responded, slowing down a fraction.

"But that's *your* address," sputtered Megan.

"Precisely. I'm serving you dinner at my house, *casa mia*."

Both women laughed, and ten minutes later the car pulled up

at the building where their host's spacious condominium took up the second floor.

After a brief tour of the abode, their host waved them to their seats at the dinner table and bade them wait while he disappeared into the kitchen.

"I only need to know one thing from each of you," he announced. "Do you like your *hamburgers* rare, well done, or medium?"

"*Hamburgers!*" his two guests exclaimed simultaneously.

"Yes, hamburgers. You are, after all, in Hamburg."

Tönnies's guests murmured their choice and he disappeared into the kitchen, humming melodiously and closing the door behind him.

The two puzzled women looked at each other silently with raised eyebrows. Their host had promised Megan a "significant" meal during their email exchange about her forthcoming visit. So this is what he meant! Before they could whisper their thoughts to one another, the kitchen door opened and a beaming Tönnies appeared with two loaded plates in his hands. He set one down in front of Mary and the other in front of Megan, returned to the kitchen, then reappeared with his own dish. None of the three heaping plates contained anything that looked like a hamburger.

"I see you're not familiar with the origin of the Hamburger hamburger," teased Tönnies. "You are looking at a pan-fried thick patty made from a mixture of ground beef, stale bread, egg, chopped onion, and pepper. Accompanying them, as you see, we have carrots, beet root, and potatoes."

"Oh, now I do see," laughed Mary. "You've made us frikadellen. I know this sort of 'hamburger' from eating them in Denmark where they're really popular. Frikadeller, they're called there."

"Right," Megan seconded, laughing at the literally delicious joke Tönnies had played upon them.

After the cheery dinner they retired to Tönnies's large living room where an old Bechstein grand piano inhabited one side. Knowing Megan's love of Bailey's Irish Cream, Tönnies had it and three glasses ready on the coffee table. He was pleased that Mary also expressed her pleasure at his offer to pour her a glass of the stunningly sweet liqueur. After they had conversed for a bit about the Mendelssohn mission that had brought Megan and Mary to Germany, Tönnies suddenly stood up and strode dramatically to his piano.

"I invite you both to step over here and see what's on the music rack."

His guests obliged and within seconds the two women were expressing their excitement.

"You have a Fanny Mendelssohn score!" gasped Mary.

"Yes, I do. And I was hoping you and Megan might perform it for me," laughed Tönnies, proud of his second surprise for his guests from America.

"Well, let's see," Mary answered, sitting down at the piano bench. Hmm. You'll like this, Megan, since you're a Goethe fan. The title is that of his most famous poem: '*Über allen Gipfeln ist Rüh'*—'Over all Summits is Peace.' Composed in eighteen thirty-five. That would be just twelve years after Schubert composed his famous version."

"For heaven's sake! Okay, you play and I'll *attempt* to sing it," said Megan. This was one thing she and Mary had never done together—perform. Thank goodness the pace of the short song was majestically slow. Mary expertly enunciated the wandering chord progressions as they articulated the search for eternal rest. And somehow Megan got through the transcendental words:

Über allen Gipfeln
Ist Ruh',
In allen Wipfeln
Spürest du
Kaum einen Hauch;
Die Vögelein schweigen im Walde.
Warte nur, balde
Ruhest du auch.

Over all summits
Is peace,
In all treetops
You feel
Hardly a breath:
The birds are silent in the woods.
Only wait, soon
You too shall rest.

After the brief song came to an end, Tönnies was ecstatic in his clapping.

"Thank you, thank you, thank you," he cried. Then his voice took on a different tone, one of seductiveness.

"There are twenty-four more songs by her on the piano top. Are you game?"

Megan was apologetically not, but Mary was, and she supplied the words as she easily sightread through the other expressive songs from different decades of Fanny Mendelssohn Bartholdy Hensel's composing years.

Time forgotten, the participants of the Hamburg Fanny Mendelssohn Bartholdy Hensel evening continued their musical explorations late into the night.

14

Bormann's troops had arrived in plenty of time to stage their first demonstration at nine o'clock that Wednesday morning. They came from Hamburg and they came from Berlin, some hundred and thirty-two of them, all with the united purpose of shaming Jews, past and present. After they had picked up their banners and bullhorns they formed two lines that would file past each other in opposite directions before the Gustav Mahler Museum and eagerly waited for their leaders to give the march signal. Their leaders were Michael Bormann of Hamburg and his respected cohort from Berlin, Johannes von Bandtrop. All wore brown shirts, reminiscent of Adolf Hitler's renegade storm troopers just before the breakout of World War II. The modern-day Brownshirts only needed one word from their leaders to begin their march.

And, at exactly nine o'clock and in concert, two abrupt nods from those two leaders initiated a demonstration that would shock passersby and soon attract dozens and dozens more to the Peterstrasse, including press photographers and various newspaper reporters.

The two columns, one led by Bormann and one by von Bandtrop, held aloft large posters showing mean period caricatures of a huge headed, large-nosed, spidery little Mahler conducting. The most repeated poster image, referring to the January 1907 premiere of his Sixth Symphony, showed a befuddled, bespectacled Mahler with his right hand clasped to his forehead, standing helplessly by a variety of hanging and standing percussion instruments used in the symphony and, at his feet, common noise-making objects such as cow horns and automobile honkers. Mahler holds one of the latter, his foot on the pump, and the cartoon's sarcastic caption reads: "My

God, I've forgotten the motor-horn! Now I shall have to write another symphony." Even the shocked spectators had to laugh at that particular cartoon as it passed by repeatedly from two opposite directions.

The protest slogan, shouted incessantly by marchers with their bullhorns, was: "Don't give wandering Jew Mahler a home in our beloved Hamburg!" A few onlookers actually joined the chant, attracting photographers and inspiring boos from the gathering crowd. Police were almost immediately upon the scene, but a permit had been obtained for the demonstration, and so far nothing had occurred that could merit arrest or halting of the carefully coordinated protest march. The whole spectacle lasted some forty minutes and then the demonstrators gathered next to two nondescript trucks parked on a side street near the scene. There they exchanged their Mahler signs for different ones and noisily regrouped, ready to march toward the nearby Fanny and Felix Mendelssohn Museum. They and their leaders Bormann and von Bandtrop were ready to raise new hell.

15

The distraction Jared Oppenheim sought in order to shake himself loose from the nightmare grip of his shocking experience at Hamburg's Jewish Cemetery had worked. Reeperbahn, the city's famous red light district, had enough variety to divert anyone seeking sexual oblivion. Jared ended up with a young redhead who, after their business was completed, took him to the Beatles-Platz on the Reeperbahn. Constructed in 2008, the memorial square—a black painted circular intersection intended to emulate a vinyl disk—displayed metal statues of the band members along with titles of The Beatles' most famous songs. Here they parted, but Jared would never forget the intensity and sheer bliss of their brief encounter.

He was still feeling tingles from last night's diversion as he took advantage of the hotel's enormous multi-mirrored bathroom and now, finishing a delicious early breakfast at his Altona hotel, he directed his attention to the day's events he planned to attend. The afternoon was dedicated to a two o'clock meeting with the director of the Fanny and Felix Mendelssohn Museum, Rachael Skylar, and he would already be in the Composers Quarter in Hamburg-Neustadt because he wished to visit the Gustav Mahler Museum there when it opened at ten.

It would be a day devoted to music as he also planned to visit the other five museums dedicated to composers in the row of restored historical red brick buildings with their multiple white-framed windows at Peterstrasse 29-39. He would visit them chronologically according to the date they were established. The first, the Mahler Museum, had been opened as early as 1971. Next, and after a long hiatus as far as founding date, would be the eighteenth-century composer Georg Philipp Telemann Museum, established in 2011.

Then he would visit the almost next-door museums, both opened in 2015, of two eighteenth-century musicians: prolific opera composer Johann Adolf Hasse and Carl Philipp Emanuel Bach, the most gifted of Johann Sebastian Bach's many children and Telemann's godson. C.P.E. Bach, as he was called, was music director and curator of Hamburg's five main churches—interestingly, a coveted post previously held by Telemann.

Jared, who over his career had performed all three composers, was especially gratified at Hamburg's treasuring of these three late Baroque-early Classical composers. Constituting their "modern frame," so to speak, were the Mahler and the Mendelssohn Museums.

But when he arrived at the Mahler Museum, visiting it proved to be impossible. A humongous, horrid, and noisy neo-Nazi demonstration was taking place in front of the newly restored building where the composer/conductor had once lived for seven years while director of the Hamburg Opera. The equilibrium Jared had newly attained was shattered as he watched the protesters shouting and marching with ugly historic caricatures of Mahler, "the wandering Jew." Revolting as he found it, Jared could not tear himself away. He watched as the police arrived but they did nothing. Just stood prepared for any violence.

All right then, let them have their violence! A coward no longer, Jared broke through the crowd of spectators and threw himself on the nearest protestor.

"*Hate your bigoted self, not Jews*!" he shouted as he fell to the ground on top of his adversary.

16

Richard Sire's one regret was that he could not make or receive calls on his cellphone. He had not taken that into account when making his abrupt and daring decision after his first full day in Berlin. Talking things over with Gabor Uninsky, owner of the prominent, eponymous gallery hosting his exhibition there, their reactions were identical. Yes. Essential, relevant, and morally necessary. Richard would initiate things immediately.

17

"My god! You're next!"

Standing at his office window and looking down at the scene on the street below, Abraham Aronson, director of the Gustav Mahler Museum, was on the phone with his treasured colleague, Rachael Skylar. He had contacted her twice. First, at the beginning of the protest with several hundred people noisily filing back and forth in front of his building, and then again after the crowd, in organized ranks, had quickly disappeared down one of the Peterstrasse side streets. Now they had just reemerged, waving new banners printed with insults against Fanny and Felix Mendelssohn and carrying large posters blazoned with a single eye-catching image showing what looked to be a short, hunchbacked man stopped by a tall guard at one of Berlin's city gates. A large caption stated "Jew Moses Mendelssohn, grandfather of 'Christian converts' Fanny and Felix Mendelssohn." The siblings' identification as converts was certainly true. They had become Lutherans, as would their parents who added to their surname the non-Jewish surname Bartholdy. Nevertheless, the hateful sarcasm of the protest poster being paraded was impossible to miss.

As Aronson, then Skylar watched in horror, the converging mob with its messages of hate took an almost military, two-column position in front of the Mendelssohn Museum building. At the whistle blow of one of its two leaders, the protestors began marching back and forth before the building in opposite directions. The whistle blowing commander was Johannes von Bandtrop, leader of Berlin's neo-Nazis. The other commander, a Michael Bormann, leader of Hamburg's neo-Nazi organization, had been knocked to the ground in front of the Mahler Museum by an angry onlooker named Jared Oppenheim.

Both men had been detained by the Hamburg police. Upon identifying himself as an American businessman spontaneously impelled to act against the Jew-demeaning protestors, he was chastised but released. The other man, it turned out, was a known Hamburg resident for whom there was an outstanding warrant of arrest. The arrest was made.

18

Megan had just completed doing her early morning exercises—a lifelong habit which she called FSAB—flexibility, strength, aerobic, and balance. Recovered from her exertions, she joined Mary downstairs at breakfast for her daily mix of blueberries, strawberries, banana, yogurt, and cereal. The hotel did not carry almond milk so she settled for cow's milk. While she was still eating, her travel mate expressed the thought that perhaps they should check to make sure Salomon Mendelssohn was still planning to be picked up by them. No sooner said than done and when the elderly man was connected by the hospice front desk, he was in an agitated state.

"Oh! I've tried so hard to find how I might contact you. I needed to tell you that I cannot, under any circumstances, go with you to the Mendelssohn Museum this morning. I am simply not up to it. I do apologize and am so grateful for your offer. Thank goodness you have called me!"

Megan realized that the old man's mind could not be changed. She told him not to worry and that they would definitely give his regards to the director. With some unexpected time on their hands they returned to their room to do some email catching up.

They arrived twenty minutes early for their eleven o'clock appointment with Director Rachael Skylar at the Mendelssohn Museum so Megan could first photograph the façades of all six museums in the Composers Quarter. But they were horrified to come upon a neo-Nazi demonstration in noisy, indeed scary progress in front of the museum. Menorahs were being thrown on the ground and stamped upon. Held aloft, along with bullhorn chants insulting the Mendelssohn siblings, were dozens and dozens of identical posters with an in-your-face image demeaning their grandfather Moses Mendelssohn. And then in precise formation the some two-hundred-plus Brownshirts, many from Berlin as their cap insignias proclaimed, suddenly quit the scene. The crowd of angry and disgusted onlookers began to disperse as well. Upon questioning one of them, Mary learned the troublemakers had disbanded in order to regroup in front of Hamburg's Museum of History. She was told that the protestors had begun their nasty business in front of the Mahler Museum an hour earlier.

It was with concern and apprehension then that the two Americans identified themselves and cited their museum business to the two policemen now standing at the Mendelssohn Museum entry door. But there was no problem: their names were on the list one of the officers held. Otherwise no museum visitors were being admitted at present. Once inside, it was not necessary to search for the director's office. Dressed in a bright blue pantsuit with a flowing yellow scarf, Rachael Skylar was striding toward them, hands held out in apologetic welcome.

"Good morning! Good morning, ladies! I am so sorry that your much-anticipated visit to us is on this day of unexpected ruckus and unrest." After shaking hands the threesome retired to Skylar's upstairs office where hot coffee awaited them. First they discussed the outbreak of antisemitism in Hamburg—two gravesites in the city's old Jewish Cemetery had been desecrated just the day before. Then conversation turned to the purpose and scope of Megan's book on Fanny Mendelssohn.

"I have read your intriguing book on Clara Schumann and I presume you intend to stress Fanny's compositions as well. Yes?"

"Definitely. And thanks to my colleague here, my musical analyses will be supervised and most likely improved."

"Ah, it's always good when colleagues from different fields can collaborate. Do you have a title for the book yet?"

"Well my much-too-long, working title right now is *From Oblivion to Fame: The Extraordinary Legacy of Fanny Mendelssohn Bartholdy Hensel*."

"I don't think that is too lengthy at all! It certainly conveys what your book will be addressing and revealing." Rachael's enthusiasm was sincere.

“Thank you,” laughed Mary. “I’ve been trying to tell her just that.” Megan modestly changed the subject.

“We heard there was also a demonstration earlier this morning in front of the Mahler Museum. How awful!”

“Yes, my colleague there phoned to warn me that the angry crowd was moving toward us. Fortunately neither of our museums has suffered any visible damage so far as we can tell.”

“It’s terrible, just terrible. We’re having spates of antisemitism in America as well,” said Mary.

“Shall we visit the showrooms now?” Rachael asked, changing the subject with relief and standing up. “I trust the demonstrations are over, for today at least.”

“Oh, yes, we’d love to see some of your museum holdings,” Mary confirmed as Megan rose from her seat nodding enthusiastic agreement.

The director led her guests to the main exhibition room first. On the way they passed a small room in the middle of which stood a beautiful brown pianoforte. As they walked by, a detection device activated an audio recording and a wistful piano piece began to sound. Smiling, they paused to listen. Over the entry, a running caption identified the piano music as “by Felix, *Italian Gondola Song in G minor,* no. 6 of *Songs without Words, op.19b, 1830.*”

When the piece was over, Rachael pointed to two small buttons at waist level by the entry to the room. They read “For Fanny Press Here” and “For Felix Press Here.” Enchanted, Megan reached over and pressed the Fanny button. A new piano piece began to sound and the running caption read “by Fanny, *Sonata (Capriccio) op.113, 1824.*” Seeing the delight on her visitors’ faces as they stood listening, Rachael smilingly beckoned them into the room.

“Take a look at this gorgeous eighteenth-century instrument from the front,” she urged her guests. They walked deeper into the small room which was lit by a window at the far end. Along the two white sidewalls ran a band of small captioned images relating to Fanny and Felix at different periods in their lives.

“What fun!” exclaimed Mary, reaching the piano keyboard first. “The keys are black and the sharp and flat keys are white!”

Megan had never seen a reverse key color piano in person and she looked down at the keys first with fascination, then with a perplexed frown.

"But it's so hard to *distinguish* the keys this way. You can't see the black spaces between the black keys very well."

"That's why the colors were changed," smiled Rachael, "even though ivory was always scarce. The seven 'natural' notes of each octave became white and the five half-tones—sharps, flats—became black. That created a brighter keyboard that was easier to see."

The visitors began studying various images along the wall. One of them showed in profile a twelve-year-old Felix playing in a large formal room with a string trio bowing behind him. Turning the pages for the boy was a figure Megan recognized as Fanny and Felix's teacher, Carl Friedrich Zelter. A prominent listener was alongside the piano, his hands clasped behind his back as he looked down at Felix approvingly. The listener was Johann Wolfgang von Goethe, Germany's greatest literary figure; the locale was his home in Weimar. His judgment of the boy, as quoted by the information panel below the picture, was "like a young Mozart...only better." Concerning Fanny, Zelter had written Goethe that "she plays like a man." Megan was reminded of another young girl who did in fact play for Goethe, Clara Wieck, later Clara Schumann. About her, the poet had said: "That girl plays with the strength of six boys!" She must get all this into her Fanny Mendelssohn book.

A very different image along the opposite wall of the room attracted Megan's knowing and mournful attention. It was the front page of an essay first pseudonymously published by Richard Wagner in 1850—just three years after the death of Felix Mendelssohn—and later under his own name in 1869. The title was *Das Judenthum in der Musik—Judaism in Music*. And the bigoted thrust was to demonstrate that, having no authentic culture of their own, culture-craving Jewish composer "parasites" merely emulated the music culture within which they lived.

Rachael noticed what Megan had stopped in front of and commented: "Hurtful and grim as the essay is, we display it because our visitors must be educated about the past and what prejudices Jewish composers have encountered. Also, of course, how Wagner's biased view influenced Hitler and his massive Jew-purging actions."

"I couldn't agree more that such history must continue to be known," said Megan. "In fact I used to mention the essay's existence in my art history classes."

"And where was that, if I may ask?"

"First at Columbia University in New York for ten years, and then Southern Methodist University in Dallas for the rest of my teaching career."

"So you are an art historian, but you are also a music historian," declared Rachael.

"Yes, you could put it that way. If I had to choose between the two, it would be music." Mary joined them just then and the director decided to tell the two American visitors about something pertinent to the Mendelssohn siblings that was not in her museum but in the city.

"By the way, should you have time in your schedule you might like to visit the two separate but 'twin' outdoor memorial images of Fanny and of Felix, identified by both their surnames, so Bartholdy as well. Their portraits, with Fanny wearing the great top-heavy hat you've seen in images of her, are affixed to standing slabs of gray granite in...wait, I'll write down the address for you."

"Wonderful! Thank you," Mary said as Megan nodded eagerly.

"And next I'd like to show you the magnificent and now 'famous' ophicleide I arranged to be hung over Felix's recently discovered original score of the overture *A Midsummer Night's Dream*—composed when he was just seventeen and a half years old. Visitors now refer to the room it's in as the 'Ophicleide Room' because of the one hanging above the score."

Her guests knew the long-lost score was one of the highlights of Rachael's museum and they were happy to be led to it. At the push of a button one could turn the pages of the score in its glass case, not physically but via a screen on the wall above. Every page of the score had been photographed for this satisfying activity and some musician visitors actually studied the entire overture this way.

After her two visitors had seen and studied the treasures of her impressive museum, Rachael saw them cordially to the door. Her personnel were now allowing visitors into the building and things appeared to be getting back to normal.

"I must tell you that a countryman of yours is also coming to see me today," she told them as they were about to part company. "He is Jared Oppenheim, founder of the Mendelssohn Complex in New York City."

"What a coincidence!" said Megan in amazement. "I had thought about meeting and conferring with him about Fanny until I learned he wasn't the actual director of the Complex; that it was someone else who was in charge."

"Aha! Well, should you still like to meet and confer with him you can do so today. Herr Oppenheim arrives at two o'clock and we should be through by three if you'd like to stop back by."

"Would you mind doing that with me?" Megan looked at Mary.

"Not at all. I think it could be quite interesting."

"All right then, we'll see you at three," smiled Megan.

"At three," confirmed the genial director of the Fanny and Felix Mendelssohn Museum of the medieval Hanseatic city Hamburg, birthplace of both famous siblings.

19

Arriving at Hamburg's Museum of History, or Hamburg History Museum, as Megan and Mary discovered it was also called, they could see smashed menorahs on the ground testifying that the Brownshirts had carried out their demonstration before the rectangular red brick building. Fortunately the protestors and their posters were gone and there was no trouble entering the museum. They asked where the permanent exhibit showing the history of Jewish life in the city was and were directed to it. To their delight the artifacts on the way there were varied and intriguing. They included a miniature re-creation of Hamburg's old multitrack railroad station and its far-flung two railroad lines, a metal walrus weathervane from 1701, exquisitely detailed wooden ship models from previous centuries, and fascinating aerial views of Hamburg revealing just how it lies on the River Elbe and is embraced by two of its tributaries, the River Alster and the River Bille. The temptation for Mary and Megan to stop and examine individual exhibits at greater length was strong and if it weren't for the fact that they were expected back at the Mendelssohn Museum at three o'clock they would have lingered and photographed various objects. Their only pauses therefore were to take panoramic vistas rather than stopping for close-up shots.

When they reached the Jewish exhibits, which ranged from examples of Hebrew book printing to the life-size re-creation of a small synagogue interior with all its fittings, they paused to speedread through a summary of the history of Jews in Hamburg posted on the entry wall. A uniformed museum guard discreetly moved away from the large plaque to give them more standing room. They read that the presence of Sephardic Jews was documented as going all the way back to 1590 when they arrived from Portugal and built a community in Altona. Altona! Mary and Megan were tickled to see a reference to something they had recently learned: the "origin" of the name Altona as coming from the town center merchants' complaint that the thriving Sephardic Jewish suburb directly west of them was "*all zu nah*." Reading further, they learned that German Ashkenazi Yiddish-speaking Jews had begun settling in Hamburg in 1600, however forty-nine years later they were driven out, but managed successfully to return some seven years later. What a checkered history!

Consulting the scant time left to them, the two friends moved ahead to data given for the twentieth century. They read that the number of Jews living in Hamburg at the beginning of World War I was around 17,000, and that at the end of World War II, during which thousands of Hamburg Jewish inhabitants had fled the country, those who remained and were slaughtered in Hitler's concentration camps numbered some 7,800 persons. The most startling statistic stated that after World War II all that remained of Hamburg's once thriving Jewish community were 674 Jews.

Just as they were quietly absorbing this last dismal fact, the sound of youngsters running and shouting broke out behind them, causing the nearby museum guard to race toward the restored synagogue from where the sounds were coming. There, two boys were tossing a small nine-branched menorah back and forth to each other while yelling "Happy Hanukkah!" Their boisterous activity was attracting a small crowd of distressed onlookers but it was not until the guard reached them that they stopped. The candle holder was put back on the altar shelf from where it had stood and the boys were rounded up by their embarrassed, apologizing parents who had just rushed to the scene.

"They saw the protest marchers doing it," they explained.

Mary looked at Megan. It was time to leave.

20

"I'm sorry, but there's nothing I can do about it. They had a warrant for his arrest."

Johannes von Bandtrop of Berlin was attempting to console the young inner circle of their leader Michael Bormann who had been handcuffed and led away from the protest scene he had helped to create in front of the Mahler Museum in Hamburg's Composers Quarter.

Faced with glum silence, Bandtrop made what he hoped would be a helpful suggestion.

"If I may say so, you might like to consider choosing a stand-in for Michael as your leader. My right-hand woman, Barbara Badubrecht, is originally from Hamburg, and she is returning here temporarily because both her parents are coping with health problems. Some of you may know her?"

Several heads nodded and one young man with shaved head and tattooed hands spoke up.

"Yeah. We know of her and some of us, including me, know her personally from when we've gone to Berlin to participate in your rallies. You're mentioning her because she could be a good temporary leader for us n-Ns until Bormann gets out of prison. Right?"

"Right on," answered Bandtrop smiling. "I think she has the temperament for the job and that you'd learn a lot from her...and she from you."

No more needed to be said. Presuming she would accept the job, the inner circle voted unanimously to invite her to be their temporary leader.

"Excellent," said Bandtrop. "I'll let her know. She's still here and could meet with you as early as tomorrow most likely. I'll be in touch with you. In fact I'll soon be requesting that some of you come to Berlin for help in an important indoor demonstration I'm planning to stage there."

"Glad to be of help," said several of the Brownshirts as they left the meeting.

"And thanks for loaning us your Barbara Badubrecht," grinned another one, daring to clap the imposing Berliner on the back.

21

Jared's two o'clock appointment with Rachael at the Mendelssohn Museum had gone exceedingly well. Both liked each other on the spot and their talk covered a number of objects from each of their institutions' unique holdings on display. The major thing Jared had in mind was agreed to willingly by Rachael. It was the idea that each museum would display on loan for three months one unusual item belonging to the other, along with the attendant information concerning the loaning institution. Rachael loved the publicity it would bring her museum in America, especially now that people were traveling more after COVID-19 restrictions had lessened to an extent.

So delightfully intense was their meeting that the museum cashier had to call to say that a professor with the surname Crespi and her companion were at the museum in regard to an arrangement to see her made earlier in the day.

"Oh, yes. Send them right up to my office, please." Rachael turned to Jared.

"Oh my god, I forgot that I'd asked two very nice American scholars who'd like to meet you to drop by when I thought we'd be concluding our conversation."

"No problem," said Jared generously. "Although I would like to browse through your impressive museum afterward."

"And so also would they, I'm sure. They only had about thirty minutes at the exhibits with me this morning."

"And who are they, may I ask? You said they're American?"

"Yes. One of them, Mary Russell, works with opera singers around the world; the other is a retired professor of art history who's now publishing books on women composers. Clara Schumann was her latest. And now she's writing one on Fanny..."

"Wait a minute! Are you speaking perhaps of Megan Crespi?"

"Indeed. How did you know?"

"I've been wanting to make her acquaintance ever since reading her book on Clara. It was an eye-opener. And now she's doing Fanny. How perfect!"

A knock sounded on the office door.

"Come in!" Rachael commanded as she and Jared stood up to greet the visitors. The next forty-five minutes were devoted to what one could call genial and interesting shop talk. After t they parted, Rachael went home to check on her son and as the museum was still open for another hour, the three Americans spent their time looking at the exhibits and discussing various unusual items.

Jared was shocked to see that the cover and pages from the infamous essay by Richard Wagner were on exhibition, but he agreed that the general public needed to be reminded of what he had written so disparagingly about Jews in music.

"Just think what Felix Mendelssohn and Giacomo Meyerbeer managed to do in their time," declared Mary.

"So why do you think Wagner wrote his essay?" Megan said angrily, then immediately answering her own question, she said, "He was thinking of *them*—Mendelssohn and Meyerbeer, members of a race apart, grossly aping the 'higher' Christian class of society."

"You know the famous dictum," pronounced Jared, "'The Jews are like other people, only more so.'" The laughter that followed cleared the gloom and as the museum closed, the trio found themselves still laughing and exchanging opinions on the street.

"Hey, do you two have dinner plans for this evening?" Jared asked, not wanting to part company with the interesting women.

"No dinner plans," Mary answered for them both.

"Then how about we share a meal at one of the most interesting restaurants in Hamburg, or at least so I've been told."

"Sounds good to me," said Megan, glancing at her friend for agreement. She was nodding.

"What is the restaurant?"

"Well, let me say first that it's very near us. We can actually walk to it from here."

"*Really*? I love the restaurant already."

"And what sort of food does it offer?" Mary wanted to know.

"How about guessing the nationality of the menu, ladies?"

"Oh, Jared, you're so mean! But I'll take a guess. German?"

"No."

"Chinese?"

"No."

"Italian?"

"No."

"I know. American?" Megan jumped in.

"No."

"Oh Jared, don't be cruel. What nationality?"

"French."

"Hoorah!" whooped Mary who, having lived in France for three decades, had a passion for eating and cooking the country's cuisine.

"And, it's highly recommended by Michelin," smiled Jared proudly.

"Does this restaurant have a name, by any chance?" asked Megan.

"Indeed. *Petit Bonheur*."

"As in the painter Rosa Bonheur! Then I'll love it. It will be a *grand* bonheur. Let's get going!"

A smiling Jared indicated the direction, and as they walked to Hütten 85 he asked Megan who Rosa Bonheur is.

"Do you want the long version or the short version?" she offered.

"The telegraph version," he said without missing a beat. Mary snorted. She knew how much Megan had to say concerning the extraordinary nineteenth-century artist.

"Rosa Bonheur was a contemporary of Gustave Courbet and, like him, a member of the French Realist style of the mid-eighteen fifties. She's best known nowadays for her enormous canvas of eighteen fifty-five called *The Horse Fair*, which you can admire when you get back to New York because the Metropolitan Museum is the proud owner."

"Well, lucky me! I don't know of her but she sounds lively if she was painting horses."

"If you do go, here's a tip about what to look for that most viewers don't know: she slyly inserted a torso-high self-portrait into the picture, just to the right of center, wearing a cap and blue shirt and riding one of the brown horses. Directly in front of her is a white-shirted man trying to subdue a rearing white horse."

"Hey! I do remember seeing that huge jumble of horse flesh picture at the Met. Didn't realize it was by a woman though. Amazing."

"Right. It's not the sort of subject matter one would imagine a woman addressing back then, or maybe even now. She watched the fair for many months, making on-the-spot sketches. And she dressed like a man so as not to be bothered by passersby."

"That was smart."

"She almost made it into the twentieth century; died in eighteen ninety-nine."

Mary touched Jared's shoulder.

"What you're not being told, Jared, is that Megan recently gave our Dallas Museum of Art a small oil painting of a sheep—a ewe—by Bonheur."

"You *owned* a Bonheur, Megan!"

"I did. But I found and bought it decades before women artists were being bought. Collecting women artists past and present was a passion of mine and I began early, so got some good deals."

"Too bad you didn't have a passion for Fanny Mendelssohn. God knows what you might have found!"

"Or still may," added Mary.

Megan was about to make a comment as they reached Hütten 85 but instead she reacted with delight at the restaurant's façade.

"Look at that façade! It's pure Art Nouveau. Elegant!"

A friendly waiter inside showed them to a table next to one of the front windows. It had a gleaming white tablecloth with two-page menus standing up between the silverware. Paintings from the chef's own collection graced the walls, the waiter informed them, and the long menu offered different meals every evening of the week. In the background one could hear Edith Piaf singing classic songs from the 1940s and '50s; the one playing as they sat down was "*Non, Je Ne Regrette Rien.*"

Jared, Mary, and Megan studied the menu in silence, made their choices, and looked at each other smiling victoriously.

"Which plate did you choose, Mary?" Jared asked.

"All of them," Mary answered with a straight face.

"Perfect! But which one for starters?" pressed Megan.

"What else but beef steak tartare *a la maison.*"

"Wow! That's what I want too," nodded Jared, opening his eyes wide in anticipation.

"You're not going to believe this, but me too!" Megan laughed. "And what wine do you, Mary, whose second home is France, recommend?"

"Only one wine, a red Beaujolais."

Their waiter seemed to approve and soon the three Mendelssohn lovers were happily consuming a perfect dinner. And now for dessert! Menus were again consulted.

As had happened with the main course, all three diners ordered the identical dessert: crêpes Suzette. What they did not know was that the delicious crêpes would be especially prepared for them right at the table. The thin pancakes were as yummy as anticipated and it was a happy trio who conversed over a concluding café and the sound of Piaf singing "*La Vie en Rose*."

"So who's going to bring it up?" asked Jared after a while, looking from one woman to the other.

"Bring what up?" Mary answered.

"Yes, bring what up?" echoed Megan

"What's happening to Ukrainian Jews these days. Here we are, all researching two German Jewish composers in Germany and right now new history is happening to Ukrainian Jews because of the Soviet invasion of the country."

"How many Jews live in Ukraine, do you think?" wondered Mary.

"I've researched that and the figures differ wildly, but I think the number is close to three hundred fifty thousand."

"A friend told me once that the Hasidic movement actually developed in Ukraine. Is that true, do you think?" Megan enquired.

"I think so. I've heard it goes back to the seventeen hundreds and was founded by a specific rabbi whose name is known to the history books but not remembered by me. Why do you ask?" Jared was curious.

"Oh, because of that Russian airstrike against Kyiv's radio and television tower that's just steps from the city's Holocaust Memorial Center. It's a memorial to the nineteen forty-one two-day machine gun killing spree of almost thirty-four thousand of the city's Jews. And I couldn't help wondering how many of them were Hassidic Jews since the men are so identifiable with their long black garments and side curls."

"And therefore the first to be recognized and the first to go," said Mary sadly.

"Whew! Let's change the subject," urged Jared. "What are you two gals up to next?"

"We're off to Berlin tomorrow morning," Mary answered. "Our flight leaves at ten-thirty, so we'll be there well before noon."

"Berlin. Hmm. I hadn't thought of going there this trip but maybe I should, especially considering how long Fanny lived there. Plenty of Mendelssohn family stuff to see and visit there. What hotel are you staying at?"

"Where I always stay when I'm in Berlin," answered Megan happily, "the Hotel Kempinski, as I still call it, or Hotel Bristol as they call it now, just off the Kurfürstendamm, number twenty-seven. In the center of Berlin."

"She says it's very swank," Mary added.

"'Swank?' I love swank. How many days will you be there? Would you object if I joined you day after tomorrow? I'll be spending tomorrow back at Rachael's museum, but after that..."

"Great idea," smiled Megan. It would be fun to continue the Mendelssohn Trio. Each had something to give and she felt that Mary enjoyed the genial young man's company as much as she did.

A minute later, after they had paid their dinner bill, each going Dutch, Jared proved her point. As they exited the restaurant he beckoned toward a small park just down the street.

"Ladies, it's still early. What say we adjourn to that siren spot of nature in this busy city and treat ourselves to a Fanny Mendelssohn performance I recently discovered on YouTube?"

"What fun," laughed Mary. "I'm game. How about you, Megan?"

"Sure."

A few minutes later they were seated on a comfortable wooden bench with a small wooden table to one side. It was in the center of the park and away from the noise of traffic. After pulling the little table over in front of them Jared sat between his two ladies and whipped out a large cellphone. It was a Samsung Galaxy 3 Fold 2 and after typing in the URL he unfolded the cellphone with its containing wallet, positioned it standing up on the table in front of them and pressed the play button. It was Fanny's Overture in C Major as performed by the Women's Philharmonic of San Francisco and conducted by Maestra JoAnn Falletta. The sound quality on the Samsung was excellent and brought out the full instrumentation, and for ten minutes and twenty-five seconds the music proceeded from lento sorrow to allegro jubilation. Unabashed homage to Beethoven sounded every now and then. Several passersby stopped to listen and actually clapped at the end of the piece. Jared was asked to play it again and a growing group of listeners gathering behind the bench watched the imagery on the screen as well. Imagery not of the orchestra playing, but of different portraits of the composer concluding with the serene 1842 oil portrait by Moritz Daniel Oppenheim. This beautiful music was composed by a *woman* then?

When Jared had read the name of the artist the first time, he had almost interrupted the recording, so dazzled was he by the idea of kinship with this Oppenheim of the past. And now, after the second playing of the overture, Jared turned to the group of clapping listeners and began a spontaneous lecture on Fanny Mendelssohn Hensel. Despite the fact that he was speaking in English, most of the crowd remained to hear what he had to say. One man, however, spat on the ground in a gesture of disgust and stormed off.

"Why don't they show the orchestra playing?" asked one spectator.

"It would seem that it was only recorded, not videotaped," answered Jared. "And unfortunately, after almost twenty-five years of existence—from nineteen eighty to two thousand four—that orchestra disbanded. But its work is being continued by the Community Women's Orchestra of Oakland, California, founded in nineteen eighty-five."

"So it takes Americans to introduce to the world Hamburg's wonderful woman composer," concluded one listener.

After a third person requested playing of Fanny's overture, the small band of people, briefly united by music, began to break up. The three Americans stood up and Jared used his handy Uber app for a ride back to his hotel in Altona. For Mary and Megan it was easier: they could simply walk back to their nearby Neustadt one. All three were delighted they would be seeing each other again and in Berlin.

They had now officially dubbed themselves "The Fanny and Felix Trio."

22

The demoralized Hamburg group of Bandtrop admirers had followed the suggestion of that galvanizing neo-Nazi leader from Berlin yesterday to meet with and nominate his Berlin lieutenant as their proxy leader. At least until the length of Michael Bormann's incarceration was known. The leader of Hamburg's neo-Nazis had been arrested on a warrant by the police yesterday and it was highly likely that his prison time would be lengthy.

And thus it was with more than normal anticipation that the diminished Hamburg group met with Bandtrop's lieutenant early that Thursday morning in the back room of Café Funk-Eck. Her self-introduction was brief and to the point.

"My fellow Hansiatics, I am Barbara Badubrecht, originally from Hamburg, presently lieutenant of Berlin's glorious n-N leader, Johannes von Bandtrop. I am here to tell you that I would serve you with as much dedication as I do him, were you to elect me your temporary leader until our inspiring Michael Bormann is released and handed back to us. We all share the same vital mission, whether we protest in Berlin or Hanseatic Hamburg."

The unusually tall woman with blonde hair pulled back in a practical bun and dressed in a black pantsuit with white blouse and a red scarf at the throat—the original Nazi colors—needed say no more. Cheers burst out and everyone, without exception, jumped to their feet. An unsmiling and deadly earnest Badubrecht shook the hand of every man and woman there. Their essential work on behalf of the party would go on.

23

Five corpses had been left in the middle of the battered highway. Heavy black tires had been dragged on top of them in an effort to conceal the dead. Fifteen miles further west a small demolished urban area with more bodies simply left on the street was encountered. Many of them were children. Silently, a lone man slowly photographed both sites with his Leika V-Lux 5.

After documenting the second group of corpses he vomited on the side of the street.

24

"Important as Hamburg was for their earliest years, it was of course Berlin that provided the dominant cultural ambience for Fanny and Felix, right, Megan?"

Mary was pretty certain what her travel mate's answer was going to be. She merely wanted to focus their talk on the great historic city to which they were flying that very moment. Her conversational ploy was successful.

"Oh, definitely. Fanny was just six years old when the family moved to Berlin in eighteen eleven and little Felix only two. And for the first few years it was Fanny who received piano lessons from her mother. At first, just five minutes at a time, then longer as the daughter's attention and endurance lengthened. Of course Felix was tutored by his mother as soon as he could begin pressing keys down in ordered progressions."

"Interesting. So their first teachers were, in both cases, their mother."

"Correct. There was no doubt that both were child prodigies, a fact that pleased their father until Fanny became too interested in what she called her 'musical urges.' That caused him to write her a concerned mandate, the words of which still sting me whenever I think of them."

"Oh, goodness! What did he write her?"

"I remember every word. He worte 'Perhaps music will be Felix's profession, whereas for you it can and must be but an ornament.'"

"That's terrible! And yet so typical of the times, the general idea that a woman's life must be completely devoted to home and family; no professional ambitions of her own."

"Right. And although you and I can name exceptions, that's the problem, isn't it? That they *were* exceptions."

"I'm beginning to understand why you've chosen Fanny as the subject of your new book."

"Yes. Funny, isn't it? Most of my scholarly books have been on male Austrian artists like Gustav Klimt and Egon Schiele and Oskar Kokoschka, but now here I am, engaged in writing about composers, first Mahler and Beethoven and Brahms, and then narrowing down to women composers and musicians, like Clara Schumann and Fanny Mendelssohn. It's a real siren call and I can't resist it."

"I can attest to its being a siren call for you. Think of how many times you've turned down my invitations to join me and Sire for a concert because, as you say, you're 'happily entrapped' inside your material!"

"It's true, and I am grateful to you both for putting up with me and for continuing to invite me to musical events."

A momentary shadow crossed Mary's face but Megan did not notice it.

"And what would you like to do first, once we've checked into our hotel?" Mary asked, almost too cheerfully.

"Oh, no wondering there. I'd like us to go see the grand eighteenth-century Baroque mansion at Leipziger Strasse number three which Abraham Mendelssohn bought and refurbished for his wife and four children. It came complete with a garden wing and it was the house where Fanny would spend the greater part of her life from eighteen twenty-five to her death in eighteen forty-three."

"Yes! Let's go there first. That garden wing is where she held her famous *Sonntagsmusiken*—Sunday recitals, isn't it?"

"Yes. At first the concerts were held on Sunday mornings; later they became soirées. They were enormously popular. Famous musicians and composers would play with or for her, and prominent members of Berlin society vied for seats. This was where Christian and Jew mingled easily."

"Must have been such a wonderful treat." Mary's tone of voice did not convey enthusiasm and Megan glanced over at her friend. Her face had a set expression and she was staring sightlessly straight ahead.

"Hey, what's the matter, Mary? You don't seem yourself."

"Sorry. It's just that I'm really beginning to worry about Sire. He hasn't called and his number doesn't go through when I call, as I did again early this morning, so I can't even...even leave a message for him." Mary's voice broke and she said no more.

"Oh, how insensitive of me!" Megan was chagrined. "I tell you what: as soon as we've checked into the hotel, let's forget about the Mendelssohn mansion; we'll go immediately to Sire's gallery and plague them for information about him. Surely they must know!"

"That's what I thought and I've called them several times already. But all I get is their receptionist who says the same thing each time. That she cannot give out personal information on artists whose works are to be exhibited."

"Then, as I said, let's go right away in person."

"Oh, yes. Thank you.

Twenty-five minutes later they had landed in Berlin and after checking in and leaving their roller bags at their Bristol Hotel, which Megan still insisted on referring to as Kempinski Hotel, they ordered an Uber to take them to the famous Galerie Gabor in Berlin's Mitte district at Oranienburger Strasse 37/38. The busy street was within what had become a thriving Jewish neighborhood. As they pulled up in front of the elaborate brick building which had once been the royal post office, both women expressed their surprise at the sheer size of the gallery which, Sire had gleefully told Mary, was known for having staged retrospectives of Annie Leibovitz, Robert Mapplethorpe, Peter Lindbergh and other big names in the art world.

"Golly, this is really serious business," murmured Megan as she stared at the capacious old building.

"Yes, that's what Sire was saying and why he was so thrilled when the gallery contacted him. Seems that one of the things the gallery is known for is its photography exhibitions."

"Perfect!"

Not noticing a small sign outside the entrance, the two women hurried past a Chinese restaurant and into the gallery, approaching the young girl seated behind a desk in the reception room. Mary smiled at her and distinctly announced her reason for being in the gallery.

"Hello. I am Mary Russell from Dallas, Texas and I am here to see Gabor Uninsky."

"Do you have an appointment?"

"I do not. But he will want to see me. I am Richard Sire's partner."

"Just a moment. I will buzz him in his office." Her call was answered immediately and after conveying her brief message, the receptionist listened for a moment, then turned to the visitors and announced that Herr Uninsky would be right with them.

Before another full minute had passed, the gallery owner appeared with a welcoming smile on his face. His glance went from Megan to Mary.

"Ladies! What a nice surprise. And which one of you is Mary Russell, may I ask?"

"I am," Mary nodded her head as Megan pointed to her. "And this is Richard Sire's and my dear friend, art historian Doctor Megan Crespi." Hands were quickly shaken all around.

"I knew you would be arriving in Berlin to attend Sire's opening, and so here you are, but too early. Something of which you are apparently unaware. I am so sorry. As our obviously too small sign outside says, and as we have announced online and in the papers, the opening of Sire's exhibition has been pushed ahead by two more days: not tomorrow, Friday, as planned, but Sunday evening. Did he not tell you?"

"No. He did not! And I am sick with worry, Herr Uninsky, because I haven't been able to reach his phone. It's as though the line has gone dead. Do you know, please, *please*, where he is?"

"I do know where he is. You needn't worry. Let's go to my office and I will explain everything to you."

Uninsky led them through several rooms, one half of the walls of each of which were hung with Sire's enlarged photographs of Afghanistan then and in 2022. The other half of the walls of each showroom was blank. Uninsky beckoned his visitors to seats in his spacious office.

"I shall explain to you what has happened and why I too have been unable to reach Richard by phone. Because of the terrible things that are presently happening in Ukraine, and because some thirty years ago Richard, as he did with Afghanistan, took a series of photos of different Ukrainian cities and their architectural treasures...oh, you did not know this?" Mary's jaw had dropped open.

"Well then. I guess you can imagine what he spontaneously

decided he had to do for our exhibition here. As you know, we had planned to show only the photographs he took in Afghanistan thirty years ago and again just this year. But now here was this extraordinary opportunity—*obligation*, he called it—to document what is happening today. And so he left for Ukraine the very evening of the day he arrived here in Berlin. We both agreed that it was a necessity. But I was unaware he had not contacted you about his sudden change of plan. I am so very sorry. No wonder you have been worried." Tears had come to Mary's eyes and Megan began lightly patting her shoulder.

"God, this is just like Sire! I should have known, should have guessed where he was when I couldn't reach him." Mary's relief was almost palpable. But immediately a thought came to her.

"How do we know he is safe, though?"

"We know, because ten minutes ago, via an MSNBC photo crew posted in the Kyiv borough of Bucha, he sent us *this*," said Uninsky, pointing to a screen on the wall behind his visitors. They turned and gaped at what they saw. In living color the black of death had been captured: seven twisted corpses, left to rot, were strewn across what had once been a tree-lined neighborhood street with a small school, now completely shelled out.

"And twenty minutes earlier, Sire got *this* to us."

The screen now showed a shelled church in the distance and a deserted highway in the foreground with black tires heaped atop five discernable bodies. All Mary and Megan could do was to wipe away the tears that came unbidden. Words were not available. Finally Gabor Uninsky spoke again.

"We are pairing these painful images with similar sites and locales photographed by Sire in their integrity thirty years ago. What a message these documents will bring to the public. And to our news media here in Berlin and beyond. And what a brave man your Richard Sire is."

"Yes, what a brave man," murmured both Americans, relieved to know where he was and deeply moved to learn the reason why.

25

Jared was surprised not to find the director of Hamburg's Fanny and Felix Mendelssohn Museum in her office. He had been researching files in the records room since the museum opened at ten and by noon he thought it was time to take a break, trot up to Rachael Skylar's office and tell her of two small but interesting finds he had made, both having to do with Felix's inspired feat of reintroducing Bach's forgotten St. Matthew Passion to the musical world. But the director was nowhere to be found, and upon questioning one of the museum guards, he learned that she had not yet arrived. So Jared went to a Burger King and had a relaxed meal. He checked the reservation he had made for a hotel in Berlin early that morning and figured out how close it was to his new friends Megan and Mary in their elegant Bristol Hotel lodgings on the Kurfürstendamm. He had been unable to obtain a room there himself but had settled for an interesting luxury hotel just off the same mile-long boulevard, the Hotel Zoo—a mere ten minute walk from the actual Berlin Zoo. If Grace Kelly and Sophia Loren had stayed there in the 1960s, it was good enough for him in the 2020s.

"Frau Doktor Skylar is here now," announced the guard Jared had queried earlier.

Jared went directly up the stairs to her office. He paused at the closed door and knocked. There was only silence. But then, just as he was about to leave, he heard a woman's strained voice command softly "Come in." What Jared encountered was a tremulous Rachael seated behind her desk and hastily wiping away tears.

"Oh, Frau Doktor! Rachael! For heaven's sake, what has happened?" Unable to stop himself he bolted to the side of the desk and took both her hands in his. Touched to the core by Jared's concern,

Rachael let escape what had held her in a vice all morning.

"I...I, we, my five-year-old son Davyd and I received some terrible news earlier today. Nazar, my, my husband, he is in Ukraine right now to help his parents flee the country and come to us in Hamburg, but, but early this morning his father called me and said Nazar had been *shot*! Russian cross fire as their bus was just eighteen kilometers from the border. He is alive, thank heaven, but his wounds are very painful, superficial they say, but painful, and, and..." Sobs overwhelmed Rachael and Jared laid one hand comfortingly on her shoulder as she dried her tears.

"Does your boy know all this?" he asked.

"No. Davyd only knows from listening to me on the phone that his father is, is... 'sick,' I told him. Our maid is with him now and will be for the rest of the day until I get home again."

"Were your husband and his parents able to cross the border in spite of his wounds?"

"Yes, oh, yes, thank god. They are on a train right now crossing Poland and they will arrive here at the Hauptbahnhof this evening supposedly at six-fifteen."

"So you can meet them at the main train station then! Isn't that wonderful?"

"Yes, yes, of course it is." Rachael smiled woefully, dabbing her eyes and cheeks with a finger. "It's just that I do not feel capable of driving our big station wagon to pick them up. I'm too nervous with such a responsibility. I'll have to arrive in an Uber and persuade the driver to wait while I locate them if their train has arrived. I know I shouldn't be crying over such a small thing when a grand thing is happening, but..."

"Do not give this another thought," Jared interrupted, placing both hands on the woman's shoulders and standing back from her, his head lowered and staring into her brown eyes. "If you allow, I will drive you in your car to the train station and bring you and your family home. All will be well, you'll see."

As Rachael murmured her thanks through a new bout of tears, Jared smiled, nodded, and took his temporary leave until the poor woman came to the records room to get him. The calming effect of Felix Mendelssohn and Bach would fill the time till then.

26

Mary and Megan were still discussing Sire's bold and sudden decision to return to Ukraine as they ate lunch near the Gabor Uninsky Gallery. The restaurant they had chosen was on the same street as the gallery, and it was its name that had attracted them: Hummus & Friends. They decided to eat indoors and chose what the extensive menu described as 'Trio Hummus for Two.' It was a healthy mixture of fresh avocado, red beets, and garbanzo beans, each mixed with hummus.

"Could not have been a healthier meal," Mary allowed as she sprinkled a little garlic on the tasty concoction.

"Mm. I agree," mumbled Megan, her mouth momentarily full.

Over a cappuccino, some email catch-up took place as well as a bit of people watching. Oranienburger Strasse was obviously a very popular commercial street in this interesting Jewish section of Berlin's Mitte and it offered all sorts of cafes and restaurants. On the other side of the street and just two blocks up from them at 29-31 they could see the façade of a building they had read about: the New Synagogue. It was still called that despite having been constructed in the mid-nineteenth century. The façade was unusual: Eastern Moorish style with one central and two smaller side domes. It had actually survived Kristallnacht destruction because of police interference when Nazi thugs began setting fire to the many treasures inside—a fire which threatened to burn down not only the synagogue but the adjacent residential buildings. However it did not survive allied bombings in 1943. What Megan and Mary were looking at was a reconstruction of the street façade with its entrance and dome and two smaller domed towers. There were now only a few rooms behind the entrance. The original enormous building behind the façade had been truncated just before the main hall of the synagogue, which once could accommodate 3,200 worshippers.

Unable to resist photographing the façade, Megan left Mary at the Hummus restaurant for a few minutes and returned with a triumphant expression on her face. "Look at this, she said, holding her phone up toward Mary. "It's a plaque on the façade that tells us the data we know plus a very touching inscription: '*The façade of this house of God shall remain forever a site of remembrance. NEVER FORGET.*'"

"Very moving," agreed Mary, staring at the photo Megan had taken. They both sat in silence for a minute and then, wishing to change the sad subject, Mary asked Megan a question about their itinerary in Berlin.

"What Fanny sites in addition to the J. and A. Mendelssohn Bank founded by her uncle and her father are you thinking we might visit, Megan, now that we'll be here two days longer than we'd originally planned?"

"Yikes! We better be sure we *can* stay two more days. Let me call our hotel and prolong our reservation." She searched for the number on her phone and called. It was a quick and successful call. The only slight drawback was that they would have to move to another but similar room for the two extra days. This made Mary realize that they should also change the day of their Alitalia flight to Rome and while making that call she asked that the flight schedule of Richard Sire also be adjusted to match theirs. The date of their return flight to the States would not be affected since they would still have plenty of days in the city. Not to be forgotten, however, was the new arrival day at their hotels in Rome. This too was accomplished without any problem. A good forty-five minutes of doing the revision work necessitated two more cappuccinos.

"Now! Mary, you were asking what Fanny sites we could visit in addition to checking out the Mendelssohn family bank building."

"Right. Especially now that we'll be staying two days longer in this rich-with-history city."

"The bank isn't the most pressing item I'd thought of visiting here but let's just find out if Jägerstrasse fifty-one is by chance anywhere near us here." Megan typed a few words onto her phone, got her answer, and smiled broadly.

"The answer is no. But good news. The bank is very near Gendarmenmarkt Square which is also here in the Mitte district, so if we go to the bank now we'll be very close to our hotel which means that afterward we can take a little lie-down as we, or rather, as I did in Hamburg."

"Oh. yes. Probably I won't want one but there's plenty I can do quietly in our room while you doze for a little while."

"Great! And then after dinner at the hotel we'll be rested and ready for tonight's performance."

Megan was referring to a revised performance of the popular 1966 musical *Cabaret* at the Schaubühne on Lehniner Platz which was conveniently located on the Kurfürstendamm. Mary had ordered tickets for them while still in the States after studying what was on in Berlin's theater world during their stay. The loud, jarring musical, set in a seedy Berlin during the rise of antisemitism and the Nazis, seemed somehow related to their Mendelssohn quest. And when Mary told Megan she'd gotten them tickets, Megan was thrilled, admitting she'd only seen the later film, not the musical in the flesh.

Filled with purpose, the two women abandoned their empty cappuccino cups and headed for the Mendelssohn Bank. If they had expected a tall, imposing building, they were disappointed. The long, two-story, white building with rows of windows was just that. Nothing regal or in your face. Only in the twenty-first century had an identifying plaque been designed for it.

Megan was quick to photograph the large, convex, shield-shaped memorial plaque. The left side showed the emblem of the Mendelssohn Bank: a vigilant crane clutching a coin in one claw with the motto "I watch."

"Darn good motto for a bank," Mary declared. Then while Megan continued photographing, she read the right side of the hand-burnished, bright bronze plaque out loud for her:

> Starting in 1815, this building housed the banking firm founded by the brothers Joseph and Abraham Mendelssohn. The Mendelssohn family lived at this address and worked here, and over many generations turned it into an inviting salon for

artists and scholars. Established in 1795, the company became Berlin's largest private bank in the 19th century. In 1938, Mendelssohn & Co. Bank was forced into liquidation by the Nazi regime.

Taking a look around the informative exhibits and objects inside the building of the Mendelssohn remise, they learned that the informative shield was unveiled on January 21, 2004, which was the two hundredth anniversary of the founding of the Mendelssohn Bank. A digital family tree covering seven generations attracted their attention and they spent some time listening to music by Felix and Fanny at a small media station.

That the historic remit of the building to the Mendelssohn family in 1998 and placement of the shield marker on the building façade took so long, was something Mary and Megan discussed on the way back to their hotel. And it had been heartening to learn that the winning design for the plaque had been submitted by a woman sculptor by the name of Annelies Rudolph.

"Fanny would have been proud," Mary commented and Megan nodded vigorous agreement.

As they began walking in the direction of their hotel, they passed by a once-regal old house in front of which, embedded in the sidewalk, was another one of those brass "stumbling stones" they had first literally stumbled upon in Hamburg. Mary stopped to read the name of the Jewish family who had been deported from their home, and then on her phone she looked up the *Stolpersteine* list for Berlin. She was stunned to read there were more than 1,400 of them throughout the metropolis all created by the artist Gunter Demnig. Also, other artists were now creating them in other countries, driven by the "Lest We Forget" principle. Heartening, the two friends pronounced reverently.

The rest of the day went as agreed upon. Back at the hotel Megan dozed; Mary emailed. An in-house dinner was relaxed and delicious and *Cabaret* met all their expectations—excellent voices and acting along with potent, jarring sets. There were even English surtitles. An unexpected bonus was the theater itself—an immense former cinema with a circular front designed by the Art Deco architect Erich *Mendelssohn*! Yet another son of yet another Mendel. Who could ask for more?

27

Members of the Hamburg neo-Nazi adherents were surprised to be called to a virtual meeting set for ten o'clock that Friday morning. Organizer of the Zoom meeting was their formidable new leader Barbara Badubrecht and her message was straightforward and simple. No time was left for questions after Badubrecht had voiced her order.

"Greetings to all you brave Hamburg n-N members. As of yesterday morning I, Barbara Badubrecht, am your new director until our greatly respected leader Michael Bormann is released from prison. The first and only order of business today is a request from our Berlin counterpart to participate in two important demonstrations scheduled there for tomorrow morning and for tomorrow evening. If you can be present for both events, please come; if only to one, then let us know immediately. At noon today a description and meeting point locations of the two separate protests in Berlin will be emailed to you according to the records we have for each of you at Bormann's office. If any of you have updates, please send them immediately to our organization's cyber address. Do not telephone; phone calls will not be answered. Any questions you may have will be responded to by contacting us via email. You will receive a revised update later today. Thank you and... see you in Berlin!"

The dazzlingly beautiful, unsmiling woman exited her Zoom screen with the touch of a forefinger.

28

Earlier that morning, on his eight o'clock flight to Berlin, Jared was reliving the unusual events in which he had been a participant the night before. His spontaneous offer to drive Rachael Skylar to and then from Hamburg's central train station once her husband Nazar and his parents arrived from Ukraine, had turned into a search and rescue mission. For starters, the train was an hour and a half late and arrived on a different track from the one announced. Then, when Rachael finally spotted the family and began running toward them, her husband's mother, also running, lost her footing and fell. Nazar was unable to help her up as he was supporting his father, whose wounds had begun bleeding again after hours of immobile sitting. And so it was Jared who ran to aid the fallen woman. One look at her was enough. Yanking out his cellphone, he quickly looked up the number then dialed 112 for an ambulance.

"Don't try to go further, any of you!" he had commanded the Skylar family. "An ambulance is coming. Stay where you are."

Rachael immediately understood how grave the situation was and knelt over her mother-in-law, urging her not to attempt to get up. Nazar guided his father to a platform bench and settled him into a sitting position. Blood was pooling from his wounds. When the ambulance crew arrived a few miraculous minutes later, Jared caught Rachael's attention.

"Just find out which hospital they're taking his parents to and we'll follow in the car."

Although they did not reach Rachael's car in time to follow the ambulance, she knew where the Albertinen-Krankenhaus was on Süntelstrasse and by the time they arrived, both of Nazar's parents were already under emergency care. The mother had broken a shoulder which was now being set and the father's wounds had been cleansed and rebandaged: all he needed was rest and food.

Not until well after midnight was Jared able to drive everyone to the Skylar home. Little Davyd, under the faithful maid's attentive care, was awakened by the noise and when he woke up to see his Táto bending over him, his cries of happiness brought smiles of joy to everyone. Rarely had Jared felt such empathy, such satisfaction. And now he was on the way to Berlin to join his two new friends in their Mendelssohnian explorations. He was also most curious to see what his Hotel Zoo was going to be like. After all, guests Grace Kelly, Romy Schneider, Hildegard Knef, Gina Lollobrigida, and Sophia Loren awaited him...in spirit at least!

An hour later Jared was in a taxi going at a fast clip from the Berlin airport to the compact, seven-story Hotel Zoo. The historic, twenty-foot high entrance facing the Kurfürstendamm was jaw-dropping while everything beyond was unusual, ranging from dark lobby to rooms that had been gutted and redesigned in 2012. The result was, in Jared's judgment, "swank." There were 127 luxury rooms and fourteen opulent suites, to which one of the panoramic latter he had treated himself. After all, who knows if his two new American "girlfriends" might wish to visit his spectacular lodgings?

The walk down a long hall to the reception desk took him along a dark green carpet lined with life-size images of hunting leopards seen from above. The nearby Zoo-indebted felines guided him to a walnut wood reception desk where he left his suitcase. Check-in time was not until three p.m. and before calling his girlfriends to see what they had planned for the day, he explored the lavish public rooms and vistas floor by floor, coming finally upon an elegant rooftop lounge and bar, its 270-degree panorama protected by glass walls. What a view of the city! Oh, yes, bringing Megan and Mary here was a must.

Lounging in one of the rooftop chairs and absorbing the Berlin skyline, Jared ordered a black coffee and called the cellphone number Megan had given him. He recognized the cheerful voice that answered.

"Megan! It's Jared. I'm here in Berlin, at my hotel. And even though Felix and Fanny never stayed here, we've got to put it on our to-do list. This place is spectacular—luxurious modern overkill. You'll love it. Swankier than your Bristol hotel, I'm sure." Megan laughed.

"Great. We'll try to get there. Our visit here has been extended because the opening of Richard Sire's show has been rescheduled from this evening to Sunday."

"Oh. I'm sorry."

"Nothing to be sorry about. In fact we're glad to have the extra time to search out our Mendelssohn spots."

"What do you have lined up for today?"

"Well, we're still at breakfast, but we thought today might be devoted to the gravesites."

A shudder went through Jared as he involuntarily pictured the sacrilege he had come upon at Hamburg's Jewish Cemetery. But he was game.

"Awesome. May I join you two ladies?"

"Of course! Hold on a second. Mary wants to tell you something."

"Sure thing."

"Welcome to Berlin, Jared!" Mary's distinctive voice sounded in his ear.

"Thanks. I can hardly wait to get together with you two ladies so the Fanny and Felix Trio can be operational again." Mary's cascading laugh sounded merrily in his ear. Megan's giggle could be heard as well.

"So what's on your agenda for today other than gravesites?" Jared persisted.

"We thought it could also be a good day to visit the Jewish Museum." A big smile animated Jared's face.

"An all-Jewish day. Why not? Shall we do the cemetery things first, get them out of our bloodstream, and conclude with a walk through history? That's what I've read that the Jewish Museum here is strong in chronicling our long history."

"Good," agreed Mary, "let's do it in that sequence. When and where shall the F and F Trio meet?"

"How about you two stay put. Since you're in the middle of breakfast and I've not had mine yet, allow me to join you. I could be there in ten minutes or less."

Jared was as good as his word, and after all had eaten their fill, they lingered over coffee finalizing the day's itinerary.

"I find it nice that all three of the most famous Mendelssohns are buried here in Berlin, even Felix, who died in Leipzig," Megan mused as they studied a fold-out map of the city she had brought with her. A firm believer in paper maps, she always traveled with ones of the cities to which her peregrinations took her.

"Yes, but even more amazing, miraculous, really, is that two of the three original gravesites survived Nazi destruction," commented Jared.

"When you say 'two of the three' of the most famous Mendelssohns, you are speaking, I take it, and in order of death, of Moses, Fanny, and Felix, yes?" Mary asked, just wanting to be sure.

"Yes, that's right," confirmed Megan. "Shall we get going? Does anyone want to visit the restroom before we leave?" It turned out everyone was pleased to do so.

"Should hate having a need to pee in the graveyard," said Jared over his shoulder.

They regrouped outside the hotel just as a taxi showed up discharging three passengers right in front of them. The F & F Trio happily took their places. First destination was the *Alter Jüdischer Friedhof*—Old Jewish Cemetery—of Berlin where Moses Mendelssohn had been buried. Megan voiced what she was thinking as they got closer to the cemetery.

"You know, from a few hard-to-read images I've seen on the Internet it looks as if the tombstone might have been inscribed in Hebrew. But other photos definitely show the inscription to be in German. Confusing but interesting!"

"Both might be true," intervened their driver. "Some years ago, in two thousand eight, the city began remodeling the cemetery."

"Interesting. But to 'remodel' a tombstone? I think not," Mary murmured quietly.

Soon they were seeing for themselves as, despite or perhaps because of city refurbishment, the isolated Moses tombstone was easy to locate. In the upright Ashkenazi style, the tall, freestanding, gray slab with curving crown clearly identified in five easily readable lines Moses Mendelssohn of Dessau and his birth date, and his death date in Berlin: 6 September 1729—4 January 1786. The inscription was in German on the front and in Hebrew on the back, so the conundrum was solved. The three visitors to Moses' grave respectfully photographed both sides of the tombstone. Touching to see were the pretty little rocks visitors had placed in homage on the grave and tombstone.

Then it was back to the waiting cab and on to their next destination, the *Dreifaltigkeitsfriedhof*—Trinity Cemetery—in the Friedrichshain-Kreuzberg district. This was where both Fanny and Felix as well as their parents were buried—in the cemetery section reserved for Jewish converts to Christianity—*Neuchristen.* Most conveniently, all their graves were within the same small plot which was protected by low black iron fencing. The contrast between Fanny's and Felix's gravestones couldn't have been more different. Fanny had died first on May 14 of 1847 and her tombstone was a large, rose-brown, standing granite slab around five feet tall and about thirty inches wide and nine inches thick. The gold inscription read: Fanny Cäcilie Hensel born Mendelssohn Bartholdy; then came her birth and death dates followed by some measures of a melody by her. A melody which, although Mary immediately hummed it, was not known to any of them. She photographed it for later research.

A stunning grave, the three visitors agreed. Then, after spotting the grave of Fanny's husband Wilhelm Hensel nearby, they turned their attention and cellphone cameras to the gravesite to the left of Fanny's. Felix's headstone could not have been more different from his sister's memorial slab. Slightly shorter than hers, it was a tall, white, cement cross. Engraved in black along the crossbar and after all his given names, was the double surname his father had taken for the family: Mendelssohn Bartholdy. The cross emphasized the Christian faith to which he had converted.

Intriguing, the visitors from America again agreed. They began reading and occasionally photographing inscriptions on the neighboring graves which were headed either by a standing white cross or a rounded, upright, granite slab; all of them were related to the Mendelssohn clan.

"It's truly miraculous that these gravestones of Fanny and Felix survived Nazi destruction of Jewish monuments," declared Mary.

"Yes," Jared marveled, "and just consider the diverse fields those Mendelssohns represented: Moses, the great philosopher, his sons Joseph and Abraham, founders of a prestigious bank, and Fanny and Felix, extraordinary composers."

"And this of course is what Nazi antisemitism strove to destroy: suppressing Moses' work, shutting down his sons' bank, and banning music by his grandson," declared Megan.

"No need to mention any banning of Fanny's work since she was unknown and unplayed at that time. Her discovery and renaissance have only come with twenty-first century scholarship," Mary said sadly. Then she continued on a happier note.

"Speaking of playing, guess what I've brought with me if we can find a piano and some privacy?"

"What?" her friends asked simultaneously.

"Fanny's '*Das Jahr*'—'The Year.' "

"How wonderful!" Megan clapped with enthusiasm.

"Wonderful what?" Jared asked.

"The twelve-piece piano cycle she composed after the happiest twelve months of her life when she, her supportive painter husband Wilhelm Hensel, and their nine-year-old son Sebastian lived in Italy during the years eighteen thirty-nine and forty," explained Megan. "How clever of you to bring the music with you, Mary. Did you bring the actual paper score with you or download it?"

"It's all on my iPad."

"Great!" Megan exclaimed.

"Can you actually play the piano reading from an iPad?" asked Jared simultaneously.

"Oh yes. The pedal is linked to my iPad by the Bluetooth system. It's a hands-free way to turn pages with my left foot. Makes it much easier than turning with my hands! And now we three are here in Berlin where Fanny gave the cycle to her husband on Christmas Day of that last year, and in a few days we'll be in Rome, the city that inspired the cycle. So I thought it would be really thrilling to play through it. In *both* cities if possible."

"In that case I think there might still be a piano in one of the basement rooms of our own hotel—I used it in previous decades before the Kempinski became the Bristol. We'll take a look-see when we get back, good?"

"Terrific!"

"Now we've seen the three main graves on our agenda," said Megan, "but there is one other Mendelssohn grave we might consider visiting."

"Whose?" Jared asked. Mary was silent.

"That of Fanny and Felix's uncle, Joseph. It was he, after all, who first ran the Berlin bank: Their father didn't join him until he moved his family here in eighteen eleven."

Silence greeted Megan's suggestion.

"Where is it?" Mary asked finally and unenthusiastically.

"It's at Schönhauser Allee, up northeast of here in Prenzlauer Berg. You know, where Käthe Kollwitz lived. Right by the park named after her."

"Who is Käthe Kollwitz?" queried Jared.

"*Who was Käthe Kollwitz*?" Megan repeated in disbelief. "She was the powerful Expressionist artist and sculptor whose depictions of working-class poverty and suffering in Berlin were so poignant during the Kaiser's time, and then later she defied Hitler with her poster 'Never Again War.' She lived for decades practically right next to the Jewish cemetery in Prenzlauer Berg and I always try to get there whenever I'm in Berlin."

"Was she Jewish?" Jared wanted to know.

"No, but she was loyal enough during Hitler times to attend, along with only thirty-eight other courageous persons, the funeral at that cemetery of Max Liebermann."

"And I take it Liebermann was an artist and he was Jewish," chanced Jared.

"Certainly was; in fact he was Berlin's most important portraitist."

"And how do you know the exact number of persons who attended Liebermann's funeral?" Jared was truly curious.

"Because thirty-nine mourners signed the condolence book, that's why. So shall we go there? Megan added a final enticement. "And by the way, grand opera composer Giacomo Meyerbeer, the 'other' important Jewish composer at Fanny and Felix's time, is also buried there. Although he died in Paris, four months later his remains..."

"Megan, it all sounds so interesting, but perhaps we should stick to our primary Fanny research," dared Mary.

"And we still haven't been to the Jewish Museum. Who knows, perhaps the Mendelssohns we're primarily interested in might be part of one of the exhibits," Jared enticed. Megan gave in with grace and they returned to their patiently waiting taxi driver. He had a suggestion based on their itinerary so far.

"Berlin has an Anne Frank Institute out on Rosenthaler Strasse you might be interested in." Megan was the one to answer for them all.

"Thank you. We *are* on the trail of a Jewish woman, but we have to limit it to just her this time. Have you ever heard of Fanny Mendelssohn?"

"No."

"I'll tell you about her while you kindly drive us to our next goal, the Jewish Museum."

The distance was more than they imagined and included passing Checkpoint Charlie, another historic entity from West and East Berlin times and through which Megan had actually driven several times in the distant past. As they finally sighted the one old and two new buildings that constituted the Jewish Museum coming into view, Jared spotted something equally important.

"Hey! Stop right here!" he commanded the driver who obliged as safely as possible. They had pulled up in front of several eateries.

"Look! That restaurant calls itself 'ONLY BAGELS'! That's the most relevant spot possible for us to eat lunch before we enter the labyrinth of the Jewish Museum ahead. Right, gals?"

"Yes. I am a little hungry," Mary agreed.

"Me too. I hadn't actually noticed I was till just now," acquiesced Megan.

She paid and thanked the taxi driver who in turn thanked her for telling him who Fanny Mendelssohn was, promising he would listen to a YouTube recording of her music.

Inside the small, crowded restaurant with driving German electronica music, a mouth-watering and varied menu awaited them. Jared ordered a guacamole bagel and orange juice; Mary, a mozzarella and tomato bagel, also with orange juice; Megan, nothing liquid, but a salmon bagel with plenty of cream cheese plus a bowl of muesli with fruit and yogurt, which she ended up sharing with her two jealous partners.

"Do you know the history of why bagels are a Jewish food?" asked Jared who had finished eating first.

"No. I just know that smoked salmon on cream cheese and bagels is associated with Jewish food," Megan answered. "I used to eat lox a lot when I lived in New York."

"Right. Well, I'll explain. Legend has it that in the seventeenth century a Jewish Viennese baker wanted to send the king of Poland a gift for having saved Austria from invasion by the Turks. He knew that the king loved horses and so he created a round roll with a hole in the middle for the shape of a stirrup—'*Buegel*' in German—and soon salmon and cream cheese served on bagels became popular with Austrian and Polish Jews and eventually all over central and eastern Europe. And it was Jewish immigration to the States in the nineteenth century that introduced the bagel to New York and other cities. So that's why we think lox when we eat salty salmon strips and cream cheese on bagels. End of explanation."

"Well, that's quite an explanation. It will lox in my brain forever," quipped Megan, a sometimes too frequent voicer of puns.

Freshly nourished, the F & F Mendelssohn Trio strode eagerly up Lindenstrasse to the trio of buildings that constituted the recently completed Jewish Museum—the largest Jewish museum in Europe. What a strange, jolting sight it was to look from the old yellow, red-roofed rectangular two-story building that once housed the German Supreme Court on their left, then look right and instantly come upon two connected, almost windowless titanium-zinc faced slabs of buildings winding backward away from the street. At first glance they seemed to have no physical or intentional connection with the staid Baroque building. Could they have seen the two buildings from the air, the Mendelssohn Trio would have realized instantly that the mournful gray edifices interconnected into what looked like a writhing serpent or bolt of lightning or broken star of David. The three buildings made a strange but powerfully symbolic grouping of the unstable but stubborn continuum of Jewish history.

After the Trio entered the museum they learned that the brilliant architect of this continuum displaying two millennia of German-Jewish history and culture was the Polish-born American architect Daniel Libeskind. What an achievement! And in the permanent collection so many things to see: dozens upon dozens of zigzagging exhibits mounted in ways and groups never attempted before and lodged in unexpected areas at different levels, most of which involved wooden or iron staircases of one kind or another, some leading to cement voids. Something Megan noted warily. Libeskind's use of angled walls, underground axes, empty concrete areas—voids—without air-conditioning or heat all purposefully contributed to visitor disorientation, echoing the addled existence of displaced Jews in history.

One of the things the Mendelssohn Trio stopped to listen to was a podcast by Libeskind speaking about how architecture, like music, creates a shared space that connects us all. The listeners' multiple head nodding conveyed their silent agreement with the architect.

The special six-month exhibition had opened just the day before and they gladly paid the price of entry—the exhibition was on Moses Mendelssohn! And the first thing they saw was multiple images of the man hung crosswise on a wall including two identical historical oil portraits, framed differently and hung sideways, one above and beyond the other. As they studied the images and accompanying documents they realized how far had been the reach of the humpbacked ghetto boy from Dessau who became Berlin's philosopher of the Enlightenment. All this they were absorbing when suddenly the overhead lights began blinking and a man's voice started speaking over the PA.

"Visitors! Silence please. We regret to inform you that ten minutes ago in Berlin's Old Jewish Cemetery the tombstone of Moses Mendelssohn was discovered to have been vandalized concealing the inscription. A hate note on cardboard was taped to it as well. The note reads: *'No museum exhibition on Moses M can correct his humpbacked hopes of assimilation. Jews will always remain Jews!'*"

29

At five-twenty that evening in Berlin an irate Johannes von Bandtrop was on the phone with Barbara Badubrecht.

"It's all over the news. If it wasn't one of your over-eager people, then who could it have been, for god's sake?" he questioned his former lieutenant, now newly elected leader at his own suggestion of the Hamburg neo-Nazis.

"All I can tell you, Johannes, is that I prepped them this morning about your two upcoming demonstrations and urged as many as could to join your people in Berlin tomorrow. Not today."

"And you're sure you said tomorrow?" Johannes was at his wit's end. Did he have an overeager follower right there in Berlin?

"I am absolutely sure, Hannes." The fact that Barbara used his nickname convinced Johannes of her adamant truthfulness. Their short-lived affair had been over for years but they still cared for and trusted one another.

"All right. Then it falls upon me to root out here what idiot took the initiative to stage a one-man protest. And at the wrong place, the wrong time, and the wrong day! And now of course we don't dare hold the demonstration in the Jewish Museum tomorrow morning. The place, the whole neighborhood will be guarded by police. Good god! Do you realize that if we proceeded, *I* could be arrested?"

"That is scary. Yes, you've got to identify the asshole who did this! And I'll double check here, of course."

"Thank you, Barbara. Notify your troopers immediately that tomorrow's morning event is canceled and that they should come to Berlin only for the other event that evening, and I'll be doing the same right away here, okay?"

"Right. You bet."

"Goodbye then." Johannes von Bandtrop hung up abruptly, turned to his computer and began typing an urgent event cancellation notification. He also increased the volume of what he had been playing to calm himself. It was what he always played when in need of serenity: the overture to Richard Wagner's *Tannhäuser.*

30

Still stunned by news of the desecration of Moses Mendelssohn's gravestone, neither Jared nor Mary nor Megan had any idea of what time it was and were surprised when they found out. It was now five-thirty and the Trio had spent more than three hours in Berlin's Jewish Museum! Too late for visiting any more "M" sites for the day, they took a taxi to Jared's Hotel Zoo in hopes that seeing his "swank" lodgings might take their minds off what had just happened in the city. Jared gave his ladies a full tour, one that, of course, included his luxury suite with its panorama of the city. The tour concluded at the rooftop bar and everyone opted for Bailey's Irish Cream. Tension was easing and only then did Megan realize she had not had her afternoon nap. The mere memory brought on a great yawn, one that was contagious, as immediately Mary and Jared yawned as well.

"Have you ever tried to make an animal yawn by pretending to yawn at it?" Megan asked. Her interlocutors shook their heads no.

"I have with my little Maltese dog Button, and it works every time. And then the funny thing is that he'll yawn at me sometimes and it's absolutely contagious. I yawn immediately. So, after researching the phenomenon, I learned that mammals, birds, and even reptiles yawn."

"I don't think a reptile would make me yawn back; I'd be out of there too fast!" laughed Jared.

"We could ask the Internet why yawns are contagious," Mary suggested, yawning involuntarily.

"I know there are competing theories about what triggers yawning, but I don't remember any of them," said Jared, suddenly yawning at the utterance of the word yawning. "What we should concentrate on, however, seems to me, is deciding where to eat this evening, or do you two have plans for tonight?"

"Not anymore, since Richard's photographs exhibition opening isn't taking place this evening after all. For tomorrow night, however, we do have something planned. And then finally the exhibition will take place on Sunday. Do you think you might still be in Berlin then, Jared? It would be wonderful if you could see Richard's work." Mary smiled encouragingly at him.

"As a proud member of the F and F Trio, I am prepared happily to remain in Berlin for as long as you dear ladies do," Jared affirmed immediately.

"In that case you could go with us to the very special event we'll be attending tomorrow evening, since Sire's ticket will go unused otherwise," answered Mary. "Megan's former university colleague, a well-known composer and conductor, is giving the European premiere of his recently completed...well, you tell him, Megan."

"His recently completed *A Jewish Requiem*. Like Brahms's specific titling of his requiem as *A German Requiem*."

"A Jewish requiem? I don't think I've ever heard of one," Jared said, awed by the majestic idea.

"I hadn't either," responded Megan. "The world premiere of, full name is *Azkara*—meaning 'memorial' or 'remembrance'—*A Jewish Requiem*, took place just a few months ago in New York at the Park Avenue Synagogue. It was a sensational, really huge success. And Simon's admiring colleagues in Berlin immediately begged to be the first to perform it in Europe."

"And here I *live* in New York and didn't know about it! But then I'm not a practicing Jew. I'd absolutely love to come with you. Where is it going to take place?"

"At the Rykestrasse Synagogue," answered Mary.

"It's Germany's largest synagogue, we learned online," Megan took up the conversation. "It was finished in nineteen-o-four and was immediately criticized as being 'too large!'"

"How so?" Jared wanted to know.

"Well, the interior initially seated two thousand people and..."

"That's *crazy*!" interrupted Jared.

"Right. It was deemed so soon enough by its congregation and when recent renovations were made, the worship space was whittled down to just a little over a thousand persons—one thousand and seventy-four, to be exact," said Megan.

"Is it liberal or Orthodox?"

"Liberal *and* Orthodox, I've read on recent Internet updates," was Megan's surprise answer.

"Ah, so separate seating some of the time," Jared mused.

"What do you mean? Separate seating for women and men?"

"Exactly."

"That's what I was afraid you meant." Megan sighed, her feminist sensibilities springing front center. Should she tell Jared what really upset her about orthodoxies? She decided yes.

"I cannot accept that the daily morning prayer of every Orthodox Jewish man thanks God for not having made him a woman."

Jared sighed.

"Yes, I understand, Megan. There are multiple explanations for that, of course, mainly that two other categories are previously mentioned in the prayer—God is also thanked for not having made the man a Gentile or a slave. But..."

"But nothing, thank you Jared. I have read all the explanations including the one pointing out that the role of woman was so constricted at the time that being thankful not to have been created female is justified and not an anti-woman statement in itself. But I can't help it, Jared, I am still offended to the core. This despite explanation of the historical setting." Jared put his hand gently on Megan's shoulder.

"Megan, Megan. I understand. The prayer could also have included thanks for not having been made homosexual. I understand your pain, believe me."

A bond of understanding had just been formed between the two new friends.

"So, since Jared can attend the requiem, tell us more about your former composer colleague Simon Saragon," urged Mary.

"Ah, S S! Well, there's plenty to tell. He was brought to America as a child from Bombay. His parents were of Saragondi, Indian-Jewish, and eastern European Ashkenazi heritage. He earned a master's degree from the Juilliard School of Music in nineteen sixty-two and I remember that date not because I knew him then, but because my second-floor apartment in New York at that time—one forty Claremont Avenue—well, the apartment had a side window that looked out directly across a vacant lot next to Julliard. So who knows, we might well have walked past each other on the street! I must remember to tell him that sometime."

"What were you doing living in New York at that time?" Mary asked. "I know you went to Barnard College, but that would have been earlier, yes?"

"Oh, yes, six years earlier. But I was back in New York after earning an M.A. at Berkeley—where I discovered Egon Schiele incidentally—um, back in the city to get a Ph.D. in art history at Columbia University. That's why I rented an apartment on Claremont Avenue, because it was only two blocks from the university. And during eight of those eleven years I was in New York that time I also taught, first as an instructor, then as an assistant professor at Columbia before I was yanked to Dallas."

"Yanked? How so?" asked Jared laughing.

"By a splendiferous teaching offer from SMU where my mother had founded the Italian Department and was still teaching. And so it came to be that my younger sister, Tina, was the student of both her mother and her sister!"

"That's amazing. What did she major in?" Jared pursued. Megan laughed.

"Well definitely *not* in Italian or Art History! She studied City Planning at SMU and then, escaping her family, she went to Florida State University to study Urban and Regional Planning."

"And she'll be meeting up with us in Rome, where she's taking a two-week course in glass and fiber arts," added Mary. "But, Megan, please tell us a little more about Simon Saragon."

"Certainly. For starters, as a composer he has written operas, symphonic works, chamber music, choral works, and Lieder. As a teacher, before coming to SMU for two decades plus as Professor of Composition, he taught at Sarah Lawrence College and at his alma mater Juilliard in America, and in Jerusalem at the Rubin Academy of Music for a number of years. *And* he served as music director of Dallas's prestigious Temple Emanu-El for some twenty-five years." Megan looked at the engaged expressions on the faces of her friends and added a question that hit its mark.

"So how old do you think he must be, with all those accomplishments behind him? I'll give you a hint. He's four years younger than I." Mary giggled knowingly, while Jared was left in the dark until Megan proudly told him which specific year in the eighties she now logged in at.

"Will he be conducting his requiem here?" Jared asked.

"He was going to do so until a slightly more famous conductor asked if he might have the honor."

"Who?"

"Nathaniel Darenborne."

"*Nathaniel Darenborne!*" Jared was impressed beyond words. He could barely wait to hear and experience Simon Saragon's *Azkara—A Jewish Requiem* in the historic Rykestrasse Synagogue.

Tomorrow evening could not come too quickly.

31

"Papa will be so proud of me. Finally he'll notice me!" declared fifteen-year-old Helmut von Bandtrop, son of Johannes von Bandtrop. He was murmuring to himself as he waited for his terribly overworked father to finish speaking on the phone in his home office. He had been talking angrily to his fellow commander in Hamburg, telling her that the Jewish Museum event scheduled for tomorrow morning had to be canceled. At last he hung up, obviously upset and in a bad mood. Helmut was about to change all that.

"Papa! I can see you're upset, but I have something to tell you that will cheer you up. Want to know what?"

"Not now, child. I'm busy."

"But you will be so pleased and happy with what I have to tell you..."

"*Not now!*" The angry father turned his back on his bothersome son.

"*Papa!* What if I tell you who already did something spectacular like you were planning to do tomorrow?" Johannes von Bandtrop wheeled around to face his son.

"*What*?"

"Papa, it was me! *I* am the one who wrapped colored tape all around the old Moses Mendelssohn gravestone from bottom to top. And *I* was the one who taped a declaration on it about Jews always being Jews. *I*, Helmut, your very own son did these things. Aren't you proud of me?"

32

Why the hell had she instructed her Zoom group to send any email address updates to her, Barbara Badubrecht asked herself angrily. Her screen was flooded with messages. Most of them were not about address updating but rather notes asking if she would consider having dinner with the sender. Some even included photos of the sender. Crap! What were these Hamburg neo-Nazis in need of? A dominatrix or something?

Fuming, she answered none of the unwelcome emails but went straight to her task: informing every member of Hamburg's neo-Nazi organization that the demonstration planned for tomorrow morning in Berlin at the Jewish Museum had just been canceled. Thus it was even more crucial for all Hamburg members who could, to join the very important demonstration planned for that evening. The start time was precisely at seven-thirty in the evening; the location remained the same as initially announced. Secrecy was crucial.

33

The stirring sounds of *Tannhäuser* had for once not functioned as the uplifting, calming agent to which Bandtrop, an accomplished pianist, was accustomed. He could not erase from his mind the fact that his very own son, by a selfish and premature act of vandalism, had forced the cancellation of a long-planned demonstration inside the obnoxious entity forced upon his beloved city in the form of the new Jewish Museum. This time he would turn to something more palpably helpful by his hero: Wagner's extraordinary essay *Judaism in Music—Das Judenthum in der Musik*. It was originally published under the testy pseudonym "*K. Freigedank*"—"K. Free-thinker"—in Leipzig's *Neue Zeitschrift für Musik* in 1850—just three years after Felix Mendelssohn's death. After a scathing characterization of Jews in general—their looks, their dialects, their pronunciation of German words—the essay focused its hateful critique on the two major Jewish composers of the time, Mendelssohn and Meyerbeer. The latter had been an early supporter of Wagner, enabling the Dresden premiere of his opera *Rienzi*. Almost twenty years later, in 1869—five years after Meyerbeer's death—Wagner published the infamous essay again, this time under his own name and with updated footnotes.

Searching for some of the most poignant and pertinent passages by his idol, Bandtrop's eyes focused on some favorite paragraphs he had copied and pasted together for himself—paragraphs emphasizing why the modern Jew could not compose true music because of innate peculiarities with reproducing common sounds. He read the lines aloud, echoing the accepted authority of the great composer whose entire life had been devoted to sound:

The Jew—who, as everyone knows, has a God all to himself—in ordinary life strikes us primarily by his outward appearance, which, no matter to what European nationality we belong, has something disagreeably foreign to that nationality: instinctively we wish to have nothing in common with a man who looks like that.

In particular does the purely physical aspect of the Jewish mode of speech repel us. Throughout an intercourse of two millennia with European nations, culture has not succeeded in breaking the remarkable stubbornness of the Jewish *naturel* as regards the peculiarities of Semitic pronunciation.

The first thing that strikes our ear as quite outlandish and unpleasant in the Jew's production of the voice-sounds, is a creaking, squeaking buzzing: add thereto an employment of words in a sense quite foreign to our nation's tongue, and an arbitrary twisting of the structure of our phrases—and this mode of speaking acquires at once the character of an intolerably jumbled blabber *s*o that when we hear this Jewish talk, our attention dwells involuntarily on its repulsive *how*, rather than on any meaning of its intrinsic *what*. How exceptionally weighty is this circumstance, particularly for explaining the impression made on us by the music.

This written iteration from a mind such as Wagner's was balm to Bandtrop's wrath. He had read the words aloud many times to his son. Yes, by his impetuosity Helmut had jinxed his demonstration plans for tomorrow morning, but the undeniable fact that even so young a person had been inspired into action by Wagner's words was something to be thankful for, not angry about. A feeling of peace descended upon Bandtrop. Peace and pride that his own son had been responsible for such a news-making public protest. He would praise the boy in front of his sisters and mother over dinner that evening.

34

Short, blond, and muscular with acid yellow-green eyes, Homer Wesselmann prided himself on being an "independent" member of Hamburg's formidable neo-Nazi organization. Independence for him meant occasionally joining the loud raggle-taggle group when the spirit moved him and their demonstration seemed worthy enough. One of his favorite self-assignments was harassing visitors after they left the city's embarrassing Fanny and Felix Mendelssohn Museum. He would follow them for a number of blocks and when other pedestrians were not around, hurl an insult as he ran up behind his prey and then, turning his back, he would retreat so quickly that his face was never seen. His favorite affront was to hiss the words "Watch out, you misguided Jew lover!" So far there had been no problems or reports to the police and Homer was encouraged to continue his satisfying pastime until a greater cause came along to challenge him. And now he believed it had.

An urgent callout had come from Berlin's super active neo-Nazis to join them on Saturday for two protest demonstrations in one day. Homer had eagerly responded to the call. In fact, he had managed to contact by phone the Berlin unit's inspiring, but never seen in public, leader Johannes von Bandtrop. They had spoken at some length and in fact Homer had accepted a personal assignment from Bandtrop that quite appealed to him as it involved "raising havoc." It was because of this that he arrived in the city that very Friday afternoon. He had first sized up the revolting building where the evening demonstration was to take place Saturday. Then he leisurely explored the sorry interior and art displays where the morning event was scheduled to occur: Berlin's new Jewish Museum. Looking with revulsion at the crowded exhibit on Moses Mendelssohn, he spotted a rapt visitor whose face somehow looked familiar. Searching his mind to place it, he found that his ears were suddenly filled with music. Music he had heard recently. Oh good god, it was by that horrid Fanny Mendelssohn! But how did he know what it was, he asked himself. Then came clarification. The museum visitor whose face seemed familiar was the man who had been sitting in the park near the Petit Bonheur restaurant Wednesday evening, playing his cellphone at top volume for a group of people who had gathered around him. Homer had expressed his disgust by spitting on the ground near the man's blaring phone as he strode by indignantly. And now here was that same man! Before he could do anything to make the Jew lover uncomfortable, the museum's PA system suddenly blared a message informing all visitors of a "distressing" thing that had just been discovered at the city's Old Jewish Cemetery: the tombstone of Moses Mendelssohn had been vandalized and a hate note left affixed to it.

How fabulous! Homer Wesselmann of Hamburg had certainly arrived in boisterous Berlin at the right time.

35

Saturday morning's exciting plan for the F & F Trio was meeting for a relaxed breakfast at Megan and Mary's hotel and then taking an Uber along the spiffy shopping and tall condo avenue of Leipzigerstrasse out to Berlin's eastern Friedrichstadt where the Mendelssohn family had held forth. Before departing the States, Megan had eagerly culled details from a number of Mendelssohn biographies, including two photographs, concerning the site at Leipzigerstrasse No. 3. Back in 1825, the neighborhood's grandiose but deteriorating complex—the former "*Reck'sche Palais*"—had been purchased and refurbished by Abraham and Lea Mendelssohn, partly with their four talented offspring in mind. The house's long tripartite street façade with nineteen upper story windows and three mansard roofs gave no indication of the vast acreage and garden that extended from the back of the building. It was exactly this that appealed to the Mendelssohn family in search of both a safehouse in the time of escalating antisemitism and a private cultural center that would soon become the setting for Fanny's popular musical matinees and soirées to which Christian and Jew, forgetting their differences, vied for invitation. The house's spacious garden wing—recorded in a winsome sketch by Fanny's husband Wilhelm Hensel—was where the two lived after their marriage in almost rural seclusion, protected from street noise by a forest of great green-leafed trees.

The center section of the house contained an immense hall suitable for court balls. There was space in it for well over a hundred and fifty people. On the garden side was a sliding glass wall, supported by pillars, so that the hall-auditorium with its view of the enormous garden could be easily converted into an open portico giving onto the garden and terrain beyond of about seven acres that at its far corner originally housed a farmer with twelve cows providing the family with fresh butter and milk.

All this was imbibed by Mary and Jared as an enthusiastic Megan read aloud from her laptop notes over their second cups of coffee. Eagerness to see the Mendelssohn mansion with its garden pavilion where teenaged Felix had composed both his Octet for Strings in E-flat Major and then his famous *Overture to A Midsummer Night's Dream*, took especial hold of Jared and finally he interrupted Megan's narrative to dial for an Uber. Five minutes later the Trio was on its way to Leipzigerstrasse 3.

"I am *ubercome*," he joked as their Uber deposited them at their destination.

But once the Uber had driven off and they had a chance to look around, something inexplicable was apparent. The enormous edifice at Number 3 did not look at all like the building in the photographs Megan had shown her two buddies over breakfast. This edifice was larger, far larger than the Mendelssohn home, and its address was not only Leipzigerstrasse 3 but also 4. A Greek temple façade adorned the middle of the building's second story and the two attached side buildings jutted out in front of the main one. If this structure had anything in common with the Mendelssohn mansion, it was only because it was composed of three buildings. A sign finally sighted by Mary informed them they were looking at a government building that since the year 2000 had housed the Bundesrat. Not a word about the Mendelssohns.

"Oh, my god!" Megan exclaimed. "I was so enchanted by the images of the house and garden that it never occurred to me to check and make sure the house still existed. I just presumed it was now a museum. Oh, no, I can't believe I didn't check it out! I'm so sorry!"

"Not to worry, Megan," Jared comforted her. "Enthusiasm just took the upper hand."

"I'm sure we've all done things like that," added Mary. But Megan was not to be comforted.

"I've never done anything this stupid concerning research before. It must be because I am becoming senile in my eighties."

"Absolutely not!" protested Mary, who had edited Megan's Clara Schumann book from a professional musician's perspective and knew what she was capable of.

"Definitely not from what I've seen of you in action," confirmed Jared. Then he grinned and held up his cellphone which he had begun consulting after Leipzigerstrasse 3 had morphed before their very eyes into Leipzigerstrasse 3-4.

"Hey, ladies. Good news. If we want to visit something Mendelssohnian today we can visit the Mendelssohn-Bartholdy-Park. Only it isn't a park, it's a U-Bahn station! Named after a small park east of it that's named in honor of Felix Mendelssohn Bartholdy. Now does that sound complicatedly exciting or not?"

"*Not*," his ladies answered in chorus. From that point on laughter was infectious as they strolled slowly along Leipzigerstrasse before resorting to the U-Bahn to return to Berlin's Mitte and their hotels. An alternate Mendelssohnian activity patiently beckoned in one of them.

36

One other visitor to Berlin had plans to visit a historic site in the busy metropolis that Saturday morning.

Simon Saragon, Megan's composer colleague from Dallas, had arrived late the night before to meet with conductor Nathaniel Darenborne for a private morning rehearsal of his *A Jewish Requiem* before its performance that evening at the historic Rykestrasse Synagogue. The rehearsal was set for ten o'clock and Simon, who abhorred being late, taking the subway line U2, had arrived some twelve minutes early at the site which was near the Kollwitzplatz in Berlin's outlying northeast Prenslauer Berg district. As white-haired, somewhat heavyset Simon stood studying the building's façade at Rykestrasse 53 with its two entry arches, he wondered how it could possibly be a synagogue. It certainly didn't look like a synagogue. Could it have been a school? And, as things turned out, the street-side building had been one since the fall of the Berlin Wall. Puzzled, Simon walked through one of the open gates of the two large arches in search of a possible courtyard-cum-synagogue and he found it: a large two-story, red brick building with a triangular roof and two pointed entryways.

Near the synagogue was a plaque with a brief history of the structure. The edifice had been opened in 1904 and, after the Great Synagogue in Budapest, is still considered the largest synagogue in Europe. Prior to the outbreak of World War II in September of 1939, Jewish elementary and religious schools were located in the street-side building. Nazi ruffians demolished the synagogue's original interior during the pogrom of November 1938. However, it escaped torching because of its dangerous proximity to next door apartment houses. In

1940 German military confiscated the building to use as a warehouse and horse stable. After the war, repairs were completed in 1953 and seating was dialed down from over 2,000-plus to 1,200 persons and under Communist rule during the sixties, seventies, and eighties it was the only synagogue used in East Berlin. In 2005 dedicated renovation restored the structure to its elegant pre-World War II state. The Rykestrasse Synagogue was Germany′s largest synagogue. Today, the congregation is Liberal-Orthodox.

Freshly informed of the building's unsettling history and realizing suddenly it was almost ten o'clock, Simon moved to enter the synagogue. But the doors were locked and a large sign stated that the synagogue was closed to the public except for certain limited times for public tours on Thursdays and Sundays. Just as his jaw dropped in disbelief, one of the doors was unlocked and Simon was waved into the building by a smiling young man well aware of who he was and his relationship with Darenborne.

"Welcome, Professor Saragon! The maestro awaits you up there before the ark, in front of his musicians."

At first Simon's eyes were almost blinded by the celestial bright light pouring in from the array of arched windows over the U-shaped, multi-arched wooden balcony and seconded by rounded windows on the ground and lining the clerestory. A gigantic lit chandelier looking as though it weighed a ton dominated the ceiling center and the tall side walls were glimmering white with differing beige articulations and connecting narrow green crossbeams. This same green was echoed by the enormous arch that framed the ark in front of which was now a small orchestra and choir. The musicians were silent at the moment, as white-haired, stocky Nathaniel Darenborne of the authoritative black eyebrows, noting the time and signaling his performers to stop, turned to locate and greet his special guest. He spotted him coming down the center aisle that cut through the wealth of bright brown rows of seats on either side.

"Simon! There you are, my good man! Our *composer*! Simon Saragon. Do join us up here. My musicians are so looking forward to meeting and performing for you."

Introductions were made and a few questions concerning tempi and volume answered. Simon was quite taken by the enthusiasm and knowledge of the performers.

"And now for your critical listening and, we hope, your simultaneous rapture, let us perform your *Azkara: A Jewish Requiem*. Musicians! From the beginning if you please!"

Rapturous approval was indeed Simon Saragon's basic response as the affirmations, questions, and urgings of his *A Jewish Requiem* commenced to sound throughout a stunning and historic 1904 synagogue in twenty-first-century Berlin.

37

That Saturday for Bandtrop Senior was unusually active. Despite last night's urgent directive calling off the morning demonstration, some idiots from both Berlin and Hamburg had shown up at the Jewish Museum regardless of his and Badubrecht's very clear cancellation of the demonstration there. Fortunately no one in the scattered group made a scene or drew attention to him or herself in front of the museum. Instead they all, without exception and unaware of each other's presence, anxiously contacted their leaders in Berlin and Hamburg. Badubrecht and Bandtrop had briefly taken time to bemoan the situation with each other, then it was back to answering panicked texts and emails. Oh, to have reliable, intelligent members in the ranks rather than crybabies who were besieging them with questions!

But at least even these pathetic members were aware of the fact that police were staging a very visible presence around the museum buildings and consequently did nothing foolish. Thus, so far at least, nothing had happened to clue police that a well-planned demonstration was to take place in Berlin that evening. This protest would occur at a different sort of site from the usual ones at Jew-related museums and cemeteries. It was highly likely that surprise would rule the day, or one should say evening, and that the courageous, independent neo-Nazi from Hamburg to whom Bandtrop had assigned a vital task would escape arrest in the pandemonium that was sure to follow. Both Bandtrop and Badubrecht had, at the last minute, decided they would be there in person for what was going to be a theatrical and apropos act of condemnation.

38

Hamburg's "independent" neo-Nazi Homer Wesselmann was spending his full day in Berlin as a tourist, visiting sites that interested him. Now that the Jewish Museum demonstration had been canceled he had all day to himself before the 7:30 evening event at the Rykestrasse. This was something he was really looking forward to as he had never been inside that kind of weird building before. He had one brief errand to make at a hardware store before taking the rest of the entire beautiful August day for himself.

Homer's private agenda was filled with quite different sorts of interesting sites. First on his list was the Monster Kabinett situated down an alley off the bustling Rosenthalerstrasse. It turned out to be a warehouse in which the visitor was confronted by platoons of various sorts of monsters varying from scampering spiderlike metal robots to wounded sculptures to aggressive, bizarrely costumed human actors. What a treat! Then it was on to the spooky, now derelict Spreepark, overgrown by grass and home to abandoned thrill rides exiting from monster mouths, a still functioning Ferris wheel and scary roller coaster and wild water journeys. After partaking of the thrills, Wesselmann studied an artificial rock display of the Grand Canyon, spiriting one small specimen away for himself.

Then it was off to the anarchist Georg-von-Rauch-Haus, a free-living collective with ever-changing residents. The large ring of graffiti around the ground level attested to the everpresent antagonism between the police and the city's left-wing squatter movement. This was the sort of thing that appealed to Wesselmann's sense of humor.

And finally, as coolant for his nerves, he took himself to the abstract-looking, multiple tent-like structure at Möckernstrasse number ten in the heart of the city. There he could spend the afternoon drifting in the Tempodrom's enormous saltwater floating pool, the Liquidrom. Large arches surrounded the famous domed and dimly lit pool with its multi-colored lights and music spanning from techno to classical meant to be heard underwater.

A perfect relaxant before turning to the noble task ahead of him that evening.

39

Seated next to the center aisle in the front row of pews with a full view of orchestra, chorus, and conductor, Simon Saragon's full attention was on the morning rehearsal of his seven-part *Azkara—A Jewish Requiem* at the Rykestrasse Synagogue. He definitely approved of how the opening section was being performed and was happy with the emotional connectivity conveyed. Also he was pleased that, because of the synagogue's recent shift from Orthodox Judaism to Reform Judaism, two cantors stood before him and one of them was a woman. Simon could hardly wait to tell his wife!

A ten-note introductory motif for cello and string bass, then repeated by the chorus, conveyed not the mournfulness of a Christian requiem but an immediate and earnest questioning of God. The cantor's opening line as conveyed by a soprano voice seemed somehow especially more potent to Simon: "Lord, What Is Man?—*Adonai, Mah Adam?*" This question, posed in Psalm 144:3, was asked not once but three times during Simon's three-and-a-half-minute-long piece: "Oh, God, what are we that you should care about us? Oh, God, what are we that you should care about us? Mortal humans that you should think of us?" Yes, Simon nodded unconsciously, such a query needs to be asked several times. Three times I've specified it ascendingly, with a descent at the very end. It does work nicely.

And now on to the second of the seven sections of my requiem, the composer mused, readying himself to absorb the four-minute-plus music to "The Lord is My Shepherd—*Adonai Roi*" as conveyed by the musicians before him. Its statement, movingly voiced by the cantor, male this time, and seconded by the choir, was a passage from

Psalms 144 and 90 that emphasized the brevity of life: "God. God, we are like a breath. Our lives are like a passing shadow. At daybreak, it flourishes and grows up. By dusk it withers and dries up." Simon's music demonstrated this process of vanishing from the earth through quiet, disappearing chords. The musical and vocal declarations moved from confidence to adamant confirmation through hard times. The composer smiled as the music concluded with an upward octave articulated by the cantor's tenor voice.

"Remember How Frail I Am—*Z'chor Ani Meh Chaw-led*"—was the plea that characterized Simon's third musical setting, and this time woodwind instruments joined the strings. The entreaty filled the synagogue for three minutes and three seconds and it was the tenor cantor again who intoned and led the imploration of the choir's answering extended repetitions in a minor key. Celestial woodwinds concluded the slow four-note motif's hopeful upward climb.

I wonder how "Jewish" this will sound to a mixed audience of Jews and Christians, Simon asked himself. Will they respond to the diminished seconds and minor modes of my Jewish Requiem as being Jewish? Will the use of scales with microtonal notes from both Ashkenazi and Sephardi traditions seem super Jewish to some and merely mournful to others? Think what Leonard Bernstein did with Jewish liturgical themes in his third Symphony, the Kaddish one. I'm hoping to do something similar. Before Simon had time to ponder further the requiem's fourth section began: "I Lift Up My Eyes—*Esa Einai*." No cantor's voice led this time; it was totally a choral piece with men's voices intoning what would be a meditative alteration of men's and women's voices repeatedly embracing what would be a diminished second in Western music. Simon laughed. Well, this harmonic leitmotif of G/B-flat/A/F/G business could really confound a mixed audience! And yet for him, the repeated five-note themes broadcast ebullient serenity.

His attention was steered back to the performers as the fifth section sounded: "The Lord Has Given; The Lord Has Taken Away—*Adonai Natan; Adonai Lakach.*" Lasting a little over three and a half minutes, a stark sforzando from the brass instruments running up a scale initiated the choir's immediate response. At first basses, tenors, and altos overwhelm; then a sudden capping of the first half of the text by soprano voices. This past gift of the Lord is marveled over by various choir voices and sections until suddenly another brass octaval run darkens the musical mood as dismayed acknowledgement that the Lord has also taken away and the chorus changes from calm acceptance to mournful realization of this second truth, with brief orchestral conclusion. Yes, yes, this is very much the way I wanted it, Simon told himself. Perhaps suggest to Nathaniel that he bring out the bass voices more; at times they sound overwhelmed by the others.

Just as Simon was thinking this, Maestro Darenborne turned his head toward him, a gentle smile on his face. He was about to perform the requiem's three-and-a-half-minute section six, "The Rock Whose Ways are Perfect—*Ha-Tsur Ta-mim P'-aw-lo*." Simon returned the smile, nodding his head, Nathaniel turned back to his players and gave a gentle downbeat. Against suspended choral notes the tenor soloist began to sing of the Rock—God, whose work is perfect. For all his ways are just, a God of faithfulness and iniquity, just and right is He. The confirming chorus repeats these calming words at length and at the end the tenor voice ascends to heavenly heights with four concluding notes, the last one of which leaps joyously into that heaven.

"Perfect!" Simon couldn't help exclaiming out loud, much to the smiling satisfaction of the maestro and his performers. To himself now Simon articulated the thrilling thought: and now cometh the sublime, I hope, conclusion. The composer settled down into his seat, his full attention centered on the last and longest-lasting music to come: a full seven minutes and fifteen seconds voicing "God, Full of Compassion—*Eil Maleih Rachamim*/ Blessed be the True Judge—*Baruch Dayan Emet*."

Arpeggiated chords in the violins articulated celestially by flutes assured the listener of serenity and safety, echoed by the gentle entrance of the tenor solo and chorus. The orchestra tenderly caressed their words and for the first time distinctively what might be called "Jewish" minor intervals and diminished-second trills were recognizable, beginning with the tenor's initial phrase and continuing throughout the tender piece. Celestial musical serenity is how Simon characterized the concluding section of his *A Jewish Requiem* to himself. And apparently the musicians felt the same. When the music came to an end it was they who applauded its composer. They and the maestro who applauded until Simon, tears running down his cheeks, stood up to receive the approval *A Jewish Requiem* had earned.

40

Jared had accompanied Mary and Megan back to their hotel, responding to the lure of a Fanny Mendelssohn-related item that for sure was extant, as opposed to the legendary family house at Leipzigerstrasse 3 which they had discovered to their dismay and Megan's mortification no longer existed. Mary retrieved her laptop with Fanny's Italy-inspired piano composition *The Year* and they followed Megan into the elevator where she pushed the button for basement. When the door opened they stepped into a hallway, one side of which was lined with mops, buckets, and other cleaning materials. Hopefully, Megan opened the first door on the far side of the hall and peeked into the room. No piano. She did the same with the other five doors and got the same negative result. Only hotel supplies and two crowded offices.

"So I guess the spiffy new Bristol did away with the convenient piano practice room supplied so generously by the old Kempinski," she announced angrily. "Such a shame, and so typical of today's values."

"Let's decide what other things we'd like to spend our day doing in this rich city before dinner and tonight's synagogue concert," Mary urged.

"We could take one of those ship tours along the Spree River," suggested Jared. "I read on the flight here that you can even take a tour of Berlin without ever getting off the ship." He looked eagerly at his fellow F & F Trio members. Megan's face was expressionless but Mary had an immediate answer.

"I like to go *inside* important buildings, not just admire them from the outside, no matter how magnificent they might be." Nodding her head in agreement, Megan offered a solution.

"We could go to Museum Island right in the middle of the Spree River here and tour both the Altes Museum and the Neues Museum—that's where the famous head of Nefertiti is, you know."

"Why would an Egyptian sculpture be in the collection of an institution that calls itself the *New* Museum?" Jared asked somewhat peevishly.

"Because the two museum names don't reflect what period of art they contain but when they were built," laughed Megan. But she realized how much Jared really wanted to take a boat trip and so she added an encouragement.

"I tell you what. If we have time after visiting the two island museums—and actually, Jared, there are five of them on the island—we could take a fifteen-mile boat tour down to Potsdam and have a look at the eighteenth-century so-called Versailles of Germany, Sanssouci Park and, from the outside at least, Sanssouci Palace—summer home of German emperors."

"How about we visit only *one* museum on Museum Island, then head for outdoorsy Potsdam?" was Jared's quick response as he looked from Megan to Mary.

"Let's see how the time works out," murmured Mary diplomatically. She loved Greek and Roman art and both the Old and New Museums had plenty of that, she had just learned upon consulting her cellphone. A further look indicated how to get to Museum Island by way of the S-Bahn to Hackescher Markt station, and from there it was only a brief walk.

No sooner read than done. Within sixteen minutes they were on the island walking toward the New Museum during which time they bought their admission tickets online. Another few minutes and they were standing in front of the museum's prize possession: the life-size, intriguingly painted limestone bust of ancient Egypt's beautiful Queen Nefertiti. The royal woman's bust was created well over three thousand years ago in 1345 B.C., they learned. A forward projection of her chin and slender neck emphasized the length of the neck and largeness of the head, a head crowned by an extended cone that extended one and a half times the length of the head. The main colors of the crown were smokey blue and dusty red, the skin tones a very light vanilla brown.

Jared was enchanted. Frozen to the spot and standing in front of the bust displayed at his height in a tall glass case, he felt as though he were looking right into the Queen's hooded brown eyes. He soon learned, however, stealing a glance at the museum handout, that he was looking into only one of the original eyes—the right one. The almost intact bust of Nefertiti was discovered in Egypt on December 6, 1912, when a German archaeologist named Ludwig Borchardt was excavating the ruins of a house at Amarna identified as belonging to a certain Thutmose, sculptor to the pharaoh married to Nefertiti. Borchardt saw a flesh-colored neck in the rubble and then the lower part of the bust and finally the conical crown. Missing parts of one ear were recovered but the missing left eye was never found—possibly because the bust had not yet been completed. So!

Jared was riveted, hypnotized by the bust so full of history and beauty. Wanting to read the museum brochure through while in front of Nefertiti, he waved for his patiently waiting companions to go on; he would join them soon. He read that during World War II Nefertiti had been hidden by the losing German troops in a salt mine but was discovered by American troops and given back to the German museum that had housed it before the war. Jared also learned that Nefertiti's name means "The beautiful one has come," and he, like the museum pamphlet, began to ponder from where.

Fifty-five minutes later Nefertiti's spell broke for a minute and a bedazzled Jared staggered toward the museum lobby looking for his friends. They were nowhere to be seen. He checked his phone. There was a text waiting for him from Mary sent twenty-three minutes earlier: "We didn't want to interrupt your homage to Nefertiti so have gravitated across to the Old Museum to see the Greek, Etruscan, and Roman art. After that Megan wants to have her afternoon nap, and I need to catch up on email. So rather than join , why don't you take that boat tour to Potsdam and Sanssouci and we'll meet at your Zoo hotel for our early dinner before this evening's concert. Text ok if ok."

Jared texted ok, then returned to Nefertiti. Never mind boat tours and Potsdam and Sanssouci. I am where I want to be.

41

Barbara Badubrecht's train arrived in Berlin precisely at four o'clock and in plenty of time for dinner at the home of Johannes von Bandtrop before the Rykestrasse Synagogue concert at seven thirty that evening. The Bandtrops lived in a roomy apartment building that overlooked the Marlene-Dietrich-Platz, so named to honor the famous Berlin-born actress and singer. Dietrich's first film, *The Blue Angel* of 1930—simultaneously filmed in both German and English—escalated her to fame as the seductive Lola Lola with her "bedroom eyes" and brash, alluring song "Falling in Love Again," complaining how men swarmed around her "like a moth to a flame."

The square itself was as impressive as its namesake. Facing it were a movie theater, the Berlin Film Museum, an IMAX theater, a casino, cafes, residential and commercial buildings, and the Grand Hyatt Hotel where Barbara would be staying overnight. She was happy to visit Bandtrop's family again as she found children easily malleable, especially young Helmut, who was so often ignored by his father. What a surprise then when Johannes praised his son over dinner, confiding to Barbara and his approving mother that it was he who, on his own, was responsible for the vandalism done to the tombstone of Moses Mendelssohn. Both women applauded at the unexpected news and Helmut's cheeks became flushed with pride. Praise from his busy, important father!

The dinner and conversation passed quickly and before they realized it, it was nearing time to leave. Helmut and his mother would also attend the concert and they were enthusiastically briefed on what to expect in the weird Jewish building where the concert was being held—the synagogue in old Prenzlauer Berg.

42

Despite his unexpected, unabashed love affair with Nefertiti, Jared was seated at his Hotel Zoo's elegant, or "swank" as he termed it, Grace Restaurant well in advance of the arrival of his two travel comrades. He had managed to obtain a corner table and after sizing up the beautifully decorated room was deeply engaged in studying the unusual menu when Megan and Mary arrived. They were in jovial spirits and soon became as entranced as Jared by the restaurant's short but richly varied European-Asian menu. Mary laughed out loud at the first item: a list of the sparkling water available. There were two kinds—"*l'eau sans souci classic*" and "*l'eau sans souci naturelle*" and they came in two sizes.

"Perfect for you, Jared, since you missed going to *Sanssouci* this afternoon," Megan jested.

"Believe you me, I didn't mind missing it at all, I had fallen so in love with that amazingly beautiful Nefertiti bust."

The food turned out to be rather pricey but as the trio discovered, well worth the cost. After ordering truffled green leaf salads all around, they chose a variety of dinners: Jared, salmon tataki; Megan, lemongrass spring chicken; and Mary, Peruvian lamb fillet. Their shared sides included sautéed spinach, jasmine rice, and Chinese cucumber. Delicious, everything was delicious, they agreed. But definitely no dessert.

"I just noticed something," Jared said suddenly. Wordlessly he pointed up to the ceiling. Both women looked up and both made exclamations of surprise. Hanging low from the ceiling in the center of the great room were five large, domed chandeliers shaped like huge bird cages. The center one was larger than the other four and all had two circular levels containing small pointed bulbs that appeared like candle flames. The center chandelier had three levels of these uncannily convincing flames and the ensemble was intriguing.

"Hey!" Mary said consulting her watch, "it's time we were going if we want to arrive at the concert early enough to get good seats."

"Right," agreed Jared. "I'll order our Uber. You gals get the check and figure out what dividing it into three comes to."

Nine minutes later they were on their way to the European premier of Simon Saragon's *Azkara—A Jewish Requiem.*

43

Another jovial dinner was taking place not far from the Rykestrasse Synagogue, at Schliemannstrasse 15. Seated at a small corner table in the restaurant, Simon Saragon and Nathaniel Darenborne were meeting for a private, preconcert discussion and meal before the big performance. The vegetarian restaurant they chose, Kanaan Prenzlauer Berg, had been recommended by an old Berlin friend of Nathaniel's as an unusual eatery that served delicious Israeli and Palestinian cuisine. And so it did. A variety of salads, fresh vegetables, crunchy falafels, and, most tempting of all, hummus dishes with a variety of sauces. The owners, one from Israel and one from Palestine, obviously cared as much for social tolerance as they did for delicious food. They as well as their waiters wore black T-shirts with lettering in white spelling out the words "Ich Bin Hummussexuell."

Simon and Nathaniel were enjoying both the food and the ambience as their conversation dwelt on various performance aspects of the requiem ranging from volume and meter to interpretation. Most of their conversation centered on the German translation. It of course made no sense to present the work in English here in Berlin but Nathaniel thought the German translation, made, he learned, by one of Simon's former students, did not convey the innate power of the words. There were several fine translators, one of them a practicing cantor, whom Nathaniel could recommend and Simon was grateful for his frankness. The white-haired old friends were in agreement on all major aspects of the music, and expectations were high concerning audience appreciation. Although the synagogue would probably be overcrowded based on ticket sales, no problems were anticipated.

What a blessing and an honor to be able to present the first

European performance of the world's first Jewish requiem!

This shared moment of joy between two friends was shattered when Nathaniel's cellphone rang. There was no exchange, only a barking command from the synagogue's business manager.

"Maestro! Walter here. This is urgent! When you arrive at our synagogue *do not use the courtyard entrance*. Use the back entrance one street behind. It's under one of the building's three blue domes. You can't see them from the courtyard. Use the entrance underneath the small dome on your left when you face them. There is a neo-Nazi demonstration going on in the street in front of the courtyard!"

44

Among the few intrepid early concertgoers who broke through the slowly marching line of neo-Nazi demonstrators in front of the Rykestrasse Synagogue street entrance was a short, muscular man with yellow-green eyes. He was holding a long metal toolbox to which several rings of electrical lines were attached. Waving the young ticket taker aside at the inner courtyard door to the house of worship, he identified himself as the emergency electrician called in to check out the fuse box controlling ceiling lighting as there was an overhead continuous blinking problem that had just occurred.

"I figure it won't take more than a few minutes to identify the problem. You sure don't want blackouts during your concert," he laughed confidently as he passed inside.

"Thank you!" called the young man after him.

What looked like a family of three adults and one young boy had paused to stare at the banner-carrying, loudly chanting protesters, all of whom were wearing the classic brown shirts of neo-Nazis. Their signs stated in large bold font: "NO MORE JEW MUSIC IN BERLIN!" The demonstrators were shouting that slogan as they walked back and forth in front of the street entrance to the Rykestrasse Synagogue. At standby on the other side of the street was a single police car. Its four occupants had confirmed the protesters had filed for permission and as long as there was no violence or entrance blocking, the police were powerless to act. When the musicians with their instrument cases had begun arriving, two of the officers had helpfully directed them to use the building's back entrance. But as early concertgoers began showing up, the police did not intervene, leaving them to use the front entryway as best they could. And so, slowly, did Badubrecht and the Bandtrop family; their route was followed some ten minutes later by the F & F Trio.

As directed, Saragon and Darenborne entered the synagogue through the back entrance and began conferring with the anxious musicians. The two cantors joined them and gradually calm was restored. After all, the neo-Nazi demonstration was outside; the sublime comfort of *Azkara—A Jewish Requiem* was inside.

45

The emergency electrician had found a perfect post in the synagogue balcony for what he had in mind and it was not examination of the building's fuse boxes. He had stationed himself next to a support arch in the front row of the left-side balcony, midway down the sanctuary. From there he had an unobstructed view of the ark in front of which a small orchestra and choir were now gathering. He would choose his moment.

Megan, Mary, and Jared were still in plenty of time to obtain excellent seating in the building that held 1,074 persons and Jared spotted an ideal position up in the right-side balcony where several contiguous front row empty seats beckoned. Most of the concertgoers had chosen to sit on the ground floor in the attractive wooden pews and Jared, as usual with him, simply could not understand why people wouldn't want to have the unobstructed view of things that balcony seats provide. Megan and Mary followed their friend up the stairs to claim their front row wooden seats. Once settled, they began studying the beautiful beige and white interior of the building with its green crossbeams and gigantic green arch framing the ark behind the musicians. All was bathed in the light of three enormous circular chandeliers hanging low over the ground floor pews from the high ceiling. Unlike the birdcage-like ones at Hotel Zoo's Grace Restaurant, these bright lights did not shine in the guise of candles.

Like so many of the synagogue audience, the Bandtrops and Barbara Badubrecht had chosen to sit downstairs and they were lucky to find seats all together some eleven rows back from the front with Johannes taking the aisle seat. Young Helmut was all eyes as he examined the unfamiliar architecture of the strange building where

Berlin Jews worshipped. And he was impressed by the presence of not only a choir but an orchestra.

"Does every syn gog have its own orchestra?" he asked his mother.

"It's synagogue, not *syn gog,* dear, and no, none of them have permanent orchestras. There's one here tonight because there's going to be a special concert. It will probably be very sad music because it's a memorial to people who have died."

"And the man who composed the music is an American Jew," added Barbara, who had been listening to the conversation.

"You mean there are Jews in America?"

"There are Jews all over the world, dear," Barbara answered, "and that's why we worry that they might take over the world. Control money, television, and the press, produce large families and thrust the likes of us out."

"Auntie Barbara is correct, *Liebling*, and that's why she and your father have so many members in their clubs," Frau Bandtrop added.

"When I grow up I want to be in *your* club," declared Helmut, turning to Barbara with large adoring eyes.

"That would mean you'd have to live in Hamburg, not here, Helmut. Remember how proud your father is of you that you vandalized that old Moses Mendelssohn tombstone. He would be very sad if you weren't in his club."

"What's this?" asked Johannes, catching the last part of Barbara's sentence and looking at his son. Barbara answered for him.

"Just that Helmut wants to be in your organization when he's of age."

"Good. And because of what you bravely did yesterday, you are already an honorary member."

"I am? Does that mean I can be mad at Jews now, like you?"

Simon and Nathaniel had finally parted company. The composer went to a seat upstairs, choosing to sit in the middle of the U-shaped balcony and in the center front seat that had been reserved for him at his request. From this position he hoped to absorb all elements of his requiem—sound, performance, and audience reaction. And he wouldn't be embarrassed to be seen taking photos at times with his cellphone even though he knew a professional video was being taken and would be sent to him. People seated nearby who had read for whom his seat was reserved were already nodding and smiling at him in recognition. What an evening for this American in Berlin!

And now the male rabbi of Rykestrasse Synagogue walked out to the one-step podium in front of the orchestra. Instrument tuning stopped immediately as the distinguished-looking man turned and smiled at the suddenly hushed audience. His greeting was joyful, genial, and short.

"Good evening to all and welcome to our historic Berlin synagogue. We are assembled here tonight for an extraordinary event: the European premiere of noted American composer Simon Saragon's '*Azkara—A Jewish Requiem*.' He is here with us as is world-famous conductor Nathaniel Darenborne who will conduct this *first* Jewish Requiem ever to be composed. *And it's about time!* Maestro, if you please...."

From what could be called the left wing of the ark the energetic white-haired Darenborne walked briskly to the low podium, acknowledged the audience applause with hands pressed to his heart, and then turned smiling to the orchestra, arms spread out in symbolic embrace. He then gave the downbeat and *Azkara* began with its imploring question: "Oh, God, what are we that you should care about us? Oh, God, what are we that you should care about us? Mortal humans that you should think of us?"

"See what I mean?" Leaning forward and pointing, Barbara Badubrecht whispered to Helmut. "So Jewish, immediately badgering with a question rather than praising God or blessing the dead or comforting those who mourn."

Helmut's mother put a shushing finger to her lips, but nodded vigorously in agreement.

"The Lord is My Shepherd" was the second piece performed and although there were some positive statements, there was a typical Jewish complaint, thought Johannes Bandtrop, this time about life being so short.

"Always whining, those Jews, always whining," he whispered to his wife who stifled a giggle.

The third number, "Remember How Frail I Am," struck most non-Jews in the audience as characteristic Jewish petulance. One person was particularly irritated by the mournful complaint. He had

had enough of Hebraic self-pity and harassment of God. Slowly stretching and leaning backward from his front row left balcony seat next to a support arch halfway down the synagogue's interior, he eased a Glock 18C pistol equipped with silencer out of his jacket and onto his lap, pointing it to the ceiling. The rapid silent fire upwards hit the ceiling fixture from which the weighty central chandelier hung. With an earsplitting sound the electric candelabrum smashed onto the heads of some two dozen people sitting in the middle pews of the synagogue. Screams of pain, horror, and desperation filled the building.

During the pandemonium that followed, the shooter was among the first to rush out of the synagogue, past the initially unaware Brownshirt demonstrators, and into the night. An abandoned tool box with dangling electric coils was subsequently discovered by one of the upstairs balcony windows.

46

Now shattered into seventeen heavy iron pieces, the circular chandelier had hurtled directly onto those audience members sitting in the center pews of the synagogue. Ambulance crews arrived soon after the four police officers stationed on the street had rushed inside the building, calling for backup. The neo-Nazi demonstration had come to a halt and many of the protesters had broken ranks, quickly abandoning the site.

Inside, bedlam prevailed as the air filled with cries of pain from the wounded and sobbing from those who discovered the dead next to them. Among the identified bodies were those of father and son Johannes and Helmut von Bandtrop. All in all some seven corpses were identified and thirteen persons had wounds ranging from superficial to critical. The F & F Trio remained so that Megan could seek out Simon and verify he was all right. She found him standing with the maestro conferring with a police officer who was taking notes. The distraught composer stepped away to embrace his worried friend.

"It's a miracle you or Nathaniel weren't the target of the gunman."

"We had thought so as well, but as Officer Schütz here was explaining, the aim of the shooter was to kill and wound as many Jews as possible with a single shot. And that is what he achieved. So goddamn cleverly."

"And you can trust that Berlin's police will not rest until we've found the man," added Officer Schütz, who had seen the friends' reunion.

Maestro Darenborne walked over to them, a slight smile on his face. He stretched his right hand out to Megan.

"Despite the horror of right now, I am gratified to meet Simon's good friend Megan Crespi *and* I have extraordinary news for all of us. I just had a call from the Berlin Philharmonic concert hall manager. They wish to perform your *Jewish Requiem* as soon as they and you can schedule it. This means that instead of one thousand and seventy-four people, two thousand and forty-four lucky persons can hear your *Azkara*!"

47

Sunday brought a bouquet of news, good and bad, relating to the Rykestrasse Synagogue horror the evening before. In their respective hotel rooms F & F Trio were watching the early morning news, and the first item to follow a long report on the shooting at the synagogue was a declaration by Berlin's governing mayor, the city's first female mayor, Francis Gottfried. Speaking from the Senate Chancellery, the address of which, ironically, was Judenstrasse 1, she announced that henceforth an annual public memorial of the horrendous event would be held citywide with places of worship and schools participating. And finally, there was distressing coverage of overnight vandalism at Berlin's Holocaust Memorial to the Murdered Jews of Europe. Near the Brandenburg Gate, the dramatic maze of 2,711 gray concrete slabs—coffins?—arranged on a sloping field in a grid pattern had been dedicated in 2005. Early in the morning two swastikas were discovered etched onto the surface of one of the slabs. "*Heil Hitler*" was also written on the monument. Police had no clues as to who the vandals may have been.

"*Ah ha! You've heard the news,*" said Jared, answering his cellphone and guessing in advance who was calling—either Megan or Mary. And he was correct: it was an indignant Mary on the line. She had the speaker on so Megan could hear. After commiserating over the new rise of antisemitism in Germany, Jared had a similar item of interest to share.

"And on another channel I heard a report that there's a big Russian fake news campaign on social media. Facebook, Instagram, and Twitter all have claims that the former concentration camp of Sachsenhausen memorial site will now be used to 'house Ukrainian refugees.' How convoluted and hateful can these antisemites get?"

"Disgusting! Let's think of something sunny. We have my dear Sire's return from Ukraine sometime this afternoon and the grand opening of his exhibition tonight. Oh? Hold on, Megan wants to talk to you. Here she is."

"Hey there, Jared! I've been listening to what you've been telling Mary. Outrageous! But I agree with her that we should try to think of something cheerful. How 'bout we three take that boat cruise to Potsdam this morning?"

"Potsdam and Sanssouci! Terrific! Sounds like the perfect place to be *sans souci*. Have you had breakfast yet? No? Then I'll come over, eat with you, and we can study which Potsdam cruise to take. I mean, if that's okay with you two?"

"Sure, that's fine. We'll meet for breakfast here, say, in about twenty minutes," laughed Megan, looking at a nodding Mary for agreement. Today was going to be a positive day, by god!

And so it promised to be, as a few minutes later Mary's phone rang and her jaw dropped when she heard who was on the line. It was her Richard! He was calling from an airport in Poland and had secured a flight that would arrive in Berlin at four that Sunday afternoon.

48

Exhausted by last night's exertions, successful as they were, Homer Wesselmann had slept well past nine in the morning. When he did wake up, he sure as hell didn't feel like starting the three-hour drive back to Hamburg right away. Why not relax a little in Berlin before going home? Yesterday's long relaxation in the Liquidrom had been heaven. Maybe he should consider more time in the water. No, not the Liquidorum again, but the Spree. One of those river cruises the ads are always talking about.

He looked them up on his phone: lots of choices. Several going to Potsdam looked good and he could get food on board on all of them. Don't want to spend all day cruising but an hour and a half or so would be good. Ah, here's a perfect one, leaves from and returns to Kronprinzessinnenweg 5. Oh, yeah, I know where that is—southwest Berlin, popular bike route along the water. Could park there and leave for Hamburg right after the boat returns. There's food and drink and a guide on board who tells you all about the "Versailles of Germany." Okay, sounds good. Boarding time is eleven. Perfect. Homer got dressed, checked out of his economy hotel, and walked to the street several blocks over to where he had parked his car for free.

The F & F Trio's research of river cruises going to Potsdam presented them with a variety of possibilities including stops at other interesting tourist sites. But Mary asked for a short cruise as she wanted to be back in Berlin with enough time to meet Sire's plane. The shortest cruise they were able to find took an hour and a half and it left from and returned to the dock at Kronprinzessinnenweg, which was described as surrounded by greenery.

"That sounds nice," said Megan, sitting with her laptop open on her knees, "we immerse ourselves in nature right away while our boat proceeds to what this URL I'm looking at describes as the so-called 'Prussian Arcadia.'"

"Arcadia?" Jared asked. "That's for me. Lots of food and drink. When does it leave?"

"At eleven."

"And what part of the city is this 'Crown Princesses Way' dock in?" Mary wanted to know.

"It's southwest," answered Megan, studying the information she had pulled up.

"Okay then, let's get a moveon! Good old Tegel airport is no more. The new Berlin Brandenburg Airport—full name, Berlin Branderburg Willy Brandt International Airport—is sixteen miles south*east* of the city and I certainly don't want to be late for Sire's arrival at four." Jared sprang into action.

"I'll call us an Uber right away. Probably less confusing than contending with the subway system."

A two-story, glistening white vessel named *Sea Surprise* with glass-enclosed decks left dock promptly at eleven from Kronprinzessinnenweg 5 and two of its passengers, instead of taking in the verdant landscape, went immediately in search of the food and drink advertised as being supplied on board. On the lower deck and in the center of the boat was indeed a small display of goodies ranging from coffee, wine, cheese, and bread to small honey cakes. Coming from different directions, the two men arrived at the same time, but their attention was focused on the inviting food and drink, not on fellow passengers. After filling their plates and selecting their beverages, one of the men did glance up. The man opposite him looked familiar somehow but Homer couldn't place him until something strange occurred. A melody began sounding in his head and he was able to place that. It was by that awful Jew girl Fanny, um, Fanny Mendelssohn. Yes! That was it. Shitty music! And the tall man standing across from him was the same man playing it on his cellphone to a group of people he'd passed by in the park near the Fanny and Felix Mendelssohn Museum in Hamburg. This was the person he'd seen again inside Berlin's new Jewish Museum just yesterday. The man had to be Jewish, and Homer had just been about to say something appropriate to him when the museum's PA system had announced the fabulous news that the tombstone of Moses Mendelssohn—must be related to Fanny—had been vandalized with a hate note affixed to it. But before Homer could open his mouth now, the man turned and left, his plate loaded with little lemon and honey cakes.

"Hey, who's ready for some breakfast dessert?" asked Jared as he rejoined his friends sitting by the windows on the boat's upper deck. Both women turned him down flat. They were admiring the scenery and Megan was taking photos.

"We just had breakfast. Are you crazy?" answered Mary, adamantly turning him down.

"How do you keep so slender with your rapacious appetite?" asked Megan, rolling her eyes and laughing.

"Swimming," was Jared's one-word truthful answer.

"Swimming? Where in New York? The Hudson River?" Megan attempted to keep a straight face.

"Nope. West fifty-sixth street at the Parker New York. The hotel is two blocks south of Central Park between Sixth and Seventh Avenues. They have a small glass-enclosed, rooftop pool and I do a half hour of laps there five nights a week at ten o'clock. Special arrangement I've made with the hotel. I'm missing swimming on this trip."

"That must be incredibly expensive," Mary reacted, turning her head away from the green river bank view and staring at Jared. "Why don't you just go to a YMCA?"

"Because they aren't convenient and because they're too family oriented for my taste." Megan and Mary exchanged amused glances but said nothing.

Another ten minutes went by and then they saw it: Frederick the Great's Rococo Sanssouci summer palace on a small rise covered with green vineyard terraces. Megan had toured it years ago and so she wasn't surprised by its looks. Instead of a traditional multi-storied palace, Sanssouci was a one-story, extremely elongated building with a low dome over the center. Six sets of low, broad steps led up from an enormous fountain pool graced by a giant water spout in the center and surrounded by a few life-size sinuous marble statues of allegorical figures.

As the passengers disembarked and the Trio began to make their way around the low fountain toward the steps to the palace, an apparent accident occurred. One of their fellow tourists, a short muscular man with blond hair, tripped suddenly and smashed heavily against Jared who in turn tumbled precipitously into the fountain pool. Only Jared heard what the man whispered to him as he was knocked down. It was just one word. "*Jew*." Dripping wet, Jared climbed out of the fountain and stared at the disappearing figure of the man who had purposely pushed him into the water. He did not tell concerned Mary and Megan what had actually taken place. Something held him back. Trying to make light of the situation, Jared sputtered: "Oh goodness! I thought I was at my Parker Hotel rooftop pool."

A short time later he had his revenge. The cruise tourists were standing in the painting hall admiring framed life-size copies of works of art that had once graced the palace walls. Megan, the amateur flutist, was happily directing her friends' attention to Adolf Menzel's large 1852 oil, *Frederick the Great Playing the Flute at Sanssouci*. As she spoke, enthusiastically pointing out that the pianist accompanying the royal was a son of J. S. Bach, Jared suddenly slipped away. He had spotted the man who had knocked him into the fountain. The fellow was standing alone, apart from the others, further down the hall, scrutinizing a lascivious depiction of three female nudes. He was unaware of Jared's silent approach behind him. Seconds later, throwing his right elbow over the man's head and neck in a chokehold, Jared pulled the immediately unconscious Jew-hater backward and onto the floor. He returned immediately to the still orating Megan and it took a few minutes before their *Sea Surprise* tour guide noticed one of his group was lying insensate on the floor. When the man was unable to be awakened an ambulance was summoned and Homer Wesselmann was conveyed to a local Potsdam hospital where he regained consciousness a few hours later. The man, whose back was broken in two places, refused to give hospital staff any explanation as to what had happened at Sanssouci.

49

Richard Sire's attempt Sunday morning to reach Poland's Rzeszów-Jasionka Airport just fifty miles from Ukraine's southeastern border had met with success, in part due to his having had to "tip" two guards significant amounts of cash at the border. But now he was on his way to Berlin's new international Brandenburg Airport where his dearest Mary would be waiting when his plane landed at four that afternoon. Once in Poland he had been able to reach her on his cellphone and the joy in both their voices was almost palpable. He then called Gabor Uninsky and conferred with his greatly relieved dealer concerning the opening of his exhibition which was postponed until today. The doors opened at seven.

"All is in place, Richard, and if anything, the delay has piqued even greater interest in your work," said Gabor. "One newspaper reporter has been here twice this week just to admire and take notes on your photographs. And another came to the gallery to interview me about you and your photographs. Her article came out in today's Sunday paper and I've saved several copies for you. Of course the revelation that the show's opening has had to be delayed because you were in Ukraine updating photographs you took there thirty years ago has been like a bombshell. I can't tell you how many calls we've received asking about your show!"

"And all my photos came through via the MSNBC photo crew?"

"Indeed they did! Wonderful high resolution, perfect for our enlargements."

"Enlargements? Enlargements the same size as my photos from thirty years ago?"

"No, actually. Your images from now are so potent they begged for resizing in the large. *Really* large. For instance the church with cupola standing in the cornfields of thirty years ago; we have it two foot by two foot, and above it we have your updated view of the devastated area in three foot by three foot format. The result is breathtaking. I don't think you will be disappointed when you see the show, Richard."

"Your description has me extremely interested, I must admit. And are the older photographs at eye level then?"

"No. That would have put the enlargements too high up. We've placed them at four feet above floor level. It works marvelously that way. You'll see!"

"I can't wait. What time is your gallery opening this evening, Gabor?"

"At seven. Will that work for you?"

"It certainly should. My plane gets into Berlin at four and I'll be met by Mary so we ought to be able to get there in plenty of time. I really cannot wait to see how you've hung the show."

"I think you'll be pleased. Just don't skip dinner."

"Dinner? Who's thinking about dinner?"

50

"Hey, it's only one-thirty. How about we have lunch while we're still here in all this greenery?" Megan asked after they had disembarked the *Sea Surprise*. Mary looked at the time.

"I'm game but only some place quick, because I want to get to the airport before four this afternoon and it takes a good forty-five minutes to get there. And I also want to move my things into the room reserved for Sire and me."

"Here's the perfect solution then: my Internet map here shows there's a Burger King a few blocks up." Jared waggled his phone at them.

"That sounds perfect! I like a cheeseburger now and then," Mary smiled.

"I do too," agreed Megan. "And I especially like what one can get along with it."

"And what's that?" smiled Jared.

"A chocolate sundae."

"Yum. Let's go!" Mary commanded.

As they were happily consuming their burgers and ice cream, Jared wondered about something. No sooner on his mind than he spoke it aloud.

"So what's your hotel arrangement going to be like when the three of you are in Rome? Will you be staying in the same hotel?"

"No," replied Mary. "Sire and I will be staying eight hundred feet from the colosseum at a nifty hotel named Colosseum Corner and Megan will be joining her sister Tina who's already in Rome and is at the Hotel Scalinata di Spagna, right near the Spanish Steps and the French Academy at the Villa Medici."

"And what's your plan, Jared? Will you be returning to New York?" Mary asked in return.

Jared thought of the situation back at the—*his*— Mendelssohn Complex of which he had thought he would be the director and then the hurtful decision of the board to choose someone else as director; that they had invited Monica Sallinger, a retired professor of musicology at Hunter College known by her students as "bulldog," had ignited his sudden trip to Germany in pursuit of Mendelssohniana in general and the new Fanny and Felix Mendelssohn Museum Hamburg specifically.

"Ultimately, but I haven't decided when yet. I'm enjoying being here in Germany and thought I might even return to Hamburg to do more research at the Mendelssohn Museum and perhaps help out poor, over-taxed Rachael Skylar there. She's trying to run a museum and take care of a suddenly extended family at home."

"How thoughtful of you," Megan commented.

The yummy chocolate sundaes were rapidly consumed and the trio called an Uber to bring them back to their hotels. Mary was able to move her belongings to the room she would be sharing with Sire while Megan took "a bit of a lie-down." At three in the afternoon after some quick online research, Mary took a bus from Ku'damm out to Berlin Brandenburg Airport and arrived with fifteen minutes to spare for meeting Sire's plane. She stood as close to the passenger exit as possible.

"Mary! Darling! Over here!" Sire hollered upon sighting her. A few seconds later they were locked in a long embrace. Sire insisted upon taking a taxi the sixteen miles into the city and as they rode, each regaled the other with summaries of what they'd been doing the past few days.

"I'm truly sorry, darling, about not letting you know of my unplanned, sudden decision to go to Ukraine," said Sire. "Everything happened so fast and it just never occurred to me that I wouldn't have phone contact from there."

"Well, you're slightly but not completely forgiven. You can't realize how worried I was, not hearing anything—nothing—from you. Thank goodness for Gabor Uninsky. His receptionist wouldn't tell us anything when I called, so Megan and I just headed to the gallery and Gabor was there. He took us past some of your photographs that had already been hung and into his office where he proudly showed us some of the images you'd sent to him, thanks to that photo crew from MSNBC. Oh my god, so moving. They tear at your heart!"

"That's most gratifying—not just for me but for the cause!"

"I'm so proud of you, my dearest." Mary wiped away a sudden tear.

"And I'm so happy to be back with you." They held hands and sat quietly in the taxi for a time. Sire broke the silence.

"What say you we go to the gallery right after we leave my things and I've had a chance to change clothes and wash up at the hotel?"

"Of course!"

"Then let's go posthaste." Sire's slight British accent and phrases endeared him to Mary. But she had a sudden thought, or it could be called a hunger pang.

"Sire, dear, could we eat a very quick dinner first? All I've had today since an early breakfast has been a cheeseburger and a chocolate sundae."

"Burger and ice cream? That doesn't sound like you. Sure. Of course we can. But let's make it some place close to the gallery. Right?"

"Sounds perfect. And I know *exactly* where we can eat. Spotted it when Megan and I went to ask Gabor if he knew where you were."

"And it's a Burger King," Sire said with a straight face.

Mary exploded with laughter.

"No, sweetie, it's a Chinese restaurant, 'Peking City.' And guess what?"

"I couldn't possibly. Do say."

"It's *next* to Galerie Gabor."

51

Jared and Megan had agreed not to make any afternoon plans together after Mary had left them. Both were content to go their own way before it was time to attend Sire's seven o'clock exhibition opening at the Galerie Gabor. Jared would come by for Megan at six-thirty, giving them a chance to get to the gallery in time for the opening. For Megan, after her revitalizing short nap, this stretch of free time meant organizing and expanding on what she had learned about extraordinary Fanny Mendelssohn at Hamburg's Mendelssohn Museum and since arriving in Berlin. Sitting straight up on the bed, she set her laptop on a pillow, positioned both on her legs at waist level, and began sorting and amplifying the brief notes she had carved out snippets of time to make. Early scholars made it a point to convey what Fanny's pianist mother, who had studied with a student of Bach, said in 1805 about her newborn daughter's possessing "Bach's fugal fingers." Fanny proved her mother right when, aged fourteen and as a birthday present for her father, she played the composer's entire *The Well-Tempered Clavier* from memory. And when Fanny had a child of her own, she gave him three names after her three favorite composers: Sebastian (Bach), Ludwig (Beethoven), and Felix (her brother).

At the age of sixteen Fanny fell in love with Berlin's up-and-coming artist Wilhelm Hensel, who was eleven years her senior. Her parents were against her marrying Hensel because of the age difference but after seven years, during which she secretly set some of his poems to music, they were finally allowed to marry. The wedding took place on October 3 of 1829. One of the preconditions of their marriage made clear by Wilhalm in writing was that Fanny's "unlimited practice" on the piano was to be *continued*. This certainly augured well for an extremely successful marriage, the three happiest factors for Fanny of which were composing and performing music, the birth of Sebastian in 1830, and the family's one year sojourn in Italy from August, 1839 to September of 1840. She later had at least two miscarriages or stillbirths, in 1832 and 1837, and thus it was Sebastian who, living from 1830 to 1898, was destined to become the family historian. This he did in 1884 by editing and publishing his parents' letters and journals, translated into English as *The Mendelssohn Family (1729–1847) From Letters and Journals*.

Ah, Megan thought to herself smiling, how Fanny loved her husband's pre-nuptial precondition, so different from the lifelong low expectations of her father and her brother Felix! She would certainly get it into her book on Fanny. She thought again of Abraham Mendelssohn's written admonition to his daughter: "Music will perhaps become Felix's profession, while for you it can and must only be an ornament, never the root of your being and doing." Oh, how the daughter proved her father wrong! If she could not go out into the world to bring music to the public, she would invite some of them to her home—her salon—where she and other musicians presented her music. *Her* compositions. One of her earliest works, after having waited in vain for the music her brother promised to provide, was composed the night before her own wedding: the music for the ceremony!

Fanny was the model for her husband's renowned painting of the biblical figure Miriam, frequently used to represent the art of music. Queen Victoria saw the painting in 1838, met the artist, and commented on Miriam's beauty. Hensel must have identified her to the queen because later, when Hensel presented the queen with the work, she gave him an emerald ring and a diamond for his lovely wife. It is possible she did this to make up for the famous embarrassment she caused Fanny's celebrated brother when, playing his published compositions for her years earlier, he had to admit that the piece the queen specifically requested—*Italien*—was actually written by his sister Fanny.

When this lovely wife, at the age of forty, decided to go against her brother's wishes and began publishing her compositions under her own name, she wrote Felix an anxious letter announcing the fact: "Actually I wouldn't expect you to read this rubbish now, busy as you are, if I didn't have to tell you something. But since I know from the start that you won't like it, it's a bit awkward to get under way. So laugh at me or not, as you wish: I'm afraid of my brothers at age forty, as I was of Father at age fourteen. In a word, I'm beginning to publish." She had been approached by two Berlin publishers and without telling Felix, had decided to publish a collection of her songs under her married name "Fanny Hensel born Mendelssohn Bartholdy." After her first work—*Sechs Lieder*, opus one—came out, Felix wrote to her "[I] send you my professional blessing on becoming a member of the craft...may you have much happiness in giving pleasure to others; may you taste only the sweets and none of the bitterness of authorship; may the public pelt you with roses, and never with sand." On August 14 of the same year Fanny wrote in her journal: "Felix has written, and given me his professional blessing in the kindest manner. I know that he is not quite satisfied in his heart of hearts, but I am glad he has said a kind word to me about it." Thus her brother remained old-fashioned in his view of women functioning only in the domestic, not public sphere.

A new piece of information mentioned to her by the all-Mendelssohn-knowing Jared in his role as founder of the Mendelssohn Complex in New York had given Megan further incentive to write an up-to-date biography of Fanny. Her 1829 *Easter Sonata* in A Major had originally been attributed to Felix. The manuscript was discovered in 1970, and when scholars saw that it was signed "F. Mendelssohn," they automatically concluded it was a lost work by Felix. However, the latest research, Jared maintained, has concluded that it was actually written by Fanny. The use of the surname Mendelssohn was due to the fact that, still at the age of twenty-three—her birthday did not occur until November 14 of that year—she was not yet married to Hensel until October 3 of the same year. Certainly a date distant in months from the celebration of Easter!

Megan noticed what the time was on her laptop. Five-forty already? Suddenly she felt hunger pangs. Oh, yes, that hurried cheeseburger lunch. Her beloved research had made the hours fly by so quickly. Well, surely there will be hors d'oeuvres at the gallery opening.

Ah, research! My real food.

52

That afternoon Jared needed to let off steam. He had tried throwing himself on the bed in his fancy room at Hotel Zoo and just closing his eyes. But the sequence of events at Sanssouci kept playing through his mind. First the intentional body slam by a total stranger who hissed the word "Jew" in his ear as he fell backward into the fountain pool below the palace. Turning in surprise as he fell, Jared had caught sight of the man's face, and during the tour group's pause to admire images in the palace art gallery, he spotted the man standing alone at the end of the hall. He was immersed in studying a large gold-framed painting. Jared had no control over what happened next. It was as if he were watching a film of himself soundlessly striding up behind the man, throwing a sudden chokehold, and then jackknifing him to the floor onto his back.

"I've got to get away from this!" Jared yelled at himself, jumping up from his bed. But where to go? The answer came to him immediately. Schöneberg. The gay center of Berlin. And conveniently it was not far from his hotel, just south of the U2 metro line Zoo station. Of course! Distraction is what I need. And I can walk to this one.

As he entered the area, site of the cabarets of the 1920s, and Christopher Isherwood's books of the 1930s, '60s, and '70s, an interesting site caught his eye. Its title identified it a Mann-O-Meter and upon closer inspection Jared discovered it was Berlin's main gay community center where all kinds of information and advice were available. He stopped and learned that there was an establishment nearby called Jude-Jutsu that had nothing to do with gay bars, but was instead a consultation center for Jewish Berliners and Jewish visitors to receive free advice and counseling.

Jared entered the locale, his spirits lifting already.

53

It was exactly as Mary had said. The small but elegant Peking City restaurant was physically adjacent to the Galerie Gabor and although Sire was eager to see how his work had been hung before the gallery opened to the public at seven, he did admit he had an appetite.

"You order," he said to Mary as he took in the quaint décor of the restaurant. On the walls were large photographs of items on the menu alternating with actual green and white China plates mounted in between the mouth-watering images.

"No need," she answered. "Just write down the number of the food that looks most tempting. See that little tablet and pencil next to your napkin?"

"Hadn't noticed. What an unusual idea. Glad I don't need glasses yet," he said, squinting at the images on the wall. Mary held her tongue.

Not surprisingly both wrote down Number 12 on their tablets: Peking Duck.

Half an hour later, at six-thirty, they had paid and were exiting the restaurant, both pausing to look with pleasure at the mini-exhibition set up on either side of Galerie Gabor's entrance. It consisted of some twenty small Ukrainian blue-and-yellow flags: the blue symbolizing the sky, streams, and mountains of Ukraine, the yellow symbolizing wheat. Further symbolism interprets the blue as peace and the yellow as prosperity. Eager as Sire was to enter the gallery, he couldn't help stopping in front of the little flags that meant so much and which since 1992 had become a symbol of freedom and democracy.

"*There you are, Sire, my dear friend, thanks be to god*!" It was Gabor's voice and he was standing at the gallery door, a huge smile on his face.

The two friends embraced, Gabor and Mary as well, and they began a tour of the empty gallery that was still closed to the public for another thirty minutes. Sire's concerns over the two differing sizes of images were put to rest almost immediately as he saw how effective the contrast was. The views captured thirty years ago held their own below the recently taken photos in spite of their smaller dimensions. Because of the timeliness of Sire's Ukraine then-and-now photographs, Gabor had placed them in the two front rooms. The contrast was overwhelming and the fact that Sire had in almost every circumstance managed to find the original site was truly extraordinary. The same held true for his images of Afghanistan filling the two back rooms. After viewing the last photographs Sire clapped his hands together, then held them out and embraced a grinning Gabor.

"My talented friend, *you* are the artist. Your hanging of my images adds just as much eloquence and dynamism as do the photographs themselves. I thank you sincerely."

Mary's blue eyes sparkled with pleasure as she watched the two men. What enduring gifts they had brought to each other.

Seven o'clock arrived and the gallery doors were punctually opened to the public. Almost first in line were Megan and Jared.

54

Monday morning saw a jolly breakfast gathering of Sire and the F & F Trio at the Bristol Hotel. An apologetic Jared arrived some ten minutes late and seemed in Sire's eyes to be in fine fettle, as he remarked to him. The New Yorker smiled but did not comment. Just as the waiter came to take Jared's order, Megan's phone rang. She looked at the caller ID with disgust.

"Oh, for heaven's sake. Just because I told him I'd be in Rome this week, he doesn't have to start calling me at eight-thirty on Monday morning!"

"Who are you talking about?" Mary asked, seeing that Megan was not going to answer the call.

"It's a crazy man from Rome who's been calling me in America lately saying he has an unknown portrait of Fanny Mendelssohn that he wants me to authenticate. I finally told him I'd be in Rome later this week and here he is already trying to get me. I'm not answering while I'm still in Berlin."

"Oh, dear. Do you get a lot of calls—requests—like that?"

"About twenty or so a year. Calls and emails. Especially concerning Schiele and Klimt. Almost without exception all of them are forgeries."

The group's conversation centered on the remarkable success of the Galerie Gabor exhibition last evening and each one cited their favorite photographic pairing. Three votes were not unexpectedly for three paired images taken in Ukraine, but, surprisingly, the fourth vote, voiced by Mary, went to two paired photographs taken in Afghanistan some thirty years apart. The earlier image, captured by Sire in the early 1990s, showed the fully loaded interior of a Lockheed C-141

Starlifter cargo plane at Kabul International Airport. It was a plane that had its origin in the Kennedy era. The second image, taken by Sire earlier this year at the same Afghanistan airport, showed what had been designed as its replacement: the C-17 Globemaster III. Its monstrous interior was filled to the overflow, this time not by stacked tanks of war but by some 640 Afghan refugees—children, women, and men—waiting to embark from Kabul for Qatar. This photograph uttered more than a thousand words. Everyone around the breakfast table agreed and more of Sire's Afghan images were discussed, this time specific ones of beautiful nature spots, now documented victims of bombs and fire.

Jared's phone rang while they were discussing various aspects of the gallery show and he glanced at the ID. What he saw made him jump up from the table, turn his back to the group, pick up the call and listen intently. A long interval took place during which the look on Jared's face changed from intensity to red-cheeked jubilation.

"Yes, yes! Immediately. Thank you, thank you and I'm sorry you had to set your alarm clock to catch me!" he said at last, a wide smile on his face as he hung up and turned toward his curious tablemates.

"What is it, Jared? Tell us, tell us!" urged Megan, astonished at his charged-up demeanor.

"It's like this. Our organization's director, 'bulldog' Monica Sallinger, just resigned in a hissy fit and the director of the board—that was him on the phone—had an invitation for me, voted upon unanimously by the board: *would I consider accepting the permanent directorship of the Mendelssohn Complex*?" Jared's cheeks were red with excitement and his beautiful white teeth glistened in the broad smile that lit his face. Mary clapped.

"Oh, Jared, this is wonderful! We're so happy for you," exclaimed Megan at the same time.

"Is nine-thirty in the morning too early to order champagne all round?" asked Sire.

55

By noon three passengers—two American women, one British man—were sitting in a lounge on the second floor of Berlin Brandenburg International Airport's U-shaped terminal one, waiting for their 2:55 p.m. Lufthansa flight via Munich to Rome's Leonardo da Vinci Fiumicino Airport with arrival at 6:25 p.m. Sire was listening with growing horror to Mary and Megan's description of the Rykestrasse Synagogue massacre. It was a subject they hadn't wanted to bring up last night during his big event.

"Thank god none of you were in direct line of the shooter's pistol," he said at last, shaking his head.

"And yet we were also sitting upstairs where he shot from." Mary began pointing at an invisible seating plan. "We were in the front row and in the middle of the right-hand balcony and could have been easy targets for the shooter who, the police ascertained, was shooting from the front row, midway down, along the left-side balcony."

"I almost wish you hadn't provided that detail," said Sire. "It's scary even to think about! Let's change subjects. Mary, what did you tell me the name of our Rome hotel is again? 'Colosseum' something?"

"Ha ha! No wonder you don't remember: the second word in its name doesn't make one think of the circular Colosseum: it's 'Corner,' 'Colosseum Corner.'"

Sire and Megan laughed in concert.

"I guess the hotel name confirms your room will have corners, not circles?" asked Megan.

"Not funny." Mary brushed her off.

"And *your* hotel's name again, Megan?" pursued Sire.

"Hotel Scalinata di Spagna, near, as the name implies, the

Spanish Steps and also just steps from...well, if you've seen that wonderful thriller film *The Talented Mr. Ripley* with Matt Damon, you'll recognize the café used in the film; it's right opposite the Spanish Steps!"

"Oh, that *wonderful* movie, yes, I definitely recall the café," laughed Mary. "Based on the novel by that amazing Patricia Highsmith."

"Right," Megan said enthusiastically. "Hey. Did you know she was born in Fort Worth?"

"No! Really?"

"Yes. And my mother and I shared something in common with her: she went to Barnard College!"

"Amazing," Megan nodded and continued speaking. "And now that we're talking about the one hundred and thirty-five Spanish Steps that begin from the Piazza di Spagna, I'll tell you Mr. Ripley's café is very near my own favorite café—the Caffè Greco. Founded by a Greek, its sign actually reads 'Antico Caffè Greco.' It's been in business since the middle of the eighteenth century—seventeen sixty—and it was and still is the favorite meeting place of local politicians and intellectuals as well as legions of visiting writers and artists, because of the nearby French Academy at the Villa Medici gracing the top of the Spanish Steps. The café, which has more than three hundred paintings on its burgundy paneled walls, mostly portraits of its famous visitors, is on Via Condotti, number sixty-eight, and the busy shopping street opens right onto the Piazza di Spagna and directly opposite the Spanish Steps. So see why I like it?"

"A café founded in the middle of the eighteenth century," repeated Sire. "Oh, that's a long time to be in business. Who are some of the writers and artists that met there?"

"Are you sure you want to know? I used to teach about the famous café and it's a long list. Of course, our plane doesn't take off for another forty minutes."

"Go ahead. I'm all ears." Mary seconded Sire's request.

"All right. Now hear this and I'm naming only a few: Goethe, Antonio Canova, Shelley, Keats, Byron, Ingres, the Danish sculptor Bertel Thorvaldsen, Swiss portraitist Angelica Kauffman, Camille Corot, Stendhal, Schopenhauer, Nietzsche, Rossini, Liszt, Wagner, Berlioz, Bizet, Brahms, Grieg, Gogol, Hans Christian Andersen, crazy

King Ludwig the Second of Bavaria, James Fenimore Cooper, Charles Dickens, Nathaniel Hawthorne, Mark Twain, Henrik Ibsen, Thomas Mann, James Joyce, Henry James, Gabriele D'Annunzio, Baudelaire, Apollinaire, Giorgio de Chirico, who like Keats lived very nearby, Buffalo Bill, James Joyce, Orson Welles, Lawrence Ferlinghetti, Sophia Loren, Audrey Hepburn, Elizabeth Taylor, Princess Diana and...shall I continue?"

"No!" exclaimed Sire. "My brain is far too boggled by all these names."

"Our plane is leaving any minute now," added Mary mischievously. Megan quickly looked at the time on her cellphone.

"Whoops! It's already left!" Two could play at this game.

"All right. Sorry. It really was very interesting, all those famous figures you mentioned."

"Mostly in chronological order," Sire allowed.

"In that case, and considering we still do have more than half an hour to wait, let me mention just two more cultural figures. And they were born with the same surnames. Any guesses?"

Her friends looked baffled. Megan beamed and presented them with a protracted but interesting answer.

"Fanny and Felix Mendelssohn! Both visited Italy at different times in their lives, Felix first, then ten years later, Fanny. Which one would you like to hear about first?"

"*Felix*!" voted Sire before Mary had a chance to utter her choice.

"All right. Fun!" Megan seemed enthusiastic. "To tell you about young Felix in Italy is also to remind you of the Goethe link which began it all. As a little boy of twelve Felix had played in Weimar with charming success for Germany's greatest author. After eighteen sixteen, when Goethe published his *Italian Journey* covering his two years in Italy in the seventeen eighties, Felix would number among the hundreds of young writers, artists, and musicians across Europe who over the decades, upon reading it were inspired to get themselves to Italy. In the spring of eighteen thirty a twenty-one-year-old Felix left for Italy, making a welcome and prolonged visit to Weimar and octogenarian Goethe on the way. When Felix finally got to Rome he found the orchestra and shoddy papal singers 'almost all unmusical,' and Gregorian chant 'unintelligible.' His musical experiences there were disappointing and he later complained, quote 'I have not heard a single note worth remembering,' end quote. He was scathing about the music scene in Naples, and things were apparently even worse in Rome: the orchestras were 'sloppy,' the papal singers 'untalented,' and the tradition of Catholic liturgical music generally 'impenetrable' to him.

"Gosh! What an indictment," Mary remarked, shaking her head.

" Right, But listen, I think he may have dropped in at the Caffè Greco because he described a 'haggard colony of German artists with terrific beards.' Doesn't that sound possible?"

"You make it sound possible, that's for sure," answered Sire. "And wasn't this stay in Italy the impetus for what's called his *Italian Symphony*?"

"Right," Mary jumped into the conversation. "And the last movement's leaping theme is borrowed from the lively Italian dance called *saltarello,* from the word for jump—*saltare.*"

"Yes," agreed Sire. "So now, Megan, how about telling us about *Fanny* in Rome?"

"Delighted to! She was thirty-four. She, her husband Wilhelm, and their nine-year-old son Sebastian traveled to and stayed in Italy for an entire year starting from August of eighteen thirty-nine to September thirtieth, eighteen forty. Of that time she lived six whole months in Rome, arriving there at ten in the evening on November twenty-sixth. With a copy of Goethe's *Italian Journey* in her hand and with tour guide Wilhelm, who had spent the years from eighteen twenty-five to twenty-eight in Rome copying Raphael for the Prussian king Friedrich Wilhelm the Third, Fanny became familiar with some of Rome's greatest sights very quickly. And Wilhelm's old friends and associates were only too eager to invite him and his extraordinary pianist wife to fancy dinners and events." Megan turned, looked at Mary and smiled knowingly.

"And yet," she continued, looking at Sire now, "in spite of constant social activity, it was there, in Rome, that Fanny had inspirations and ideas for what later became her piano cycle *Das Jahr—The Year*. Mary has downloaded it onto her laptop and will play it for us as soon as we can find a private piano. Do you know it, Sire?"

"Um, no, I can't say that I do. What is it?"

"Well, it's a cycle of twelve illustrative 'scenes' for piano, each one depicting a month of the year. It's a sort of musical diary and conveys Fanny's thoughts, observations, and her emotions during each of the twelve months of her year abroad in Italy. So for instance, commencing with the beginning of the year, the family's second full month spent in Rome, the cycle begins with what suggests a cool but not cold January, just as the weather actually was when Fanny was there. This is conveyed in adagio form, and the music is regally declarative, suggesting determination and energy."

"'Determination and energy.' I like that," approved Mary, who knew the music like the back of her hand.

"As also does February, with a hustle and bustle via a scherzo and a presto, but also with a lingering meditative theme." Megan hummed it.

"Nice!" Sire declared.

"I agree. But with March, by way of a prelude followed by a peaceful chorale, finally a gentle lift to the music is communicated, as, in actuality, Rome had been surprised by a fine sprinkle of snow when Fanny was there."

"I can hear how tinkling piano keys could suggest snow drops," mused a smiling Sire.

" You got it. And then April introduces a capriccioso full of good cheer, contentment, and appreciation. May is truly a song of spring, with an allegro viva conjuring nature itself in optimistic thematic statements. And June, Fanny's last month in Rome, while beginning woefully in a serenade farewell, is full of allegro jumps and runs and happy declarations as she travels to other Italian towns visited by travel guide Goethe. Her last month in Italy, July, is characterized by a meditative larghetto."

"So, if I follow you correctly, *The Year* begins with the calendar month January and not with the beginning of Fanny's full year in Italy beginning in November, when she was already in Rome?" Sire wanted to be sure he was matching the mood of each month to the composer's actual stay in Italy.

"Exactly! After she and her family had visited Milan, Venice, and Florence. Thus, musically, we arrive at the eighth month of the year, August, when, in eighteen forty, the family left Rome to visit other famous Italian cities, primarily Naples, on their slow way back to Berlin."

"How does her music reflect that?" enquired Sire.

"The music for that departure month begins with a formal andante con moto 'At the river' announcement of travel and downright excitement and cheer-flowing energy, sort of like the American song 'I'm on the Road Again.' Do you know that song, Sire, you Brit you?"

"I do indeed. 'Well, I'm so tired of cryin' but I'm out on the road again . . .'" He began proudly singing and Mary, then Megan joined him in a rousing rendition.

"Okay, Megan, back to Fanny. Tell us about September's music," Sire requested.

"Well, September, with an 'at the river' cue, is characterized by a cheerily flowing forward movement of themes in both clefs. And October is rushing tourism portrayed in a happy allegro con spirito. November conjures up not only the winter cold of eighteen thirty-nine but also the personal excitement of finally arriving in Rome, which, as I've said, the family did on the twenty-sixth of the month at ten o'clock in the evening. So late!"

"All that was recorded in her travel diary or letters home?" asked Sire.

"Right. At length. And finally December, the last calendar month of *Das Jahr*, begins in excited allegro molto time sounding like a snow flurry but also at first cleverly unnoticed citations, then unexpectedly, triumphant quotations from Bach's chorale cantata '*Ein Feste Burg ist unser Gott.*'"

"Oh, like brother like sister then!" exclaimed Mary. "Felix has Martin Luther's chorale melody '*Ein' Feste Burg ist unser Gott*' in his *Fifth Symphony* of eighteen thirty."

"So Fanny's use of it in *Das Jahr* which she began composing a year after her return to Berlin, definitely followed brother Felix's lead," concluded Megan, just a tad bit reluctantly. She cheered up immediately when she thought of what else to tell her friends about the composition.

"And by the way *Das Jahr* is a very long cycle and also has a postlude. Even without that, it can take forty-eight up to fifty-two minutes to play—as per several YouTube performances of it. That puts it along the size of Beethoven's hour-long *Diabelli Variations*. By contrast, to mention another contemporary woman composer, Clara Schumann never composed any music that lasted more than half an hour. I think Fanny's *Das Jahr* is equal to Liszt's own musical diary of traveling through Italy composed a few years before Fanny's."

"Liszt's *Années de pelerinage*. Oh yes, that very long, showy piece," commented Mary.

"Two last words about Fanny's piece, if I may," said Megan, all smiles. "When she put the whole manuscript together months after they'd returned to Berlin, she wrote down the musical months on sheets of colored paper, with a short poem for each one, and with each month illustrated by her painter husband."

"How sweet," said Sire.

"And the second thing I wanted to share with you both is part of a letter Fanny wrote Felix during this sojourn in Rome. At this point in her musical thinking she had not yet come up with the idea of characterizing the twelve months of a year. Here is what she was being inspired by. I'll read it to you—have it right here on my laptop." Two minutes and a couple of clicks later she began reading aloud to her intrigued audience of two.

"Quote: 'I have been composing a good deal lately, and have called my piano pieces after the names of my favorite haunts, partly because they really came into my mind at these spots, partly because our pleasant excursions were in my mind while I was writing them. They will form a delightful souvenir, a kind of second diary.'" Megan looked at Mary and Sire. Silent expectancy was their response.

"Don't you see? She writes '*my favorite haunts*.' Based on this, I could theorize that Fanny Mendelssohn Hensel might have been, along with her artist husband, at the Caffè Greco, possibly several times even, between the end of November and the family departure six months later."

"Hmm." Sire was dubious. "Could women even go *inside* cafés at that time, I wonder?"

"I can give you an exact answer concerning the historic Antico Caffè Greco," answered Megan with obvious excitement. "On a wall inside this café is a painting dated seventeen ninety-seven and signed by a forty-year-old Marianna Dionigi, known not only as a salon hostess but as an artist who in a published monograph illustrated to the smallest detail the famous archaeological sites just outside Rome in the Lazio region."

"We definitely have to visit some archaeological digs," stated Sire.

"And get this," Megan said, not to be sidetracked, "she knew Shelley—another frequenter of Caffè Greco. And speaking of women artists, the noted Swiss painter Angelica Kauffman, living right here in Rome, was also a frequenter visitor."

"Fascinating!" Mary was tickled by such unexpected positive information about the status of privileged women in Rome at that time.

"Good," added Megan. "When we get to Rome, one of things we absolutely must do is have a cappuccino at Caffè Greco and then you can study this painting in the flesh. It's right there on the wall by the table where she sat to paint her detailed view of the café's interior."

"That should be most interesting," commented Sire, supporting Mary's enthusiasm.

"And this is actually one of the reasons I want to be in Rome," answered Megan earnestly. "Perhaps the present-day owner of the Caffè Greco knows whether Fanny was an actual visitor there. If he doesn't know, then I'll begin really researching before I make such a claim in my biography of her."

"Well I'm glad to hear that," Mary murmured. Her friend's enthusiasm regarding the famous café and its potential female clientele had begun to worry her just a bit.

"But there's nothing nowadays in the twenty-first century that prevents you and Megan from entering and having a coffee," proclaimed Sire, smiling.

"Oh yes! By all means we have to visit the café, and together." Mary was enthusiastic."

"But of course!" Megan could imagine nothing otherwise. "And we'll be there in the company of another artist."

"Who?" Sire asked. Megan turned to Mary.

"Surely *you* know who, Mary."

"Your sister?"

"My sister."

"Nice! I am looking forward so much to meeting Tina," Sire said. He eyed his watch.

"Zounds! *Our plane leaves in six minutes!*"

56

Jared's New York-bound Lufthansa flight also departed from Berlin's new international airport that day but not until 5:30 p.m. with a layover in Munich and a comfortable JFK arrival the next morning at 10:05. Just the sort of commodious good sleep in his comfortable blue jeans and savory breakfast timing he liked.

But what had occurred earlier that afternoon in Berlin was a different thing altogether and Jared was of two minds about it: a sense of disgust and a revengeful approval. The event took place around three-thirty and was instantly reported on all media, including cellphones and that is how he learned the outrageous but thrilling news while sitting at an outdoor café, passing the time before ordering an Uber to the airport. He immediately entered the lounge of the first hotel he could find and watched spellbound the large screen TV coverage of the bloody incident.

A lone California tourist at the Trinity Cemetery coming upon the location of the graves of Fanny and Felix Mendelssohn encountered a shocking scene. An unusually tall woman with blonde hair in a bun and wearing a black pantsuit was kneeling next to a can of spray paint and carefully photographing the two adjacent tombstones in front of her. To her right a tall standing granite block's gold inscription identified the grave as that of Fanny's and below her birth and death dates were some bars of music notation. But Fanny's name and dates had been almost obliterated by zigzagging black spray paint, and the same for the bars of notes below. The gravesite to the left of Fanny's was that of Felix, headed by a tall, white cement cross. Across the identifying script a single word had been sprayed in thick black letters: "*SACRILEGE!*" The avid photographer was obviously documenting her own vile work!

The silent witness to this obscenity cautiously retreated and when far enough away not to be heard, placed a whispered call to the police. Within minutes and without making a sound, four officers simultaneously surrounded the unaware, still photographing woman. On a signal they yelled at her to stop, that she was under arrest. She stood up immediately and, pulling a pistol from her belt, waved it menacingly at them.

"Let the world know that I, Barbara Badubrecht, former commander of Hamburg's neo-Nazis, have righted the terrible wrong done to Johannes von Bandtrop, commander of Berlin's neo-Nazis, and his young son Helmut, when they were *murdered* during a concert two nights ago by a heartless assassin at the notorious Jewish stronghold, Rykestrasse Synagogue!"

Reversing the direction of her pistol, Barbara placed it at the center of her forehead and pressed the trigger. A newspaper photographer who had followed the police caught the grisly scene on video and this is what the television channels were showing over and over again.

And over and over again Jared accused, then excused, himself for feeling exultation.

57

The new trio of Megan, Mary, and Sire had managed to make it to the gate with no seconds to spare and unmasked looks of exasperation from the flight staff. A beckoning row of three empty seats five rows down from the entrance to the main cabin was theirs, and Sire stood aside as first Megan, then Mary slipped into their seats with Megan happy to have the window seat, and Mary content to be sitting next to the precious man returned to her from Ukraine's bloody war.

While the reunited couple chatted happily about a thousand things, Megan remained glued to two paperbacks she'd brought with her: one was Goethe's *Italian Journey*; the other, a collection from the letters and journals of Fanny and Felix plus later ones from Fanny's son Sebastian Hensel, who lived until 1898 and became the biographer of his famous parents. What a world the latter book contained! And how often Fanny referred to Goethe as she experienced the architectural tourist points he had visited and commented on. One scene, conveyed in a letter of December 16, 1830, to her sister and confidante Rebecka, gave such a fine example of Fanny's irrepressible sense of humor that Megan interrupted the chatting couple next to her and begged them to listen as she read aloud Fanny's description of the goings-on at a solemn meeting of the Roman Archaeological Society, the invitation to which she and her husband could not have politely turned down.

> ...everybody was talking in whispers, and the whole thing has such a comically solemn aspect that I felt inclined to burst out laughing even before anybody had spoken. But when the speeches began! Kestner, Braun, Otfried Müller, and Abeken all spoke in *Italian*,

> but their pronunciation—well, it was as Italian as their names. Kestner went through his introductory remarks like a sensible old horse that cannot help stumbling at every step, but by dint of walking slowly managed to avoid breaking down altogether. Then Braun took the lead and galloped away...he distinguished himself by mixing up his b's and his p's, his d's and his t's, like a good Saxon, as he is.... Then Otfried Müller the lion of the occasion.... He set to work to prove from ancient writers the exact position of a certain building on the Forum, and at first I really fancied it interested me, but soon found out my mistake, and then it all proved so chimerical, and it would have been so easy to prove the exact contrary of what he was saying, that I felt half inclined to mount the table and add my voice to those dear old moles.

The delighted laughter expressed by Mary and Sire was reward enough for having interrupted their chatter with a touch of Fanny. Entertaining herself in this manner caused the time to race by and a different noise emitting from the plane's motors along with a jolt caused Megan to glance at the view out the window and to her surprise they were in Munich. The flight on to Rome allowed her to return to Goethe and Fanny and renewed the cheerful chatter of Sire and Mary.

And soon it was 6:25 p.m. and they were landing in the welcoming, historic city of Rome!

58

"No, no, Megan, we'll drop *you* off," insisted Sire as they climbed into a taxi at Rome's Fiumicino Airport. It was nearing seven o'clock and, realizing that, Megan countered with a practical suggestion.

"How about this? We go to your Colosseum Corner hotel first, you drop off your bags while I wait in the taxi, then we *eat* at a wonderful rooftop restaurant I know within walking distance to your hotel, and later I'll call an Uber for my own hotel. I phoned my sister while we were waiting for our suitcases and she knows to look for me starting from around nine o'clock on. She's out at a friend's right now for dinner."

Sire looked at Mary inquiringly. "What say, darling? Hungry yet?"

"Starving. Let's go eat!"

They did as Megan suggested and after a five-minute stop at the Colosseum Corner, where the entry door was hard to find and Sire had to ring a bell to enter. They checked in with their bags while Megan remained in the Uber chatting with the driver. Then they drove on to nearby Via Labicana and the restaurant Aroma, situated on the top floor of the Palazzo Manfredi, with its outdoor terrace tables directly facing the Colosseum.

"Oh, wow, this view is even better than I imagined," said a bedazzled Mary. "And isn't it gorgeous in the night lighting! Hey, I just realized the lights are in the three colors of the Italian flag—green, white, and red!"

"That's nifty. How did you know about this place?" Sire asked Megan.

"Friends introduced it to me during my last stay in Rome. And not only is the Colosseum so incredibly close, the food is fascinating and definitely different."

Silence prevailed as the trio studied their individual menus all of which offered in Italian translation a famous remark by Andy Warhol about food: *"Credo che sia un'artista chiunque sappia fare bene una cosa; cucinare, per esempio.*—An artist is one who knows how to do one thing well. Cooking, for example."

"Well, excellent cooking is certainly what they offer here," Megan affirmed. "In small servings. Just look at this seven-item 'tasting' offering we could share. It begins with marinated amberjack couscous and sprouts followed by marinated beef carpaccio, truffle and ricotta cheese."

"Oh, I catch on now," murmured Mary. "So the next combination is soft egg, hazelnuts, and provolone cheese foam, oh, and 'with green tea.' And then we can try red turnip oyster and risotto, or go on to ravioli stuffed with buffalo Stracciatella cheese, scampi, and Bottarga. Does anybody know what some of these ingredients are in English?" She looked meaningfully at Megan.

"I don't even know what they are in Italian! Maybe we'll find out when we taste some of these goodies. The whole object is variety in small portions—see those elegant little plates and bowls." Megan pointed to the table next to them where a waiter was clearing empty bowls and loading up a tray.

"Look, that bowl has an image of the Colosseum made of gluey cheese!"

"Charming," commented Sire. "Let's continue looking at the menu's seven choices where we left off. Here we are: smoked butter John Dory, sea urchin Bernese, and artichokes. Then..."

"Who's John Dory?" interrupted Mary.

Sire ignored the question and continued reading aloud.

"Then we have grilled lamb, cevapi, and fried lamb sweetbreads. And finally, the seventh offering, is sour cherry and ricotta cheese. Shall we spring for it? It costs two hundred and twenty euros but divide that by three and it's seventy-three euros."

"Let's treat ourselves!" Mary was enthusiastic.

"Sure." Megan less so. What she liked about the Aroma restaurant was the closeup Colosseum view, not so much the tiny snippets of food. But she was game.

Their waiter appeared and Megan gave the order, asking for a side serving of neutralizing grissini. Only Sire wanted wine; the two women opted for sparkling water.

"What shall we do tomorrow?" Sire asked after they had pretty well emptied all seven bowls of their delicious contents.

Megan's phone buzzed before she or Mary had a chance to respond.

"Oh, good lord! That Nathan Bartholdy fellow is trying to contact me again. Can't he at least let me *arrive* in Rome?" She tucked the phone away without answering. "Day after tomorrow, the fifteenth, is Ferragosto, the big holiday in Italy and I'll say I can see him then when almost everything of interest in Rome is closed."

"You certainly don't seem to be very eager to meet him, I must say," laughed Mary.

"In due time, yes. But I have a strange feeling about him and his claim that he's discovered an unknown oil portrait of Fanny. And then there's another thing: early nineteenth-century art is not my field of specialization. So how did he even get my name?"

"This mystery should be cleared up when you do answer his call," laughed Sire. "Would you like us to go with you to meet him?"

"Not a bad idea, I guess. But let me find out what he has in mind first. As for tomorrow, I know you have plans for the morning but I think you know what I'd like us to do in the afternoon."

Sire and Mary looked at each other blankly for only a half second.

"Meet you at the Protestant Cemetery at three o'clock and go to the Caffè Greco afterward!" Sire proclaimed.

"Exactly. Shall we confirm and say three o'clock?"

"Three o'clock it is," Mary pronounced. Sire nodded enthusiastically.

No one felt like dessert or coffee, so when all the small bowls were empty, they settled the bill and descended to the street where in a few seconds the Uber Megan had ordered pulled up to the curb.

"*A domani*!" Megan called as her Uber pulled off.

"*A domani!*" Megan and Sire answered, waving happily.

Roma!

59

Another airplane leaving Berlin later that Monday had also touched down in Munich before arriving at its final destination. One of its seasoned occupants had slept comfortably through the night and was enjoying finishing up the small but delicious breakfast offered by Lufthansa. The standard announcements preceding landings were given and at exactly five minutes after ten in the morning, Jared's plane touched down on a runway at New York's JFK airport.

Some forty-five minutes later the experienced New Yorker and founder of the Mendelssohn Complex was in his Fifth Avenue apartment not far from Lincoln Center and the home of his generously endowed Mendelssohn Museum/Library/Concert Hall. Should he drop by immediately or take a refreshing mid-morning swim at the nearby Parker Hotel's rooftop pool? He would have to arrange for special permission to do his laps at that time because his regular swim time was late at night, but that was no problem and that is in fact what he did.

Feeling deliciously restored, he returned home, switched out of his jeans to more formal dress, and walked to his Mendelssohn Complex office, ready and prepared to assume directorship.

The greeting he received once he entered the establishment was as relieved as it was enthusiastic. Having learned of his immediate return from Europe, several members of the board were there as well, and each had stories to tell about the disastrous reign of the dictatorial "bull dog's" battery of complaints, goofy goals, senseless reorganization, and demeanor rules for the staff *and* attendees of the live music salons.

Jared learned a lot by listening to these accounts and resolved never to introduce anything that might smack of such dictatorship. After all, the project's continued viability lay equally on his shoulders and his committed staff. He invited all persons present as well as those missing his office arrival to a celebration/business meeting three afternoons hence, during which all were welcome to present ideas and goals for *their*, Jared stressed, Mendelssohn Complex. Although he missed the recent F & F Trio action in Germany, he was happy to be back home, with inspiring goals concerning the introduction of Felix and especially Fanny to the performance world of his beloved New York City. Yes, now Jared had a life purpose. And as far as composing was concerned, he was already envisioning writing a one-act opera starring the extraordinary Mendelssohn siblings. Or perhaps a three-act opera featuring the entire family from Moses through his son Abraham, through his grandchildren Fanny and Felix, and concluding with their son Sebastian who, perhaps, might possibly be the narrator knitting the acts and scenes together. He didn't know yet. He only knew he was in fast forward and up to it.

60

It had been a joyous reunion between the two sisters Megan and Tina that night at their Hotel Scalinata di Spagna. Megan had stayed there several times before and loved the fact that the little hotel with such a panoramic view of Rome from the rooms, balconies, and covered rooftop terrace was at the top of the 135 Spanish Steps and therefore conveniently close to Via Condotti and the Caffè Greco. The whole neighborhood had been especially loved by English visitors and over the years dozens and dozens of Brits had elected to live within it. In fact, in previous centuries, it had often been referred to as the British section of Rome.

The Crespi sisters' hotel was also on the same level as the nearby former palatial home—no longer extant—of Fanny's wealthy uncle Jacob Bartholdy. He had lavishly supported the Catholic Austrian/German Nazarene artists in Rome by commissioning frescoes for one of the large rooms of his palace. Their realistic religious scenes were carefully preserved when Bartholdy's villa was about to be torn down and are now in Berlin. But Megan decided against telling all this to her sister because Tina had art of her own recent making to show her.

They went through some thirty photographs of her fiber art work structures, including one of a 3-D "mosaic" utilizing different shades of blue paper and blue sea glass to represent the melting of icebergs due to global warming. It had won first prize at the end of the two-week workshop.

"And they're shipping it to me in Dallas without charge as soon as their exhibition of this summer's work is over." It was clear that Tina was thrilled by the turn of events and Megan was proud and happy for her.

Early Tuesday morning found the sisters happily planning their day's itinerary as they sat at a small table on the partially covered rooftop terrace. Their hotel's buffet breakfast offered bacon and scrambled eggs, as well as cold cuts and cheese plus fresh fruit. Megan had fretted a bit over the fact that there was neither cereal nor yogurt since both formed the basis for her regular strawberry, blueberry, and banana breakfast—a breakfast she had eaten regularly for the past three decades. Munching her eggs and bacon, Tina had successfully bypassed her sister's predictable pronouncement on how healthy her yogurt breakfast was by asking her if they would be visiting the Protestant Cemetery while in Rome. Both sisters loved to visit cemeteries, especially those of their Italian ancestors. A cemetery had come into play during their recent trip to Vienna where Megan had been asked to resume her old teaching role as a professor of art history and deliver a few lectures on the short-lived, massively talented Austrian artist Egon Schiele. On their last day in Vienna a dear Schiele colleague named Lilli Dutz drove them to the Roman cemetery of Carnuntum about an hour away to see something very special. It was the four-foot high tombstone of their indirect ancestor Lucius Crespibus, who, the inscription stated, had died far from his own country at the age of twenty-one, and was buried by his two brothers. No cemetery experience could equal that!

Nevertheless Rome's Protestant Cemetery held great appeal for them, especially for Megan who had found in one of Fanny's first letters back to the family in Berlin, a specific reference to visiting it and the grave of her uncle, Jacob Salomon Bartholdy.

"So whose graves would you like to visit?" Tina asked. "Think we might have any distant relatives in Rome?" she laughed.

"I suppose it's possible, but I have other, famous persons in mind. The first two are both British by the way, and that's why I've invited Sire and Mary to meet us at the cemetery before we all go on to Caffè Greco at four."

"Oh, good."

"But before that, you and I should visit a small museum related to two Brits just a stone's throw from here at the bottom of the Spanish Steps, first building to our left as we descend, second floor."

"Who lived there?"

"The great Romantic poet John Keats, that's who. After being diagnosed with tuberculosis, he was advised to go to a warmer climate and for him that meant Rome. And a couple of rooms in that building were his home. But he got worse and his devoted painter friend Joseph Severn came and nursed him till he expired in his arms. That was in eighteen twenty-one. He was only twenty-five years old and considered himself a failure as a poet. The bedroom where he died has been preserved in what's now called the Keats-Shelley Museum. It's so close we'll go there first. In the Protestant Cemetery when we come to Keats's tall gravestone which is recognizable from the lyre with broken strings on top, you'll see a sad inscription, embellished by the grieving Severn that goes something like this: 'This grave contains all that was mortal, of a young English poet, who on his death bed, in the bitterness of his heart, at the malicious power of his enemies, desired these words to be engraven on his tombstone: Here lies One Whose Name was writ in Water.'"

"But that's so sad," said Tina.

"Well, his free-thinking poetry had drawn vicious criticism at home. But he is identified by name on the neighboring tombstone of Severn, who died decades later at the age of eighty-five. And *his* slab is decorated with a large palette and brushes. There's a small gravestone between the two large ones that commemorates Severn's baby boy. And then not so far away is the grave with the ashes of Percy Bysshe Shelley, who as you probably know, drowned off the coast of Tuscany."

"But of course I know!" said Tina with a twinkle in her eye. While the sisters were very close in many ways, they often teased each other over their different interests, especially what Megan called their "taste in literature." Tina's literary world was not that of her sister's. Her demanding volunteer work with homeless animals left her little time for reading and when she did read, it was either contemporary writers or for specific knowledge. Right now her sense of humor prevailed.

"You know what, Megan? The wonderful thing about your description is that now we don't need to visit the Protestant Cemetery in person." A moment of stunned silence followed. Then came Megan's huffy reaction.

"Well, *I'm* going."

"Well, *I'm* going with you, Big Sis. *Andiamo!*"

61

A similar breakfast conversation was taking place on the rooftop terrace of the Hotel Colosseum Corner situated just 800 feet from the famous oval amphitheater of Roman times.

"Am I correct, Sire, in presuming that you must have photographed every famous site here in Rome?" Mary asked, munching happily on a croissant.

"Actually, love, I've not. Too busy absorbing the history rather than documenting the imagery."

"So perhaps that's what you'd like to do today then. Make up for lost photographs?"

"Not really. I'd simply like to enjoy *being* in this ancient city. It's been ages since I was here and, if you feel the same, perhaps we could skip the obvious tourist spots and just revel in being in Rome. Doing just ordinary things like walking, listening, eating, people watching."

"Well, yes, that does appeal to me. There is, however, one famous Roman site I'd really like to visit, and I'm hoping you'll come with me so we can recreate a famous movie scene."

"'A famous movie scene'?"

"Indeed. Can you call it to mind?"

"Um. Um. No."

"Think nineteen fifty-three. Think Audrey Hepburn, think Gregory Peck."

"*Roman Holiday!* Of course, Their visit to the Bocca della Verità! They went to the Mouth of Truth to make sure no lies were being told in the early period of their relationship."

"Right! And if you like we could take a selfie, or ask someone there to take a photo of us reenacting the scene when Audrey is asked to insert her hand into the wide-open mouth of the giant marble head carved into a large marble disk. If she were lying, the huge mouth would instantly close down on her and her hand would be bitten off."

"Ha! Okay, I'm game. Where is the Bocca della Verità?"

"It's displayed at the church of Santa Maria in Cosmedin which is, surprisingly, in the Piazza della Bocca della Verità. We can get there by subway; I've checked."

"Fine. Let's go! And then we'll be meeting Megan and her sister at the Protestant Cemetery at three. But that's the only tourist thing I want to do—that and the Caffè Greco afterward."

"Agreed."

Arriving at the church, they located the now cracked, round, massive marble face standing against the left wall of the church's portico. It presented the ambiguous face of an unidentified pagan god.

A nearby plaque informed them that the Piazza della Bocca della Verità was the site of Rome's ancient cattle market, the Forum Boarium. Some scholars thought that the heavy—around 28,000 pounds—circular marble face with its open mouth, nostrils, and eyes was used as a drain cover directly under the open oculus of the nearby circular Temple of Hercules Victor. Fancy, scary drain! Or alternatively, other scholars believed that cattle merchants employed the open-mouthed face to drain the blood of cattle sacrifice to Hercules.

"I'm not so sure we want to put our hands inside its mouth," Sire said warily, after reading the informative plaque about the Bocca.

"Why, Sire! Haven't you been telling me the truth all this time?"

"Of course I have! It's just the thought of the mouth having been a sewer. But never mind." Sire turned to a fellow tourist and asked if he would take a photo of Mary and him with their hands inside the immense bocca. The tourist happily obliged and within seconds the two affirmed their love for one another while bravely positioning their hands deep inside the giant mouth.

The mouth remained open.

62

"Today is already Tuesday. That Megan Crespi professor woman expressly told me when we spoke on the phone last week that she would be in Rome this week. Apparently she was not yet here yesterday. Or when she sees the caller ID, she doesn't answer. As irritating as it is, I shall try her phone number again after we conclude our business. And she damn well better answer!"

Nathan Bartholdy, direct descendant of Rebecka Mendelssohn Bartholdy, looked indignantly at the experienced artist standing in front of the handsomely framed oil portrait of Rebecka's older sister Fanny Mendelssohn Bartholdy Hensel that hung over the angry man's desk.

63

As the Crespi sisters exited the Keats-Shelley Museum at the bottom of the Spanish Steps, Megan's phone rang. She decided to ignore the call but her phone rang incessantly. Finally pulling it out of her shoulder bag she winced when she read the caller ID. The name given was that of the long-winded man who had phoned her just as her Hamburg-bound flight was about to take off from Dallas.

"Oh, that's right!" she exclaimed to Tina, "I did tell this strange man that I'd be in Rome this week and that he could call me here. Nuts! I better take the call. Sorry." Cautiously she lowered herself onto the second lowest step of the Spanish Steps. Tina nodded, sat down on the step above her, and began going through messages on her own phone.

"Hello?" Megan tried to sound pleasant.

"Is this Professoressa Dottoressa Crespi?"

"Yes?"

"Here is speaking Nathan Bartholdy of Rome. We spoke briefly last week and you told me you would be in Rome this week and that I could call you."

"Of course. I remember, Signor Bartholdy. You said you possess an unknown oil portrait of Fanny Mendelssohn and that you would like me to authenticate it, that you would send me high quality photographs of it. And I told you I'd have to see the portrait in person. That's when I told you I'd be in Rome."

"When can I show you the portrait? It is of high importance to me that I have it confirmed that the portrait is actually of Fanny Mendelssohn Bartholdy Hensel and that it is authentic."

"I understand that. But what I do not comprehend, Herr Bartholdy, is why you have contacted *me*. My field of expertise is not nineteenth-century European art; it is of twentieth-century European art and with a specialty in Austrian art. So why would you want to show me the painting, interesting as it sounds?"

"I have contacted you, Professoressa Dottoressa Crespi, because I have read your latest book, your astute biography of Clara Schumann. And although I am aware you are not a nineteenth-century specialist, it seems to me that your understanding and sensitivity to Clara and her times equips you to be the scholar to identify and authenticate a portrait of her fellow composer."

"I see. Well, that's all very flattering, Herr Bartholdy, but surely there are art historians right here in Italy or Germany who could help you with this confirmation of subject matter. I truly do not see that I am the correct person to contact in this matter."

"I beg to differ. Your publisher has informed me that you are presently at work on a biography of Fanny Mendelssohn. So who better than an art historian who is an expert on Fanny and her family? Could you at least allow me to show you the portrait? It is truly exceptional."

"All right. You have my interest, this is true. So yes, I shall look at your Fanny portrait. What arrangement would you care to make?"

Tina's eyes opened wide when she heard her sister agree to something that might cut into their time in Rome.

"If you would consent to visit me in my office, that is where the Fanny portrait hangs in all its glory. I am located on the left bank of the Tiber just opposite the little island on the Tiber at Via Portico d'Ottavia."

Megan was struck by the fact that Herr Bartholdy did not mention that his street was in the heart of the historic Jewish Quarter.

"Yes. I know of that neighborhood. But I've never been there."

"When might you be able to come see the portrait?"

"Well, my day today is full, but I can be free tomorrow in the late morning."

"That is good. Let me dictate for you my full address and shall we say that you come at eleven o'clock?"

"Yes, that's fine. But please just text me your address at this number. All right?"

"Of course. I shall do it immediately."

"And may I bring my sister? She is traveling with me here in Rome." There was a brief silence.

"If you wish." Nathan Bartholdy' s voice suddenly sounded strained and somewhat disappointed.

"All right then, Herr Bartholdy. Until eleven o'clock tomorrow morning."

"Until then." The man's voice definitely had taken on a different tone.

Tina's voice also had changed in tone as she expressed her disinterest in going to someone's private office to see an oil portrait. She had been doing something really interesting while Megan was on the phone: admiring a sprightly little Maltese dog being walked back and forth by an elderly man, each perfectly in tune with the other. Such harmony after seeing the unpredictable feral cats who dominated the streets of Rome.

"Oh look, Megan, isn't she, or he, adorable?"

"Yes, so sweet. Makes me want to check in on my little Button right now."

"Yes, it's an unusual situation, both of us being without our doggies. But how often do you and I get to travel together, after all? It's great that because of Ring Security Europe, we can check in on them—*talk to them!*—at Bill's house when the timing is right."

"True, that's true," Megan's eyes were still fixated on the Maltese as the little white dog led its master in the direction of the nearby American Express.

"Your Maltese's ancestry is supposedly from the island of Malta, right?" Tina asked.

"Right. Although there are now differing theories as to the where of their origin," murmured Megan as she strained to catch a last sight of the trotting little Roman Maltese. "You know, they were used in ancient times as more than status symbol lap dogs. They were bed warmers and flea diverters. Still are!"

"Yes. And think what a comfort her Maltese was to Mary Queen of Scots!"

"Huh?" What was Tina talking about?

"Oh, don't you know? Legend has it that right after she was beheaded, it was discovered that her faithful little Maltese had been hidden under her petticoats."

"How touching!"

"And then when Marie Antoinette was forced to walk to the guillotine in front of a huge crowd, her despairing Maltese companion jumped to its death from the Saint Michele Bridge."

"I didn't know that! How do you know all these Maltesey things, Tina?"

"Because that's *my* 'taste in literature,' Big Sis. Dogs."

The sisters beamed at each other. In the span of a few seconds they had become closer.

64

"And now what would *you* like to do that's out of the ordinary and non-touristy here in Rome, Sire? I'm sorry that I dragged you to a tourist spot after you said you wanted to avoid such sites today," Mary apologized.

"Well, actually I'm not sorry because I don't think I ever would have thought of going there on my own. No, no, La Bocca della Verità was a true delight. I'm happy we went. And now you ask what *I'd* care to do while we're here in Rome? Well, I'd like to get *out* of Rome. At least until three o'clock when we're due to meet the Crespi sisters at the Protestant Cemetery. Or at the *Cimitero Acattolico*, as the Italians call it. Although 'non-Catholic' sounds a bit discriminatory in my opinion."

"No more discriminatory than what it's also called: the 'Englishmen's Cemetery.'"

"Ha! Good point."

"So, Sire, please tell me what it is you'd like to do."

"What I'd like is for us to take a walk on a road, not a street, a famous road that leads out of Rome and down south all the way to the port of Brindisi: the Appian Way."

"The Appian Way! What an interesting idea. Sure, I'm game and I have the perfect shoes on." Mary pointed to her comfortable blue tennis shoes.

"You do indeed. So let's return to our hotel because the bus we need to get to the Via Appia leaves from in front of the Colosseum. There's one every twenty minutes or so, I've read."

"Excellent. At least our Appia outing will get us away from the piles of trash we're encountering all over the city. Insufficient garbage removal has become quite a factor in the bitter politics at play here in Italy."

Sire was correct about their transportation. They had scarcely arrived back at Hotel Colosseum Corner when the number 118 orange bus pulled up two buildings away. They hopped on board and happily took one of the brochures offered them by the bus driver. It was full of data and presented details of several different things to be visited, including two different catacombs. Once they reached the road leading out of Rome, the first stop was at the visitor information center. Deciding they needed more information, they left the bus and began exploring different displays and studying brochures. The most practical thing they learned was that e-bikes could be rented for traversing the Via Appia Antica. Neither Sire nor Mary had ever ridden an electric bicycle and were gung ho about trying out such a mode of transportation. After all, as Mary remarked, the road was an extremely long one—all the way over to Italy's southeast coast and the Adriatic Sea! The purpose of the Appian Way, with construction begun in 312 B.C., was for transportation of two things: soldiers and cargos. By 244 B.C. the Appian Way had extended 230 miles to the port of Brindisi right in the heel of Italy's boot.

At almost the same moment, Sire and Mary turned to each other.

"Enough data?" Sire asked.

"Enough data. Let's go rent those e-bikes!"

65

"Just what is it you want of this American professor, Herr Bartholdy?" Giorgio Complice asked his pouting employer. "Could you not acquire what you wish from an expert here?"

"You do not understand. I want to protect the family honor."

"What do you mean by 'family honor'?"

"You! You're supposedly an artist and yet you do not see what's in front of you, Giorgio?"

"I see at waist-length, well, thigh-length since she's seated, looking at the beholder, a woman possibly in her early forties with long, thick eyebrows over very large, dark eyes with a steady gaze, a long nose, generous lower lip, and locks of brown curls extending down along the sides of her cheeks to her neck.

"Yes, and?"

"Well, her head is ever so slightly tilted to the right, she has a faintly sad look on her face, her arms are folded in front of her, the left hand over the right. She is wearing a shawl over her shoulders and a brooch below her throat.

"*And this is all you see*?"

"I see the hand of a master, if you know what I mean." The man allowed himself a chuckle and a compliment."

"Just get out, Giorgio, go! And do not come back until I call for you."

The agitated direct descendant of Fanny Mendelssohn Bartholdy Hensel waited until he saw the painter's back, then lit a cigarette to regain his calm.

A painter who sees not what he paints, Nathan told himself disbelievingly.

66

"Would you rather go to the Protestant Cemetery by bus or subway?" Megan asked Tina.

"Either way is fine with me."

"Well, the subway isn't far from us and I remember it's line B to the Piramide station. So let's take it."

"*Pyramid* station? Why would we be going to a pyramid? Pyramids are in Egypt, not Italy."

"True. But remember many centuries ago Rome conquered Egypt—think Antony and Cleopatra, and not so strange to say, there is one steeply pitched pyramid right here in Rome, going back to the B.C. era—the enormous tomb of one Caius Cestius. It's quite tall, faced with white Carrara marble slabs and it's right next to the double-towered main entrance of the Porta San Paolo on, not surprisingly, Via Caio Cestio. And you'll see that both the pyramid and Protestant burial grounds are now linked by the old Aurelian Walls which were once Rome's defense system."

The line B subway speedily delivered them to their goal and Tina stopped in her tracks to admire the gleaming white, impressively tall pyramid made of Carrara marble to the left of the Protestant Cemetery entry.

"Please wait, Megan! I need to see what that sign says about the pyramid."

Megan smiled and happily waited while her sister trotted over and read, then photographed the sign as well as the pyramid itself and an inscription on it. Exactly what she herself had done some thirty years ago. One can certainly tell we're the daughters of a professional photographer she thought, picturing to herself the successful portrait studio her father, fresh from Italy, had founded when the family moved to Dallas.

"Golly. that thing is tall!" Tina exclaimed upon returning. "It's a hundred and twenty-one feet high and its base is a hundred feet square. It was built in twelve to eleven B.C. and, as stipulated in the will of Caius Cestius, it was erected within three hundred and thirty days!"

"I'm glad you photographed the information—so helpful later."

"Now which way do we go after we walk through this nice, cool portal? Straight ahead?"

"No, we turn left where all those pines and dark green cypresses and those roses in full bloom are. Come on!" With an unusual show of energy, Megan strode ahead of her sister and toward the far corner of the old part of the Protestant Cemetery bounded by the Aurelian Walls.

"See! Here we have them: the tall tombstones of Keats on the left and his dear friend the painter Joseph Severn on the right. It was Severn who nursed Keats in his dying days and, as I told you, the poet literally died in Severn's arms. And even though Keats wanted his name 'writ in water' and to remain unidentified on his grave, you can find his name 'writ large' right there on Severn's own tombstone. See?"

"Oh, yes, I do," answered Tina. "Fascinating. And there in between, just as you said, is the small grave and tombstone of Severn's baby son. Very touching. Wow, I want to photo all three of them in detail plus the ensemble," she said, stepping up close to Keats' grave. After she finished taking a long series of photographs, she had a question for Megan.

"And where is the tombstone for his poet friend Shelley? I want to see and photograph it as well."

Megan was tickled that her sister had entered into cemetery documentation mode because she had a special surprise for her. But she decided to keep it under wraps in case Tina noticed it for herself. If she did, she would go crazy photographing!

"Shelley's is on the opposite side of the cemetery, in what's called the New Cemetery and it's a bit of a hike from here," she said, beginning to walk in the direction of the simple flat marble slab on the ground that covered his ashes. "Are you aware of how Shelley died?" she asked her sister.

"No, but I'm sure you'll tell me," Tina laughed.

"It's quite tragic. And just one year after Keats did. Shelley drowned in eighteen twenty-two during a sudden summer storm off the west coast of Tuscany, just after having visited Lord Byron. After several days his body washed ashore, was discovered and cremated right there on the sandy beach in the presence of Byron. Only his heart remained unburned and it was given to Mary Shelley who kept it until she died."

"Is that the Mary Shelley who wrote *Frankenstein*?" Tina was excited.

"Right you are. Now, the touching thing about Shelley's death is that when his body was found on the shore, there was a copy of Keats' poetry in his pocket. The small book was folded double back, as though it were open to a specific poem on one of those pages."

"Oh, that *is* touching! I'm glad you told me the story. No wonder the apartment where Keats died is called the Keats-Shelley Museum."

"Yes, two of England's greatest poets of the Romantic age. And it's sad to think that the other great contemporary British poet, Lord Byron, died just two years after Shelley did, in Missolonghi after joining the Greek War of Independence against the Ottoman Empire. He's still a big hero in Greece."

"Is his grave also here?"

"No. England."

"Good," murmured Tina inaudibly.

Finally, at the end of a sun-dappled path rich with tombstones and graves on either side, they reached Shelley's gravestone. Under the three words "Percy Bysshe Shelley" at the top, was an inscription of two words, "Cor Cordium"—Heart of Hearts. And at the bottom of the marble slab under Shelley's birth and death dates was inscribed a quotation of Ariel's song from Shakespeare's *The Tempest*: "Nothing of him that doth fade, But doth suffer a sea change, Into something rich and strange."

As the sisters silently took all this in, something rich and strange occurred. A large calico cat suddenly appeared out of nowhere and jumped possessively onto the flat gravestone, meowing loudly and looking demandingly at Tina in particular.

"Can you believe this?" Tina whispered excitedly.

"Yes I can. I've been expecting and waiting for it to happen. It seems that this cemetery, including the area around the pyramid, was and is a cat sanctuary. It's a semi-feral colony and is taken care of by a group of devoted volunteers."

"So you *knew* all this and you didn't tell me?"

"Wasn't it more fun this way?"

"I'm still stunned. Oh boy, I'm going to get some great photos. Look! There are more cats!" Tina pointed to the crowded, modern part of the cemetery and its thousands of graves with famous and not so famous inhabitants, and where at least eight felines could now be spotted. The cats were lounging on benches, scampering along walls, dozing in shady alcoves, and dramatically draping themselves over gravestones. What a paradise! Tina began photographing furiously with Megan in amused pursuit.

Just as they reached the nineteenth-century American sculptor William Wetmore Story's beautiful life-size *Angel of Grief* thrust across a raised tomb under which his wife and later he are buried, two voices called out to them, one female, one male.

"*There you are! Megan! Tina! Hey! Over here!*"

It was Mary and Sire and it was fifteen past three in the afternoon.

"We thought we were supposed to meet at three by the Pyramid entrance," said Mary, who sounded slightly and rightly exasperated.

"So sorry! We got carried away by the cemetery cats. About thirty of them live here and are fed by volunteers. Tina just had to document them with her phone."

"All is okay," soothed Sire, "we enjoyed looking at the pointy pyramid and then some of the graves before we decided to come find you. And find you we did! Happy to meet you at last, Tina." They shook hands warmly.

"And we saw the graves of both Keats and Shelley while crisscrossing the cemetery looking for you," Mary added enthusiastically.

"Good! Then we're all up to date. There is just one more grave I want to find and that's because in January of eighteen forty, Fanny Mendelssohn and her husband and nine-year-old son Sebastian went to visit it."

"Whose grave is that?" Sire wanted to know.

"That of her uncle, Jacob Salomon Bartholdy, who had died just fifteen years earlier. He was a Prussian diplomat posted in Rome and he became a patron of the German Nazarene painters who lived and worked in Rome. They painted frescoes for the reception room of his Casa Bartholdy near the Spanish Steps, so near our hotel. But we couldn't see the palace because, we discovered, unfortunately, it had been torn down some time after his death in eighteen twenty-five. At least Fanny and her family got to tour it when they were in Rome. Although, because her uncle had died fifteen years earlier, the house was then, in Fanny's words, 'inhabited by some English people.'"

"You know what?" observed Tina. "All the graves we're visiting today seem to be for people who died in the eighteen twenties."

"Interesting!" Mary nodded.

"Can you clarify something for me, Megan?" Sire obviously had a pressing question.

"I'll certainly try."

"This cemetery is called by a lot of names, I've noted. Ranging from Protestant Cemetery to English Cemetery to *Campo Cestio* to *Cimitero Acattolico*—Non-Catholic Cemetery. So does that mean Jews could be buried here? Bartholdy was Jewish, wasn't he?"

"He came from Jewish parentage, yes, but he, like so many other German Jews of this period, and in particular like so many of the large clan of Mendelssohns living in Berlin, converted to Reformed Christianity. Others, like Fanny and Felix and later their parents became Lutherans. In fact it was Jacob Salomon Bartholdy who persuaded Fanny and Felix's parents and most of their adult children not only to convert but to take on or add the non-Jewish one of Bartholdy—a name taken from a Berlin property owned by his family."

"Thank you, Megan. That explains what I was wondering about as far as the appellation *Cimitero Acattolico* is concerned."

"Do we know *where* this Jacob Salomon Bartholdy is buried here?" Mary asked.

"I've asked several people and they all tell me it's near the grave of Goethe's forty-year-old son which is in the first crowded zone, grave fifty-three. That's about twenty rows from here and also near the Aurelian Walls. So why don't we head down there and look around? Four pairs of eyes are better than two."

After quite a bit of walking past dense rows of tombstones they finally came upon row 22 near the Aurelian Walls and grave number 53. There was a sizable headstone with a profile head of Goethe's son, and above his death year of 1830, an inscription stated:

GOETHE FILIUS PATRI ANTEVERTENS OBIT

"'Goethe Son Died Before Father.' Have I got that right?" asked a puzzled Mary. Megan nodded her head in affirmation.

"Pretty egotistical of Goethe, I'd say," Sire commented dryly.

"Sounds so but I suppose it was necessary," answered Megan. "After all, in those days everyone knew who the famous author Johann Wolfgang von Goethe was but who the heck was August Goethe? Well, he was a drunkard, left his wife and three children, and died of smallpox in Rome in, as the inscription goes on to say, eighteen-thirty," explained Megan. "Actually Goethe pater was upset over the death of Goethe filius and he commissioned the Danish sculptor Bertel Thorvaldsen to create the bronze portrait profile we're looking at here. And by the way, Thorvaldsen was one of the regular visitors to Caffè Greco!"

"Well, folks, back to Bartholdy and his grave. Do you want us to spread out and try to find it?" Tina was willing but were the others? Megan looked at her watch and gave a gasp.

"Yikes! It's ten to four and I've invited a very important person here in Rome to meet us at the Caffè Greco at four!"

67

"My third cousin, you say?"

"Yes, I am your third cousin, initially via Moses Mendelssohn's great-grandson Carl, whose father was Felix, whereas your relation to me is by way of Moses Mendelssohn's granddaughter Fanny, whose son Sebastian produced sons who produced sons until you came along," explained Salomon Mendelssohn of Hamburg to Nathan Bartholdy of Rome over the phone.

"Well! I suppose I am pleased to make your acquaintance but how did you discover my whereabouts?" Nathan was of two minds about this astonishing telephone call. What was the reason for the call? Just to tell him they were distantly related or because this distant "relative" wanted something from him, knew his reputation was that he was a retired, prosperous banker. Ha!

"I recall from family legend that your Italian-opera-loving grandparents migrated to Rome in the eighteen hundreds and that you are their grandson. Which makes us more or less the same age."

"Interesting. How old are you?"

"I am ninety-seven. And you?"

"Ninety-two. What was your work and where do you live?" Nathan was becoming interested in the man who maintained they were related and who knew about his grandparents' long ago move to Italy.

"I was vocal coach for the Hamburg State Opera for some forty years."

"That warms my heart. How pleased my grandparents would have been!" Nathan found himself saying. His suspicions were allayed and the thought that he might have a still-living relative more or less his own age was remarkable.

"And you?" Salomon inquired.

"Banking; long since retired." Nathan did not mention his near bankruptcy and enormous debt.

"Happily, I hope."

"Indeed. My mainstay now is art." Nathan immediately moaned to himself *Oh my god, did I actually say that?*

"Art! Well that is the reason I wanted to contact you, Nathan. Last week I was visited by an American art and music historian named Megan Crespi who is writing a book on Fanny Mendelssohn. I was favorably impressed and she seems to have most of her facts together. She's extremely interested in portraits of Fanny."

"But Salomon, this is wild! I just telephoned her in America last week and now she is in Rome and we'll be seeing each other at my office tomorrow morning!"

"Marvelous! She made a good impression on me. The one thing she wasn't aware of yet was Fanny's inheritance of familial dysautonomia. I was glad to put her on the right track about that."

The two relatives continued to chat about family matters for a good fifteen minutes more. It was Nathan who ended the call with his newfound third cousin by promising to give him a report on what transpired the next morning, Ferragosto, by chance.

Salomon on his side was pleased to have conversed with a relative he had never spoken to before. And he wondered what tomorrow's meeting with Professor Crespi might bring. What Nathan would have to tell him afterward. Even at age ninety-seven, life can be full of surprises.

68

Chubby, genial, middle-aged Alessandro Divitore, his black hair now streaked with white, was the first to have arrived at Antico Caffè Greco. A leading member of Italy's broad national unity party, he had served with pride as public relations manager under the dazzling prime minister Mario Draghi—the man whose technocratic coalition had guided Italy through COVID-19 with an effective vaccination campaign, instilling competence and confidence into the country. All the more tragic, then, that Draghi's reign had collapsed a month ago after the revolt of the 5 Star Movement, the anti-establishment party led by Draghi's predecessor as prime minister, Giuseppe Conti. The turnabout had brought an end to a period of political stability for the country and pushed Italy back into the former political turmoil which had paralyzed it for decades. Alessandro was looking forward to talking to Megan and her hopefully like-minded friends about the unstable political state of things in his beloved country.

In the meanwhile he stood up and relocated away from his chosen location in one of the back rooms of the café's series of small rooms where he had thought five could sit comfortably, up to the room into which the entrance opened. Fortunately still free was one long red velvet sofa against the red velvet paneled walls opposite two small marble tables against the café's twin street windows. Alessandro's reason for the change was too much boisterous noise emerging from the room across from the small one he had originally chosen. Glancing at the guests in the rowdy room as he passed by, he realized immediately why things were so deafening. A cheerful group of relatives and friends were celebrating the bar mitzvah of a red-cheeked boy at the center table. He looked to be all of thirteen, and although Alessandro certainly understood the reason for such loud joviality, he wanted to make sure his group of five could hear each other.

The plush new location was much quieter and the walls were hung with portraits of notable figures who had visited the café over more than two and a half centuries. Alessandro took a seat that would place him directly underneath a striking photograph of playwright and journalist Gabriele D'Annunzio in the pilot's uniform he wore during his celebrated World War I flight over Vienna to drop propaganda handbills on the city. Alessandro was fascinated by the mesmerizing man whose politics had moved from initial Far Right to Far Left to an enduring Italian Nationalism that, unfortunately, had once sparked the interest of Mussolini. All this was leveled by the practical common sense that had made Alessandro indispensable for the just-ousted prime minister Mario Draghi.

Alessandro turned to gaze up at the image of the extraordinary man.

"*Alessandro!* Here we are. So sorry to be late!"

He wheeled around at the sound of Megan's voice and smiled at the sight of the cheerful quartet of persons approaching him. Introductions were made and seats were chosen, either on the couch or on one of the few chairs facing it.

"Professor Crespi, have you told your friends and your sister that I was once your student?"

"*What*?" Tina was flabbergasted. Mary and Sire were equally surprised.

"Yes, that's true. Alessandro was my student some years ago."

"Thirty-seven years ago, to be specific," the man smiled and turned to the group. "And I've never forgotten her classes: not only what she taught but *how* she taught."

"Goodness! Thank you for such a compliment."

"How is it that you, an Italian, were in Dallas?" asked Mary.

"My father was in the diplomatic service and he had been assigned to the Italian Honorary Consulate in Dallas for a couple of years when I was a teenager."

"And did you like my sister's long classes? As another student of Megan's, Tina probed mischievously. Alessandro did not fall for the bait.

"I adored them. That's in fact how I first learned about the man above us on the wall: in America, not Italy.

“How did you maneuver D’Annunzio into a class on art history?” Sire wanted to know.

“Easily. Via the great Italian actress Eleanora Duse who was his lover for a time and by his writing a play specifically for the equally great French actress Sarah Bernhardt.” Even more mystified, Sire asked another question.

“But what did they have to do with art history?”

“The subtitle of all my courses was ‘the cultural content of artistic form.’”

“And we students loved the breadth of her classes. But Professor Crespi, may I say, you look so *young*!” Alessandro stared at his teacher with happy astonishment. “How do you do it? What’s your secret? Tell us.”

“Yes, how?” the others chimed in.

“Healthy meals with yogurt and fruit and daily exercise. Plus I dye my whitish hair brown.” Megan’s answer was brief, frank, and to the point. She wanted to find out how her former student was faring after the political upset of last month that shocked all Europe.

“Enough of past classes and about me,” Megan protested. “Here we are in the city of great historic past...and perturbed political present. How are you and Mario Draghi taking the resignation?”

Alessandro sighed. “As best we can. Italy is now falling apart, going back to its old provincial ways, ignoring what is good for the nation. What can I say? As for Giuseppe Conti, now that he’s prime minister again, he won’t even allow funds to be allotted to build Rome a proper garbage incinerator system. You must have noticed how littered our streets are. It’s not just the wild cats anymore, it’s the stink of the trash-laden streets...”

The sound of an AR-15 pistol interrupted all conversation at the Antico Caffè Greco. No one had noticed the Covid-19 masked assailant who had entered from the kitchen door, bolted past the startled staff, swiftly located the noisy bar mitzvah celebration, and shot the young boy being honored as well as the two persons on either side of him—his parents. All this took only seconds after which the shooter returned to the kitchen and just as swiftly ran out the door and into the labyrinth of Roman alleyways.

Three Jews lay dead in Rome’s legendary Caffè Greco.

69

For the next hour the very efficient local police were in charge of things at the murder scene. Owner, staff, and clientele were all interviewed and then, because of the thick throng of passers-by and reporters crowded outside the main entrance, diners were directed to leave by way of the kitchen's alleyway. After the forensics team arrived and examined the three shooting victims, three non-siren-blasting ambulances ferried the bodies away via the alley. By that time two press photographers had figured things out and were outside the kitchen door awaiting more subject matter. Among those dismissed persons to issue forth was Alessandro Divitore, Secretary to former Prime Minister Mario Draghi. He was in the company of four persons, identified as Americans, and all five were photographed in time for the evening papers.

The newly formed Rome Quintet, ready for something calming after the Caffè Greco catastrophe and wishing somehow for a closeness to Jewish history in Rome, agreed to having an early dinner on the miniscule island around which Rome's great river Tiber flows. The island—smallest inhabited island in the world—was next to the historic Jewish Quarter on the mainland. Intriguing views of it were to be had from the two mezzanine floors of the island's hallowed Tiberino Ristorante and the food was delicious and varied.

Despite their efforts, conversation kept circling back to the horrible occurrence at Caffè Greco and so, as they were not able to leave the malice-toward and hatred-of Jews subject, Alessandro told them about the Tiber Island's legendary, still-functioning hospital Fatebenefratelli, founded in 1585. Because of the island's isolation from the rest of Rome, it had become a convenient location to send the sick, plague victims in particular. A school to teach staff members medical procedures was founded near the island in 1911. During the Holocaust of 1941-1945 the hospital sheltered Jewish refugees who were told to simulate symptoms of tuberculosis by pretending extreme illness and producing unremitting hacking coughs. For fear of contamination German soldiers simply skipped searching the hospital wards. Now it had become the Israelite Hospital.

The group's spirits were raised by Alessandro's historical account of heroism, so much so that he told them something about himself which none of them knew, not even his old professor Megan Crespi.

"I myself am Jewish on my mother's side. Her surname was Rappaport." Megan was stunned.

"I had no idea! Then perhaps you can tell us the answer to the great mystery, for me at least, as to why is it that Jews have historically been resented, and persecuted right up to and through modern times?"

"Yes," added Sire, "why, why have they attracted and borne such hatred?"

"Oh! Where to begin? The existence of Jews as a race, or, the existence of a Jewish religion? In other words, were the first Jews religious? As for Jews as a race, certainly Jews have developed a degree of genetic homogeneity over the centuries that can be visible in DNA testing. Thus a genealogical DNA test can confirm that a person has a Jewish origin. And so it has been with me, for example." Alessandro glanced at his dinner companions. All four had ceased eating and were fixated upon what he was saying. Encouraged, he continued.

"People often say that a person 'looks Jewish.' As with your Felix and Fanny Mendelssohn, Megan. Both 'look' Jewish, yes?"

"That's true. I do think so. And I have to admit that I most likely would have thought so just by their portraits, even if I didn't know who they were."

"And why is that?"

"Golly. I guess because of the dark eyes and dark, pronounced eyebrows, long fulsome nose and full lips..."

Alessandro cut her off. "So you could also be describing individuals coming from the four basic races of humanity: Caucasoid, Negroid—yes, there are black Jews—Mongoloid, and Australoid."

All his listeners looked perplexed. Alessandro decided not to press his point. He returned to his original line of thought.

"However, the basic factor for racial classification is and remains genetic composition. And that manifests itself as one's external, anatomical appearance." Alessandro smiled.

"So am I correct then," asked Megan, "and not insulting when I—without prejudice, I do believe—describe Fanny and Felix as 'looking' Jewish?"

"Superficially then and stereotypically, yes, along with culture, traditions, language, social practices, and biological aspects. One can consider even the professions Jews–who were not allowed to own property–gravitated to early on, when allowed: banking—think of Joseph and Abraham Mendelssohn, Megan—interest paying money-lending, journalism, science, clothing manufacture, jewelry, and medicine especially."

It wasn't clear whether or not Alessandro's dinner companions had totally digested his words but certainly they had been absorbed for contemplation later. He decided to approach one more Jewish topic with his genuinely interested friends.

"You asked why is it that Jews have been persecuted from early centuries right up to and through our own times. In early centuries it was often a question of inhabiting the 'wrong' territory—land belonging to other 'races' or nations. As, supposedly, and note I say *supposedly*, recounted in the biblical account of Exodus, with the 'enslaved' Jews in Egypt and, as pictorialized in that stunning nineteen fifty-six film *The Ten Commandments* with Charlton Heston as Moses, the tension between the Pharaoh and Moses became so razor sharp as the God-sent plagues worsened and, according to the Old Testament and to legend, the Pharaoh released the 'enslaved' Jewish people, then changed his mind and sent his army to bring them back. You know the rest: the Jews reached the Red Sea with the Egyptian army behind and 'miraculously' the sea split and the Jews crossed over to safety while the pursuing army was drowned when the sea instantly closed back in on them."

"So why do you emphasize all this is 'supposedly?'" asked Mary.

"Because modern science and modern thought hold that all this is mythical, not actual. And also the new consensus questions that Jews were 'enslaved' in Egypt."

"Those are pretty sweeping statements," murmured Mary.

"Certainly I do not mean to argue with or offend you," Alessandro smiled at Mary. "We may each believe what we think is true. My work as a politician, however, has forced me to question many a tradition. But let me jump ahead in history to something about which there is no doubt."

"And what's that?" Sire asked, looking protectively toward Mary.

"The position of Jews right here in Rome at the beginning of the thirteenth century under Pope Innocent the third."

"What was it?" queried Megan.

"Well, although on the whole Jews had been treated well under previous popes—mind you, Jews had been present in Italy during the pre-Christian Roman period—well, this pope threatened excommunication to anyone who allowed Jews to be in public positions. This was the beginning of restriction of professions for the Jews. In fifteen fifty-five, Pope Paul the Fourth commanded by papal bull that the Jews who lived in Rome must all be gathered into one section of the city, at one point reducing them to fish and rag sellers. The worst thing about his papal order was that every Jew always had to display in public that he or she was a Jew by having to wear a conspicuous yellow badge of some sort—often hoods."

"God! That sounds like Nazi times!" exclaimed a horrified Tina.

"Certainly that's where they got the idea from," Alessandro agreed. "Finally the Jewish ghetto became 'the Jewish quarter' in eighteen seventy, when the unification of Italy was at last achieved."

Conversation concluded as they discussed Italy's political role in Europe—one that Alessandro sadly characterized as glorious in the past but questionable in the future.

70

"My mainstay now is art."

Seated at his desk in the office of his two-room apartment in the Jewish Quarter of Rome, Nathan Bartholdy still could not believe he had uttered that possibly giveaway phrase to his third cousin, Salomon Mendelssohn of Hamburg. The cousin didn't know him in person, only knew of him as a distant but direct descendant of Fanny Mendelssohn. No one must know of the two-stage plan he had in mind and on behalf of which, if things turned out as he hoped, he had gone to extreme but brilliant means.

Tomorrow morning at eleven o'clock he would test his plan.

71

That evening after the simpatico Alessandro had taken his leave and the Quintet had become a Quartet again, Mary had an unusual but welcome invitation for her friends. There was, she had learned, a grand piano in one of the Colosseum Corner Hotel's private banquet rooms. To lift the gloom which they were all admittedly still under, why didn't Megan and Tina return to the hotel with her and Sire and she would play Fanny's *Das Jahr* for them and herself. It would be an hour free of today's horrendous memories and it would be an hour in which they could all get to know Fanny better.

Mary's musical invitation was welcomed with glee and within half an hour the ancient Bösendorfer was once again serving as musical ambassador to a delighted audience and performer. Now, with Mary's authoritative playing of the first month of the year, they could feel the cool weather in her adagio and picture to themselves, even if they had not found the actual grave, Fanny's visit to the vast Protestant Cemetery and its thousands of famous and less famous inhabitants. What a connection! Every month brought beauty of phrase and vividness of image and when Mary got to September, with its ceremonial Andante con moto 'At the River' announcement of motion, the appropriateness of the music to their just-concluded dinner on the Tiber River was overwhelming. What a wonderful prelude to Ferragosto, then and now!

72

The dawn of Ferragosto that Wednesday morning, August 15, augured that it would indeed be, as almost always usual, the hottest day of the year. Half of Rome had already fled to Naples as midsummer was initiated that festival day in Italy. Mary and Sire had departed Rome in a rental car at eight for a day. At the last minute Tina had joined them, saying she'd rather go to Naples than accompany her sister to a business appointment.

The reason for the choice of that southern city was not only the cooler temperature, however. It was the attraction, for Sire, of having the chance to visit and photograph the famous nineteenth-century Acquario di Napoli and its collection of over 200 fauna and marine species. The aquarium was part of the even more famous Anton Dohrn Zoological Station, an extraordinary combination of aquarium, herbarium, historical archive, library and zoological collection. Whereas ordinarily Mary would not have put an aquarium at the top of her tourist attraction list, Sire's description of what they would see at the oldest aquarium in Italy was hard to turn down. In addition, when Mary googled who the heck this Felix Anton Dohrn actually was, she had learned that his godfather was Felix Mendelssohn Bartholdy! Anton, as he was known, had been blessed with wealthy parents who were patrons of the contemporary music world and had hosted the likes of virtuoso violinist Joseph Joachim and Swedish opera singer Jenny Lind. No wonder Megan had urged her sister to go. Tina needed no urging to be in the close neighborhood of Mount Vesuvius. She would happily take a tour there while Mary and Sire fished around, as she put it. But in the end they agreed to drive with Tina to the top of Mount Vesuvius and there were no regrets, as from the rim of the crater they stared down into the cavernous black depths.

And Megan was quite content to visit the insistent Nathan Bartholdy on her own. After her forty-five minutes of morning exercises and a relaxed breakfast on the hotel roof, she studied on her cellphone various maps of the Jewish Quarter—known for centuries as the Jewish Ghetto—and at last felt ready to locate Via Portico d'Ottavia 72. She ordered an Uber rather than figure out public transportation. The street was adjacent to the historic Teatro Marcello and, as the Uber began to slow down, Megan realized that the street surrounded Rome's monumental synagogue with its unusual square-based dome. So Bartholdy could not have lived in a more historic neighborhood. As she debarked her Uber, glancing down at the ground, she saw something she had first seen in Hamburg: the stumbling stone with the names of local Jewish inhabitants on that street who had been deported and murdered during the Holocaust. She felt a shiver as she rang the bell corresponding to Bartholdy's apartment number. The front door unlocked and she entered the building. It was exactly eleven o'clock.

A plump, middle-aged woman with dark hair and scowling expression was descending the stairs from the second floor where Bartholdy lived and she stopped when she saw Megan ascending from below. They passed each other and then the woman turned around and came back up the stairs to see where the visitor was headed. She actually stood in the hallway, hand on hip, until she saw at what apartment number the unknown visitor came to a stop.

When Megan reached Bartholdy's apartment, the door was already open and just inside a short, thin man with white hair nodded his head at her in silent welcome. This was followed by a question if not a smile.

"And where is your sister, Dottoressa?"

"Oh, she went to Naples with friends to celebrate a cooler Ferragosto than here." This bit of information actually triggered a wide smile from her host. Megan commented further on what she had just observed.

"I see, Signor Bartholdy, that directly facing your apartment house there is a brass *Stolperstein* set in the street. So tragic!"

"Ach, you know what are *Stolpersteine,* Frau Doktor." Any remaining tension had disappeared and Bartholdy was unaware that he had automatically switched to German upon the trigger sound of *Stolperstein*.

"Yes indeed. I've seen them in Hamburg and Berlin and I've been told they are now all over Europe," replied Megan, also switching languages.

"Quite correct. If too late," Bartholdy said.

Megan sought to take the man's mind off the terrible fate of Jews during the Holocaust.

"By the way, Herr Bartholdy, a strange thing happened as I was going up the stairs to your apartment. A woman who passed me on the stairway on her way down, turned around and followed me back up to your floor. She just stood there, watching me, until I got to your door."

"Ach, ja! That has to have been be my cleaning lady, Signora Ursula. Yes, she is very possessive and watches over me, well, not like a nurse, but I'd say like a disapproving mother watches a potentially naughty child. Makes me a bit nervous at times. Nevertheless she has been with me so many years and is such an excellent house cleaner that I can find no fault with her. But please, do come inside!"

Bartholdy waved his guest into a medium-sized room that was obviously his office. Directly facing her was a large framed portrait hanging on the wall above a capacious desk. The portrait was definitely of Fanny Mendelssohn Bartholdy Hensel. The overly large gold wooden frame looked to be quite old.

Megan voiced this thought to her host, and then added a caveat.

"But is it a contemporaneous portrait? Painted from life? That we must establish immediately. Would it be too much trouble for you, for us, to take the portrait off the wall?" She wondered whether the elderly man was capable of removing the heavy framed painting from the wall by himself. Strangely enough Bartholdy almost ran to the painting.

"Yes," he said, "we can take it down by all means, and yes, I should appreciate your help."

Megan set down the slim briefcase she had brought with her and joined him behind the massive desk that dominated the room and, standing opposite the fragile man, worked in tandem with him to lift the artwork off the wall and over to a nearby, once sumptuous leather couch.

"No, no, I don't want to examine the front yet. It's the back I need to look at," she said to Bartholdy's surprise. Or was it surprise? He seemed to be in immediate agreement as, without a word, he swiftly helped turn the portrait around, face to the couch back. He turned, moved away slightly, and watched his American art historian visitor with keen interest. From what looked like a leather eyeglasses case hanging from her neck, she withdrew a round object with a black handle. It was a lightweight Fancii LED magnifying glass with an oversized lens and three magnification levels. With it Megan studied various parts of the canvas as well as of the frame, and the binding connection of canvas to frame. Then she ran the fingers of her right hand lightly over the canvas stretcher and wooden support framework. She nodded to herself and repeated the motion on the canvas backing itself. Then she put her nose close to the canvas for some seconds, and afterward continued examining the back of the painting. Once again she nodded to herself, then stepped back away from the work.

."All right. Let's see the front now, please." Bartholdy instantly obliged and they carefully turned the artwork around and Megan repeated the procedure she had employed with the back of the canvas, including the sniffing. With her magnifying glass she searched for crackles—the pattern formed on the surface of the top paint layer of a painting. A few more minutes of silence ensued, then Megan stepped back and looked directly at the old man, a sympathetic, sad smile on her face.

"I am sorry to say, Herr Bartholdy, that I do not believe this work of art was created in the nineteenth century, especially not in the first half of the century, which would have to be the case since Fanny died in eighteen forty-seven. From the pristine condition of the linen canvas, its high thread count, the depth and number of layers of paint, the lack of a crackle pattern formed over time on the surface of the top paint layer, and the use of a light-grain pine stretcher on the back, I would say it dates from our own twenty-first century. Furthermore on the far lower left part of the canvas back itself, almost hidden under the wooden stretcher, there is, admittedly difficult to see at first glance, the well-known stamp of the canvas manufacturer: the twenty-first century Italian supplier Savino Del Bene." Megan paused, waiting to see disappointment on the man's face. But his expression was blank and gave no hint as to how he was taking her negative news.

"In other words, and again I am sorry to say it, you have an artwork that was created sometime in the past twenty years; not in the first half of Fanny's century and on, not a low thread count nineteenth-century German canvas, but on a modern higher thread count Italian canvas. I so regret disappointing you, Herr Bartholdy."

But instead of looking dejected or angry, the man was actually smiling at Megan's words!

"Frau Doktor Crespi, *you have passed my test!* I am fully aware that this is not a contemporaneous portrait of dear Fanny. The real portrait is in the next room and I shall be delighted to show it to you now. But I first had to be assured that you are knowledgeable enough to spot a modern copy."

"Well, I am so relieved that my judgment of the work did not distress you. And I am glad I 'passed' your test. Have you tried it with other art historians?"

"Yes I have. Three—two Italians and one German. They were all immediately eager to tell me what a treasure I have here."

"In that case I should also tell you what I did *not* see in this portrait. Any indication of Fanny's slightly askew shoulders due to her unfortunate inheritance of the familial dysautonomia that had so affected her grandfather."

"*Prima!* This 'correcting' of the shoulder imbalance is exactly what I dislike in the work—a copy done at my behest by a painter of my acquaintance. I suppose he wanted to make right what seemed to him a painterly fault and thus make the portrait more pleasing. I'm afraid I gave him hell for that. All right then, *gentile Dottoressa*, let us take a look at what I believe is the genuine portrait of Fanny."

He led the way into the adjacent room which turned out to be two rooms in a sense, as one third of what turned out to be a bedroom was curtained off from the rest of the room. From the scent emanating beyond the black plastic curtain, Megan ascertained it was a small kitchen. Unusual! Her attention was immediately diverted, however, to the framed portrait over the double bed. It was a duplicate, or better said, the prototype for the one she had just examined except for the fact that the asymmetry of the woman's shoulders was pronounced, if simultaneously softened by means of the shawl draped over them. Suspenseful silence prevailed as Megan moved closer to the painting which, like the one in the office, was held in place by an old, gold wooden frame, noticeably lighter weight than the one over his desk.

"Should we remove the portrait from the wall?" Bartholdy asked after a quiet minute had gone by.

"Not yet. Unless I am totally mistaken, I can say right now that this painting is not only genuine, but this is also an unknown portrait by the Jewish painter Moritz Daniel Oppenheim, whose celebrated bust portrait showing the Fanny of eighteen forty-two is so well known that the Republic of Liberia has used it for one of its postage stamps."

"*Aber!* You echo my thoughts, *Frau Doktor Crespi*! You echo my thoughts. I have urgently investigated all that has been written about this amazing artist who became the first Jewish artist to succeed—and massively so—in the gentile world of his time. He was called 'the painter of the Rothschilds and the Rothschild of the painters.' Did you know that?" Nathan Bartholdy was all smiles.

"I did, in fact, and I love it. And do you know that Oppenheim painted a picture of Goethe in his home, sitting with Felix Mendelssohn?"

"Yes! Goethe had the image created when Felix stopped by at Weimar to visit him—he'd played for him as a boy—on his way to Italy in eighteen thirty.

"Right. And do you know about *Fanny's* connection to Goethe?" Megan's ninety-two-year-old host shook his head.

"No, please tell me!"

"Well, it goes back to eighteen twenty-one. Having heard so much about the two talented Mendelssohn children of Berlin from his music savant Carl Friedrich Zelter, Goethe invited them both to visit him in Weimar. Twelve-year-old Felix was allowed to go with Zelter, but sixteen-year-old Fanny was told she must stay home. Nevertheless, Felix saw to it that Goethe heard some of his sister's compositions and the poet was simultaneously enchanted by the music, and unhappy that she wasn't there to play for him in person. So right away he wrote a short poem dedicated '*An die Entfernte—To the Distant One*' who, he hoped, might set it to music after Felix brought it back home to 'the distant girl.' And I'm tracking down that Lied right now, hoping to find out that it was indeed composed."

"Ah ha! Your publisher was certainly right to bring out your Clara Schumann book and now to want your developing Fanny Mendelssohn biography. We had quite a flattering talk about you, as a matter of fact. That's one reason I kept trying to reach you!"

"Well, you finally did and aren't we having fun!"

Megan paused, then dared to ask a question that had been nagging at her ever since their first contact.

"Tell me, if you don't mind, why is your surname Bartholdy when it might have been Mendelssohn, as with your grandparents?" Nathan laughed.

"That's due to my ultra-sensitive father. He desperately wanted to sound more Italian to his school comrades here and continued to parade that surname as an adult; in fact he changed it legally to just Bartholdy. So that's why. And I have to confess I, too, prefer Bartholdy to Mendelssohn and for the same reason."

"But you *live* in the Jewish quarter of Rome!"

"Yes. Well, we Jews can be quixotic."

The spirited conversation between Megan and Nathan continued while, working as an experienced pair, they lifted the painting down from the wall and laid it carefully on the bed, front face down, verso facing upward. As they both backed up, Bartholdy stepped too quickly and would have fallen to the floor if Megan hadn't wheeled toward him and caught the flailing man under the shoulders with her arms. Frail Bartholdy was so shaken he could do nothing but gasp from fright while Megan tried to soothe him. Finally, she steered him to the head of the bed and helped him sit down beside the portrait. She talked to him quietly for some time and slowly he came round and his breathing became normal again.

"Thank you, thank you, dear lady," he muttered gratefully.

"But of course. You would have done the same for me. Now, would you like for us to have a look at what we've taken down from the wall?

"Yes. Please."

"Good. Why don't you stay put and just watch for now, all right?"

"All right. Thank you."

Megan examined the stretcher and back of the canvas as thoroughly as she had the previous painting. The stretcher was made of slow-decaying Nordic pinewood, confirming for her the authenticity of nineteenth-century, European origin. The linen canvas back was lightly stained, another sign of longevity. Slowly she turned the painting over and silently studied it intensely, including the sniff-

and-crackle pattern tests, nodding to herself all the while. Finally she lifted her head, turned to the old man, smiled, and spoke.

"Congratulations, Herr Bartholdy. To quote your three previous incompetent experts, 'You have a treasure.' A treasure indeed." Nathan Bartholdy gasped and his eyes opened wide. His American expert continued.

"We have here a new-to-the-world, genuine portrait as far as I can tell, of Fanny Mendelssohn Bartholdy Hensel by the artist Moritz Daniel Oppenheim. We see her at the age of possibly forty—as you know she died at forty-one—seated, waist length, head tilted a bit to the right, gazing steadily at the beholder. She exhibits the features we know from her devoted husband's many sketches of her with her stable gaze and large brown eyes, her prominent long nose, generous lower lip, conspicuously thick eyebrows and abundant hair, the long curls of which are level with her lips."

"Yes, yes, this is all so true."

"What is new to us from this excellent portrayal is the white shoulder shawl that covers her shoulders but does *not* seek to mask the disparity between her high right shoulder and her distinctly lower left shoulder. We are looking at an honest portrayal of what the artist saw in front of him. She and Oppenheim were only five years apart in age, got along well, as we know, and had every opportunity to be frank with one another. Whether or the portrait was well received is unknown to us so far. But the fact that it has only come to light recently—perhaps not for you or your family—weighs in favor of close family disapproval. Certainly her son Sebastian never alludes to the painting." Megan stopped and looked directly at its owner.

"Might you enlighten me, Herr Bartholdy, and tell me as much as you can or wish to concerning how this painting came into your branch of the family?"

"Certainly. But first let me say how impressed and of course happy I am with your conclusions. And secondly, the story is very simple. It is true that Fanny was not particularly crazy about the portrait. She liked the painter but not the painting, we could say. Sebastian must have known that, growing up with it, and it is most possible that it was simply stored out of sight, and that when he inherited the unflattering portrait, he did the same with it. This could have continued for generations. When, however, my grandparents moved from Berlin to Rome, this painting was one thing they brought with them, and we children grew up with it. Didn't really give it a thought." Nathan looked away suddenly and spoke no more. Megan was silent out of respect for his sudden change of mood. But finally she spoke.

"May I ask you what has prompted you to reveal the fact that you own this extraordinary portrait of Fanny to me and to three other art historians?" Nathan did not respond. Then he turned and put his right hand on Megan's arm. Tears were in his eyes.

"'Prompted'? Me? *Poverty*, that's what has prompted me! People know me as a retired banker by reputation. But they do not know that I am a ruined retired banker. That I have lost everything I once owned. Including this apartment building. Yes, I once owned it! But a foolish land venture did me in. And I am alone. I have no family left, no living offspring. My debts are now overwhelming and I have been given notice that when my lease on this miserable, small apartment of two rooms expires next year, it will not be renewed. In short, *Dottoressa* Crespi, I am desperate and must *sell* this painting! And I don't really know how, to whom to go, which auction houses to approach!" Megan began gently patting the ninety-two-year-old man's hand.

"I understand. Thank you for confiding in me. And I think I may have a solution to your problem."

"A solution?"

" Yes, solution. A good American friend of mine recently founded a new Mendelssohn foundation in New York City. It's called the Mendelssohn Complex and contains a fine archive of over four hundred recently discovered works by both Fanny and Felix, as well as a rich library and a performance area for weekly Mendelssohn live performances. It's extremely popular and quite a financial and scholarly success as well. I am certain that the director, who is my friend, would be willing to pay top dollar—euro—for such an extraordinary addition to the Mendelssohn Complex as this painting of Fanny. Shall I call and send him a few photographs—if you permit—and ask him? Would you like that?" Nathan's answer was immediate.

"Yes. I should like that. Simplicity. No going from auction house to auction house, from expert to expert." Tears of relief were forming in the man's eyes.

"And allow me then to tell you one more thing that would make your portrait of Fanny of unique importance to the Mendelssohn Complex of New York."

"And what is that?" Nathan asked weakly.

"The founder and director's surname is Oppenheim."

73

Signora Ursula Ladro did not appreciate her husband's sarcasm when he arrived home late that afternoon. A hearse driver for Rome's *Obitorio Scaduti e Figli*, Carlo had experienced cap leak carburetor trouble with his loaded limousine on the way to the Mausoleo di S. Elena. Seventeen minutes had passed before the problem was fixed and he could feel the silent anger around him. His morose mood became even glummer as he listened to his wife prattle on about her eccentric employer of over fifteen years and that recently he was talking about needing her only once a month instead of weekly. She told Carlo about the unusual visitor to her morose employer Nathan Bartholdy late that morning—an older woman dressed in slacks and carrying a small briefcase rather than a purse.

"Can't you see, Ursula? He was interviewing your replacement!" had been Carlo's sardonic response. This had set off a virtual tirade from Ursula concerning the straightened circumstances under which they already lived.

"Even here in crowded Centocelle, we're never going to make it, Carlo, if Bartholdy reduces my wages like that or replaces me altogether! Years ago he said he wanted to leave me something when he died, but how can I be sure he still has that in mind?"

"So what do you want me to do? Let's be thankful I have my job."

"It's not going to be enough, don't you understand? We'll never get out of this dilapidated old neighborhood so far from the inner city if we don't have more money. Listen to me. Bartholdy is rich—has two large gold-framed old paintings on the wall—but he's a real penny-pincher. We know he's in his nineties and doesn't have long for this world. I've watched him get weaker. *And* he has no living relatives; he's told me that himself."

"And so?"

"My thinking is this. When the old man dies, his belongings will be taken over by the city and that will be that. But what if one of his belongings, something that is real valuable, was to leave the apartment *before* he kicks off?"

"Like what?"

"Like one of the two paintings on the wall I just told you about. The old, gold frames alone must be worth a lot. And the weird thing is that the paintings themselves are just alike! Identical twins, you could say."

"Are you serious?"

"Yes, I'm serious. They are duplicates. Same size, same woman, same look on her face. Maybe his deceased wife or someone he was once in love with, since he has one of them in his bedroom."

"So, Ursula, you're suggesting that one of these two identical pictures could be removed and the old man would still have the other one so he wouldn't be too upset?"

"That's exactly what I think. God knows, he's so old he might not even notice one of them is gone!"

"Which one, since they're both alike?"

"I got that all figured out. Because the gold frame on the bedroom painting is smaller and less fancy than the elegant one in the office, the office painting is probably worth a whole lot more."

"Sounds like a plan except for one thing."

"What?"

"If the old man is a light sleeper, he could wake up at any time. You could, as a precaution, temporarily knock him out by spraying a pesticide at his eyes, nose, and mouth. Do you think you're up to that?"

"Of course I am!"

"All right. You've got to be prepared for anything. We can get one of the pesticides you use for our windowsill plants and we'll take it with us. Plus a blanket to hide the painting from anybody who might see us loading the thing. *Va bene?*"

"I love it."

"So when would you want to do this?"

"Now."

"*Now!* When?"

"The later the better. Say at one a.m. or so?"

Carlo's sarcasm was a thing of the past. If his wife's plan succeeded, their financial state of affairs could be hugely improved. Maybe they really could move out of the crowded, working-class neighborhood they lived in.

"One a.m. it is."

74

It had been arranged that the Naples battalion of three would rejoin events commander Crespi in Rome at the Colosseum Corner Hotel as close to eight in the evening as possible. Megan had made dinner reservations for them all at a highly recommended restaurant quite nearby and now, early at seven-thirty, she was sitting waiting in the Colosseum Corner lobby and enjoying watching a Japanese family with two young children grapple with the hurdle of checking in. At one point she almost jumped up to help with the language barrier but it proved unnecessary after all when the father of the family and the reception clerk switched to English.

Happy to have witnessed a satisfactory conclusion to the little event, Megan looked again toward the hotel entrance. Still no returnees from Napoli. She was jolted then, when Tina's cheerful voice sounded right behind her.

"Hey, you, Megan! You're so involved in watching people check in that you didn't even notice us waving to you when we entered the hotel!" All three members of the Naples battalion were standing behind her. After happy reunion hugs and a quick round trip to their room by Mary and Sire, they decided to try the other great restaurant so near the hotel. Oddly enough, or perhaps not so oddly, the Ristorante Aroma was located on the roof of yet another building near the Colosseum: the Palazzo Manfredi Hotel.

"Since restaurant air conditioning is so rare here, it's going to be cooler eating outdoors on the roof terrace," Mary commented happily as they walked toward Via Labicana 125. Reaching the hotel within seven minutes, they immediately took the elevator up to the roof terrace where a cashier positioned by the entry politely asked if they had a reservation.

Upon being given Megan's name the woman nodded, left her post, and showed them to their table.

"I had no idea this place would be so small," commented Mary, as she and Sire took seats opposite Megan and Tina.

"Ha! Yes. That's why I called and made a reservation this morning. The restaurant has only twenty-eight seats because of the small area possible for open seating on this particular roof terrace. But from what I've read, the cuisine more than makes up for the limited seating. And just look at that spectacular view of the Colosseum!"

Tina had already stood up to photograph the amphitheater.

"I don't mind the limited seating at all; makes it more intimate," said Sire, looking meaningfully at Mary.

"And I like the candles on the table," Tina uttered as she sat down again. Megan looked at her dinner-mates and said what was on her mind.

"I have to warn you: it's not cheap here. But the emphasis, as you see on the menu, is on the freshest food ingredients possible and the choices are nicely traditional."

"Well, great, I'm in the mood for some pasta pesto," declared Mary. When their orders arrived, conversation ceased as everyone was hungry and the food, ranging from pastas to beef and vitello tonnato with fresh vegetables on the side, was indeed excellent.

During dessert—cooling ice cream all round—the Naples Battalion gave an enthusiastic report of their very full day. A compromise had been made: if Tina would join them at the Anton Dohrn Zoological Station and Aquarium, they would drive Tina to Mount Vesuvius. They had climbed right up to the crater top and studied the black depths below! A little scary.

Megan then happily recounted the twists and turns of her complicated but vastly successful visit to Nathan Bartholdy.

"I wouldn't be surprised if when I call Jared tomorrow morning, he will book a flight to Rome immediately," she said.

"And you are the only person who realizes that this ancient Bartholdy man owns the real thing?" asked Tina.

"I was just going to ask the same question!" Mary exclaimed.

"Definitely. He has this test with showing you a copy of the real thing, as I told you, and the three previous experts failed it. Pronounced the copy as genuine."

"Well, then, *three other people* at least know about the painting's existence, even if they weren't shown the real thing, isn't that right?" questioned Sire.

"Um, yes, if you put it that way."

"What other way is there to put it? Where do these three art historians come from? You said Bartholdy told you two were Italian and one was German. Did he say whether they were all from Rome?"

"No."

"Well, that's why I think it would be wise you call your American director friend as early as you can tomorrow. If there is a financial transaction and removal of the painting from the premises, it should occur as soon as possible."

"You are absolutely correct, Sire. And come to think of it, somebody in Nathan's building was aware that he'd had a visitor. On the stairs going up to his apartment, I passed an unpleasant woman who seemed irritated to have encountered me. She actually climbed back up the stairs behind me apparently to see which apartment I was going to. I thought she was a busybody, that's all. But when I mentioned her to Bartholdy, he said she was his cleaning lady and she was just that way, sour. And overly protective, I guess."

"Quite possibly," said Tina, unhappy at the relentless questioning of her sister.

"Now you've made me nervous, Sire," Megan confessed. "Let's see. There's a six-hour time difference between Rome and New York—Rome being ahead of New York. If I call Jared at noon tomorrow it will be six in the morning for him and I'd catch him at home for sure. That's what I'll do and perhaps this will appease you."

"Dear Megan, I don't need to be appeased. I'm only worried about how quickly knowledge spreads that there is an elderly man in Rome who believes he owns an original oil portrait of the nineteenth-century composer Fanny Mendelssohn."

"Well then, I guess we can all remain calm about it because how many people know or even care who Fanny Mendelssohn was?" Megan sounded bitter, or was she also now just plain worried?

75

"Pick me up one block down on the right side of the street, Carlo, so I don't get into the hearse right in front of our place," Ursula Ladro directed her husband.

"Good thinking. I'll go get the limousine now and should be back here in under ten minutes."

They met precisely as planned and Ursula guided Carlo to the building in the Jewish Quarter where Nathan Bartholdy lived. It was a little after one in the morning and the old man should be sound asleep by now for sure. Carlo parked the hearse, its *Obitorio Scaduti e Figli* logo now covered over by tape, a few apartment houses up from where Bartholdy lived. After reaching and entering Bartholdy's building with Ursula's key, the couple climbed up to the old man's apartment door. Ursula looked around, then soundlessly unlocked the door.

"Let me go in alone at first, just in case he's up," she whispered to Carlo. "If he is, I'll just say that I forgot my wallet and didn't want to bother him. If he's sleeping soundly, I will spray him with the pesticide. Either way I'll come back to you and open the door as soon as I know it's safe to come inside. Look to your left and you'll see the desk with the painting above it. That's the one we want. And you decide if you can take it down by yourself or if you want me on the other side helping." Carlo nodded his head.

"Are you sure you have the can with you?"

"Right here in my handbag." She removed it and showed it to him.

"Okay. Good. I'll be waiting right here. Good luck!"

Ursula tiptoed inside the apartment and listened. She could

hear regular snoring coming from the bedroom. I don't really think pesticide is necessary, she thought to herself, setting it down on the side table next to the bedroom door, just in case it was required after all while removing the painting from the wall behind Bartholdy's desk. She stood outside the man's bedroom a minute longer as the loud snoring continued and then changed her mind. Better safe than sorry! Stealthily she entered the room, sprayed the snoring sleeper's face up and down, and was out of the bedroom seconds later, replacing the can on the side table just in case it should be needed again. And now to get her husband inside.

The whole silent operation took less than six minutes. Carlo was able to remove the painting from the wall swiftly without help and they were out of the apartment. Bartholdy's snoring continued as, on purpose at Ursula's whispered suggestion, they left the apartment and the building entry doors wide open.

"That way no suspicion will fall on me since I have a key to his apartment and would of course have used it to enter and exit."

"Clever," murmured Carlo.

Once they had carried the painting downstairs, they draped it with the blanket they had brought along and Carlo carried the framed canvas to the hearse while Ursula strode away in the opposite direction. So far they had seen no one and it remained that way as Carlo picked up his wife two blocks down from Bartholdy's building.

"We did it!" Ursula cried triumphantly, as they left the Jewish Quarter.

"And the pesticide did its job too." Carlo said with a smile of satisfaction on his face.

"Oh, yes, the pesticide." Carlo did not notice his wife suddenly grow pale. Oh well, what the hell, she told herself. Just another cleaning agent she used around the old man's apartment.

76

"*Meeeee gan! Do you realize what time it is here*?"

The incessant ringing of his phone had awakened Jared Oppenheim from a deep dream in which the sound of a fire alarm was becoming ever more piercing.

"Yes, I know. It's six a.m. your time. So noon my time. But you'll forgive me when you hear why I've called you at this hour."

"What the hell do you mean? Wait! Gotta piss. Be right back."

Megan waited impatiently, feeling both elan and guilt.

"Okay, I'm back. What's going on that's so important it can't wait until a decent time to call?"

"Something incredible enough to make you fly to Rome immediately."

"Ha! I doubt that."

"Listen to what I have to say and then see how you feel. Okay?"

"Okay."

Megan gave a detailed account of what had happened during her visit to Nathan Bartholdy and how, after thoroughly examining the painting's verso and recto and the state of the canvas, she was absolutely certain that the riveting portrait he possessed was genuine and that it was done from life as well.

"Take a look at your email. Photos of it are waiting for you."

"Hold on. I'm walking over to my laptop." Megan could hear him striding across the floor and opening a door into another room. Another minute and Jared announced in a wide awake voice that he was looking at the photographs and that the portrait was stunning.

"Exactly what I hoped I'd be hearing you say. Now listen. Nathan is in terrible debt, has no family, and is eager, in fact desperate, to sell the painting. Right away! And word could spread rapidly about that. I've told him about you and your founding of the Mendelssohn Complex in New York and that I was sure you would be interested in obtaining the portrait. I am right, am I not?"

"You are so goddamn right, Megan, that I'm getting a night flight to Rome the minute we finish talking. If I'm lucky I could be there tomorrow morning. What's your hotel? I'll come right there. Try to book me a room. If not we'll have to double up."

"Sorry, buddy, I'm already doing that with my sister. But don't worry. I'm pretty sure I can get you a room here because this whole week is celebrating Ferragosto and most of Rome is drained. Even tourists have gone elsewhere. Our hotel is at the top of the Spanish Steps, and that's why it's called Hotel Scalinata di Spagna. Your taxi driver will know exactly the best way to get you up those one hundred and thirty-five steps."

"All right, gal, I'll see you tomorrow morning if all falls into place. It will be good to meet your sister, great to be the F & F Trio again, and grand to see Fanny with my own eyes! Till then."

"Wait! One more thing you should know."

"What?" Jared had almost hung up.

"The name of the artist who painted Fanny's portrait is Oppenheim. Moritz Daniel Oppenheim!"

77

Megan had called Jared at noon her time that Thursday. Now three and a half hours later her phone rang and it was Jared on the line. His voice echoed how he felt.

"Hi, Megan. 'Tis I. And I have disappointing news. All afternoon and evening flights to Rome are filled; of course I'm on standby, but my reservation now is Alitalia tomorrow morning at seven. It's an eight and a half-hour flight so I won't be getting in until three-thirty tomorrow afternoon. Bummer!"

"Don't worry, Jared. It will be okay. I'll call Bartholdy and tell him we'll be at his place around five o'clock. All right?"

"If you say so. The main thing to tell him is that I do indeed want to buy his painting of Fanny and that I'll be bringing the euros with me for direct handover. Of course this means I totally trust your judgment about the authenticity of the work."

"I'm absolutely certain about that."

"Great work. About how large is the painting, including frame? What are we talking about here?"

"Well, from handling the work to get it off and back again on the wall, I'd say the work, including the four-inch frame, is about forty-four inches tall and about thirty-eight inches wide. But that's only an estimate. Math—any form of it—is not my best subject."

"How do we do the follow-up? You know, get the painting to a packing and shipping company?"

"I've found out about that too, Jared. Called several and liked best a crate and cargo business called Mancini Aerotrasporto here in Rome. Here's why: they would be willing to pick up the painting at Bartholdy's place. They say they can do a rush packing job within an hour, if you want. We could plan your return flight based on that information. You can either try to have them ship it as freight on your own flight—confirmation is tenuous, they say—or have it shipped to arrive later, which is what they highly recommend."

"Hey, Megan, would you please come work for me as my manager at the Mendelssohn Complex?"

"Ha! I'm not interested in living in New York again. Been there, done that. Twelve years in total."

"About my return flight. I booked a tentative one from Rome for next Monday evening at nine, so perhaps this Mancini firm you've found could get a loading confirmation that far ahead."

"Oh? Planning to live it up in Rome are you?"

"No, not at all. I thought that as long as I'm going to be in Europe again I might as well drop in on poor Rachael Skylar in Hamburg for a day—Sunday—and see how she's doing."

"How sweet of you! I think maybe you have a crush on her."

"Not impossible, but it's the whole family I'm thinking of."

"Have you told her yet?"

"No. I wanted to confer with you first about our major business."

"Well, then, let's agree now what time I should tell Bartholdy we can come by."

"Right. You said we could be at his place sometime between five and six tomorrow afternoon. Let's plan on that. I'll come straight to your hotel from the airport—should arrive around four-thirty—and we'll go together from there to Herr Bartholdy. Good?"

"Not just good, Jared. I'm thrilled that you want Fanny for your Complex and that you're coming to Rome to get her! We've missed you."

"And I've missed our F and F Trio. I just didn't realize how much."

78

The Rome Quartet—Megan, Tina, Mary, and Sire—had agreed to meet later that afternoon and engage in a Fanny activity: going to the Villa Medici, home of the French Academy, at the top of the Spanish Steps. This was something Fanny and her husband had done quite frequently. Their very first full month in Rome they had been befriended by the director of the French Academy there, the famous neoclassical artist Jean-Auguste-Dominique Ingres. He was in his early sixties when they were there and heartily appreciated that they were musicians as he was one as well, in addition to being France's leading neoclassical painter. After dinner he performed on his violin, or as Fanny described it "there is no dancing to Ingres's fiddle for he will have nothing but ultra-classical music." Fanny had also described in one of her letters home witnessing, at what became regular Sunday evening Villa Medici dinners with Ingres, the type of clientele to be seen at the Caffè Greco: "the whole French Academy were assembled there, all looking *thoroughly jeune France*, with beards and hair *à la Raphael*, and nearly all handsome young men."

These were the images Megan shared with her friends as they entered the hedged grounds of the Villa Medici at two that afternoon. The French Academy itself, temporary home across the decades to over two thousand fellowship recipients, including Hector Berlioz and Claude Debussy, was closed to visitors so it was only the grounds they could walk around. But fountains and fragments of ancient sculptures as well as the floral variety and beauty of the gardens with their spectacular views of Rome certainly made up for that. Stopping in front of one particularly lavish fountain, Mary reminded her companions that a musical evocation of the Medici garden fountains highlights Ottorino Respighi's *Fountains of Rome* tone poem. It was a most relaxed afternoon and at dinner nearby afterwards, Megan's friends were riveted by her account of visiting Nathan Bartholdy with the result that Jared Oppenheim would be arriving in Rome tomorrow afternoon. Mary clapped with joy at that news.

Their big event for the evening was two-fold: experiencing the third century B.C. Roman public baths of Caracalla ruins—fortunately not far from Mary and Sire's Colosseum Corner Hotel—and attending an opera there outdoors. It was the final offering of the summer season: Giuseppe Verdi's early opera *Nabucco*, written when he was just twenty-six and premiered in Milan in 1842. Megan was enthusiastic about having a chance to see the opera because of its Jewish subject matter and therefore its interest for that contemporaneous Mendelssohn circle of the early 1840s. In a desire to touch all possible cultural bases for her book on Fanny, she believed seeing the opera performed could be fascinating if not indeed useful. The rest of the Quartet needed no motivation. Seeing an opera outdoors in what was once a huge Roman public bath was incentive enough!

Around five o'clock, after Megan had finished napping back at the hotel, Tina asked her sister to prepare her for what they were going to see and hear that evening.

"But make it brief. I don't need all the details, my scholarly older sis."

"Don't worry. The plot is terribly complicated: you only need know that the two, quote, daughters, end quote, of the Babylonian King Nabucco—Nebuchadnezzar in English—are in love with the same man while at the same time we are presented with the historical plight of the Jews as they cower from advancing Babylonian troops in the Temple of Solomon—which makes the ruins of the baths of Caracalla a perfect setting—anyhow, they are about to be conquered by Nabucco, subjugated, and finally expelled from their homeland as..."

"*Stop!* Your summary is already way too complicated for me!"

"I'm sorry. Let me put it another way. All of the opera's *music* is beautiful and heart-rending but the high point, what every audience waits for is Act Three and the chorus of the Hebrew slaves as they sing the opera's world-famous *Va pensiero*, urging their thoughts to return to their beautiful but lost homeland."

"That's better. What are the opening words of this chorus; just the opening, please."

"They go like this. Megan began to sing:

Va', pensiero, sull'ali dorate;
Va, ti posa sui clivi, sui colli,
ove olezzano tepide e molli
l'aure dolci del suolo natal!
Del Giordano le rive saluta,
di Sionne le torri atterrate...
Oh mia Patria sì bella e perduta!
Oh membranza sì cara e fatal!

"Well, the melody is beautiful. Now what do the words mean?"

"I'll translate them literally, paraphrase the lines for you. And I'll speak them because singing the words in English to Verdi's moving melody just wouldn't work."

Go, thought, on golden wings;
Go, settle upon the slopes and hills,
Where smells balmy and delicious
The sweet breeze of our native land!
Greet the banks of the Jordan,
The destroyed towers of Zion...
Oh my Country so beautiful and lost!
Oh remembrance so dear and fatal!

"Those last two lines are really so sad," murmured Tina.

"Yes, well, Verdi felt that way about his divided Italy before the *Risorgimento*—the Unification. And you can see how this chorus has been used in many situations across time and around the world. Think of Ukraine."

"That gives me the shivers. Hey, do we dress up for the opera?"

"Absolutely not. We won't be sitting in regular seats. The opera is at the Caracalla ruins, remember?"

"Huh?"

"*We'll be sitting on the ground.*"

Was Megan joshing her?

79

Rome's chief of police, Cesari Cacciatore, still continued to keep his dear friend Alessandro Divitore apprised of certain events. The two men had met at the beginning of prime minister Mario Draghi's time in office and hit it off immediately. Both were, in their limited spare time, avid followers of the *Giro d'Italia Donne*, the cycling sport that brought international women athletes to towns and villages all across Italy. When the race involved any town near Rome and they were both free, the two bachelors—plumpish Alessandro and noticeably thin Cesari—would drive to the lucky site and be among the spectators waiting to cheer the dogged cyclists on. Their favorite contender was the thirty-nine-year-old Dutchwoman Annemiek van Vleuten who had recently won the overall title at the 2022 *Giro d'Italia Donne.*

Another event, coming up in a few weeks, was scheduled at Frascati, just twenty kilometers from Rome. So when Cesari phoned Alessandro, the latter instantly assumed that he was calling about the Frascati cycling event. But no, the call was about something quite different: a leak that a "disturbance" was planned for that evening at an unspecified popular site in the city. This after yesterday's dissemination of anti-Israel fliers among the perpetual crowds in front of Saint Peter's: fliers calling for the boycott of Jewish-owned businesses and listing some forty stores, restaurants, hotels, and even bars suspected of being owned by Jews. Italian hatred of Israel and its conduct toward its neighbors had become the country's new, almost justifiable and certainly convenient form of antisemitism.

"So I wanted you to be aware of what might occur this evening and just be on your guard if you or your parents are out and about."

"Thank you so much, Cesare. Tonight is a stay-at-home night for me and my family, but I shall certainly advise some of our neighbors. Oh, and also a visitor to Rome who might be doing something touristy this evening. Just imagine! She, Megan Crespi, is my former fantastic professor when I was a college student in Dallas, Texas and..." He coughed suddenly and had to clear his throat mightily before he could continue.

"... I will always remember what I learned in her classes." Alessandro described a few of the exciting classes he had taken with her.

"And one time, when we were covering the French Revolution, in preparation for studying the artist Jacques-Louis David, she had a few members of the class march up the aisles to her podium on the stage humming the Marseillaise while from the back of the auditorium a music student in the class, by prearrangement, belted out the anthem on his trumpet!"

"What wonderful memories you have of your professor, Alessandro! What did you say her name is?"

"Crespi, Megan Crespi. I'll never forget her classes. And she's just as much fun to be with now as she was then."

"I don't doubt it. So. See you in Frascati!"

"*Sì, certo*!"

80

It was good the Crespi sisters had agreed to eat near Mary and Sire's hotel because the Baths of Caracalla, near the Appian Way, were not too long a walk south from the hotel. All four members of the Rome Quartet had dressed down, sharing the notion that seating in front of the stage and orchestra would be "*on* the rough," as Sire described it. They were pleasantly surprised, then, to see that even rows of folding wooden chairs faced the stage in front of the entry ruins. Nevertheless, their informal clothing matched that of most of the other audience members and they felt right at home in their blue jeans and slacks. Their seats were about twenty rows back from the orchestra and Megan arranged things so that she would be sitting in, what was for her, the prized aisle seat.

"You know, Fanny mentions visiting here in a letter back to her family."

"Ah ha! So that's why you wanted to come here. Not because of the opera but because your sacred Fanny had been here!" teased Tina.

Although they had arrived about fifteen minutes early, most seats were already occupied for the nine o'clock performance and the sky was still light that mid-August evening.

Taking in the immense scope of the original baths from the imposing architectural remnants left, Megan could not help thinking of the equally gigantic 1910 Pennsylvania Station in New York, the scope of which was inspired by the Terme di Caracalla. She was living in New York in 1963 when deconstruction of the busy transit station began in order to build a more modern station. Too bad a more up-to-date version had not been built of the Caracalla Baths, she mused.

Expectations rose as the orchestra members strode to their

positions in front of the raised stage. The podium was also raised and enthusiastic applause greeted the conductor as, at nine o'clock on the dot, he stepped up to it, acknowledging first the orchestra and then the audience. Silence ensued and the opera began. The acoustics were much better than Mary had expected. There were no intermissions between the acts and when the much awaited Act Three was about to begin with the chorus of the Hebrew slaves, "*Va pensiero*," one could have heard a pin drop. Tina nudged her sister in anticipation. Megan's literal translation for her would make the chorus so much more meaningful.

And meaningful it was until the seventh line, "*Oh mia Patria sì bella e perduta*," was sung. Immediately afterward all hell broke loose. Out of nowhere two marching ranks of chanting men on either side of and in front of the orchestra joined forces before the flabbergasted conductor's podium. Although not dressed in any sort of uniform, each man wore a cloth fasces hanging from his neck picturing five contiguous, erect fence rods from out of the top of which the head of an axe emerged—that symbol of power adopted and perverted by Mussolini from Roman times.

And what they were shouting was the odious chant: "*Hebrews! Get out of Italy! Go back to Israel!*"

This hate-filled demonstration that stunned orchestra, maestro, and audience alike lasted some five minutes before the police arrived to arrest the sixteen chanting culprits. Even as they were led away, they continued their demand that Jews "return" to Israel. After conferring with the orchestra, the maestro faced the audience and shouted "Shall we continue?" The ear-splitting "*Yes!*" that followed restored everyone's spirits, and Verdi's opera was performed to the very end. The Rome Quartet was as inspired as the rest of the audience as the great Baths of Caracalla were filled with the inspiring music of *Nabucco*.

81

Only slowly did Nathan realize where he was. His deep dream had him in Hamburg at the senior living facility where his third cousin Salomon Mendelssohn lived. They were having a jolly time reminiscing about family members and family legends. But no. He wasn't in Hamburg. He was in Rome. In his own bed!

But what time was it? He half-opened one sleepy eye and looked over at the small clock on the bed-side table. *What*? Ten in the morning! He never slept that late. He was always up well before seven. How could that have happened? Well, now that he was awake he'd better get the morning paper. It would still be leaning against his entry door in the corridor. Galvanized, he got out of bed carefully and entered his study. The first thing he saw was that the door to the corridor was open. Wide open! The second thing he saw was that the portrait of Fanny over his desk was not there! What the hell? After scooping up the newspaper with great difficulty, he staggered to his desk chair and let his body collapse into it. Time and again he leaned forward, slowly twisted his head up and back only to confirm that the portrait was not there. Missing!

What to do? Report the theft? Call the police and become the center of a gathering throng, perhaps the object of avid press coverage? No! Never. Thank heaven it was the copy and not the original that was stolen. Nathan realized he was as horrified that someone had been in his home as he was that a painting had been stolen. What to do?

The answer came: call Megan Crespi.

82

"What an evening!" Tina exclaimed as she and her sister lingered over a second round of breakfast goodies on the roof terrace of their hotel.

"I'll say. Just wish I'd thought to take photos of the demonstrators and their arrest."

"Not to worry. The world will survive without your constant documentation, you know."

"Well, certainly the newspapers gave it good coverage. And..."

The throbbing of Megan's cellphone caught her attention and her eyes opened wide when she saw the caller ID. She answered immediately.

"Yes, this is Megan Crespi. How are you, Herr Bartholdy?"

"Ach, Doktor Crespi, I am so glad to reach you! Something terrible has happened. I have been robbed and I believe I was drugged in order to steal from me the Fanny portrait!"

"Oh, no! Are you all right?"

"Yes, I am now, but I slept many hours late into the morning as if I had been drugged. And when I awoke, the door to my apartment was wide open out to the hall corridor and one of my Fanny portraits was gone!"

"Oh no! Which one?"

"The wrong one, god be thanked!"

"But you, your health. Shall I call a doctor to come to you, Signor Bartholdy?"

"*No, no!* This is what I want *you* to do, if you would be so kind. Please come here. I need to be with someone who knows the truth about the two Fanny portraits. I do not want doctors or police or newspapers."

"Of course I will come, and right away if you want. Or..." A thought struck Megan. "Or if you like and if you could wait a little, I can come to you with Director Jared Oppenheim of the Mendelssohn Complex this afternoon. He arrives from New York here in Rome at three-thirty and we could be at your home sometime between four-thirty and five."

"Ach! I was completely forgetting about Herr Oppenheim. But of course this is the thing to do. We can, the three of us, talk over things and perhaps even conclude the business we have already discussed concerning the sale of the original Fanny portrait by Oppenheim."

"The good thing is that matters can be arranged quickly. I know he is bringing a generous potential payment with him." Oh dear, Megan thought to herself, should I have let Bartholdy know that? How imprudent of me.

"Ah. With such news I can take the time to attempt, perhaps, to calm down. To eat something and rest. Yes, Doktor Crespi, let us meet in the late afternoon as you have explained. Talking with you has already had a good effect. I feel better now. Thank you."

"Until later today, then," Megan said.

"Until later today," a calmer Nathan replied.

83

As study material on his flight from New York to Rome, Jared had brought along two sets of materials. The first was a conglomerate of data pertaining to recent auction house sale prices of mid-nineteenth century portraits of recognized German personages by identified and well-known German artists. The sales were not as steep as he had imagined but they were impressive.

Additionally, Jared had printed out several high quality images and image details of the two Oppenheim portraits of Fanny Mendelssohn Bartholdy Hensel for comparison purposes. The contrasts were significant. The earlier, familiar 1842 oil portrait showing a bust view of Fanny approaching her mid-thirties, thus in her prime, with her eyes concentrated on inward thoughts, belonged to New York's Jewish Museum. The second oil portrait, perhaps painted a year before her death, was owned by Nathan Bartholdy of Rome, and it recorded a very different Fanny. She had probably just turned forty, perhaps the occasion for the portrait—done just one year before her premature death at forty-one, thought Jared sadly. Here she is shown seated and at waist length; one might better say at lap length. Unlike the earlier portrait, her head is tilted slightly to the right and she seems to be gazing almost imploringly at the beholder, the hint of a wistful smile on her face. Her abundant hair, the long curls of which extended to neck level in the 1842 portrait, only reached to lip level in this later portrait, as if self-grooming had become more of a task.

But the most important feature about the Bartholdy portrait, Jared thought, was, if one didn't know, Fanny's uneven shoulder height, so frankly recorded this time by Oppenheim. Not even the white shawl worn over them concealed the discordancy of her shoulder levels, with the left one distinctly higher than the low right one. Most telling about the sitter's mood as noticed by the artist was the total covering of her pianist hands. They were positioned across her lap and tucked into the wrist-length arms of her dress. What a different Fanny! Gripping, supporting herself. And yet, why? She was fully in command of her talents. Jared recalled that it was during her home rehearsal of Felix's cantata *The First Walpurgis Night* for that Sunday's salon concert that she suddenly lost sensation in her hands, asked a colleague to substitute for her at the piano, declined calling for medical assistance, instead rubbing her hands with vinegar, and just as she was about to return to the rehearsal suffered another, more severe attack, a stroke, rendering her unconscious and taking her life a few hours later. It was the fourteenth of May, 1842; she was only forty-one. And Felix, in deep grief over his sister's death, would die within six months, apparently also from a stroke. Modern medicine, Jared had recently learned, regards subarachnoid hemorrhage as the likely cause of death for both Fanny and Felix, just as it had been for their parents and for their grandfather, Moses.

Oh, how eager he was to see with his own eyes Oppenheim's second portrait of Fanny. If he could acquire it, what interest it would stir up when installed at his Mendelssohn Complex! It would not only rival the Jewish Museum's earlier Oppenheim portrait of Fanny; it would be of far more historical interest. And, Megan had assured him, Nathan Bartholdy was more than ready to sell the unique portrait. Once again that early afternoon on board his Rome-bound flight, Jared researched whether or not he might be genetically related to the painter. And once again he was frustrated at his inability to track any convincing link. Never mind. He could already visualize the newspaper headlines: "Director Oppenheim acquires painter Oppenheim portrait of Fanny Mendelssohn Bartholdy Hensel for New York's Mendelssohn Complex."

84

Discussion between the Ladro couple late that morning about what to do next with the Bartholdy portrait had come to a temporary dead end.

"In our rush to get the picture, Ursula, we just didn't take the time to think ahead what to *do* with the picture afterwards," Carlo summed up their worried conversation. He continued.

"And when we invite persons from auction houses and galleries to examine the portrait, we sure don't want them to know where we live. For instance, if we were to turn down somebody's offer to buy the painting because we think the sum is too low, it's possible they could get angry, even suspicious, and give our address to the police. And we sure don't want that!"

"You're right, you're right Carlo," his overwhelmed wife whined. "When the old man finally wakes up and tells the police his painting has been stolen, they might want to interview *me*. *Dio!* They could be on their way here right now! They can't miss the thing under the blanket in the hall!"

"Calm down," Carlo urged. "I think the painting and its frame could be slipped under our bed if I raise it a few inches."

"Oh, Carlo, you're brilliant! You are..."

Ursula's cellphone in her purse rang loudly. She rushed to see the caller ID.

It was Nathan Bartholdy.

Ursula held up the phone so Carlo could see who was calling. Should she answer, she whispered?

Yes, he nodded vigorously. Obediently she did, summoning all her courage.

"Signor Bartholdy?"

"Yes. It is I. Ursula, I have something extremely upsetting to tell you. Last night after I fell asleep around ten as usual, somebody burst into my apartment, entered my bedroom, and sprayed me with a pesticide that knocked me out for many hours. In fact I didn't wake up until ten this morning. And then I discovered that one of my paintings had been stolen!"

"Oh my god! How terrible! Did you call the police?"

"Heavens! Certainly not. The last thing in the world I want is nosy policemen and detectives here sifting through my things and asking me questions."

"Of course. You are right. Would you like me to come there? Did the burglar leave the place in a mess?"

"Oh no, that's not why I called you. I want to know if you have noticed anything unusual in the building lately. Something like a man hanging out in the hall of my floor or in the lobby. Someone watching my place and the comings and goings. Whoever this person was, he left my door wide open.

That was the first thing I saw—the door to my apartment left swung open into the hall. I can't tell you how upsetting that was to see."

"I can imagine, Signor Bartholdy." An idea suddenly came to her. "You know, come to think of it, I did see something strange yesterday as I was leaving your building. A woman passed me on the stairs as I was going down and she was going up. I had a bad feeling about her so I returned to your floor and I saw her standing in front of your apartment door."

"Oh, well, that was a visitor from America whom I was expecting. But I thank you for being concerned enough to come back up the stairs and check on things."

"Oh, Signore, I do care and worry so much about you!"

"Well, thank you for that, Ursula."

"Um. You said the person who broke into your apartment sprayed you with a pesticide. How did you know that?"

"Because he left the can on the table outside the bedroom door."

"That would mean his fingerprints are on the can. Are you going to show it to the police?"

"No! *I do not want police in my home*. I am having a locksmith come tomorrow—the earliest they can come—and he will install a new lock. I'll get you a copy of the key, of course, and next time you arrive here, just ring my apartment number at the building entrance and I'll let you in. Then when you get to my floor, I'll be there waiting for you." Nathan could not see the victory sign his cleaning lady was waving at her husband.

"What a good idea, Signor Bartholdy. And about something you said concerning this terrible break-in. Did you say that one of your paintings had been stolen?"

"Yes. But fortunately it was simply a copy I had made of the portrait in my bedroom. Kind of you to worry about that, Ursula. But that office copy is, thank god, worthless."

"*Worthless*?"

"Yes, worthless. Goodbye."

Hanging up his phone, Nathan did not hear Ursula's loud gasp.

85

"So, what would you like to do today, Tina?" Megan asked as they went back down from the roof restaurant to their hotel room. "Like to come along with us to the Women Composers recital at noon?"

"Um, don't think so. There's something I've really been wanting to do here but I didn't have a chance to do while taking the art courses. And I wouldn't have missed those courses for the world."

"What's it that you want to do?"

"Spend two and a half hours with a small private tour group at the Colosseum and in all its underground halls and chambers. I just confirmed my reservation this morning while you were doing your exercises."

Megan shouldn't have been surprised. She knew her sister loved visiting and working at archaeological sites in Texas. She just hadn't visualized Tina exploring Italian artifacts. And the Colosseum certainly was a super artifact.

"Well, more power to you! Of course you want to spend quality time there, and today is a perfect day to do it."

"Glad you understand, Big Sis. And also I'm having a farewell dinner with some of my fellow art class students this evening. So I hope you'll excuse me if I don't join you all."

"Ha! Join the crowd. Mary and Sire are also having dinner separately tonight with one of his old investment bank buddies who lives here. Plus Jared is arriving late this afternoon and we have a very important visit to make that could ultimately include dinner as well. So I guess our Rome Quartet will be playing separately tonight!"

"Yep, seems that way. Hey, I gotta get going now," Tina announced, gathering her things up.

"If you can wait for just a minute I'll come with you. We're heading in the exact same direction because I'm meeting Mary and Sire at their hotel."

A patient Tina waited as she watched her sister deftly go through the new dental routine imposed upon her by her caring dentist: floss, rinse with a special premixed liquid, and Waterpick brush. Then it was off to the Colosseum via the reliable bus line 51.

At the Colosseum stop Megan headed for the hotel as Tina hurried off to the giant Flavian amphitheater. In the lobby Megan encountered a smiling Sire, who indicated that Mary would be there any minute.

"It takes her hours to brush her teeth," he explained.

Megan laughed out loud but didn't explain why. Her own tooth routine was probably twice as long as Mary's.

"Hi there!" Mary greeted them after a few minutes. "The Ottorino Respighi School of Music is just two metro stops away, so follow me!"

Twelve minutes later and in plenty of time for the concert, they emerged from the underground and laughed with glee when they caught sight of the school. About eighty students, a predominant number of whom were black, were standing around the entrance holding banners that read "*Benvenuto Grace e Troy!*" The two African-American performers being greeted in this festive manner were the famous wife-husband team who had made a name for themselves in America and Europe presenting songs by women composers both past and present. Along with their accompanist, pianist Joseph Terald, they were on their second concert tour of Western Europe. One of the notable aspects of their performances was that they were held not only at crowded concert halls but also at music schools with the aim of presenting an encouraging model of to what their listeners could aspire.

"I'm so grateful that you found out about this extraordinary event and got us all tickets for it," Megan said as they entered the school auditorium where only a few seats were still available. For the next hour and a half they enjoyed a variety of ear-pleasing songs as Grace and Troy alternated presentations or, some dozen times at least, sang duets. Troy's deep baritone voice blended perfectly with Grace's lilting soprano voice and the emotions conveyed by the texts ranged from mourning and nostalgia to hope and joy.

Surreptitiously during one extended applause, Megan studied the printed program she had been handed. With a heavy sprinkling of British and Americans, the composers ranged from the twelfth-century multi-talented German Benedictine abbess Hildegard von Bingen to Mozart's gifted sister Maria Anna, to Fanny Mendelssohn and Clara Schumann to Mathilde von Rothschild, Ethyl Smyth, Amy Beach, Nora Holt, whose skin color was that of Grace and Troy's, Wanda Landowska, Alma Mahler, Nadia Boulanger, Maria Rodrigo, Mary Howe, Germaine Tailleferre, Imogen Holst, An-Ming Wang, Yoko Ono, and Cecilia McDowall.

There was no intermission and the program lasted an hour and a half. Time had been scheduled afterward for audience questions and the mood of the audience was both inquisitive and cheerful. The music school's students were inspired and as the audience began to leave, they lingered behind, taking photos and holding up books and paper for autographs from the two obliging singers. All in all a joyful and educational experience, the Rome Trio agreed as they walked back to the metro station.

"Makes me proud to be almost American," Sire allowed.

At the metro he and Mary parted company with Megan who needed to get back to her hotel and make more Fanny notes. Aye, and so she might even be able to slip in a wee nap before Jared's arrival, she told herself in what she fancied was a Scottish brogue.

86

"Just two more hours. It won't be long now," murmured Jared to himself excitedly. He had finished his research on recent auction house sale prices concerning paintings comparable to the Fanny portrait in Rome. He had also put aside all attempts to find any ancestral connection between himself and the nineteenth-century artist Oppenheim who had painted the moving portrait of Fanny owned by Nathan Bartholdy. Internet data pointed out that he was the "first Jewish painter of the modern era," and certainly, as Jared found online, the image he had created of young Mendelssohn visiting Goethe in Weimar on his way to Italy was masterful, catching the spirit and looks of both men.

And now he was about to meet a direct descendant of the composer: the nonagenarian Nathan Bartholdy who owns an unknown portrait of Fanny! A portrait, if genuine, he was determined would soon be hanging in New York's Mendelssohn Complex!

87

"I've called you, Alessandro, because I had to tell someone how relieved I am that a planned demonstration for today was thwarted by my men. Had it taken place, it would have been a terrible smear on our country." One could tell by the sound of his voice that Rome's Chief of Police Cesari Cacciatore was upset.

"Oh no! What was it?"

"A concert was scheduled at one of our music schools today at noon and it had attracted the attention of our local white supremacists because of who was performing. It was a vocal performance of songs by women composers and while that alone shouldn't have raised any eyebrows, the performers did: a married American couple who are Black. Fortunately, word of the plan leaked and we were able to arrest the leader this morning. It would have been a debacle, I can tell you, with all those youngsters present. And nationally as well. Not only is there this outbreak of mounting antisemitism fed by disapproval of Israel's treatment of Palestine, but our local white supremacists are multiplying: there are a number of private clubs of them right here in Rome and their disapproving focus is on Afro-Italians. What a world full of malice we live in now!"

"And how thankful our city is to you and your dedicated staff for the work you do." Alessandro's praise was sincere. The two friends spoke a few minutes longer and both felt better by the time they had finished. It was after he hung up that Alessandro realized with some guilt that he had completely forgotten to warn his former professor Megan Crespi, now visiting in Rome, of possible public demonstrations last Thursday. Oh, well, considering her advanced age, she was probably sound asleep when the demonstration at the Baths of Caracalla occurred during a Verdi opera.

88

It was a little past two o'clock and Megan made one quick stop on the way back to her hotel. There, after bringing the Fanny notes up to date and with nothing pressing on her schedule until Jared's flight landing at three-thirty and his arrival about half an hour later at the hotel, Megan partook of one of her favorite activities—a short, reviving afternoon nap. "After all, I'm no longer in my seventies," she would justify this activity to herself and, if necessary, to others.

Thus she felt rested and ready to go when her cellphone rang and it was Jared, just a few minutes after four o'clock.

"Hey there, Megan! 'Tis I. I've cleared customs and am in a taxi on the way to your, uh, to *our* hotel."

"Wonderful! How nice to hear your voice. I'll be waiting in the lobby, or maybe standing just outside the entrance so I can hop right into your taxi. See you soonissimo!"

Half an hour later Megan, wearing a small backpack, was indeed standing outside the hotel entry when Jared's cab drove up.

"Hi, Megan! Let me just drop my bag off inside at reception and I'll be right back—here, you get inside and hold our taxi."

Megan obeyed, smiling and nodding at the driver, and before she could even get settled, an unencumbered Jared was back. Megan gave the address and off they went in the direction of the Jewish Quarter. She gave Bartholdy a call and he was overjoyed to hear they were on their way to him.

"Just ring my apartment buzzer at the building entrance and I'll let you right into the building and be waiting for you," the old man said in German.

"He's bilingual—his grandparents and parents saw to that—and seems to prefer German," explained Megan.

Some twenty-five minutes later their taxi pulled up in front of Via Portico d'Ottavia 72 and within another few minutes they were at Bartholdy's apartment door. It was slightly ajar and a feeble male voice called out.

"Come in!" a welcoming voice said in English. Ah, ha, master of one more language, thought Megan.

Introductions were made and Nathan, who was seated at his desk, waved them to the leather couch facing him. Megan spoke first and earnestly.

"Before we talk about your wonderful Fanny portrait, please tell us, Herr Bartholdy, how you are after the terrible thing that happened to you last night?"

"Thank you, Frau Doktor. I am still, physically and emotionally, in the thralls of having been sprayed with a pesticide in my sleep. But let us not dwell on that. I think it is a fine thing you have created a Mendelssohn Center in New York, Herr Oppenheim."

"Mendelssohn Complex," instantly corrected Megan sotto voce.

"Ah," replied Jared graciously, "with the Fanny portrait it will become a Mendelssohn center."

"And you, you must be eager to see my Fanny portrait, having come all this way from America."

"Most definitely, sir."

"You know of course that it was painted by a namesake of yours."

"Indeed I do. How I would love to be able to say that Moritz Daniel Oppenheim shares my family tree, but so far I have not been able to discover any confirming data. But I haven't given up!" Nathan smiled at Jared.

"Keep trying, young man, keep trying."

"It is strange to see the wall behind your desk vacant now, Herr Bartholdy. Even though it was only a copy, are you sad about the painting's being gone?" Megan asked.

"I am horrified and sad that a burglar has invaded my home and I am also sad that the copy is gone, as she would have been somewhat of a comfort to me should you decide to acquire the original, Herr Oppenheim. However, if you leave it here a day, I can have my copyist paint me another, and this time an exact copy. Previously he glossed over an important detail."

"What was that, if I may ask?" enquired Jared.

"He 'cured' her uneven shoulders inherited from Moses Mendelssohn. Made them straight. Outrageous falsification. But I've kept you from the original too long. Follow me," Nathan said, laboriously rising from his desk. Slowly he led his guests into the bedroom. The overhead lights were already on and a strong flashlight stood on the bedside table.

Instantly Jared gasped. God! Megan had been so right to notify him about the existence of this extraordinary portrait.

"May we take it off the wall and examine it?" he asked, eager to see and confirm to the best of his ability the authenticity of the painting.

"But of course!"

The New Yorker, accustomed to limited home spaces, was instantly at the bed, leaning in and gently removing the painting from the wall in what seemed to his two observers one fluid movement. Just as Megan had done, Jared placed the portrait face down on the bed in order to examine the back of the canvas and its moorings.Some minutes later, satisfied that everything really dated from the nineteenth century, he slowly turned the painting over, and with the use of the handy flashlight on the bedside table and a magnifying glass he had brought along with him, he began meticulously examining every inch of the portrait. This lasted a long time, even though he never applied Megan's sniffing test. Finally, he stood back and took stock of the pronouncedly uneven shoulders, so different from Fanny's devoted husband's many portrayals rectifying the imbalance just as Bartholdy's copyist had done.

Turning to the old man who had taken a seat on the far edge of the bed, Jared smiled.

"In concert with Doctor Crespi, I am satisfied that this unique portrait of Fanny Mendelssohn Bartholdy Hensel is genuine. And I am certain that infrared radiation and multispectral scan will confirm this. So I shall rehang this portrait on your wall for now, and then, if you like, we can return to your office and discuss the business details."

With a look of peaceful ecstasy on his face, Nathan Bartholdy led the way back to the first room and took his place at the desk while his guests returned to the couch. The Americans conferred for a minute. Jared pulled out his phone and the two studied it briefly as he pulled up various previously studied URLs and their content. At last Jared looked at the smiling man across from him and spoke slowly.

"Herr Bartholdy. By my calculations of recent auction house sales of a mid-nineteenth century portrait of an identified German celebrity by an identified and well-known German artist, as was Moritz Daniel Oppenheim, your Fanny portrait is likely worth between eight and nine hundred thousand euros."

He paused, allowing the projected value information to sink in. Then he continued.

"What do you say to my offer of one million euros?"

Nathan Bartholdy looked joyfully overwhelmed. He had done his own Internet checking and come up with very high monetary figures. But none at the level of one million euros. He was more than pleased. His answer was given immediately.

"Herr Oppenheim, your calculations match those of mine and I accept your generous offer."

Jared immediately stood up, strode to Nathan's desk, and genially, gently shook the old man's proffered hand. Megan applauded with glee, and smiles lit their faces.

"Furthermore," said Jared, "fully understanding your desire to have an exact copy of the original Fanny and realizing this could not be carried out in a single day by your artist, I am prepared to pay you right now in euros one third of the sum just agreed upon and leave the portrait with you for the next two days, Saturday and Sunday. I shall arrange with Mancini Aerotrasporto to pick it up Monday morning and have it crated for bringing it back to New York with me on my return flight that evening. I shall make out a check to you right now for the remaining two thirds euros. I am not in the habit of carrying one million euros around with me."

"But this is marvelous! Thank you, thank you!" Nathan was on a cloud.

"Yes, that makes a lot of sense," said Megan, happy for both men and the mutually beneficial business arrangement.

"Ah, but you do not know *how* grateful I am," Nathan continued, "and what I now intend to do in appreciation to Doktor Crespi for bringing us together without any tiresome auction house bargaining. Herr Oppenheim, you may or may not know that Doktor Crespi is at work writing a biography of Fanny Mendelssohn Bartholdy Hensel."

"Indeed I do know." Jared smiled proudly at Megan.

"I am sure it will be as insightful and valuable as her recent biography on Clara Schumann is. So listen closely. What I have not told Doktor Crespi, or you, or anyone in Rome or Berlin, is that I have in my possession, handed down by my grandparents, twenty-three letters written by Fanny to her sister Rebecka dating from her year in Rome. And these letters I will give to you right now *as a gift*, without any payment, but with the proviso that, when you are done with them for your biography, you will donate them to either the Mendelssohn Archive at the Staatsbibliothek in Berlin *or* to your Mendelssohn..." Nathan cleared his throat and said distinctly, "*Complex* in New York. That would be your choice."

Megan clapped her hands in astonishment and joy and her clapping was seconded by an equally delighted Jared.

"I cannot wait to have them in my hand and read them. But first!" she exclaimed, reaching toward the backpack she had placed in one corner of the couch. "It is now almost eight o'clock and none of us has had dinner. Herr Bartholdy, *caro Signor* Bartholdy, I have brought along dinner for three and if you will just allow me the brief use of your kitchen, I shall return in a few minutes with our food—pasta pesto tortellini and green salad. Is this agreeable? And is moving to a first-name basis also agreeable?"

"Both highly agreeable, Megan," laughed an enchanted Nathan and seconded by a totally surprised Jared. So that's why Megan had a backpack with her!

Nathan turned to Jared and beamed.

"*Pranzo a casa! Magnifico!*"

89

Carlo Ladro did not finish work that evening until eight. Two afternoon funerals at different and distant cemeteries had kept him out late. When at last he was through, he had rushed home to be with Ursula. She was spooked and had called him multiple times while he was on the job.

"We're going to think this thing out," he consoled her, swiftly walking to the bedroom to change out of his tight chauffeur's uniform.

"*Oh no!*" his voice shouted an instant later. "What have you done, Ursula?" She hurried into the room after him.

"I was just trying to hide the goddamn painting. What if Signor Bartholdy has changed his mind about not wanting police in his home? What if he sent them to talk to me? If the police had come today that would have been the first thing they would be looking for. And they would have immediately seen it in the hall."

"But you have it half-crammed into the closet! And with a bathrobe over it. That only attracts attention; hides nothing."

"Because I couldn't get it with its frame under our bed and I had to put it somewhere. The police could have, can come at any moment!" Tears began flooding Ursula's cheeks.

"All right, woman, stop crying. I'll get it under the bed." Carlo was true to his word. After looking in vain for anything helpful in the kitchen, he put together a huge stack of old magazines from the living room, brought them into the bedroom, and began dividing them into four compact piles of identical height. Then he lifted the head of their bed up on end, had Ursula hold it in place, and positioned two even magazine piles where the weight of the bed would rest when lowered again. The same routine was applied to the foot of the bed and when

Carlo tested it, the balance was perfect. It was now possible to slip the framed painting under the bed and out of sight. Ursula laid a large open quilt over the end of the bed, and the coverup was complete.

"Fantastic," she said, kissing her husband on the cheek. "Now I'll fix us a good dinner and we can discuss what we need to do later tonight." Her composure had returned and she was rapidly thinking ahead.

"'Later tonight!' What are you talking about?"

"Carlo, we've simply got to go back to Bartholdy's. We must get the genuine painting out of there as soon as we can. No waiting. The longer we wait, the more dangerous and the more difficult it gets. The old man has a locksmith coming tomorrow! *We only have the right key tonight*. And it will be safe. He'll be asleep and snoring when we enter real late like we did last night. And you heard the old man declare on the phone that he wouldn't call the police; absolutely did not want them in his place. So it will be *safe* for us."

"But didn't you say the real painting is in his bedroom and actually on the wall over the head of his bed?"

"So? We simply squirt him with more pesticide." She did not mention that she had forgotten that she had left the can at Bartholdy's place. Best to bring another anyhow.

"You do have a way of figuring things out, Ursula, I have to say."

"As long as I'm in charge of the situation, yes. But not like it was for me today, panicked and trying to hide the painting for just in case the police might come. Now you sit down and I'll fix you some delicious ravioli. How's that?"

90

"You know, Megan, dear," commented Jared after they had taken their leave of Nathan Bartholdy and were on the street again awaiting the Uber they had ordered, "I just don't feel right about frail old Nathan's not having reported to the police that bold break into his apartment and then the theft."

"Oh, Jared, I was just thinking the same thing!"

"I know he does not want the police nosing around his apartment, but I've thought of an alternative. Having a private detective keep watch over his place as soon as possible. Nathan need never even know."

"That's a super idea! But how are you going to contact a private detective at this time of the evening?"

"I've got that figured out. I came prepared with a number just in case one might be needed. But I'll need your help, Megan, because you speak Italian and I don't very well."

"Sure, that's fine. Who are you going to call? "

"The name I have noted down here—see? Name and number." Jared held up his phone.

Megan studied Jared's entry: the name was Amadeo Seguire and the phone number for calling from America was 1.315.723.4242.

"So you'd be calling from your U.S. phone to this man in Rome, correct?"

"Yes. I'll dial and you talk and explain the situation. Here's Nathan's street address below the phone number, see?"

"I do. Okay, let's try it. It's ten-thirty; he should still be up."

Jared dialed the number, put the phone on speaker, and handed it to his co-conspirator. They could hear a man's voice answer: "*Pronto*."

"*Signor Seguire*?"

"Sì. *Chi sta parlando?*"

Megan explained who she was, who Jared was, and what they would like him to do, beginning with this very evening. Would it be possible? Signor Seguire answered that he did not take night jobs any longer but that he had a young associate who could, if not already assigned, take on the job immediately. He would call right away, find out, and call them back.

"*A questo stesso numero*?" he asked.

"*No, no, Signor Seguire. Meglio a me per il problema della lingua.*"

Megan turned to Jared, pointing to herself as she gave the detective her phone number and thanked him. Then she smiled at Jared as she handed back his phone and asked him a question.

"Do you know what that nice detective's surname means in English, Jared?"

"No. What?"

"Follow. *Seguire* means to follow. Rather appropriate, yes?"

"Love it! Let's hope it brings good luck."

As they talked, their Uber drove up and they were comfortably seated, Megan with Fanny's letters safely in her backpack which she had removed and put on her lap for the ride back to their hotel. There was no answering call back, however, and still nothing after they had tipped the Uber driver and entered the hotel. But then her phone rang at last and she answered immediately. She listened, smiled, nodding her head in agreement, and thanked Signor Seguire.

"You're going to like this," she said.

"What?"

"Amadeo Seguire's young man, Vittorio Trovato, fully informed of the case, is already parked across the street from Nathan's building and keeping a close watch over Via Portico d'Ottavia seventy-two."

91

Before Megan went to bed that night she could not restrain herself from quickly going through the twenty-three letters Fanny had written Rebecka, her younger sister by six years, during her year in Rome. Usually Fanny's letters were addressed to the entire family back in Berlin, but this trove was exclusively to Rebecka and therefore almost twice as interesting, since Fanny had such a special relationship with her sister. An indication of this greeted Megan's eyes at the beginning of a letter dated Rome, December 16, 1839 written just to her and detailing a dull event Fanny had attended. Megan read it out loud with increasing amusement, especially at her final words to her beloved sister: "I should have been as frolicsome as a rabbit, if you had been there too."

What a treasure! And such great timing for my biography of Fanny, thought Megan to herself. The evening's prolonged excitement at Nathan's and now this first glance at Fanny's letters to her sister beckoned Megan into a deep and restorative sleep.

92

Since his arrival at Via Portico d'Ottavia 72 in his black two-door Fiat 500 shortly after ten that evening, Vittorio Trovato had observed nothing out of the ordinary concerning the apartment building across the street from where he had found a parking space between two cars that placed him several feet north of the apartment house. So far only three people had entered edifice: a single man in his late fifties and a young couple. "Vitto," as his friends jokingly called him—a shortening of his name that meant "food" in Italian—knew he was in for a long night of surveillance but, after all, that's what being in such an unpredictable profession often entailed and he always had enough food with him. This time it would seem he was lucky, however.

At one-thirty in the morning a slow-moving motor vehicle pulled up and stopped next to a parked car that was one car length down from the entrance to the building he was keeping tabs on. The car was a Cinque Posti hearse. What the hell was a hearse doing out at this time of night? And why would it be parked out in the street parallel to a parked car rather than by the sidewalk? It certainly would make for a quick departure parked that way and the hearse was perfect for long loads, in particular a large framed painting. Could this be the reason for what Vitto read as quick-exit parking?

Sliding over to the front passenger seat and crouching low, Vitto switched his cellphone camera to video and began filming. First to get out of the hearse was a woman. Dressed in black pants and a long-sleeved black blouse, she was gesticulating to someone in the driver's seat. When the figure stepped out of the hearse and toward her, it was clear that it was a man. Gazing around briefly toward the parked cars before and beyond his own vehicle, the man then gave a long look at

Vitto's side of the street. Nothing seemed worthy of further scrutiny and the man turned back to the woman who had now joined him on the sidewalk. They walked to the entrance of Nathan Bartholdy's building. The man opened the door readily with a key and the couple entered without any fuss or noise.

The lateness of the hour for all this made sense to Vitto. Why would any legitimate occupant park in the street, presumably overnight, parallel to and blocking parked cars? Time to call the police.

But wait! If the couple actually lived there, perhaps they left the hearse where it was because they intended to return to it shortly, reasoning that they would not be blocking any parked cars at that hour of the night, or rather at one-thirty in the morning. Perhaps out of eagerness to spot something suspicious for his boss, Vitto was overreaching? He had done that once and that set him back with Amadeo Seguire for quite some time. So never again would he make an impulse judgment.

He would simply wait and watch.

93

Once inside the building the Ladro couple quickly climbed the two flights of stairs to Bartholdy's floor and walked silently down the hall to his door. Ursula quietly inserted her key into the lock and turned it. But the door did not open. Carlo pushed gently but the door did not give. He pushed again a bit more forcefully and the door opened some six inches. Looking inside he could see that a small upholstered armchair had been pushed up against the door. Well, that was easily remedied. Reaching his left hand through to the chair, he pushed it away, then pressed against the door again. It swung open silently. Another moment and they were inside the apartment.

A familiar sound greeted them. Loud, regular snoring. The pesticide can they had brought with them the first time still sat on the side table next to the bedroom door, and Ursula quickly blocked Carlo's possible view of it. Taking no chances as they entered the bedroom, Ursula sprayed the snoozing man's face thoroughly. Then Carlo stepped over and, leaning across the sleeper, very slowly lifted up the painting hanging on the wall over Bartholdy's head. That was it. Mission accomplished. In just under ten minutes. Pushing the fallen chair to one side, the Ladros purposefully left the apartment door open into the hallway as they left.

And this time they did not bother to wrap the painting in a blanket before leaving the building. Who could possibly be around at this hour of the morning? There was a blanket already laid out in the hearse. Suppressing the desire to gloat over how easy the removal had been, they quickly loaded the framed painting into the back of the hearse.

All this was filmed by Vitto from his vantage point across the street, and while the couple was still loading the painting he called the police, quickly identifying himself, giving his location and describing the couple and what they had just done. He would follow their vehicle when they drove off and he would stay on the line with the officer who had answered his call until police cars silently caught up with the hearse.

The time was exactly one forty-five in the morning.

It only took another six minutes before two police cars passed Vitto, fanning out on either side of the hearse with sirens sputtering.

"Damn it! The police must have seen us," cursed Carlo.

"We could never outrun them. Best just to stop. Let me do the talking," commanded Ursula.

A tense Carlo slowed down immediately and the police car to his right made way for him to park next to the sidewalk. The police car on his left swooped around in front of him. After Carlo parked, he rolled down his window and smiled weakly at the officer who was approaching him on foot.

"Hey, Officer, what's the matter?" Ursula called across her husband to the policeman.

"What's the matter? You're in big trouble, Signora, that's what's the matter. Now both of you, get out of your vehicle." The driver of the second police car was walking toward them, pistol raised. Not only did Carlo quit the car, so did Ursula, hurrying around the hearse to speak to the police.

"Why are you stopping my husband, Officer? He's done nothing wrong! And we haven't run through any traffic lights." Ursula crossed her arms in front of her chest.

"Your driver's license. Now!" said the officer, confronting Carlo and ignoring the woman. Carlo obliged instantly.

"Everything should be in order," he said.

"*Why are you stopping us*?" demanded Ursula as the officer examined Carlo's license.

"Open up the back of your hearse, immediately!" the second officer commanded, paying no attention to the woman.

"No, Carlo, no! Don't do it. They have to have a *reason*." Neither husband nor wife noticed the black Fiat 500 coming to a halt several parking lengths behind the hearse.

"The reason is that some ten minutes ago a witness saw you carrying a large framed painting out of Via Portico d'Ottavia seventy-two and loading it into your hearse. He also saw you enter the building some fifteen minutes earlier."

"There's an explanation for that," exploded Ursula. "My husband works late nights and it wasn't until way after midnight that we could pick up the exciting gift my husband was given by a wealthy friend of ours."

"A gift? That's not how our sources describe it. We know that one night ago, a first picture was stolen from the home of Signor Nathan Bartholdy, who during the robbery was rendered unconscious with a pesticide spray."

"Oh, really? Did this man *report* such a theft to you?" Ursula said sarcastically.

"No, he did not. But he did confide to a friend who immediately had a private detective assigned to watch the building. Your arrival and departure was caught on video and we have dispatched an officer along with a medic to check on Signor Bartholdy—they should be with him now."

For once Ursula Ladro was speechless.

"No more delay, Signor Ladro. Open up the back of your hearse now!"

His head hanging low, Carlo obediently walked to the back of his hearse and slowly raised the trunk lid. There, wrapped in a thick blanket, was the painting that had so recently cheered Nathan Bartholdy in his bedroom.

"But that portrait is a *gift* to us from Signor Bartholdy," Ursula shouted.

"Officer Sicuro!" shouted Vitto, running up, his phone still to his ear.

"The medic just called. They found Bartholdy's apartment door wide open and the old man unconscious, pesticide of some sort sprayed on his face! They're trying to bring him round now."

Officer Sicuro immediately turned to the Ladro couple.

"*You are both under arrest on charges of breaking and entering, assault and battery, and theft.*"

94

Placed for the night on Jared's hotel bedside table, the cellphone's insistent ringing woke him up at six that Saturday morning. Hardly the time he preferred but he was pretty sure who it would be and he definitely wanted to get the report he was expecting.

"Yes?" he asked. Megan's voice greeted him.

"Hi! It's me. Great news! Detective Amadeo Seguire just phoned me. Your assignment to have a watch kept on Nathan Bartholdy's place proved to be crucial in the arrest by the police of the two persons who had broken into his apartment, doused him with pesticide, and stolen a painting two nights ago."

"Great! How did the police know that?"

"Because the couple returned for another one last night!"

"Oh my god! Did they hurt Nathan?"

"He's all right now but yes, they did the same thing they'd done to him before: knocked him out with pesticide again. A police medic got to him and was able to revive him."

"And did they steal a painting again?"

"They certainly did. *Yours*!"

"Yikes! That's the other thing I was worried about when we left Nathan after dinner last night. Was I really foolish enough, I chastised myself, to have paid him a down payment in euros on the spot but leave the painting? I've never done a thing like that before. But I wanted to give him time and the funds to have an exact copy made, just as he said he wanted to do."

"Hmm, let's just say you were foolish but big-hearted."

"I'll take that as a compliment, Megan. But tell me, how was the robbery carried out and how did the police find out? Was it my detective on the spot?"

"You bet it was! Seguire's man Vittorio parked in place across from Nathan's building, spied the two persons—a man and a woman—drive up, park in the street parallel to a parked car, enter the building, to which they obviously had a key, around one-thirty this morning and then exit about ten minutes later with what they had come for: another painting..."

"Unbelievable! What nerve. What happened next?"

"Well, this Vittorio was videoing the entire street scene and when he saw what the couple were doing—loading the vehicle with a framed painting—he immediately called the police and they tracked it down almost instantly, with Vittorio following close behind. And guess what the mode of transportation was! A hearse! Rather easy to spot, wouldn't you say?"

"Ha! Definitely. A *hearse* of all things!"

"So just think, Jared. Because you thought of having Nathan's building watched overnight, you have solved a crime in Italy!" All Megan heard in response was a long, loud yawn.

"Thank you Megan, but you give me too much credit. It was Seguire's detective who spotted and reported the crime."

"And who hired him? You!"

"All right. Thank you. The good thing, the important thing is that not only is the painting in police possession, I take it, but that Nathan is okay."

"Yes! Thank goodness for that. I want to call him later today. Hey, shall we meet on the roof for breakfast at seven, then? Tina and I will be there by that time."

"Definitely. What time is it now? Fifteen after six. I need to do some exercises first, but seven is doable."

"Oh, that's right, you're the dedicated swimmer, aren't you!"

"Try to be."

"Well that's fine with me. I have a morning exercise routine too."

"Really? What do you do?"

"Maybe I'll tell you at breakfast if we run out of Bartholdy conversation. Till seven then, Mister Crime Stopper."

Jared was the first to arrive at their Hotel Scalinata di Spagna's charming rooftop restaurant and he was still standing, taking in the Roman panorama when Megan and Tina joined him. They were early enough to get one of the tables with the best view and while Tina stuck to her bacon and eggs, Megan and Jared helped themselves to a breakfast of bananas, blueberries, strawberries, cereal, yogurt, and milk. Tina zoomed through her breakfast, however, because she had something "special" starting at eight o'clock.

"And what might that be?" Jared asked. He and Megan were surprised to see that Tina almost blushed as she answered his question.

"I'm meeting this wonderful and very witty tour guide who led our group around the Colosseum yesterday. His name is Tullio Guido and the two of us got along so well yesterday that he offered to pick me up this morning and give me a personal tour of some of the fascinating archaeological sites outside the walls of Rome. Rome isn't the only thing worth seeing in the Lazio region, he insists. Thousands of remnants of ancient monuments and buildings are at one of the sites he's taking me to, plus a small museum with the very best finds. Isn't that exciting?"

"Absolutely," beamed her sister as Jared nodded his enthusiasm. "How long do you think you'll be gone?"

"I really don't know because there are so many sites to visit in the Lazio area. But I'm pretty sure you shouldn't count on me for lunch. How about I call you when we're on the way back and we can decide when and where to meet. I'm sure Tullio would be happy to drop me off wherever you all might be at that time. Are Mary and Sire going to be with you today?"

"No, they're not. They want to rent a car and go out to explore Calcata today."

"*Calcutta*?" Tina couldn't believe her ears.

"No, Tina, not India; Italy," chortled Jared.

"Well, that's certainly more believable. What's so special about 'Calcata?'"

"Yes, what makes it a tourist spot?" Megan asked.

Jared, who had actually been there once on a grand tour of Italy, answered the uninformed sisters.

"For starters the miniscule medieval village is situated high up on top of a cliff of volcanic rock and ringed down below with beautiful green forests. But what must be of interest to Sire and Mary is the fact that Calcata—which is only an hour's drive from Rome—has emerged from being an almost abandoned ghost town with empty houses randomly stacked on top of each other—in the nineteen sixties, when artists began arriving, buying, and restoring small buildings and then setting up ateliers and galleries—some actually in caves cut into the side of the mountainous cliff which is the ground floor for the town."

"Well, I can see why the attraction! It's now a picturesque, popular commercial center for contemporary art." Megan was impressed.

"Yes, that and one other thing," murmured Jared slowly and mysteriously.

"What?" Tina demanded.

"Are you sure you want to know?" he teased.

"Of course," urged Megan. The two sisters were now all ears.

"Calcata was once the possessor of a unique religious relic."

"Oh," said Tina with no interest.

"Yes. The papal-approved foreskin of the infant Jesus."

"*What?*" exclaimed the Crespi sisters simultaneously.

"I kid you not. In fifteen twenty-, uh, twenty-seven, I think it was, during the sack of Rome, a German soldier stole the relic, which for centuries had been kept in Rome's Sancta Sanctorum—the original private chapel of the papacy. He absconded with it and other treasures to Calcata but was caught, arrested, and jailed there. *But* the foreskin was nowhere to be found. That is, not until some thirty years later when it was discovered hidden in the soldier's jail cell! Can you imagine, picture where?"

Tina only made a face but Megan responded.

"I can indeed picture where, but let's not go there, please."

"Aw. I take it you're not *for skin* then?" Jared was unable to fulfill his friend's request. So he was not surprised when Megan socked him lightly on the jaw. Nevertheless he stubbornly continued with his foreskin narrative.

"It became a pilgrimage-to-Calcata attraction until about the beginning of the twentieth century when the Vatican began to regret the small-town whereabouts of the religious relic and the unreligious aspect of what it was. Nothing happened, however, until nineteen eighty-three when suddenly news broke that the relic had mysteriously disappeared. The only explanation I can see is that it was stolen from Calcata by the Vatican itself. God only knows where it is kept now, and I won't ask you to picture where this time."

Silence reigned until Tina departed for her archaeological outing.

"Who would have guessed that we like so many of the same things for breakfast!" exclaimed Jared to Megan, attempting to guide their thoughts elsewhere.

He pointed to their partially consumed breakfasts. They had differed only in that Megan liked coffee and Jared took tea. In between bites of breakfast they discussed at length the events of the past twenty-four hours. Fortunately for Megan, Jared forgot to ask what her morning exercises were and she did not offer them. She used to be proud to describe the exacting routine that took forty-five minutes of stretching, weight lifting, treadmill, and balance. But in the past few months she had been forced to adjust a few of them due to a sudden, but longtime in the buildup, debilitation of her right foot called "posterior tibial tendon dysfunction"—PTTD—that makes the foot and ankle roll uncontrollably outward or inward. Megan blamed it on her years of ballet training which had endowed her with fallen arches, something that physicians had named "adult-acquired flatfoot." Determined not to be relegated to using a cane or crutches, Megan had religiously followed the "RICE" formula: Rest, Ice, Compression, Elevation, as well as wearing copper compression bands during the day and engaging in all sorts of stretching exercises while standing and also on her bed. The pain had been very severe in the beginning but was better now.

The second "gift" from aging was a hemorrhaging retina in the right eye, being successfully treated with tri-monthly shots in that eye. When horrified friends asked how painful that was, her answer was always the same: the instrument used to position and hold her eyelids open was far more painful than the lightning quick shot itself. Now she was having to enlarge and bold typeface on her computer, use a magnifying glass more often, and remember not to research and write for hours without taking a break to rest her eyes.

"You know what, Megan?" Jared's rich basso voice interrupted her thoughts. "I no longer swim as many laps as I used to. Age is beginning to nibble at me." He was bewildered when instead of consolation Megan burst out laughing.

"Don't make me explain, Jared. It's just that I was thinking exactly the same thing myself. No, no! Not about you!" Jared had pulled back in bewilderment. "About me!" she clarified.

Laughter cleared away the gloom and they began to plan what they would do during their last few hours together before Jared flew to Berlin to visit Rachael Skylar and her recently united and enlarged family. His plane didn't leave until nine that evening and so they had plenty of time to do just about anything they wished.

"What two things would you most like to do, Jared? Something having to do with museums, music, archaeology, monuments, shops—you name it."

"Only two?"

"Of course more if you wish. I was only keeping the time in mind; quality over quantity, you know."

"Just joshing you, Megan, just joshing. All right," he rubbed his hands. "It's eight-fifteen. I need to organize crating and flight arrangements for the Fanny portrait by my great-granduncle David Moritz Oppenheim. And then.... "

"*Wait! What*? You *are* related! How did you find out?" Megan scrutinized Jared's grinning face. "Are you teasing me?"

"Yes."

"Wow, you certainly are in a good mood today, boy."

"I am because the Fanny portrait is going to New York and Nathan is all right, no longer in danger. Now, the two things you asked me, what I'd most like to do—they are shopping and café-ing."

"Shopping and 'café-ing'? I hadn't thought of you as that type."

"See if you think so after I tell you where."

"I'm listening."

"You know what the Rinascente is in Milan, don't you?"

"Of course! Whenever I visited my Italian grandmother there decades ago I always used to go to that wonderful, one-and-a-half-centuries-old department store next to Milan's cathedral square—the Piazza Duomo. They carry the most interesting, non-predictable things. Incidentally, the name, which means 'rebirth' was coined by Gabriele D'Annunzio—sounds like the Italian word for Renaissance—*Rinascimento*—which also means rebirth."

"Right! Well, a few years ago, in twenty seventeen, Rinascente established a second flagship store and it was right here in Rome!"

"Oh! That's wonderful. I didn't know that. But somehow I still don't think of you as an avid department store habitué customer."

"I'm not. But this Rome Rinascente, which occupies a renovated eight-story building on Via del Tritone with a wonderful view of the city, has an amazing feature which is what I want to see. It's the archaeological site opened up in the basement and containing the remains of the Aqua Virgo aqueduct which goes back to, get this, nineteen B.C."

"Well! That's more like it! I'd be happy to see those archaeological remains. And won't my sister be jealous!" They both chortled.

"And what's this second 'Café-ing' thing you'd like to do after that?"

"Have a cappuccino and a long sit-down in the famous Antico Caffè Greco where I've never been."

"Great idea! And by the way, speaking of D'Annunzio, he frequented that famous café."

"Megan, what is this thing you have for Gabriele D'Annunzio? He seems to come up somehow in lots of our conversations, especially now that we're in Italy."

"I don't really know, Jared. I guess I do mention him a lot. And our being in his native land just brings him closer to me. Visiting his huge estate and lavish house on Lake Garda, which he named *Vittoriale degli Italiani*, made a terrific impression on me, and especially his words on the great entry gate: '*Io ho quell che ho donato.*'"

"'I have that which I have given.' Hmm, yes, that's quite a concept."

" For me, that phrase sums up my years of teaching. Sort of like saying I have—still retain—the knowledge and the enthusiasm that I have given to my students, if that makes any sense to you."

"Thanks for explaining. Now, what do you think of our spending some relaxing time in the Caffè Greco? Just people-watching?"

"Actually, I was there just this past Tuesday. Although, it turned out, not under the most pleasant of circumstances. But I'll tell you about that when we're there."

"Then thank you, Megan, for being willing to go there again with me. See you downstairs in the lobby at nine o'clock?"

"At nine o'clock sharp, you bet."

95

It was eight-thirty that Saturday morning and Nathan Bartholdy was feeling almost himself again. The medic who came with the police officer last night was extremely kind and very much an expert at his job. He had brought Nathan around to a state of awareness after much effort. The officer gently explained to him what had happened and that his stolen painting was safe and sound at the police station nearest the Jewish Quarter, Arenula/Cairoli. He himself was ready to bring it back to Signor Bartholdy's apartment when the frail, elderly man felt better. Nathan told him about the first stolen, almost identical painting as well, and the kindly officer said he would look into that as well.

"Ah, I feel better already just knowing my beloved painting is safe. And I would be so very grateful to you if you could bring it back to me as soon as you possibly can," had been Bartholdy's wide awake answer.

"If I can skip the paperwork, and I think I can, the painting will be here by ten o'clock this morning," promised the simpatico policeman. "And Signor Bartholdy, let me advise you to think about changing your apartment door lock as soon as possible." The hint of a proud smile animated Nathan's face as he responded to the suggestion.

"That I have already tended to, Officer; a locksmith is due here later this morning."

"Excellent. All right then, I shall see you with paintings in hand in about..." The officer consulted his watch, "eight hours."

"Ah, wonderful! Thank you so much." Nathan fell back to sleep within minutes after the two men had left. He awoke again some five hours later and was not only feeling significantly better, he was ravenous. After he had fixed himself breakfast in his miniscule bedroom kitchen, he dressed and began working at his desk.

"*Oh!*" he exclaimed out loud. "I must tell Doktor Crespi and Herr Oppenheim what happened!" He picked up his landline phone and, consulting a rotating spindle of cards, spooled through to the recent one he had created for Doktor Megan Crespi. He dialed the number notated and she answered within a few seconds.

"Frau Doktor! Megan ! It is Nathan, Nathan Bartholdy. I must tell you the terrible thing that happened to me last night."

Megan started to say she knew all about it, but realized it was important for him to articulate what had occurred for his own sake.

"And even the heavy chair I pushed up against the door did not block the intruders," he concluded, out of breath.

"It is a terrible, terrible thing that has happened to you. And two nights in a row! But even worse is *who* did it. You do know, don't you, Nathan?

"What? The police know who entered my home and stole my painting?"

"Yes. It was your cleaning lady and her husband. Both times!" There was a loud gasp and after that a long silence on the other end of the line. Then a very different sounding Nathan spoke.

"So it was Ursula. What a betrayal. And to think, ten years ago I left her a sizable amount of money in my will!"

"You might want to cross out her name now."

"I shall, I shall! My will is right here in my desk drawer."

"Good, Nathan, good. And now, of course, you will be getting both of your paintings back—the original temporarily of course before it's flown to America on Monday—and things will be almost the same for you as they were."

"Oh, but things will *never* be the same again for me! I must get out of Rome. Of Italy!" Nathan sounded quite hysterical all of a sudden.

"Oh, surely in a few days you will be feeling better about everything. Rome is your home after all. Your parents' and your grandparents' home."

"Perhaps. How is it, Megan, that you know so much about what happened to me?"

"Well, after we left your home last night, Jared was so worried about you that he hired a prominent private detective here who immediately dispatched a man to keep watch on your building overnight. The man saw and videoed the arrival and departure of the Ladro couple with your painting and it was he who called the police. They flagged down and arrested the Ladros within six minutes."

"Ah, Megan, I owe so much to that wonderful man Jared! Not only has he rescued me financially, he has set into motion the foiling of two robberies at my home. And now I will be able to have an exact copy of Fanny's original portrait over my bed. I already have my copyist Giorgio Complice booked to arrive here at noon today and this time he will paint exactly what he sees—Fanny's uneven shoulders. By then the original painting will be back, thanks to the kind police officer who is handling the crime case and who has promised to return both paintings to me at ten o'clock this morning."

"Speaking of the time," Megan said, "I am supposed to meet Jared at nine, and it's after nine right now."

"Please greet and thank him for me, won't you?"

"Of course! And I'm so happy to have spoken to you just now and to have your good news and to hear that you are feeling better after that second dose of pesticide."

"And the last dose ever, please god! One last thing and I won't keep you. Might you find time to telephone me again before you leave Rome and return to America?"

"But of course I will! Goodbye for now!"

Megan scooped up her things and rushed to the lobby. When Jared spied her he put his hands on his hips and looked at her accusingly.

"Nine o'clock, we said. So what's kept you? It's four minutes after nine." Both laughed and Megan explained to Jared's immense interest the touching conversation she had just concluded with Nathan Bartholdy. She told him how very grateful Nathan was to him for having put into place an overnight surveillance of his building with such fortunate results. Jared beamed with pleasure.

"And I've made arrangements with the crate and cargo business Mancini Aerotrasporto to have the painting ready to be loaded aboard my nine o'clock return flight on Monday back to New York. They'll be picking the painting up from Nathan's apartment at ten o'clock Monday morning. Why don't I call him when we're comfortably settled at the Caffè Greco, tell him all this and make my goodbyes to the dear man."

"Absolutely do it. I know he'd be thrilled to hear from you."

"And now off to Via del Tritone and Rome's greatest department store, La Rinascente! While I was waiting for you I arranged the best way to go—ah, here it comes now. Now just don't get Uberexcited!"

Megan couldn't stop from laughing in disbelief at the crafty and totally unnecessary way Jared had handled things, booking an Uber for such a short distance—five blocks south from the bottom of the Spanish Steps! His explanation was "it's hot outside." And when it came time to move on to the Caffè Greco—just five blocks back up toward the Spanish Steps on the narrow Via Condotti, Jared had also extravagantly booked an Uber. It would be parked at Rinascente's main entrance at two o'clock, giving them plenty of time to explore all aspects of the store as well as the famous archaeological remains in its basement. For Jared it was a treat to travel in outrageous style with his dear scholar friend from Dallas.

What Megan and Jared saw as they pulled up alongside the department store entrance on the wide Via del Tritone was a beautifully refurbished eight-story building, the complex reconstruction of which, amid the historic buildings of central Rome, had taken eleven long years. Inside, the eight floors were arranged around a central atrium reaching from the ground floor to the roof. Wide, zigzagging escalators brought people to each floor and a large elevator system was in service as well. They decided to explore all eight floors before descending to the basement's archaeological climax—the remains of the nineteen B.C. Virgo aqueduct.

The first floor featured jewelry, sunglasses, accessories, and an enormous display of various watches and timepieces which held their attention for some time. The second floor was devoted to perfumes, lingerie, and toiletries—not so interesting for either Megan or Jared. The next two floors were devoted to men's clothing, while the upper two floors displayed women's clothing.

"That's sexist," whispered Megan into Jared's ear. "Why do men's clothing come before women's clothes?"

"Because women's clothing is superior to men's," he whispered back.

They were still laughing when they reached the seventh floor which was devoted to delicatessen type foods and wines, fine chocolates, and a few small eating nooks.

And finally, via a small stairway, they reached the eighth floor—the roof level—which presented truly magnificent views over the rooftops of Rome as well as their culinary goal, the Terrazza Borromini restaurant and bar.

"Are we hungry yet?" asked Megan.

"I would be starving if we eat *after* we see the remains of the Virgo aqueduct."

"It's probably a good idea since the food at Caffè Greco is outrageously expensive; even just a cup of coffee costs around six dollars!"

"A good way to make up for lost revenue, I'd say, when people spend hours over one cup of coffee," mused practical-minded Jared.

They took one of the elevators down to the basement where, in addition to the archaeological exhibition, there was an interesting selection of lighting, electronics, and office supplies.

"Wait!" Megan commanded her friend as they passed by the latter. "I see they carry the kind of Italian leather diary I use. Let me see the variety." She practically pulled her patient friend over to the display of notebooks, calendars, address books, and "agenda" booklets, as the diaries were called in Italian.

"But they're all so small!" said a baffled Jared, holding one up. It measured a mere four inches tall and two and a half inches wide. He opened up the diary. There were two days to each page, displaying four days when the agenda was spread out flat for writing.

"That's what I like about them. And they even have address book pages at the back."

"Wow, your handwriting must really be small!"

"You mean like this?" Megan pulled her current agenda out of her shoulder bag, slid back the small leather closing strap and opened it up for Jared to see.

"How can you even *read* what you've written?" he asked, staring at the miniscule handwriting summing up four days of activities.

"Take a try," commanded his friend invitingly and handing him the diary. Jared squinted and slowly read out loud but with difficulty as there were multiple words he just couldn't understand.

"What, for example, is this word—'*ieri*?'"

"Oh, it means 'yesterday' in Italian. I use the shortest words I know for long words in English."

"Now that's clever considering the space you have to write in. Just in Italian?"

"No, no. In whatever language I know the word is the shortest."

"What languages beside Italian?"

"Well, Spanish, for example. I always write '*a mi casa'* instead of 'at my house.' Shorter than the Italian '*a casa mia.*' Hey! You just made me think of an even shorter way to say it in French: '*chez moi.*' Thank you!"

"I bet you don't have any shorter substitutes in German, do you?"

"Very few that I've thought of. But the word '*Mut*' is shorter than the word 'courage' in those other languages, and '*wo*' for 'where.' And I use the Danish word '*pjat*' for disgust or nonsense."

"Don't tell me you also speak Danish?"

"Very little. But I have dear Danish friends and hear them exclaim dismissively with that particular word."

"So, how long have you been keeping a diary, Megan? Since retirement?"

"Ha! No. A bit longer than that. Since the year I graduated from Barnard College. So that makes an uninterrupted, um, sixty-something years. I'm not going to be more specific than that."

"Come on now. That's impossible."

"Yep. Sixty-something years. And extremely useful for when I get called in by the IRS for an audit. But enough. *Pjat*! Let's go take an archaeological bath!"

It turned out there were not as many ruins to see at first hand as Jared had imagined. Instead, a multimedia device presented the history of the area and of the other Roman remains found there. These included an insula, a domus, and parts of other aqueducts—most all of which had been reburied after archaeologists had studied and photographed them in detail. This constituted the material shown and explained in a continuously playing multimedia presentation which concluded each time with the surprising information that the ancient aqueduct Vergine still brings water to the nearby Trevi Fountain and to other wells in the city. Jared was blown away by this.

"Imagine! From the year nineteen before Christ right up to today!"

They were still discussing this when they sat down to lunch on the Rinascente rooftop. They both ordered the same refreshing Hugo cocktail with sparkling white wine, elderflower syrup, some sparkling mineral water, and a few leaves of mint—the perfect drink for a hot summer day.

"What do you think goes best with this?" Jared asked.

"You're going to look down on me, but what I'd love to have with my healthy Hugo is a pizza margherita, nothing further!" Megan answered unabashedly.

"I'm not going to look down on you. I'm gonna join you! I am a huge pizza lover."

While waiting for the pizza, Megan studied the informative menu asides concerning Rinascente restaurants. She wrongly thought there were only two—the original one in Milan and then this one in Rome. But now there were two in Rome, she read, and nine others around Italy! She began reading in what cities they were until a personal, just-the-right-size hot pizza was suddenly set down in front of her.

"Shall we take the next Uber you've ordered for us and go to the other Rinascente in Rome, wherever that might be?" she joked as they devoured their tasty pizzas.

"Perhaps not, if you don't mind. I'm beginning to get eager to absorb the atmosphere of Caffè Greco."

"It's really so close, you know. Via Condotti. We could walk."

"Not on your life. In another fifteen minutes our Uber will be waiting for us and we are going to arrive in style."

"Wonderful!" Megan gave in. And her PTTD right foot silently thanked her.

96

No sooner that afternoon had Rome's chief of police learned of the curious crime in the Jewish Quarter than he called his buddy Alessandro Divitore. It would seem, he told him, that his former professor in America Megan Crespi, about whom he'd heard good things after Alessandro's reunion with her a few days ago, had been involved in the solving of a brutal crime involving theft and bodily harm.

"I don't know about that," said Alessandro after he heard what Cesari Cacciatore had to tell him, "but nothing about her can surprise me. Tell me about it."

"The crime was theft, theft of the same kind of thing each time, and it occurred in the same apartment two nights in a row. Well, actually each time around one-thirty in the morning. The victim is a retired banker, Nathan Bartholdy, a man in his early nineties. Seems his housekeeper of many years and her husband decided to steal one of the old man's paintings—a portrait of a distant relative—a woman supposed to be the sister of the great composer Felix Mendelssohn."

"Ah, Cesari, you're speaking of Fanny Mendelssohn, also a fine composer."

"Interesting. So perhaps that's why her portrait was stolen. Bartholdy must have told his housekeeper the painting was of a well-known composer. But the strange thing is that the thieves weren't content with just this one portrait. The very next night they returned and stole a second, and curiously, identical portrait of the woman! But thanks to Crespi and an American friend, who by this time had hired a private detective to maintain twenty-four-hour surveillance of Bartholdy's building, the arrival and departure of the housekeeper couple were observed and immediately reported to us. Two of our units tracked them down within six minutes of the crime's being perpetrated. In both cases Bartholdy had been rendered helpless by use of a pesticide spray that knocked him out for a number of hours."

"That's terrible! So where are the housekeeper and her husband now?"

"In jail, both of them. Charged with breaking and entering, assault and battery, and theft."

"And Signor Bartholdy?"

"Faring reasonably well, I am told by Officer Sicuro at our Arenula/Cairoli station. The old man has begged to have his two stolen paintings brought back to him as soon as possible and I have given permission to do so as soon as fingerprints are taken from both. The first portrait stolen was found, apparently undamaged, under the couple's bed in their small apartment out in Centocelle."

"Centocelle. That miserable working class district?"

"Exactly."

"Thanks for telling me about this, Cesari. I'll have to call Megan and tell her I've heard she was arrested for stealing artworks."

"You're such a helpless jokester, Alessandro. See you in Frascati!"

"In Frascati!"

97

Some five minutes after two that afternoon at the command of one of his two passengers, an astonished Uber driver slammed to a quick halt at the top of the Via Condotti, a narrow packed street five blocks north of his pickup point at La Rinascente. The overly generous tip lessened his indignation if not his surprise.

After a look back at the expanse of Spanish Steps so physically close to them, Megan and Jared entered the historic Caffè Greco—host over some two hundred and sixty years to a number of Europe's most famous intellectuals, poets, painters, authors, goliards—wandering scholar poets—journalists, adventurers politicians, writers, rulers, prelates, wise women, gigolos, and figures from the world of music. The café was open for twelve hours—from nine in the morning until nine at night. There was no showing of clients to tables; you chose what appealed to you among the tables that were free in the café's multiple rooms. At this time of day the choice was slightly greater than at most other times and Megan hoped to have the luck to find the table from which Marianna Dionigi had painted her 1797 view of the Caffè Greco's large front room with its great, glass-blacked bar. The framed picture was supposed to be hung next to that table.

First, however, Megan wanted to give Jared, and frankly herself, an idea of the scope of the café and its many small rooms. She steered him down the main hall which was densely hung with different size paintings, some of them landscapes of the Roman countryside, and they took a quick peek into each of the art-filled small rooms across from each other along the hall and stretching deep into the back of the building. Passing a spiral staircase apparently leading to further chambers, they returned to the front room which was larger than the others and from which they could get a glimpse of any interesting individuals who might enter the café during their visit.

But their search for Dionigi's painting was in vain. No table in the café's entry room had a depiction of that room hung next to it, and people were beginning to point and stare at the American couple as they moved earnestly from picture to picture, often over the table occupants' heads.

Giving up the search for now, they chose one of the miniscule circular marble tables across from the entry and opposite the busy bar. They settled down with satisfaction into the two lightweight red velvet armchairs that faced each other across the table. Jared's vista was of the large and busy bar across the room, while Megan had a good view of the portrait-hung wall behind him. Although the noisy room was quite full, an alert tuxedo-wearing waiter appeared almost immediately to take their order. Both elected to have one of the café's famous cappuccinos. While waiting for their drinks, they discreetly studied the people around them. Three quarters of them seemed to be tourists. The other quarter looked like inhabitants of the city, totally at home in the establishment. From their comfortable seats they began studying the various small, framed portraits interspersed with a few small landscapes on the walls. Supposedly there were over three hundred individual portrayals housed at the hallowed establishment. The portraits were of famous or briefly famous visitors to the coffee house over the many decades of its existence. A few of them, even from a distance, either Jared or Megan were able to identify with growing and competitive excitement.

"How wonderful to be in Rome," Megan sighed after their brief competition had ended. "Just think! Being in Rome for Fanny produced *Das Jahr* of eighteen forty-one and for Felix, the *Italian Symphony* of eighteen thirty-three. Both completed after they had returned from Italy to Germany."

The waiter came back with their order and they spent some drawn-out minutes inhaling the delectable odors and sipping the delicious beverage, the preparation of which—brewing coffee grounds with water in a special coffee pot—had been introduced to Western Europe by Ottoman Turks in the fifteenth century, so the small menu told them. Even when hard economic times had forced other cafés to cut back on coffee grounds in Rome, Caffè Greco had maintained this original preparation.

Suddenly Jared put down his cappuccino and turned to Megan.

"Oh heck, I've completely forgotten to call Nathan!"

"It's not too late. Why don't you do so right now?"

"Good idea," Jared agreed, dialing the man's number and putting his phone on speaker. Nathan answered immediately with a wary, questioning, single "Yes?"

"Nathan, it's Jared here. I just wanted to give you a call before I leave Rome tonight for Berlin and then America." He did not bother to specify that he'd be returning to Rome Monday morning for his flight connection to New York.

"Ah, I am delighted to hear from you, Jared. You of course know about what happened here—again!"

"Oh yes, Megan has filled me in. I am so, so sorry for what you have gone through. How upsetting that must have been."

"I was upset only after a brilliant medic pulled me out of pesticide slumber that same night. But now things have calmed down and as a matter of fact both stolen portraits have been returned to me and actually my copyist is here right now, creating an identical substitute portrait for the original that your cargo company will be picking up on Monday. And *this time* the disparity between Fanny's shoulders is not being 'corrected.' My copyist is painting exactly what is to be seen."

"What good news, Nathan, what good news. I also called because I wanted to find out personally how you are feeling physically after having survived two brutal bouts of pesticide poisoning."

"Why, thank you! A great deal better. Pretty much back to my old self. And when I say old, I mean it! I'm not sure how much longer I can bear to live in a Rome where such frightening, life-threatening things have happened to me. But on the other hand, you only live twice."

"Ha! If you can joke about it all, you are definitely on the mend. Well, I just wanted to check in with you and say goodbye for now."

"Thank you so very much, Jared. I am, needless to say, hugely happy to have met you and to have conducted the business we did so rapidly with such beneficial outcomes for both of us. Please give my greetings to Megan if you see her before you leave."

"I certainly shall," said Jared, smiling at Megan and putting a finger to his lips.

After he had terminated the call, Megan thanked him for not letting on that she was present during their conversation.

"I think it will give him more pleasure if he gets yet another call from his two new American friends," she said, "and I do intend to call him tomorrow and perhaps even one more time before I, too, return to the States."

"And when do you and your sister and the others go home?"

"We are all flying together back to Dallas on Tuesday evening, so just one day after you."

"Nice. Say, shall we order another cappuccino?"

"Brilliant inspiration!" said Megan, holding up her hand to catch their waiter's attention.

Jared suddenly froze, his eyes fixated on something.

"Wait!" he commanded. "Hold off ordering them for a minute. I just noticed a portrait on the wall to the right of the bar by the inner rooms that I absolutely have to take a closer look at. Two customers had been standing there, blocking it."

He bolted over to the image he had sighted. It featured a young man facing the beholder with locks of thick black hair reaching down to his shoulders. Long sideburns framed his cheeks and a short, black mustache and trimmed beard completed his hirsute appearance. After staring intently at the portrait for some long minutes, Jared took a number of photographs ranging from full view to miniscule detail, and then returned to the table. The ecstatic smile on his face revealed his white teeth, and his wide-open brown eyes silently broadcast his exhilaration.

"What is it, Jared? Your cheeks are red. You look so excited."

"I can't tell you yet, dear, too much to find out about first, back in New York, but as soon as I can, I'll call you and let you know."

"Megan?" a familiar voice said. Hidden momentarily by a passing waiter, the figure of Megan's friend and former student Alessandro appeared. He was alone and, pulling a red velvet covered stool over from an adjacent empty table, he happily joined them at their surprised and simultaneous invitation.

Megan introduced the two men to each other: Alessandro as the public relations manager to Italy's former prime minister, and Jared as the founder and director of New York's Mendelssohn Complex.

"But I just don't think of you as a habitué of cafés, Alessandro," said Megan.

"Oh, but I am now that I'm no longer working for the government.

I have to recalibrate myself, and how better than to be in the midst of things?"

"I would have thought just the opposite," Jared murmured.

"It's my nature, I suppose, as my profession has always been to take the pulse of the public."

Noting there was another client at the Americans' table, the waiter who had just appeared with two new cappuccinos looked inquiringly at him.

"*Lo stesso*," said Alessandro, nodding. Then he turned to Megan. "I am truly surprised to see you here, considering what a horrible thing happened when you and your friends were with me here before."

"Yes, what did happen, Megan?" Jared asked. "You said it was something unpleasant."

"Ha! Far more than that!" She narrated for him the terrible series of events that had resulted in the especially brutal shooting murder of three of the participants at a bar mitzvah celebration—the young boy being honored and his parents. The shooter had escaped the way he had entered, through the kitchen door giving on to the alley.

"And so far the police have no suspects because the assailant was wearing a COVID-nineteen mask," added Alessandro.

"Oh, Megan!" Jared exclaimed. "How brave and generous of you to come back here for my sake with such brutal, fresh memories. Thank you and I am so sorry."

"The police are pretty sure it was one of the neo-Fascists who have been individually frequenting Caffè Greco for the past few years," Alessandro informed them.

"Neo-Fascists here?" Megan asked, frowning.

"Indeed," Alessandro lowered his voice. "For example—don't look now—there is one—a sentinel, we call them—sitting at the end table to your right, across from the bar. These watchkeepers are easily identifiable by their wearing of a miniature fasces button on their lapels in the Fascist colors of red, white, and green. Some tourists occasionally call them neo-Nazis but here in Italy they are and call themselves 'neo-Fascists.' Just think of them as neo-Mussolinis *because that's exactly what they are*." Alessandro's voice had become a bitter hiss.

"I'm sorry, but what is 'fascis?'" Megan confessed her ignorance, despite having taken five years of Latin in high school and college.

"Fascis is the Latin word for bundle. A bundle of rods with an axe blade sticking out was carried by lictors in ancient Rome as a symbol of a magistrate's power, and thus used as an emblem of authority in Mussolini's Fascist Italy. So the miniature insignia pin worn by Italian neo-Fascists shows a bundle of rods with an axe blade sticking up and out."

"But why would they want to keep watch over things here at this café?" Jared wanted to know, stealing a glance at the fasces-wearing-pin man whom Alessandro had indicated.

"They've been keeping continuous watch here ever since the terrible battle that began in twenty seventeen over Caffè Greco's either paying its raised rent or facing eviction."

"What's that? Explain, please," requested Megan. She, too, could not pass over the chance for a split-second glimpse at the man wearing the fasces button. He was in his thirties, had black hair, a short, dense mustache, and he appeared to be reading a newspaper.

"It's a bitter financial dispute over rent between Caffè Greco and the building owner, which is the privately run Israelite Hospital here. Its initial location was on the little island on the River Tiber you may know about."

Alessandro's audience of two nodded a vigorous yes. Along with Mary and Sire, they had eaten dinner on the Isola Tiberina just a few evenings ago!

"So the problem with the Israelite Hospital—they now have three locations in Rome and make over a million euros every year—the problem is that the 'impoverished' hospital now wants to raise Caffè Greco's rent from eighteen thousand euros a month to one hundred and twenty thousand euros a month."

"From eighteen thousand to one hundred and twenty thousand euros for thirty days rent? Six times the amount they pay now! That's outrageous!" Jared almost shouted. "This is the sort of thing that engenders malice and resentment among Gentiles. I am Jewish, but I certainly don't approve of such gluttony!"

"Most of Rome thinks so as well," answered Alessandro. "And the Roman unit of a heritage organization called Italia Nostra has been running interference. There's some hope because as early as nineteen fifty-three the Italian government stipulated that regardless of who manages the premises, the Antico Caffè Greco must remain intact, including its artworks and furnishings. The case has been handed to court after court for years now and it's still not settled."

"Wow, such suspense," breathed Megan.

"One way the café has handled it is to double the price of coffee—which they still make with the aromatic Turkish beans—and to downsize the cups; just look at the ones we're drinking from! And yet who would begrudge the café, considering that for the price of one coffee or cappuccino you can sit at your table all day!

"So why would this attract neo-Nazi, I mean neo-Fascist attention?" Megan asked.

"Just think of it," Jared answered for Alessandro. "An Israelite Hospital owns the property. This can be seen immediately as a grabbing of Christian property by Jews." The politician nodded in vigorous if sad agreement.

"At this stage the mayor of Rome has stepped in and things are at a standstill for now," he sighed.

"Golly, what a debacle," said Megan. "And what an ideal opportunity for neo-Fascists to inflame hatred of Jews. I'm surprised that the Israelite Hospital didn't anticipate such a reaction."

"Well, so far, the Neos have just been practicing surveillance in the guise of a single customer or two who sit here for hours at a time, pretending to be absorbed in their newspaper, often taking observation notes. But if the city of Rome loses its case, what an ideal opportunity—unique, really—to fan rage and organize a gigantic, angry antisemitic demonstration that would include Christian protesters as well!"

At that moment they were approached by a wiry, black-haired man of about fifty in a loose-fitting, blue smock, holding a small blank canvas and a minute palette and brushes.

"*Mi scusi, Signori*. I am Renato Ritratto, the Caffè Greco's resident artist of more than twenty years. You three clients look most interesting, and you, Signore," he said, pointing to Alessandro, "are a regular, I would say, as I've seen you here many times. May I know what your professions are and if perhaps you are well known, even famous?"

All three of the addressees laughed uproariously. Megan pointed to Alessandro, Jared pointed to Megan, and Alessandro pointed to Jared.

"I knew all of you looked important!" responded the café's

resident artist happily. Can you kindly be specific?" Alessandro volunteered an answer.

"The Signore there is founder and director of the Mendelssohn Complex in New York City, and the signora is a famous professor who has been awarded Austria's medal of honor. I? I am not famous but the man for whom I was public relations manager is: Mario Draghi."

"*Dio mio!* What an impressive trio. I knew I was right. Now comes the big request. May I portray you individually or as a trio?"

"No, but thank you," responded Megan quickly, "in fact Signor Oppenheim and I should be leaving quite soon now." She looked at Jared for conspiratorial confirmation since his flight did not actually leave until nine that evening. But, she figured, he must feel the same about having his portrait done as she did. And sure enough, Jared was nodding his head in affirmation. On an impulse Megan turned back to the inquisitive portrait painter.

"But let me ask *you* a question. Do you know where the little picture by Marianna Dionigi showing an indoor scene of this café's clientele is? Painted in seventeen ninety-seven?" Renato Ritratto looked bewildered and shrugged his shoulders.

"No. I am sorry, Signora Professora. I do not know of this person or painting." He turned to Alessandro, whose attention was directed toward the neo-Fascist sitting a few tables away who was observing their little scene with interest.

"And you Signore? I do not even know your name yet."

"Let's keep it that way, as I am unimportant."

The hopeful artist's face fell. There would be no portraits today. He made his farewells then walked away. It was high time to check in with his employer Homer Capo whose office was up the spiral staircase near the bar side of the café.

"Well! We certainly dodged the bullet with that one!" Alessandro exclaimed. "Although I do think, Megan, that you, my brilliant professor and famous author, should be portrayed by that eager artist."

"Not on your life!" Megan snorted. She looked at her frequenter of the Caffè Greco friend and suddenly realized that he might know exactly where the indoor scene of cafè clientele painted by Marianna Dionigi might be.

"Are you familiar, Alessandro, with the little painting on a wall here showing Caffè Greco patrons? It was done by a woman named..."

"Marianna Dionigi. I heard you ask that would-be artist. But of course! It's marvelous."

"Oh, wonderful! Jared and I have been trying and trying to find it. Can you show us where it is in here? You wouldn't believe how hard we've tried to locate it."

"Or how many people we've disturbed." Jared laughed.

"Ha! That's because it is no longer on display. Too many people were photographing it and bothering the patrons sitting underneath it. Also, the painting was showing signs of deterioration. So it's been removed to the proprietor's office."

"Good! And you must know this boss personally, right?" Megan was full of hope now.

"No. Never had the pleasure."

"Oh, dear. I would have thought you.... But I've *got* to get into his office and see it," said a desperate Megan. Alessandro smiled and turned to Jared.

"There speaks the relentless art historian I've known from the classroom. She never gives up until her mission is accomplished. But I'm afraid this time she won't succeed."

"But at least I can try!" Megan started to slide her armchair back to stand up just as their waiter appeared. He was waving a business card at her.

"Signora! Our Caffè Greco padrone invites you to his office and holds the hope that you and your companions can come to him as soon as possible."

Megan was not the only astonished person at the table. All three rose and followed the waiter to the spiral staircase. Renato Ritratto was just descending. He stood to one side and beckoned them to ascend.

"Nuts!" Megan said beneath her breath. "Climbing those spindly stairs with my foot. Thank god for the banister." She did so slowly and reached the top, her patient friends right behind her. A white wooden door faced her and she knocked. It swung open almost instantly and a pleasant-looking white-haired, portly man stood smiling at her and the two men behind.

"Thank you for mounting the difficult stairs to my office, Signora, Signori. I am Homer Capo. Our resident artist Renato Ritratto has told me about you and of your strong desire to see the Marianna Dionigi painting of our Caffè Greco clientele as they and our entry room looked in the eighteenth century." He looked at Alessandro.

"And because you, Signor Divitore, are well known as a regular visitor here, I decided your wish should be granted. And you, Signora, are?"

"I am Megan Crespi, retired professor of art history from Dallas."

"Ah ha. So of course you are interested in seeing the Dionigi!"

He turned last to Jared with a questioning look.

"I'm Jared Oppenheim, founder and director of the Mendelssohn Complex in New York."

"Ah ha! So that is why you are here. Because of Felix Mendelssohn's and his uncle Jacob Salomon Bartholdy's visits to our Caffè Greco."

Simultaneously Jared and Megan asked two questions.

"Do you have portraits of them?"

"Were they also portrayed?"

Amid general laughter the proprietor regretfully had to say no. There were no known portrayals of either Mendelssohn or Bartholdy at the café. It was just handed-down legend that both notables visited Caffè Greco, Bartholdy with some of his Nazarene artists.

"But," he continued, "we do, in addition to the oldest known rendition by Marianna Dionigi, keep some of the more interesting unknowns up here in my office, as you can see." He waved his hand around at the office walls.

"Of course! Have a closer look at any of the paintings you like. And there behind my desk is the Dionigi. Feel free to photograph it as long as you do not use a flash." Megan almost leapt over the proprietor's antique wooden desk in her eagerness to see the beckoning work.

She studied it with discerning admiration and without any further words while her friends went from one area of framed portrait paintings to another. Homer Capo continued standing, clasping and unclasping his hands in front of him and smiling at the intensity of his visitors' viewing.

Finally they seem to have had their fill and it was time to thank their host and leave. But Jared had something to say.

"Signor Capo, you say there are no portraits of Felix Mendelssohn here at the Caffè Greco. But I think I may happily be able to prove you wrong. Would you like that?"

"Of course I would like this! Whatever do you mean?"

"To do that we must go downstairs and head toward the bar."

Jared's mystified audience was willing to do as he suggested and made a slow progression down the spiral staircase, Megan last, at her request, not wanting to slow them down. She joined the group just to the right of the active bar and standing in front of a life-size portrait on the wall. It had the usual dimensions of a Caffè Greco portrait painting—sixteen inches across by twenty inches high. What they saw staring out at them was a serious young man of twenty or so with a high forehead, large, luminous brown eyes under pronounced eyebrows, and a finely chiseled long nose. He looked directly at the onlooker. His copious black hair reached down slightly past his shoulders and his face was mostly hidden by a thriving mustache that joined long sideburns and a short, clipped black beard. He looked for all the world like one of the Villa Medici students with, as Fanny Mendelssohn had written, their beards and long "hair à la Raphaël."

The group of three onlookers appeared open-minded but dubious. One by one they leaned forward, then backed away, and then, when there was space, came up close with noses only four inches away from the canvas. They looked at each other with questioning glances but received no affirmative nods. Finally Signor Capo spoke up.

"I share your wish, Signor Oppenheim, that this be a portrait of the young Felix at the age of twenty-one and twenty-two during his extended ten-month visit from October to July to our Italia, to our Roma, and to our Caffè Greco. Believe me I do. But there is no reference to that or to his ever growing a mustache and beard or having such long locks of hair down past his shoulders. Not that I know of. Does anyone here know of such a reference or portrayal?"

They all shook their heads. The resident artist, Renato Ritratto, now bearing a folded wooden easel on his way to paint a prominent client in situ, noticed the unusual sight of his boss downstairs standing and earnestly talking to a few persons in front of one of the wall portraits. He slipped over to the bar next to it, out of the visual orbit of the portrait admirers, but near enough to follow their conversation. Well, imagine that! They were the same trio of people who had turned down his invitation to have him paint their portraits!

"Signor Capo," Jared spoke again. "On the subject of whether or not Felix Mendelssohn ever patronized your historic café, allow me to read to you out loud the short initial paragraph Felix wrote to his parents back in Berlin on November eighth, eighteen thirty, after his first week in Rome." It would seem as though the entire Caffè Greco had fallen silent as Jared opened up his Samsung phone to the item he had downloaded.

"Quote: 'Picture to yourself a small house, with two windows in front, in the Piazza di Spagna number five which all day long enjoys the warm sun, and an apartment on the first floor, where there is a good Viennese grand piano: on the table are some portraits of Palestrina...I come into the room early in the morning, and see the sunshine...such is my present abode.'"

An "ah" of amazement was voiced by all who heard and understood Felix Mendelssohn's words through Jared's reading them aloud in English. The tall American immediately continued speaking, in his own voice now.

"How many of you realize *how close Piazza di Spagna number five is to our historic Caffè Greco here*?"

Gasps were heard nearby as more and more clients had begun trying to follow the interesting recitation intended for three persons standing in front of a framed portrait on the wall. The American tourist continued speaking.

"Now although we know that Felix, during his many months in Rome, met mostly with high class foreign families living here, rather than hanging out in cafés, we do also know that in his letters home he often wrote in closing, 'I want to meet Italians!' Well, what better place to meet Italians than right here?" He held his hands out in an embracing gesture.

A group gasp was heard, for now the listeners involved were not just the café's proprietor, Megan, Alessandro, and the eavesdropping resident artist, but also more of the number of clientele sitting nearby. Everyone was mesmerized by the scene taking place in front of one portrait of a bearded young man on the café wall. Even Megan, who, she had thought, was acquainted with every portrayal of Felix as well as of Fanny, was nonplussed. Jared spoke again, lifting his cellphone up to eye level for his two friends and Signor Capo.

"I have with me, always at hand, my portable *archive* of all known Felix and Fanny images. And while looking earlier at this unidentified portrait before us here, I remembered the portrait Fanny's husband Wilhelm Hensel made of a twenty-one-year-old Felix in Berlin, not here in Rome. True, both had been in Rome but not at the same time: Hensel for five years beginning in eighteen twenty-three until eighteen twenty-eight, and Felix for ten months in eighteen thirty and thirty-one at the age of twenty-one beginning that October. Hensel's Berlin image that you see here on my phone was in oil and showed the Felix whose countenance we all know of him at the age of twenty-one—clean-shaven, with long narrow sideburns, and abundant shoulder-length hair.

"With one of those amazing facial manipulation apps available online I have been able to superimpose the long hair, light mustache and beard we see in the wall portrait onto Felix's clean-shaven face as portrayed by whoever the resident artist was in eighteen thirty. Have a look here. *It is the face we see in the portrait in front of us. It is Felix Mendelssohn!*"

He held his Samsung up horizontally which juxtaposed the clean-shaven face of Felix with the facial-haired face for his friends to look at, then passed it around among them. By now several of the café's clients were standing close behind them, hoping to have a chance to see what was being shown. Jared generously held his phone up high so they too could see. One of the eager clients at the end table near the bar was a black-haired, mustachioed man wearing a small red, white, and green fasces pin on his lapel. He was still holding his fresh cup of coffee, so quickly had he joined the scene playing out near his table. Suddenly he raised his coffee cup up high and shouted.

"*So there's a portrait of a dirty Jew in the Caffè Greco? Let's see it drink a cup of coffee!*" The neo-Fascist lifted his cup up so that when thrown, it would splatter its contents directly onto the portrait.

The three legs of Renato Ritratto's jettisoned easel knocked the coffee cup out of the crazy man's raised hand. Two men wrestled the shrieking neo-Fascist to the ground and another three men helped them proceed to drag the lunatic to the door. They were met there by Signor Capo.

"Don't let him loose!" he commanded. "I've called the police. They are coming to arrest this insane would-be-vandal and I hope he'll be put in jail."

The cheers inside Caffè Greco could be heard outside on busy Via Condotti.

98

Tullio Guido's history of the region of Lazio was continuous and fascinating as he drove his enchanted guest Tina Crespi to their first and main stop some thirty miles northwest of Rome, the old Etruscan town of Cerveteri where archaeological sites ranged from the ninth century B.C. to Roman times. Of special interest, Tullio pointed out, were the nearby Etruscan cemeteries.

"Oh great!" exclaimed Tina, "I love cemeteries. The older the better."

"Good. Because the Romans learned and took many things from the Etruscans. The ancient Etruscan civilization was at its height from about the eighth through the fifth centuries B.C. and that is the period so heavily represented here."

Some minutes later Tullio turned his 2021 Fiat Strada truck off the main highway and parked by the Etruscan necropolis at Cerveteri. He had apologized to Tina when he picked her up for taking her there in a truck, but she assured him that she loved trucks and had a beloved Ford Sport Trac in Dallas.

They began to walk toward the necropolis. What a spectacle! There were literally thousands of tombs. Many were large structures in the shape of houses or dome-shaped huts. Others were carved into rock.

Tina felt a little overwhelmed. She was wearing a sun hat and sunglasses, cellphone in its belt case, and in her miniature backpack she had her usual dig items: measuring tape marked in inches and centimeters, small flashlight, sunscreen, bandages, and pencils, plus, of course, a water bottle. But where to start? The necropolis was well over one square mile in size and laid out like a small town. Tullio had told her that fragments of paintings remained in a few of the tombs and that some had intricate carvings inside, as well as some funerary objects that were buried with the dead. Where to begin?

Her amiable guide sensed her confusion and smiled.

"I wanted you to have a feeling for the size and layout of the necropolis and now you have, Tina. So what do you say we walk around as long as you wish, but then return to the truck and I will drive us to Ruspoli Castle—see it up there overlooking Cerveteri? Well, the castle is now the site of our National Archaeological Museum of Cerveteri and that's where you can really study some of the tombs and their contents."

"Excellent suggestion, Tullio. Let me walk around here a bit and then, as you say, we will return to the truck and drive to the museum. I can't wait!"

Longing to see what recovered objects were in the castle museum, she made a shorter survey walk than usual, Tullio right behind her. Then she nodded to him and they rejoined the truck. What she had not expected to see in the castle's huge collection were the many large sarcophagi and memorial stones. So much to see, right down to the hundreds of funereally decorated ceramics! And the museum gift shop was full of small treasures as well.

No wonder it was already four o'clock in the afternoon when she glanced at her watch. She needed to give a sign of life to Megan! Agree when and where to meet. Better to do it immediately.

"There you are!" exclaimed her sister when she picked up Tina's call. "Where are you? Back in Rome?"

"No, we're still in Lazio at the Etruscan necropolis at Cerveteri. So about forty-five minutes from Rome. What's going on with you and Jared? Anything fun?"

"I wouldn't say fun, but certainly exciting. Explain later. Right now we're at the Caffè Greco and will be for a little while longer. So I'm really glad you called me now because I was thinking that, because Jared's plane leaves at nine, we should have an early dinner, say as early as five-thirty so it can be relaxed and without hurrying. Would you be up for that?"

"Since I forgot to eat lunch because it's so fascinating here, yes, an early dinner would be just fine with me. What restaurant should I meet you at?"

"Don't know yet. Too much going on here. But I'll ask and get recommendations, then call you back. Good?"

"Fine. And I'll make sure we start back right away."

"That would be best. *Ciao!*"

"Bye, Big Sis."

99

Calm had descended once again upon Caffè Greco. Megan and Jared had resumed their conferring with the café's proprietor. Tina's short phone call was only a brief diversion of attention and now the three again consulted with one another as to what was to be done with the portrait. Alessandro had, with regret, to excuse himself from the scene because of an appointment.

"How can I thank you, Signor Oppenheim, for presenting such strong and convincing evidence that this portrait is actually of the great German composer, young Felix Mendelssohn? There must be some way I can repay you. Just tell me. Anything!" Jared looked thoughtful for some seconds, then replied with gusto.

"Thank you, Signor Capo. If you truly mean what you say, I can indeed suggest a way you could repay me, and, I might add, receive international press and television coverage of the portrait, and of you, and your celebrated Caffè Greco."

"Aha, and what might that be?" Capo tried to hide his excitement.

"Allow yourself to lend me the portrait for a few weeks. I return to New York on Monday and I should be thrilled to exhibit it at the Mendelssohn Complex along with another unknown portrait, not of him but of his sister Fanny, who was also a composer. I am bringing the sister portrait back with me to New York and I could take the brother portrait along with me on that same flight. Think of the publicity that exhibition of these two portraits side by side would excite! And of course I would pay for the necessary cleaning of your portrait aforehand." Jared paused to let his words sink in. Finally he looked questioningly at Capo. The proprietor of Caffè Greco responded with an enormous smile that revealed somewhat yellowed but even teeth.

"It is with great joy and honor that I accept your extraordinary proposal, Signor Oppenheim. Let me carry the painting upstairs and wrap it securely for you to take with you today." The two men engaged in a long handshake. Megan quickly took a photo of the two entrepreneurs. She also had something to say as she exchanged her cellphone for something else in her sling purse.

"If you both would wait a few minutes before removing the painting from the wall, there is something rather rare about it I should like to point out to you."

"But of course!" Capo said as Jared nodded eagerly. What arcane bit of art historical information had Megan held back?

"All right. Stand as close as you can to the painting."

The two men obliged.

"Now look carefully at the wide open eyes of Felix. The irises are large enough to reflect the light in the room in which the portrait was being painted. Now this sometimes happens in portraiture and it's something we art historians are always on the watch for. Because, as in this case, sometimes in the iris we can see reflected the room environment in front of the sitter, as well as the figure of the painter standing at his easel. This is exactly the case here. Here, take my magnifying glass and have a close look."

Capo took the offered item and examined one eye in the portrait carefully, then the other eye before voicing his amazement.

"*Dio mio!* I see exactly what you mean! I can see the artist!"

"Oh, let me look!" cried Jared, almost grabbing the magnifying glass out of the man's hand.

"Gosh! I see what you mean. So the objects reflected off the iris here are the front of the painter, the back of the canvas on his easel, and a patch of reflected sunlight from what must have been a small, high window on the right. Absolutely amazing!"

"Signor Capo, have you any idea where this portrait could have been painted?"

"Yes, that I do! It is still used today by our artist in residence. We have a very small room in the back with a little window to the right up high. It used to be a lavatory in the eighteenth century but it was converted into a small supply room at the beginning of the next century. And from then on it was also occasionally used by our different artists in residence for privacy if doing an oil portrait rather than pencil or charcoal sketch." He sized up the portrait on the wall. "It is time I pack up the painting for you. Perhaps you will help me remove it safely from the wall, Signor Oppenheim?"

"Of course!"

"And while you two do that I'll just take a quick look at your miniscule storage room, occasionally painter's atelier, if I may," said Megan.

"Yes, of course. If anyone stops you just say that il capo sent you.:

"Thank you!"

Megan walked straight back to the small storage room and opened the door. Bundles of towels and linen napkins took up most of the area, but Megan saw what she wanted to: a small window at the far side of the room high up to the right. A helpful confirmation of what they had seen reflected in the Felix portrait. She returned to Jared who was still working with the proprietor to remove the painting from the wall. At last they were successful.

"Well, hell," Jared berated himself in front of Megan after Capo had left with the precious painting in his hands. "When I first examined this portrait today I took a bunch of photos but it never occurred to me to do extreme close-ups of just the eyes!"

"Don't feel bad, Jared. As I said, it's not common, but happens often enough to be on the lookout when examining oil portraits," Megan said comfortingly. "But something you and I should confer about and right now is having dinner earlier than usual today because you should allow two hours for getting out to the airport, checking on the Fanny portrait and..."

"Yes, Mother, you're right. And we should factor in a quick run back to our hotel for me to pick up my suitcase after dinner. It's all packed and at the concierge's desk waiting for me. So it would be best to stay in this neighborhood wherever we decide to eat. Do you know of any decent restaurant nearby?"

"I do as a matter of fact. And it's so nearby that I really think you ought to order an Uber to ferry us there." Jared's delighted guffaw could be heard several tables back.

"I'm game. So what's the name of the restaurant and where is it? What's the address?"

"Now try to remain calm. It's called Babington's Tea Room and it is the very first shop in the building to the immediate left if you're standing at the foot of the Spanish Steps. Its address is Piazza di Spagna twenty-three. So that's just a few buildings away from Felix's abode at number five and only a few more buildings from here."

"Super location. But tea rooms? For dinner?"

"If you like Scottish smoked salmon, Irish bacon, Chianina beef, rice pilaf, chicken, eggs, especially all sorts of eggs Benedict..."

"Okay, okay, you've sold me. I certainly don't want anything heavy before my flight, that's for sure. How old a place is it? Sounds rather dated to me, oh, but in a nice way, of course. 'Historic,' I mean." He had seen the dour expression growing on Megan's face.

"Your offensive offense not taken. It was founded in eighteen ninety-three by two pioneering British women, one of whom was named Anna Maria Babington. Between them they had a hundred pounds. They were inspired by the idea of providing something rare and much sought after by their fellow Brits, who dominated the Spanish Steps area at that time. That 'something' could only be found in pharmacies at that time—tea. Their establishment would not only provide a friendly place to relax and sip tea—and they do also have what's called 'British coffee' by the way—it would also be a place where you could read newspapers to your heart's content. Just like its older neighbor in which we sit now. Within two years of opening their tea room the women were such a success that they managed to move to their superb, multiple room, present location. "

"Well, how about that! This sounds ideal. As soon as Signor Capo comes down with the packed painting ready to go, let's amble on over there. Or do you still want me to order an Uber?"

"You choose, Jared." The two friends looked at each other fondly.

Megan's phone rang. She pulled it out of her purse and replaced the magnifying glass while she was at it.

"Hello?"

"Hi, Megan, it's Mary."

"Oh, wonderful! Where are you two?"

"Very near your hotel."

"Perfect. Listen. We need to eat early because of Jared's flight at nine tonight. We're about to go to Babington's Tea Room for a light dinner. Ask Sire if he knows it and..."

"*Babington's Tea Room*? Even I know of it! Sounds like a great idea and we're not that far away. Where is it?"

"It's a well-identified corner building practically a stone's throw across the fountain of the Barcaccia if you're at the bottom and the middle of the Spanish Steps. We're just finishing up an amazing time at Caffè Greco, so very near Babington's. Tell you all about it when we meet there. Did you two have a good day in the Lazio region?"

"Fabulous! We'll swap stories when we're together again."

"You bet. See you soonissimo."

After they had hung up Megan called her sister. She answered immediately.

"Well, hi, Megan! I was wondering when I was going to hear from you."

"Sorry. Things have been developing fast here. I just heard from Mary and Sire and we're aiming to meet them in about fifteen minutes for early dinner. Remember that Babington's English Tea Room I pointed out to you at the bottom of the Spanish Steps by the Bernini fountain? Opposite side from the Keats/Shelley Museum?"

"Sure. But dinner at a *tea room*?"

"It serves the things you like, trust me. How soon do you think Tullio could drop you off?"

"He just did. I'm at our hotel."

"Wonderful! You could probably reach Babington's before any of us do."

"I plan to." The sisters giggled and hung up.

After a few more minutes Signor Capo appeared at the top of the spiral staircase, the securely wrapped painting in his hands. Jared jumped up to meet him and the precious cargo was transferred to his hands.

"Have you heard anything more about that neo-Fascist who almost ruined this portrait?" Megan asked. Capo suddenly looked indignant.

"Yes, I have. Just minutes ago. The police rang me in my office and told me that the ruffian, a confirmed neo-Fascist named Arlotto Zitto, had received a warning and a fine but he was not arrested. More's the pity!"

Goodbyes were said and soon Megan and Jared were off to the nearby Babington's Tea Room where they would blend with the other members of the Rome Quintet.

100

After being released at last from police custody, Arlotto Zitto called his superior at the *Ordine Ario Romano* (OAR)—the Aryan Roman Order—to report the event at Caffè Greco and his courageous action. Imagine his surprise when the comandante did not compliment him; he *chastised* him.

"Idiocy! Action must be gauged according to the specific situation and its possible aftermaths, not by your spontaneous reaction to one. And with no advance reasoning out what your action could ignite. We are about *action* not *reaction*."

"But don't you see, Comandante, it was a moment to be grabbed! Everything happened so fast that I *had* to do something or it would be too late." Zitto was almost whining.

"Consider this. *Why* were you assigned this watch post at the Caffè Greco?"

"Umm. To be able to report the clientele's reaction when the long lawsuit by Israelite Hospital against the café is finally decided."

"Yes. What happens there is crucial for our plans as far as tapping into and shaping public response. Which reactions could be beneficial to our party and what our own considered response should be. Understand, Zitto, that while we aim for violent public reactions, our own actions must be informed and rational. Not the sudden brandishing of a cup of coffee with the threat of defacing a little painting!"

"Yes, Comandante, I see. I understand now. I shall try from now on not to act on impulse but to be guided by reason."

"All right. Good man. Now as an incentive, since you can no longer serve as our temperature taker at the Caffè Greco, I am giving you a temporary new assignment. You will attend and report back to me about our just convened OAR conference taking place this coming Monday."

"Oh, thank you! May I know why OAR is meeting so suddenly?"

"Yes. Because with the recent victory of that woman Gioia Cantaloupe to be our next prime minister, we need to know how many of our OAR goals she intends to follow and not just give lip service to. Will her government follow our goals of designating our country's enemies, including migrants, especially those with skin colors different from true Italians, LGBT people, and of course our justified antisemitism."

"Yes, Comandante! I would be honored to take on this assignment. Thank you. Where is the conference taking place? Here in Rome?"

"No. We do not wish to attract public or media attention. The conference takes place at noon in the vicinity of the small town of Terracina. Are you familiar with it?"

"Yes, Comandante, I am. It's about sixty kilometers south of Rome on the Via Appia and it's on the coast. Great place to have a conference at. Especially if you're interested in antiquity—the town goes back to Roman times, I think."

"Well, don't you. We want you to be super alert to the *present* and what the general mood is concerning this Cantaloupe woman. How far right is she really going to be?"

"Absolutely. "

"All right. I told you that our conference is taking place in the vicinity of Terracina. Now I need to tell you exactly where. Because Terracina has become such a popular and packed tourist spot, our OAR representatives are meeting in an even more isolated location, although it too is a tourist goal. It is the small island called Ponza. Not far out from Terracina, just fifty kilometers. I advise you to take a ferry out to the island no later than ten in the morning. As you slide into the small harbor, the little town climbs up from there. And right as you land, if you look straight ahead and up, you will see a small domed church. Look to the far left of it as the town rises up to culminate in a couple of buildings that are noticeably larger than the houses below. There, the top white building, mostly abandoned, but used as a gym now, there is where our OAR meeting takes place at exactly noon. It should last, most probably, until late into the evening."

"Comandante, thank you for giving me a second chance. I shall not let you down."

101

Just as she had predicted, Tina was the first to arrive at Babington's Tea Room and she chose two connected tables at the back of the second largest room of the buzzing, animated, multi-roomed establishment, knowing the space would be the preferred, less distracting, and more private area for the Rome Quintet to talk and be heard. A large and amusing image dominated the space she had selected: the figure of a young boy sitting on a cliffside wearing a hat and blowing a trumpet that attracted legion flocks of birds to it. Glancing at the pithy menu where forty varieties of loose-leaf tea were offered, Tina read that the back of Babington's was used by members of the Resistance during World War I. Perfect place, Tina thought, with escape through the kitchens.

Next to arrive after Tina were her sister and their jovial New York friend Jared, and bringing up the rear were Mary and Sire. They all greeted each other as if long lost friends, so much had occurred for all of them during that long Saturday. A variety of herbal teas was ordered all around, and in addition, everyone chose the inventive "dinner" proposed by Megan of the only non-sweet tea house offerings: rice pilaf, chicken, eggs, Irish bacon, Chianina beef, and Scottish smoked salmon. A variety of burgers had been added to the menu since Megan had been there last but no one was tempted. As for dessert, sweets ranging from exotic pastries to homemade cakes were visible at different counters around the rooms and were also listed on the menu. The cheerful China cups and plates had blue rims populated by small sunflowers.

Mary had looked up Babington's online and regaled her friends with the names of famous film stars who had frequented the tea house.

They included Elizabeth Taylor, Richard Burton, Charlton Heston, Robert Taylor, Peter Ustinov, Audrey Hepburn and the filmmaker Federico Fellini.

"I love everything about this place," pronounced Jared, who had originally questioned Megan's choice. The precious Felix portrait was resting discreetly and safely between his legs and his chair legs. After the reunited Rome Quintet had devoured their food and chosen desserts, Tina looked around at the four happily chatting people. She truly wanted to hear their stories but she also really wanted to tell about her exciting day. She plunged in.

"Shall I start things by telling you what I did today?"

"Go for it!" Mary encouraged her while the others stopped talking and nodded encouragingly.

For the next ten minutes Tina described what she had seen and experienced at the Etruscan necropolis at Cerveteri and then what sort of giant tombs and sarcophagi were housed at the National Archaeological Museum in the nearby Ruspoli Castle overlooking Cerveteri. The museum is now the site, she told them, of hundreds of funereally decorated ceramic pots and plates, some local, others imported, with astonishingly evocative scenes of individual figures—women as well as men—crossing over symbolic rivers or simply floating upwards. Tina held her phone up, sharing some of the most poignant images she had recorded. Then she opened her commodious purse and pulled out a small flat circular object. She held it up so all could see.

"And this is what I was able to come away with."

It was a small black circular plate rimmed in red with the small figure of a woman seen in profile, her hands held upwards and climbing up a two-step ladder.

"Superbly simple symbolism, don't you think? And there are no guards around. Superbly simple to slip away with."

"*What!*" Megan was horrified. Was her own sister boasting that she had stolen an object from the museum? Mary was also reluctantly wondering the same thing.

"No," laughed Tina. "I was pulling your leg. It was superbly simple to *buy* an exact copy of the plate at the museum gift shop! Just wanted to make sure you were all listening. Now here's something that should interest all of you and I swear that I paid for it." She reached into her purse again and pulled out a book about six inches high and eight inches wide. Megan uttered a sound of surprise when she saw the cover. It was a modern reprint of Marianna Candidi Dionigi's comments and archaeological drawings for her book *Viaggi in Alcune Città di Lazio—Trips to Some Towns of Lazio*, first printed in 1809.

Sounds of surprise and glee issued from Tina's tablemates. They knew of the book in which, in the form of a series of letters written by a fifty-year-old woman—Dionigi, of course—archaeological sites are not only described but meticulously illustrated in a series of etchings that included transcribed inscriptions, plans, and elevations. And now, thanks to Megan's dogged hunt for her painted view of the place and its clients, everyone knew that she was one of the regular women visitors to the Caffè Greco.

Desserts arrived and silence ensued for some contented minutes as the Quintet consumed the various mouth-watering goodies that ranged from strawberry cake to Scottish scones to two apple tarts to peppermint ice cream.

"Okay," Tina asked after finishing her last bite of apple tart, "who's going to tell us about their day next?" Sire looked questioningly at Mary and she nodded affirmatively. He began speaking, a look of pure joy on his face.

"Well, after we picked up our rental car we drove straight to Calcata—or as you would have it, Tina, Calcutta." Tina was the first to laugh as her companions looked at her affectionately.

"It's only a forty-mile drive northeast from here," Sire continued, "so about an hour's drive and the weather was perfect. Our first sight of the little medieval town was *spectacular*. Right ahead of us, as we pulled out of a dense green forest, was a mountain with a miniature town on top! Okay, the mountain was a tall cliff, but it was over five hundred feet high and that was certainly impressive. Have a look!"

Sire held up his cellphone for all to see and his friends gasped in amazement. They were looking at a view of the forest-surrounded volcanic cliff on top of which sat a packed ensemble of small buildings, all of almost equal four-story height except for a small church and the tower of a miniature castle. Everything was crowded against everything else in an area the girth of which seemed no wider than the height of the volcanic cliff on which the village sat.

"How did you ever even get inside the towering town?" Megan

asked, beginning to feel slightly jealous that she had not visited the site. Mary answered her.

"We had to park the car at the official parking lot which is close to but above the town. And you have to pay for the privilege. Then you follow a footpath down that takes about fifteen minutes. Finally you get some good views of the village on your left as the path leads into the entry gate and finally into the main square where the little church and miniature castle are. All the other old brick buildings are living quarters, we were told, for only some seventy, we were told, permanent residents."

"And did you learn anything about any religious relics the little town might once have had?" Jared asked, feigning ignorance.

"No," answered Sire calmly, "unless you mean the Holy Prepuce."

"*The holy what*?" Jared was no longer feigning ignorance.

"The Holy Foreskin of the infant Christ which was once stolen from the Vatican and hidden in Calcata for a while. But of course several churches in Europe have claimed to possess that foreskin, sometimes even at the same time. It is much venerated because of miraculous powers ascribed to it."

Tina and Megan could not hold back laughter, and Jared joined them.

"Oh yes, sure, the Prepuce," he blurted out finally. "I never heard of the Holy Foreskin referred to that way, so I'm glad to be *fore*warned."

"You should always be *prepuce*d," answered Sire without losing a beat.

"Enough, fellows, please!" chastised Mary, who was not amused by such feeble attempts at punning.

"So let's hear about *your* day, you two," Sire looked commandingly at the two members of the Rome Quintet who had not chronicled their day.

The next half hour passed rapidly as Megan and Jared narrated the chronology of increasingly interesting events with its totally unexpected, breathtaking finale.

"It could have been really dangerous," a worried Mary pronounced.

"But what an outcome for Jared's Mendelssohn Complex," Sire

said. "And you actually have the Felix portrait with you right here and now?"

"I sure do. Right here underneath my chair," the New Yorker pointed.

Discussion turned to what the diminished Rome Quintet, regrouped as the Rome Quartet, would be doing after Jared, along with his Felix Mendelssohn portrait, took off for Hamburg that evening.

"Just a minute," Tina asked, "who is this woman museum director in Hamburg you're returning to see? Is there more to this than meets the eye?"

"Only that we're getting married tomorrow. Otherwise nothing out of the ordinary." Tina gasped while Megan, Mary, and Sire laughed heartily at Jared's naughty lie. The inveterate joker continued to answer Tina's question, but seriously this time.

"Rachael Skylar is the capable director of the new Fanny and Felix Mendelssohn Museum in Hamburg and it will be a pleasure to talk with her again, especially since I am now about to exhibit two previously unknown portraits of sister and brother. Also, Rachael has been through some tough family times recently and I want to give her a shoulder to lean on. It will be a Sunday well spent before I fly back to Rome early Monday morning and check on the second portrait, the big Fanny one, for my flight back to New York."

"Where are you picking them up from?" Mary wanted to know.

"Well, I'll have the Felix one with me as I want to show it to Rachael, and the other, larger one of Fanny is being picked up and crated early Monday morning and will be delivered to my plane's cargo reception area in the early afternoon. Things should go smoothly, but I'm a fussy person, you may have noticed, and will be checking on everything a number of times."

Megan had something to say to that.

"Jared, it is just because you *are* a fussy person and see to every detail that I want you to know something. After I've finished reading and xeroxing them, I intend to send you, for the Mendelssohn Complex, the twenty-three letters written by Fanny to her sister Rebecka during her year in Rome. My only request is that you mail me a formal gift receipt for my income taxes."

"Oh! Unbelievable! How absolutely fantastic. Megan! So generous of you to do this. From Nathan's largesse to you and from your largesse to the Mendelssohn Complex. I am thrilled beyond words. Thank you, dear friend."

Jared reached over and gave Megan a kiss on the cheek. Mary and Sire applauded. Tina patted her sister on the shoulder, inadvertently noticing the time on her watch.

"Yikes!" she exclaimed. "It's six forty-one! Jared, you better get going if you want to have a full two hours for getting to the airport and checking on things before your nine o'clock flight."

"Gosh! You are so right! It's amazing how our time together has raced past."

Jared stood up and, carefully sliding the portrait of little Felix out from under his legs, he made his farewells. Everyone was sad to see him go. Just before he walked out of the tea house he turned to Megan and slipped some euro bills into her hand.

"That should cover our magnificent Babington's Tea Room dinner for five."

Blowing kisses to his friends with his free hand and pressing Felix close to his side, Jared headed up the Spanish Steps to the hotel where both his suitcase and his Uber would be awaiting him in three minutes.

102

It wasn't too long after Jared's departure that the remaining four, all of them exhausted by their long day of travel, also broke up. Mary and Sire had miraculously found a parking place on the Via Borgogna, not far away from Babington's, and the Crespi sisters only needed to climb to the top of the Spanish Steps and turn right to reach their beckoning hotel.

Just before they took off in separate directions, they confirmed the plans for tomorrow, Sunday. Although none of them were Catholic they were all in agreement that the Vatican was not to be missed, and what greater day to visit than on a Sunday? Sire had thought ahead after they arrived in Rome and when he learned that all four of them wanted to visit the Sistine Chapel and St. Peter's, he suggested they take a private tour. He did some Internet research and then booked a small and very special "skip-the-line tour" for them. It included not only art in the Vatican Museums and the Sistine Chapel as well as the basilica and dome of St. Peter's, but also a visit to a "church opera concert" in one of the many churches "in the heart of Rome with dinner at a nearby select restaurant" afterward that offered "limitless wine." What a tour!

Sunday would also be a day for relaxation in the morning, since they all desired to have a nice, drawn-out breakfast on the roof level of their respective hotels. Each couple—Mary and Sire, Megan and Tina—claimed their hotel had the best view of Rome. Thus they would not meet that morning until eleven-fifteen at Via degli Scipioni number nine, where a bus and private guide would take them to the Vatican City.

Megan was especially happy to have much of the morning to

herself because that would give her time to review the letters home Fanny had written concerning her trips to the Vatican and St. Peter's. What better way to add to her biography of the fascinating woman than to visit the treasures there with her eyes?

While Megan reread the Fanny items from the years eighteen thirty-nine and forty, Tina worked on an intricate new fiber art idea and the morning passed more rapidly than either one realized. In fact they almost had to run to catch metro A to Cipro, the Vatican City stop. It was a ride of just seven minutes with four stops. As they emerged, they spotted Sire and Mary talking to a tall, thin, authoritative-looking, gray-haired lady wearing a green baseball cap and green armband, both with the words "*BONELLI GUIDA*" on them. The woman turned and with a nod of the head acknowledged the two hurrying Americans. She began walking toward them, her face expressionless.

"Welcome to Bonelli Tours, last-minute ladies. I am Charlotte Piacevole, your tour guide. A word about myself before we commence. I have been giving tours of the Vatican for over thirty-three years and am considered Bonelli Tours' most valuable tour guide. As such, I am the most highly tipped."

Megan and Tina exchanged wide-eyed looks. Their "most highly tipped" guide continued without a break.

"And now, people, let us join the eight other tour members who have been waiting and I shall escort and enlighten you on this grand private tour of the walled Holy City. Covering just over one hundred and ten acres, the Vatican is the smallest nation on earth. We will commence in the Vatican Museums, descend to some famous grottoes, and end inside the dome of the tallest building in Rome, Saint Peter's Basilica."

Tina smiled at Megan sympathetically as she attempted to hide her shock at the thought of climbing all the way up to Saint Peter's dome. Surely there must be an elevator by now? The difference of fifteen and a half years between the two sisters' ages did sometimes lead to just such navigation problems.

"There you are! We were beginning to get worried about you," said Mary while Sire beamed them a smile of relief as the two sisters joined them.

"Time just passed so quickly this morning and we were both totally involved in projects!" explained Tina. "And Megan was loading some of the Fanny letters into her cellphone that she thought might be of interest to all of us inside the Holy City."

"Yes," Megan added, "but as far as I can tell, every reference is to events in Saint Peter's and the Sistine Chapel she and her husband attended, and *not* a description of the art works, unfortunately. But we shall see."

A few minutes later the Rome Quartet and eight other expectant tourists, all Americans including two teenage girls, boarded the multi-windowed yellow bus awaiting them. Within minutes the bus pulled up at the large official entrance to the walled city on Viale Vaticano, at the opposite side of the entrance to St. Peter's. Because some twenty-five thousand visitors pass through the Vatican every day, lines for tickets stretched for blocks. Holding her green cap high up in the air and twirling it, Charlotte led her private Bonelli tour group imperiously past the Swiss guards and those ordinary tourists, through the metal detector, and onto the grounds. Because it was a Sunday the group was not allowed to enter the Papal Gardens off to the right with their stunning array of statues, fountains, and early autumn flowers, but walked directly into the first building. There they immediately mounted a very broad spiral staircase that took them to a series of magnificent halls which opened at last into one of the two thousand rooms of the Vatican Museums: the Pio Clementino Museum featuring the most important Greek works owned by the Vatican. The star, of course, was the almost life-size white marble statue of the Trojan priest Laocoön and his two sons. They were shown fending off the giant serpents sent to punish him by Apollo because Laocoön had warned his fellow Trojans not to trust the huge wooden horse sent by the Greeks to the gates of Troy. The warning was in vain, and thinking it was a "peace offering" from the Greeks, the Trojans pulled the horse inside the city gates, and during the night Greek warriors hiding inside the hollow horse emerged and the city was conquered.

The knowledgeable, if somewhat grim guide Charlotte informed her attentive group that the extraordinary ensemble had been discovered in a Roman vineyard and excavated in 1506 and that, along with the pope, a young Michelangelo—at that time better known as a sculptor than a painter and one who would also become an architect and a poet—was among the first to visit it. Some parts were missing, including Laocoön's right arm and although other artists reasoned its position must have been outstretched, Michelangelo, with his knowledge of anatomy and sculpture, argued that the missing arm had been bent backward to the shoulder. He lost that argument, however, and within a few years a heroically outstretched right arm was given to Laocoön along with a few other restitutions of missing parts.

Laocoön was considered such an important example of Greek sculpture, guide Charlotte continued, that when Napoleon conquered Italy in 1799 he had the statue shipped to Paris where it was put on display in the Louvre the next year. After the fall of Napoleon in 1816, Laocoön was returned to the Vatican, its outstretched right arm intact. And so it remained until the year 1906 when the Prague-born classical archaeologist Ludwig Pollak discovered part of a marble, backwards-bent arm in a yard near the site where Laocoön had been unearthed. Pollak would not live to see the arm restored, however, because he was murdered in 1943 at Auschwitz. Years later the "Pollak arm" was added to the statue, after it was demonstrated that a drill hole in the arm fit perfectly with a corresponding hole in the shoulder. And thus Michelangelo's theory of five centuries earlier was proven correct.

Another set of corridors led them through the Gallery of the Candelabra with a plethora of fine Greek sculptures and into the Gallery of Tapestries, some of them designed by Raphael, in vibrant colors depicting in detail scenes from the Bible.

"There was a common-sense factor to these tapestries," announced Charlotte in a low voice, bringing her group closer together. "Because they were woven in wool as well as silk and gold thread, they could trap the heat in a room, thus insulating stone or brick rooms in wintertime."

The last huge showroom before reaching the Sistine Chapel was the Gallery of Maps which featured forty fresco panels of medieval maps detailing the geography of Italy and in such a manner that, amusingly, Sicily looked upside down, as guide Charlotte pointed out rather disdainfully. She also sternly warned her group that this was the last chamber in which photography was allowed.

They finally arrived at the pope's chapel: the Sistine Chapel in all its Renaissance glory. After commanding complete turnoff of cellphones and warning that no loud talking was allowed in the Chapel, their guide proudly whispered to her small group that the rectangular brick building with its six high, arched windows and elevated, barrel-vaulted ceiling was used by the Sacred College of Cardinals for election of a new pope. Good, but of far greater interest to Mary, Sire, Tina, and Megan were the frescoes on the two side walls by Michelangelo and other celebrated High Renaissance artists, depicting among other subjects, ancestors of Christ and past popes. Their guide skipped identifying any of them, hissing "No need to look at those; look at *that*!" as she pointed upward.

On the long, sixty-foot-high ceiling beginning above the altar and divided into three sections above the length of the nave, Michelangelo, commencing at the age of thirty-two, painted from 1508 to 1512 a heroic narrative. It started with *The Creation of the Heavens and Earth*, followed *by The Creation of Adam* and *The Expulsion from the Garden of Eden*, and finally *Noah and the Great Flood*. Alongside these scenes, sitting in various poses and identified by painted marble tablet inscriptions, were the figures of classical sibyls and biblical prophets. And of course also present were the *ignudi*—nude, male, muscular young men who frame some of the ceiling's central scenes.

"Hmm, Michelangelo certainly doesn't leave anything out," murmured Sire sarcastically to Mary, pointing to some of the male figures' distinctly portrayed private parts.

"Well, why shouldn't an artist show them?" she responded, slightly vexed that the question of Michelangelo's sexual orientation be brought up.

"That's more of a twenty-first century question; here we're in the sixteenth century," replied Sire.

The centrally placed, iconic *Creation of Adam* stole the show, of course. Free of a plethora of distracting details, the dynamic white haired, bearded figure of God, clad in white, descends swiftly from heaven on the right to give life to an earth-bound, passive, naked Adam on the left, who struggles to raise his left hand to receive the spark of life. The first finger of the hand reaches out to the extended first finger of the right hand of God and the suspense of the scant but distinct space still between the two approaching hands can be felt if not seen from the chapel floor. It was hard to look away and at other images after this one!

The group's guide, or rather commander, Charlotte took this pause to explain in a low voice, forcing the group to circle close around her, the fresco technique: a method which involves damp plaster. The wet lime must still be able to react with oxygen to create calcium carbonate which protects the pigments from environmental factors.

"I don't understand one single word of what she's explaining," Tina whispered to her sister who nodded.

"Took me years to understand. Tell you later," whispered Megan back.

"*Myth or true?*" asked Commander Charlotte suddenly. "That while suspended hundreds of feet painting the ceiling frescoes over a period of five years Michelangelo lay on his back, wiping plaster and perspiration from his eyes as he slogged away year after year."

All but one of the group raised their hands in indication they believed the account was true. The art historian in the group, Megan, had something to say, however, and the guide hardly hid her impatience.

"I do know," she whispered to the group, "that Michelangelo invented his own method of suspension *up* to the ceiling and *not down* from the ceiling as has often been suggested. He was furious that people would think of drilling holes in 'his' ceiling. And he did not lie down to paint; he stood to paint, craning his neck back and so, yes, plaster flakes and perspiration did indeed fall onto his eyes over those five years."

"Correct," answered the Commander almost grudgingly. "That was just my form of a trick question to make sure you are all following what I say." Universally the entire group frowned. Why was this obviously experienced guide worrying about whether or not tourists were all listening to her all the time?

"And anyway," Sire whispered, "how can plaster bits and sweat droplets in your eyes possibly be a myth in an unairconditioned building during a hot Italian summer back then?"

Commander Charlotte ignored the man's practical question. It was time for one of her favorite anecdotes; issued again in a loud whisper.

"Now something we know is *absolutely* true is that upon seeing the ceiling frescoes in progress, young Raphael, eight years Michelangelo's junior, dashed back to his *School of Athens* painting and added the pensive, black-bearded figure of Michelangelo sitting just to center left at the bottom of the steps of the school. Unfortunately, the Raphael Rooms are not on this tour schedule but I urge you to book another tour—the 'Raphael Tour'—with Bonelli Tours and ask for me, Charlotte Piacevole. But now follow me closely and let us make our way over to the altar and digest Michelangelo's mighty *Last Judgment*. It was begun twenty-two years after he had completed the ceiling frescoes, thus from fifteen thirty-four to fifteen forty-one."

"So how old would that make him?" Mary asked.

"Fifty-nine or sixty, depending upon what month he began work. He was born in March, March sixth of the year fourteen seventy-five."

"Gosh! That's pretty old to be climbing back up on his ceiling lift," mused Mary.

"Yes, but by this time sunglasses had been invented, so he was free of plaster bits," Tina murmured with a straight face.

Commander Charlotte looked furious as every member of her group tried hard to mask a laugh. Disrespect was not something to be suffered in her Sistine Chapel. With some twenty-five thousand persons visiting the Vatican every day of the week, it was enough work just to keep her people moving; not standing around making stupid jokes.

Hissing a command to follow her, the grim guide led her small group forward to the altar which was uncharacteristically on the east wall—the exit wall—of the giant chapel. Standing pressed against dozens of other eager tourists, they devoured with their eyes the colossal, hugely populated—over 300 figures—multi-leveled, terrifying panorama of Michelangelo's *Last Judgment*. A widespread compositional turmoil touches both the anticipation of heaven and the dread of hell, the latter undeniably reminiscent of Dante's ferocious *Inferno*. And indeed one of Michelangelo's heroes was this great fourteenth-century writer and his epic *The Divine Comedy*.

Centrally placed, almost naked, and—highly unusual in being beardless—is the athletic figure of Christ. He sits in a white vortex with a demure mother Mary seated at his right side. Christ's raised right arm, bent at the elbow, brings his hand dramatically above his head as he looks at the knots of figures on his left, the viewer's right. These are the souls who will go to hell.

Gazing at that Christ, one sees the elect surrounding him: various saints, martyrs, and angels. To his left, the beholder's right, are prominent apostles like Saint Peter, holding the keys to heaven. To Christ's right is St. John the Baptist.

Looking at such an assemblage, one or two of Charlotte's small group might have first thought they were viewing the Resurrection of Christ, but no, they were looking at the Second Coming of Christ with the Resurrection of the Dead on Judgment Day. The tortures of hell awaiting those who have sinned were everywhere to be seen within the waterfalls of mostly naked, mostly male, beings. All of them exhibit varieties of angst while Charon, the ferryman who transports souls to the underworld, stands in his small boat holding his oar up, ready to swing it at the souls in front of him. The figures are met by one of the judges for those entering hell, Minos. He has donkey ears and a serpent wrapped around his body biting his genitals.

Megan so wanted, but did not dare, to point out to their group the figure of Saint Bartholomew just below Christ. A martyr saint, he had been flayed alive and Michelangelo showed him sitting on a cloud with the skin of his body in his hand. It was widely thought that the gruesome, black-haired, black-bearded face on the end of the skin is actually Michelangelo's sardonic self-portrait. But before she worked up the courage to say so, the abrupt sound of Commander Charlotte's harsh whisper suddenly interrupted everyone's intense concentration.

"Notice, people, how a sense of depth is created by Michelangelo with the overlapping of so many figures, and with the figures further back depicted in paler tones."

An incongruous if correct technical fact to be pointing out at that dazzling moment, Megan thought, when there was so much to explain about what was going on in so many groupings, literally hundreds of them, including a few figures in hell with African features and dark skin colors. And how to explain such wholesale, muscular nudity? Of course Michelangelo was a sculptor before he was a painter—just think of his *Pietà* or his *David.* For him the perfection of the nude human form was the purest expression of the divine. And the nudity here was pervasive.

As if she had read her thoughts, Charlotte spoke again.

"In fifteen sixty-three the Council of Trent, responding to the Counter-Reformation, issued a specific decree stipulating that all naked images in the Sistine Chapel should be covered. The covering over of genitals was ordered and carried out one year after Michelangelo's death in February of fifteen sixty-four by the Mannerist artist Daniele da Volterra—ironically a pupil and close friend of the master. He was given the nickname *Il Braghettone*—the breeches-maker. And after that, over the seventeenth and eighteenth centuries other artists added more underpants."

"Just tell us, please, if you don't mind: when was all this nudity we've been looking at restored?" Megan really wanted to know, having been embarrassingly unaware, as an art historian—granted not in the field of sixteenth-century art—of all this coverup business. The answer came quickly from their undeniably knowledgeable guide.

"All right, this is what happened and it did not happen until the twentieth century. After the Sistine Chapel's ceiling frescoes were restored in the nineteen eighties and early nineties, it was decided that *The Last Judgment* should also be cleaned of centuries of dirt and grime caused by candles and oil lanterns. But the restorers discovered that most of *Il Braghettone's* breeches could not be eradicated because Volterra had scraped away and destroyed much of the original fresco. They were only able to remove seventeen of the forty underpants."

"Only seventeen out of forty? What a pity," commented Sire who had previously been flippant about the abundance of uncovered male genitalia. Mary smiled in pleased surprise. Knowledgeable Charlotte looked directly at Sire.

"If you really want to see what Michelangelo's *Last Judgment* naked males looked like before Volterra's cover-up, then go to the Capodimonte Museum in Naples. That is where you can see an exact copy of the original, a copy which was painted in anticipation of the Council of Trent's censure of pictorial nudity. The artist Marcello Venusti was commissioned to copy the entire fresco by a prescient Cardinal Alessandro Farnese in fifteen forty-nine. He had anticipated what might happen to Michelangelo's masterpiece by way of the impending threat from the Council of Trent."

"Fascinating!" responded Sire and other adult members of the tour group. "And if we don't have time to go to Naples, we can probably study it online."

"Correct, if you don't care about not seeing art in the flesh. Now listen, people, I'll give you another five minutes to gape at the great, then we must move on to Saint Peter's basilica," announced Charlotte. Stubbornly staying in place, despite the pushing, impatient tourists behind them, her mesmerized group "gaped at the great" until the last second of the time allotted to them. And then it would be on to the world's largest basilica. "Built over the bones of Saint Peter,"

Charlotte announced spookily, referring to the graveyard where the Apostle Peter had been buried and on top of which the church's apse had been built.

As they waited impatiently in front of the exit door for the laggers to arrive, Megan quickly read aloud in a low voice to her tightknit group what Fanny had written home about the Sistine Chapel.

"'Yesterday were at the Sistine Chapel and I saw the Pope, and all the cardinals as well as they passed by. We poor women fare badly at these ceremonies, for we are made to sit in the background, behind a trellis, and those who, like myself, are short-sighted, cannot see much, though we are obliged to sit still for three hours, listening to the *incorrect* and indifferent singing of the Pope's choir, and to the not-very-interesting performance of the mass by a few old cardinals with quavering voices.'"

"Not a *word* about the frescoes!" Megan remarked wonderingly. "Even though *her husband was a painter*! Only complaints about the *musical* performances. Well, doesn't that tell us a lot about Fanny?" The gravelly voice of their tour commander sounded above Megan's whisper.

"Now, because you are on a private Bonelli tour with me, you do not have to return through the Vatican museum rooms we visited, back to the entrance we came in, exit, and make the long walk on Viale Vaticano Portico to Via di Porto Angelico around to the front entrance of the basilica. Available only to us guides is a special passageway directly from here into the basilica. Follow me!"

The Rome Quartet took one last look at the 5000 square feet of breathtaking Michelangelo frescoes, and then, almost reluctantly, followed Commander Charlotte through a door on the right into St. Peter's. What and who could be on the same level as Michelangelo?

The answer, they soon saw, was Michelangelo. His *Pietà*, sculpted when he was only twenty-three. His white Carrara marble pyramidal ensemble of the dead, limp Christ held in his mourning mother's arms across her lap was movingly stunning. Fortunately their guide refrained from recounting the horrendous vandalism it suffered in 1972 at the hands of a deranged Hungarian-Australian geologist—something Mary knew about, but also refrained from mentioning to her friends.

Instead, Commander Charlotte, now able to speak in a normal, in her case, loud voice again, directed her group's eyes upward to yet another masterpiece by the sculptor and painter. This one was designed by Michelangelo the architect. It was he who, starting in 1546 at the age of seventy-one, designed the massive, seemingly weightless dome that soars loftily toward the sky and at the same time hangs lightly like a gigantic crown over the presumed tomb of St. Peter directly below the high altar of the basilica. At the very end of Michelangelo's long life, in early 1564 when he was eighty-nine, construction of the dome had reached the drum. Gabled windows alternated with protruding double columns and, slowly, the best was yet to come. The completion of the double-capped dome—the tallest church dome in the world—was completed in 1590.

Commander Charlotte, having delivered herself of this truly fascinating information, then paused to explain to her tour group the order of what they would be doing next.

"Ordinary tours end after an underground visit to the artifacts and papal tombs beneath this great church. And this is where they then exit Saint Peter's. But we at Bonelli Tours feel this is a depressing way to finish a tour and so, instead, we schedule the climax of our tour to be Michelangelo's great dome with its vast vista! I hope you agree."

Heads nodded and the faces of the two teenagers lit up for the first time on the tour.

"And people are more likely to tip generously with a grand finale like that," Tina whispered to her sister, who giggled out loud.

Twirling her raised cap, Commander Charlotte led her obedient group down the nave toward the church portico through thick streams of incoming tourists until they got to the statues of St. Helen and St. Andrew. Here they stopped by a door that led down into the immense Vatican Grottoes—a massive spread of papal tombs and artifacts spread out underneath the entire basilica.

"To understand the immensity and number of the grottoes under this vast church to which we shall descend, picture to yourself the figure of a colossal giant standing and facing us, arms extended out from the sides and from the knees more side extensions. *This huge figure is the length of the entire church of Saint Peter's!*"

"Spooky," one of the teenage girls whispered to the other.

"This enormous area is the final resting place of over *ninety* popes, royalty, and other dignitaries," continued their Commander

"Are there any *women* buried in Saint Peter's?" interrupted not feminist Megan, but Sire, admirer of his Mary's extraordinary activities in the world of music. Obviously Commander-in-Chief Charlotte had been asked this particular question many times before, because her memorized, pithy answer was immediate, interesting, and unexpectedly long.

"Yes. There are actually *six* women buried here, although most guides and guidebooks will tell you there are only three. But I shall give you the full list because this is what Bonelli Tours does: we provide trustworthy, complete information. Of the six women we have here in Saint Peter's, one is a saint, three are queens, another is a great countess, and the last one, a noblewoman. I can tell you briefly about them in chronological order. Would you like that?"

All members of the tour group vigorously nodded yes.

"All right, then. The first was Saint Petronilla, possibly the daughter of Saint Peter, and described as a virgin martyr killed in either the first or second century. By the fourth century she was venerated. After Old Saint Peter's Basilica was demolished and this new one we're in was begun in the sixteenth century, Petronilla's relics were taken to an altar dedicated to her in the upper end of the right-side aisle from where we stand. Her chapel was partly decorated by Michelangelo. So far so good?"

The group nodded affirmatively.

"All right. The second woman buried here was powerful Matilda Canossa of Tuscany, mediator between the popes and King Henry the Fourth during the last quarter of the eleventh and beginning of the twelfth century. If you look past my head and directly across the nave, there is her life-size statue by Bernini within a monument to her. Her body lies inside. It is the only one of three monuments to women buried here in which this is so."

Delighted stares followed the Commander's bidding. Two of her group quickly took photos, partly for the sheer pleasure of being able to do so again.

"The third woman buried here was the fifteenth-century Queen Charlotte of Cyprus. She is buried in the grottoes to which we will soon descend. Charlotte, my namesake you will have noticed, was queen for five years, *beginning at the age of fourteen.*" Commander Charlotte looked meaningfully at the two young girls standing in front of her. "But then she was pushed off the throne by her grasping, illegitimate half-brother, and after being blockaded in a castle for three years, she fled to Rome in fourteen sixty-three and was received by the pope in what was described as 'chairs of equal height.' She died at the age of forty-three, her funeral paid for by the reigning pope, and she is buried in the chapel of Saint Andrew and Saint Gregory."

The American teenagers were thrilled to hear about a teenage queen, and the younger girl even jumped up and down in excitement. Commander Charlotte actually smiled for a split second before continuing.

"The fourth woman, also buried in the grottoes, was the noblewoman Agnesina Colonna. She died in fifteen seventy-eight and is buried within the wall inside the Chapel of the Patron Saints of Europe. Unfortunately, it is not accessible during the day, but we can remember her as the mother of not one but two sons who became cardinals. So now let us climb down the spiral stairs here—*slowly!*—and into the Vatican Grottoes."

The two reinterested teenagers scooted to the front of the line.

Reassembled in the dark labyrinth under the altar, the curious tourists followed their fearless commander to the dark-stoned, humble chamber just under the high altar where some secret archaeological excavations during the middle of World War II had revealed what appeared to be St. Peter's bone remnants.

"Whether or not they truly are is still being disputed, as scientific data points in two directions," Guide Charlotte explained.

"The fifth woman, and the most important in my estimation, was Queen Christina of Sweden, who lived from . . ."

"*Wow!* There's a Bridgerton series about her on Netflix!" Tina exclaimed to her sister. "But you're probably too old to know about Bridgerton."

"And you're too young to know there was a movie made on her in nineteen thirty-three starring Greta Garbo and . . ."

"*Silenzio!*" Commander Charlotte barked at the two giggling idiots. "So disrespectful."

"You're right, it was. Sorry," Tina apologized, pretending to spank Megan's behind. The two teenagers' mouths fell open at the sight while an unamused and unmollified Commander Charlotte continued her lengthy but riveting spiel. Megan, Tina, Mary, and also Sire were beginning to reconsider the earnest woman's bid for high tips, which at first had seemed unseemly. Knowledgeable Guide Charlotte continued.

"The unconventional seventeenth-century Queen Christina of Sweden is famous for her conversion from a reigning Lutheran Queen of Sweden for twenty-two years to a Catholic Queen without a country to rule. But she reigned over the world of culture with her tremendous interest in art, theater, music, literature, and philosophy."

None of the Rome Quartet knew that much about the fascinating former queen and they were all ears. The teenagers not so much.

"During her reign of twenty-two years she persuaded the French philosopher René Descartes to come to Stockholm and, fascinated by her company, he stayed for two years. But difficulties with problems of taxation, governance, and foreign relations plagued Christina's last years as queen, and in sixteen fifty-one she herself proposed that she abdicate. She had also secretly converted to Catholicism and in sixteen fifty-four she abdicated the throne and made her way—first dressed in men's clothing and on horseback to escape detection—to Rome where she was the honored guest of *five* successive popes. She persuaded Pope Clement the Tenth to ban the custom of chasing Jews through the streets during the Carnival season and later she issued a declaration that Roman Jews were under her protection."

This time the teenagers as well as their parents gasped, as the family happened to be Jewish.

"After several disappointing returns to Sweden, Christina made the Riario Palace right here in Rome her home for the rest of her life. And the sumptuous palace provided a suitable setting for her vast art collection which included works by Titian, Veronese, Correggio, and Raphael."

Looks of boredom reappeared on the teenagers' faces. Trooper Tour Guide Charlotte was undeterred; the best was yet to come.

"When Christina, asking for a simple funeral, died of pneumonia at the age of sixty-two in sixteen eighty-nine, the pope—Alexander the Eighth—ignored her wishes and gave her a fantastic four-day public viewing at her Riario Palace. For her burial here in the papal grottoes, she was embalmed, dressed in white brocade with fur-lined ermine, and with a silver mask, scepter, and gold-leafed crown. Her intestines were placed in a high urn and, as with many of the popes, Christina's body was placed in a series of three coffins—the innermost made of cypress, the next of lead, and the final, outside one made of oak."

Interest had peaked with the teenagers: a silver mask? Intestines in an urn?

"And she was buried right here in the papal grottoes—one of only four women ever given this honor."

The long-standing, stationary tour group began surreptitiously glancing right and left. There was only one other woman to be identified and then maybe they could see their tombs at last. Observant Guide Charlotte, sensing the group's impatience, quickly named the sixth and last woman to be buried in Saint Peter's.

"Then, finally, the early eighteenth-century Polish-born princess, Maria Clementina Sobieska of the enormously wealthy Sobieska family, who through marriage at sixteen to James Stewart, a thirty-year-old Catholic claimant in Rome to the British throne, was titular queen of England, Scotland, and Ireland."

The teenagers frowned their total bafflement.

"She traveled to Rome where she and her husband were housed in the Palazzo Muti by the pope, a supporter of Stewart's claim. But relations broke down between Clementina and her politically obsessed husband. She went to live in a convent for two years and afterward spent the rest of her short life working with and for Rome's poor. When she died of scurvy, leaving the bulk of her vast fortune to the church, the pope ordered a state funeral and burial in Saint Peter's because of her proven devoutness and piety.

"What's scurvy?" both teenagers quietly queried their parents.

"You will be able to see the dramatic ensemble dedicated to her when we are up in the cupola, but now while we're in the grottoes let us proceed to the tombs of Queen Charlotte of Cyprus and Queen Christina of Sweden."

Happy to be on the move again, the group practically ran after Galloping Guide Charlotte toward the area directly underneath the basilica's great Papal Altar. Then their guide suddenly turned right. Facing each other in a small chamber were the two tombs: Queen Charlotte on their right, and Queen Christina on their left in a great white sarcophagus containing the three stacked coffins with her remains inside. The tomb had raised corners and a large bronze plaque that read "Here lies the body of Christina Alexandra / Of the Goths,

Swedes, Vandals / Queen / Died 19 April 1689."

It was as if Guide Charlotte sensed the group's next question.

"Yes, Christina's remains were *here*. In the grottoes. Not in the monument to her upstairs even though her remains were later removed from here and placed in the wall above the monument to her." Their detail-driven guide ignored the befuddlement of her group and continued with yet another unexpected fact.

"And I must give you an update from the year seventeen forty-five about our Polish Maria Clementina Sobieska. Originally buried here in grottoes, her remains were moved that year also to a place in the wall above her monument."

In continued befuddlement, Mary had a question.

"May I ask what the difference is between 'remains' and 'relics' in regard to the dead?" Patient Guide Charlotte answered immediately.

"Yes. It can be confusing as the two nouns are often misused interchangeably. The difference is that 'remains' means what is left after a person dies—their corpse, while 'relic' is that which is left after the loss of most of the corpse or its decay—a remaining portion."

Many of the group were pleased at having been given this distinction since they had indeed been a bit perplexed by the interchangeable usage of the two words they had encountered elsewhere.

"Now if you'd like to wander about here, I can give you ten minutes, and after that I'll have a surprise for you."

The Rome Quartet and all the other members of the group wandered in different directions, each on their own, admiring various sarcophagi and working at reading informative inscriptions in Latin. All returned on time, eager to find out what Commander Charlotte's mysterious surprise was.

It was a very welcome one. There was an elevator in the grottoes that ascended directly to their last stop, Michelangelo's dome!

"And Bonelli Tours pays the extra euros that taking the elevator costs each passenger." Guide Charlotte allowed herself a proud smile. "The elevator will be full when it opens its doors down here, but once passengers have exited, there will be just enough room for the thirteen of us to enter. And as you can perhaps imagine, I shall make certain no hitchhikers join us."

The group guffaw this remark triggered was one of pure delight along with a touch of gratefulness. Megan was even thinking that Commander Charlotte's immediate description of herself as the highest tipped guide at Bonelli Tours wasn't so much a bid for a big tip but rather simply a matter of pride after thirty-three years of guiding tourists. And right now Megan felt inclined actually to leave a generous tip.

Some minutes later Charlotte's group was in the elevator and on their way up to the top of St. Peter's. When they exited, Helper Guide Charlotte suggested they take a look over the edge of the basilica down at the top of the Sistine Chapel before walking over to the entrance of the cupola, the inner side of the dome. What memories of Michelangelo's amazing frescoes that Sistine glimpse brought back already!

And then it was time to enter the inner drum of the dome with its mosaic-covered walls and from where there was a stunning view down into the basilica. The group looked long at the top of the famous, ninety-five-foot-high, bronze baldacchino canopy over the Papal Altar which was designed by the famous sculptor-architect Gian Lorenzo Bernini. Charlotte's group now understood how Saint Peter's grotto tomb could be exactly underneath that altar.

"Isn't Saint Peter's a cathedral?" asked the father of the two teenagers.

"You would think so because of its enormous size, but a cathedral is the seat of a bishop, so no, Saint Peter's is a church and it is a basilica, but not a cathedral," answered all-knowing Charlotte helpfully.

Looking down beyond the altar from the cupola, the group marveled at the many thick throngs of people who were wandering around the nave and up and down the aisles. From this amazing vantage point, Responsible Guide Charlotte pointed out to her privileged group the packed crowds gathering to see the three monuments to women she had told them existed on the ground floor of Saint Peter's. Although her group couldn't see them, as only the crowds lining up on the floor directly in front of them were able to, the monuments were for Queen Christina of Sweden, Maria Clementina Sobieska of Poland, and Matilda of the Canossa House of Tuscany. Of these three, Charlotte also pointed out that only Matilda's monument is an actual tomb, as the other two do not hold remains. And it didn't count that Queen Christina's remains were later moved to a place *above* her monument. Conscientious Charlotte's group smiled at the recent clarification they had been given concerning the difference between remains and relic.

"And now," Guide Charlotte actually smiled at her group, "those of you who wish, may climb the three hundred and twenty steps to the top of the dome."

"Be careful!" shouted the parents of the two teenagers, who had immediately turned and bolted up the steps. Other athletic, game members of the tour group also began to climb up the steps eagerly, if at a slower pace, toward the dome's top with its amazing view of the far flung city of Rome. The Rome Quartet was not among them nor were a few other staid members of the group. Instead they remained at the roof level for their equally stunning vistas. The mid-afternoon sunlight was at first almost blinding, but they soon adjusted and were all happily taking photos and panoramas of the Eternal City—*la città eterna*—so called because the ancient Romans believed that no matter what might happen in the world, Rome would continue to exist.

Proud Guide Charlotte allotted her group some fifteen generous minutes before rounding them up and leading them down in the much-appreciated elevator and back past the Sistine Chapel toward the great opening in the Vatican City wall from which they had entered the Eternal City—entered some three and a half hours earlier!

As they walked single file past Commander Charlotte of Bonelli Tours to board their waiting bus for the music concert ahead of them, each adult member of the group handed their knowledgeable, articulate guide one of the largest tips they had ever given.

103

Jared's visit to Hamburg to see Rachael Skylar on Sunday had proven most successful. They met at "her" Fanny and Felix Museum at ten o'clock that morning and first caught up on things concerning their personal lives. Rachael's darling five-year-old son Davyd, now reunited with his father—his Táto—back from the Ukraine and, along with his own refugee parents, had been transported to Rachael's home by Jared and he wanted to know how they had adjusted.

"It is wonderful the way father and son have reconnected and how doting Davyd's grandparents have become over their little grandson," Rachael told Jared happily.

Then they turned to equally delightful Mendelssohn business. Rachael told Jared proudly that her museum attendance was continuing to grow and that she had finally had a chance to visit Salomon Mendelssohn at his retirement home just outside the city. Their animated, mutually helpful meeting had lasted almost three hours!

Jared told Rachael about meeting another descendant of the Mendelssohn dynasty: Salomon's third cousin, Nathan Bartholdy. He described Nathan's apartment home in the Jewish quarter of Rome and the double physical attacks and painting thefts the poor man had gone through. Thank goodness the thieves were apprehended by the police and both paintings—the one original, and the other a copy of the original—had been returned to him undamaged. In fact Signor Bartholdy had agreed to sell the original to Jared and it would be featured in an exhibition he was about to stage at his Mendelssohn Complex. The New Yorker did not reveal the price his Complex had paid for the painting and discreet Rachael did not inquire.

"And can you guess of whom the portrait was?" Jared had asked Rachael. She had spread her hands out and answered that with his luck it could be an unknown portrait of Moses Mendelssohn! Hastening to disabuse her of that exciting idea, he gave his friend the identity: Fanny! A portrait from her later years by the well-known eighteenth-century painter Moritz Daniel Oppenheim—no, not a relative although he would welcome that august connection—in which for the one and only time the hunchback-caused disparity between her shoulder height was boldly shown.

"Amazing!" Rachael had responded. "Is that what you have in this package wedded to your right arm?"

Jared had laughed, then explained things, concluding with a detailed narration of the exciting events that had occurred at Caffè Greco the day before concerning his recognizing the unidentified portrait as being that of young Felix, and afterward, the neo-Nazi attempted attack on the painting. Rachael's astonished excitement had been almost palpable.

And then Jared had finally unwrapped the Felix portrait he had spotted at the Greco, holding it up proudly in front of Rachael. She was flabbergasted.

"No wonder you asked me to have my museum photographer on hand when we met here," she had marveled. "I'll tell him to join us now."

Closeups and details of the charming work were taken and Jared told Rachael that he would be happy to make the portrait one of their first exchange loan swaps. Such a benefit for both their institutions!

But then came another surprise: Rachael found herself joining the exhibition excitement and proclaimed: "In that case, I'd like to loan to the Mendelssohn Complex the small portrait drawing we have here of Felix: you know, the closeup of his face around the year eighteen thirty-five that Wilhelm Hensel made."

This, and dinner with Rachael's family, was how Jared's successful Sunday trip to Hamburg ended. He could hardly wait to call Megan the next day and give her the good news before he caught his Monday evening plane back to Rome, where he would make sure the Nathan Bartholdy Fanny portrait was picked up, crated, and was ready to be loaded into the cargo section of his evening flight to New York.

104

Bonelli Tours' yellow bus was awaiting the Rome Quartet as they passed through the Viale Vaticano gates. The ride to their next event—the "church opera concert"—took only ten minutes or so. The late nineteenth-century Chiesa Evangelica Valdese was indeed "in the heart of Rome," as the tour Sire had booked for them advertised. Located at the beginning of Via IV Novembre, it was halfway between the Pantheon to the west and the Colosseum to the east. The rather stark interior was not yet full when their tour group entered and took seats in those wooden pews closest as possible to the front. Megan was tickled that flat, red cushions were provided. Although there was a fine pipe organ above the apse in the small church, it was clear that the instrument to be used for the church opera concert was going to be the Fazioli grand piano standing to the left of the altar. Apparently only two vocalists would be performing, at least as suggested by the two chairs in line with the piano on the right and facing the audience. On each red cushion in the pews was a program sheet, and as Megan read it, she was impressed by the array of aria offerings. They ranged from Albinoni and Vivaldi to Verdi and Puccini.

Also on the program were a few Neapolitan songs; those melodious dialect songs were something near and dear to Megan's heart since, in her long-ago folk singing days in San Francisco when she was in her mid-twenties, she had learned and performed them on her twelve-string guitar at a long- since disappeared local venue. It was after that short career as a folk singer that she earned her master's degree at the University of California Berkeley, where and when the universe of Gustav Klimt and Egon Schiele encompassed her, dictating her future profession and life in art.

But that was then and this was now!

The Evangelical church had filled and three musicians walked to their places: a male pianist, who took his seat at the Fazioli, and two vocalists—most likely a soprano and a tenor. It was sad, Megan thought, how there is not much solo repertoire for baritones and bassos; a bit more for contraltos, but on the whole, sopranos and tenors won the day. And so it was here. The church acoustics were impressive, the two singers likable and excellent, and the piano pleasing, with the bass notes in particular standing out as being brighter than one might expect. The duets received the greatest applause and the single encore was the popular two-minute duet from Verdi's *Rigoletto,* "*È il sol dell›anima, la vita è amore.*"

The Bonelli tour guests were then rounded up for the final event: dinner at a "typical Italian restaurant nearby." And it was truly nearby; no bus needed, just a short walk to the Pasta and Social International House, a large and lively establishment where they ordered from a tempting menu of intricate pastas, unusual pizzas, flamboyant salads, and, as Bonelli Tours had stated, "limitless wine." Their dependable yellow bus was still in front of the church when the group finished some hour and a half later and they were dropped off where they had started—Via degli Scipioni, number nine. The Rome Quartet broke up into duos and returned by metro to their respective hotels. What a a fulfilling experience—Michelangelo's unforgettable frescoes; six intriguing women buried in Saint Peter's; the spooky, history-filled grottoes; and the mesmerizing dome vistas of the Eternal City spread out before them!

Thank you, Fanny Mendelssohn Hensel!

(Even if you did not mention art.)

105

When Megan woke up at seven-thirty Monday morning, her last full day in Italy before flying back to Dallas, she suddenly remembered her promise to call Nathan Bartholdy before leaving Rome. Oh dear! He must think I didn't remember. Which is true. But let me make up for it now. She stole a look at Tina: she was still sleeping. Skipping her beloved exercises, Megan stepped out onto their bedroom's small balcony, closing the glass door quietly behind her to make the call without waking her sister.

Nathan answered immediately; seven o'clock was already late for him. He usually arose at six in the morning. Delight animated his face when he saw the caller ID.

"Ah, Megan! There you are! I thought you'd forgotten about me."

"You wouldn't believe how busy we've been, Nathan, since we saw you last. And this evening our dear Jared departs Rome for New York with not only your superb portrait of Fanny, but also a smaller one of a very juvenile Felix."

"Yes, all is good with the shipment of my, or rather the Mendelssohn Complex's Fanny portrait; in fact, Mancini Aerotrasporto just called to say their men are arriving for pickup at eight this morning. But tell me: what has kept you and Jared so busy?"

Megan narrated for Nathan the exciting events that had taken place during her and Jared's visit to the Caffè Greco and the glorious aftermath of the loan of the young, mustached Felix. Nathan was intrigued, then shocked by the attempted attack on the portrait, and finally very pleased by the conclusion of Megan's narration with the loan of the Caffè Greco's Felix portrait for the Mendelssohn Complex exhibition.

“I will send you a photo of it soon,” she promised a delighted Nathan.

“And now I have a piece of Mendelssohn news to give you,” he said.

“Oh my gosh! What?”

“I am leaving Rome at the end of the month and joining my third cousin in Hamburg, Salomon Mendelssohn!”

“Ah, what a wonderful idea! A visit to your relative whom you’ve never seen is just the right medicine after what you’ve gone through here.”

“But you do not understand, Megan. This is not a visit. I am *joining*, as I said, Salomon. I will be living in a vacated apartment on the floor beneath his apartment in the assisted living facility where he lives, he assures me, with a fabulous view of the Elbe.” Megan’s jaw dropped as she gasped with amazement.

“What a surprise,” was all she could find to say at first. She wasn’t sure if this was a good idea. What a world he would be leaving behind if he were to move to Germany. His parents, his grandparents had made their home in Rome and it had always been his as well. How could he just suddenly up and leave? Then she thought about it a bit more. The double invasion of his home, the physical attacks on his person, and the two robberies had dramatically changed his world and drastically so. What must it be like for him to continue living where his home had been invaded, sabotaged twice? And did he still have any actual friends? Hadn’t he said something about outliving all his friends here in Rome? As she pondered, Megan began to understand how a move to Germany, back to his roots, might present a healthy environment and permanent distraction for Nathan. The company of an actual relative could be stimulating as well as anchoring. And he wouldn’t have to deal with undependable cleaning women or noisy food deliveries in a senior living establishment. No, this sounded like a perfect next stage in life for the man. And she said so.

“Nathan. I think you have made a wise and excellent decision. And one that could well prolong your presence here on this planet.”

“Well, thank you, Megan. I am glad you agree. Rome is a totally different city to me now. I feel threatened and vulnerable here. And I have genuine curiosity about meeting Salomon. We’ve been having very long, wonderful phone conversations ever since I made up my mind to do this. He’s such an interesting man!”

"I can certainly second that. When I visited him last week our conversations covered a hundred different subjects. He is a fountain of knowledge and knows so much about your common ancestors. And you will most likely meet the director of the new Fanny and Felix Mendelssohn Museum there in Hamburg, Rachael Skylar. She is a kind and fascinating person, totally dedicated to the history and works of your ancestors."

"What you say, Megan, only encourages me that I have made the correct decision. Now tell me: what else has our indefatigable friend Jared been up to?"

"Well, he visited Hamburg again yesterday to confer with Rachael Skylar and he'll be flying back to the States from Rome late this evening."

"Ah. Perhaps he will be giving me a call before he goes."

"He might well do so." Megan immediately resolved to suggest that to Jared, depending on when they got in contact. She had no idea what time he'd be flying back to Rome today.

There was a sudden tap on Megan's balcony's glass door. It was a sleepy looking Tina and she was holding up her cellphone so her sister could see. On the screen was a live look at their dogs playing with each other after midnight at Bill's house. His two Chins had joined in the fray and it was just charming to watch all six doggies chase each other. Megan signaled she would be coming inside as soon as she could. Nathan's voice sounded again.

"Megan, it's been just wonderful talking with you and catching up on things. I hope we will continue to be in contact when you're back in Dallas."

"Most certainly, Nathan. Just be sure to give me your new phone number when you relocate to Hamburg!"

After they had said their goodbyes, Megan joined Tina inside and the two sisters continued to watch their doggies at play for another five enchanted minutes before they began getting dressed for breakfast. The special activity for their last day in Italy had been planned out well in advance and carefully coordinated with Mary and Sire, who would be picking them up in a rental car at ten o'clock for a final Fanny-related activity.

Megan's cellphone rang again and, only half-dressed, she hurried out of the bathroom to get it. Most likely it was Nathan wanting to tell her something he'd forgotten to say. She picked up without looking at the ID.

"Hello again," she said cheerfully.

"Again? I've only just called you now!" Jared's deep voice proclaimed.

"How wonderful! I thought it was Nathan Bartholdy calling back after we'd just finished catching up; thought, perhaps, he had something more to say. Where are you? Still in Hamburg?"

"Nope. I'm in Rome; touched down at Fiumicino about thirty minutes ago and have checked on the status of Nathan's Fanny portrait. It's being picked up from Nathan's place just about now and will be boxed into a sturdy case and ready for loading onto my evening flight. What are you all up to on your last day?"

"Let me ask you a question first. What time, again, did you say is your flight this evening?"

"Nine o'clock. Why?"

"And what do you plan to do in Rome today?"

"Haven't thought about it yet. Of course I'd love to be with you guys again."

"Ah ha! That's exactly why I'm asking you questions. How'd you like to join us on a very special Fanny outing? We'll be driving a rental car this time and we're off to the small city of Terracina, a beach town where she, her husband, and son stayed overnight on their way from Rome to visit Naples."

"Terracina. That's one Italian site I've never been to. How long a drive is it and what is it?"

"Well, it's exactly halfway from here down to Naples, so about seventy miles. It should take us only about an hour and a half at a good speed to get there. And guess what road we will be taking?"

"The Via Appia?"

"You got it! The Via Appia—Europe's first super highway and now Italy's national road Appia SS seven, direct from Rome to Terracina on the sea. Fanny wrote that they were building a harbor when she was there. Driving on that two-thousand-year-old historic route could be worth the trip by itself! So, Jared, my dear, would you like to come with us?"

"Try and stop me. What time are you all leaving?"

"Mary and Sire are picking us up at our hotel at ten this morning.

And you certainly know how to get to your former hotel here!"

"Sure do. Have you and Tina had breakfast yet? I'm starving."

"Then come join us! One last yogurt health breakfast of your trip. We're still getting dressed, but will certainly be at the roof restaurant by the time you get here from the airport."

"*Perfetto*. The Rome Quintet reunites again!"

"Oh, that's right. Our Rome Quintet will be together again. Neat!"

"Gwad, Megan, you are so old-fashioned, saying 'neat' like that."

"What would you suggest to make me up-to-date?"

"How about 'awesome'?"

"Yuck. No. Sorry, can't do that; it cheapens the word."

"See you *prestissimo* then," said the savvy, contemporary musician.

"*Al più presto* then," said the old-fashioned art and music historian.

As soon as they had hung up, a frowning Tina came out of the bathroom to confront her sister.

"You invited *Jared* to join us on the drive to Terracino?"

"Yes. So what's wrong with that? I thought you liked him."

"I do like him. I like him a lot. That's not the problem. Don't you realize how *tall* Jared is? Over six feet. He'll need to sit in front with Sire. That'll mean us three short females have to sit in a crowded back seat."

"Oh, come on now, Tina. That's not so bad for such a short trip. Just an hour and a half. Isn't it more important that Jared can actually come with us to Terracino?"

"Of course. Hurry up and finish dressing. We've got to get going if you want to have one of your famous 'relaxed' breakfasts."

Ten minutes later found the sisters ensconced at their favorite table on the hotel roof with healthy food on their plates and hunger pangs in remission. Twenty minutes later found Jared sitting with them bolting down a fruit, cereal, and yogurt breakfast like Megan's, while telling them about his genial and successful visit with Rachael Skylar.

"And she actually lent you one of her museum's images of Felix for your exhibition?" asked an impressed Tina, trying not to access openly just exactly how tall Jared was. Probably six foot-two.

"Yes she did. It's Wilhelm Hensel's closeup drawing of his young brother-in-law's face when Felix was around twenty-six or so. It's quite a commanding portrait, catching the young composer's intensity as well as his dark good looks. Pretty interesting, huh?"

"Certainly is, Jared. And I have something interesting to tell *you*," smiled Megan.

"What's that?"

"I talked to Nathan Bartholdy earlier this morning and he told me some astonishing news about his future plans."

"Future plans?"

"Future plans, yes. He is leaving Rome, quitting Italy in fact, and is moving to Hamburg."

"Wow! *Why?*"

"Makes sense if you think about it. He's moving into the senior residence where Salomon Mendelssohn lives. They're third cousins, after all. It should be wonderful for both of them as they find out how much family history they have in common."

"Oh, I see. Well, that makes sense. Rome can only have bad memories for him now and this way he'd have company he can trust."

Megan glanced at the time.

"Well, fellow travelers, if we want to be downstairs when Mary and Sire pull up at ten, we'd better go down to our room for one last hurrah." Tina nodded agreement and asked Jared if he'd like to use their bathroom before they did.

"So kind, but I'll say hello to the one downstairs off the lobby and shall be waiting outside in front of the hotel in case they get here early. They'll be pretty surprised to see me, I bet."

"Perfect. See you very soon," Megan answered.

All went as planned—Mary and Sire were delighted to see Jared again—and soon the Rome Quintet was off in a beautiful Peugeot 5008 heading for the Appian Way, now the national Appia SS 7, to Terracina. Their swank rental car had three comfortable seats in the rear and Jared offered to sit in the middle one in order to be "between my two beauties," Megan and Mary. A happily surprised Tina sat in front with genial Sire at the wheel. All occupants were content and had plenty of leg and head room. Megan began singing a Neapolitan song quietly to herself. Too bad, she thought, we're not going on to Naples the way Fanny, her husband, and little nine-year-old son Sebastian had in eighteen forty. But she only bemoaned this for an instant because the thought of that family reminded her of the brief mention Fanny had made of overnighting at Terracina in a letter home written in July of that year. I must read it out loud to everyone, she resolved. No sooner thought than done. She opened up her MacBook Air, found the pertinent letter, and enjoined her receptive fellow travelers to listen to what Fanny had written concerning Terracina:

> I was very sleepy, and should certainly have gone to sleep but for Sebastian, who watched me with Argus-eyes and never allowed me to indulge in the shortest nap. At Terracina, where we spent the night, the scenery becomes suddenly beautiful, with palm-trees, the sea, and grotesque rocks up which the town seems to climb. It has a decidedly more southern aspect than Rome, my own beloved Rome.... Terracina has a splendid hotel, actually on the sea, which when we arrived was sparkling in the last rays of the setting sun. A harbor is being built besides other things, so Terracina is actually the first town in which I have seen any building going on. We ate our supper, and fell asleep to the murmur of the sea.

"Is that all? Didn't she write anything more about Terracina?" a disappointed Mary asked.

"No, but that's enough. We're going to find that, quote, 'splendid hotel, actually on the sea' end quote."

"How are we going to do that?" Sire inquired, not taking his eyes off the road, which so far gave no glimpse of the vast Tyrrhenian Sea between Italy's west coast and Corsica and Sardinia.

"Actually, I already have. Unfortunately, Fanny's 'splendid' nineteenth-century hotel of eighteen forty exists no more. It was on the site of what is now Terracina's Grand Hotel Palace, erected in nineteen fifty-two and it really is, in Fanny's words, 'right on the sea.' Well, a few feet of beach from it. And, I hope you all agree, that's where we'll eat lunch after we've explored the town and its surroundings a bit through Fanny's eyes."

"What fun!" Jared exclaimed, tickled to have joined this suspenseful detective trip on behalf of his Mendelssohn Complex. Who knows what they might possibly discover? Mary announced a funny fact she'd just found on her phone about the modernized Appian Way they were on.

"Guess what! This stretch of SS 7 is called '*fettuccia di Terracina*' due to its straight line."

"Um, just the thought of it makes me hungry," Jared said, smacking his lips.

"*Hungry?* Why hungry?" asked Megan, frowning with incomprehension.

"Well...aren't we talking about pasta, like fettuccine Alfredo, which I absolutely adore?"

"Ha! No, hungry Jared. We're talking about *fettuccia*—which means ribbon. So the highway is stretched out like a ribbon, see?"

"No wonder I've never seen that word in any Italian aria."

More straight *fettuccia* miles, more small villages, none on the coast yet, but at last, when they made a long, left-hand swooping turn south, the sparkling Tyrrhenian Sea appeared on their right in all its glory! Almost immediately they sighted their destination, the ancient city of Terracina. A mighty, 656-foot-high cliff abruptly blocked one end of Terracina's natural, now modernized harbor all the way down to the sandy beach. The harbor had been used, aggrandized, and modernized repeatedly since ancient times—witness Fanny's 1840 comment about a harbor being built. And thanks to Emperor Trajan's desire to improve the route of the Via Appia by having the giant obstruction of the great Montano cliff cut 120 feet right into the rock to make passageway, the two-thousand-year-old road led right through the old town. Its minute, timeworn cathedral was densely hemmed in by narrow twisting streets, small houses with common walls, and a few larger buildings. Since Fanny's time the harbor had indeed been enlarged, not once but several times. It would have been possible to visit the ancient Temple of Jupiter high up on the cliff overlooking Terracina, but after walking along the modern harbor and beach fronts and exploring a few of the shops—"not with Fanny's eyes," remarked Tina—the Rome Quintet began to experience hunger pangs. They parked as closely as they could by the beach hotel, the Grand Hotel Palace, and made their way through a crowded and very noisy lobby to the capacious dining room lit by large windows overlooking the beach. At this time the restaurant was pretty full but an empty table for six was available next to one of the windows with its vast view of the sea. As they approached the table Mary stopped and pointed out something rather curious to her friends.

"Hey, look here. There are dinner mats on all these tables we're passing by and they all have the same identical black and white image on them, see? All with inscriptions reading, and I'll translate, 'Children cry when they leave our hotel. Please bring them back soon!'"

Megan came to a dead stop. She could not believe what she was looking at. Her eyes met Jared's. He, too, had stopped in his tracks. With wide eyes he silently nodded his head in confirmation of what his friend was thinking.

They were looking at, reproduced on every single dinner mat, a portrait sketch of a sobbing young boy. It was, unmistakably, a drawing of Fanny's nine-year-old son Sebastian, tears rolling down his cheeks! And it was obviously the work of his father, Wilhelm Hensel! How could this possibly be?

Wondering why two of their group were rooted to the spot at one of the vacant tables they had passed, Sire and Tina turned back.

"What's the matter?" asked Tina.

"Nothing. Everything is suddenly *wonderful!*" Megan laughed loud and long, clapping her hands in enthusiasm. Jared put his arm around his excited art historian friend and smiled gleefully at their mystified friends. Several waiters had stopped their work, worried something was wrong. And now the head waiter joined them.

Finally Megan pointed to one of the dinner mats and announced joyfully: "This weeping boy is the son of Fanny Mendelssohn Hensel and her husband Wilhelm Hensel."

Her extraordinary information fell on deaf ears. Who were these foreigners and why were they so excited about their hotel's signature table mat?

"Is your hotel director here?" Megan asked the head waiter.

"*Sì, sì Signora*, he is in his office."

"Please take us there immediately. This is very important!"

While three of the Rome Quintet remained discreetly behind, Megan and Jared followed the worried head waiter to the office of the hotel manager. He stood up from his desk immediately.

"How may I help you? I hope nothing is wrong?"

"On the contrary," Megan assured the perturbed man. "We are

here to ask if you know who is pictured on your dining room table mats?"

"Oh, our 'Crying Child'?"

"Yes," Jared emphasized.

"Well, we don't actually know who the boy is, but the large drawing was left here in one of the original hotel's rooms ages ago, back sometime in the first half of the nineteenth century, actually. The then owner, Signor Daniel Rossi, of this hotel, which was constructed on the site of the old one, thought right away that this wonderful, believable image could be used as unique publicity to urge our guests to return, and since so many of them bring children along, this image of a child weeping when he has to return home seemed perfect. As you can see, tears are streaming down his cheeks."

"Ah ha. Well, that was certainly good thinking. Is there any way you can put us into immediate contact with the present owner of your hotel?" Megan pressed.

"Definitely. Since its founding, the hotel has been family owned and the descendants live right here in Terracina. I can call them for you, if you like."

"Yes! Please! It's very important!" Megan's excitement was mounting. Perhaps the family still had the original.

Contact was made right away and a Signor Medad Finzi listened to Megan's words with growing interest. After identifying herself and Jared and their connection with the Mendelssohns, she identified the artist and his subject for Signor Finzi.

"So. Our crying child was drawn by a famous artist and husband of a famous composer! How very interesting." Megan's next question lunged at her interlocutor.

"You say 'our' crying child. Does this mean you own the original drawing?" She pressed Jared's arm tightly in suspense.

"Yes, my wife does and we have the original in our home. I could bring it over to the hotel for you to see, if you like." Megan's response was immediate.

"Oh, how kind of you! Yes. Please do bring it over if that is not too great an inconvenience."

"I can be there with it in about half an hour to forty-five minutes."

"Perfect. We'll be eating lunch in your hotel dining room by one of the vista windows. You can't miss us: we are a group of five. We drove down from Rome today specifically to find the hotel, well, the site of the hotel where the famous parents of your crying boy stayed along with their nine-year-old son. What incredible luck to encounter your table mats and learn that you have the poignant original!"

"I do agree. And I'll bring my wife. She will love to learn of this, since she inherited the picture from her parents, the owners of this hotel. It has been handed down by the Rossi family through generations."

Once seated at the window table, their food ordered, Jared and Megan explained the sequence of events to the three "left-outs." They were enchanted and became as eager to see the original drawing as the two sleuths.

"You know," meditated Sire, "if this drawing is as interesting as you say it is, perhaps you can get the owners to lend it to your exhibition in New York."

"My thought exactly!" a suddenly coughing Jared responded, trying to control his excitement. "I'm just hoping it's in good condition."

Time passed quickly; in fact the group had just finished paying their lunch bill when, in only a little over half an hour, the Quintet saw a widely smiling woman and man approaching them, obviously the couple they were expecting. But neither one carried the work of art with them.

"Hello. I am Devora Rossi Finzi," said the woman extending her hand to Megan and Jared and nodding at the others, "What you have identified for us as Sebastian Mendelssohn Hensel's portrait awaits you with joy in our office upstairs."

Introductions were made quickly as the seven people walked to an elevator around the corner, took it, and exited on the hotel's top floor. As they entered the sizable Finzi office another stunning vista of the shimmering sea greeted them and the distinct outlines of the Pontine Islands could be seen in the distance--islands temptingly beckoning to Terracina tourists who had felt overwhelmed by the prodigious numbers of noisy fellow tourists.

The framed portrait sketch by Hensel of his young son lay on a conference table facing them. And the Finzis watched with pride as their guests reverently circled around the table studying the tender portrait with hushed attention. The drawing was in excellent condition.

A bust portrait, the boy was shown holding onto his shirt collar and pulling it forward with both fists. His distress was also expressed by his lips clamped together, the lower one protruding downwards. Tears rolled down his cheeks, his eyelids were squeezed almost closed, and a great frown furrowed his forehead. Handsome locks of long, dark curly hair fell to his little shoulders.

This was indeed a summary of sadness and Sebastian's artist father was obviously compelled to record it. Perhaps he hoped that concentration on the task of sitting still for a portrait might divert his son's thoughts. But obviously not. Perhaps it was the recorded moment of his child's unhappiness that was responsible, in the rush to depart for Naples the next morning, for the drawing's having been left behind in the hotel room. At least that was the explanatory theory Megan expressed to the Finzis.

"Was Sebastian's father famous as a painter?" asked Devora.

"Yes, quite well known and admired in his time. Early in his career he was sent to Rome to copy some of Raphael's works for the Berlin court. He was the royal court painter to King Friedrich Wilhelm the Third, and his special interest was in portraiture—he executed more than a thousand drawings; many of them are of his famous family circle."

"And what about his and Fanny's son Sebastian? Did he grow up to be famous too?" Medad Finzi probed, his interest in the art work growing by the minute.

"Not in the same way his parents were. But he was successful in life and lived a long time. He was born in eighteen thirty and died just two years before the beginning of the twentieth century, in eighteen ninety-eight." Megan was happy to be able to fill in the details for the Finzis.

"Just how was our Sebastian 'successful'?" Devora Finzi wanted to know more details of the boy's life. "Perhaps he was in the hotel business?"

"Ha! Late in life, yes, actually! But first let me tell you the three given names of this boy in your portrait because they were the given names of the three composers most respected by his parents. His full name was Sebastian, for Johann *Sebastian* Bach, Ludwig, for *Ludwig* van Beethoven, and Felix, for his uncle *Felix* Mendelssohn. Interesting, huh?"

"Yes, yes," agreed the unmusical hotel owner Devora Finzi. "But what was he successful in, then? You said 'yes' in regard to hotels."

"Quite right. I did, didn't I? Well, after a career in agriculture, he joined a hotel and construction company and in eighteen seventy-five he was responsible for building the grand Hotel Kaiserhof in Berlin."

"My god! What a *connection* we have with this boy!" exploded a delighted Devora to her beaming, wide-eyed husband.

"Right!" he replied, then contributed what he considered an extraordinary link.

"And there's another connection. My middle name is Mendel—a nickname for the Jewish name 'Menachem' which means one who provides comfort. So this crying child we have here is the son of Fanny *Mendel*ssohn Hensel, and I am, have been, and will be his comforter!"

Every person in the room nodded with surprised pleasure.

"Tell me, Dotoressa Crespi and Signor Oppenheim," demanded Devora, "whatever can I and my husband do to repay you for giving us this fascinating and important information that will add even more interest in our restaurant's table mats? Especially after we hang the identified portrait in the lobby with an explanation of the circumstances underlying the charming image. So please, what can we do for *you*? A free week here at our hotel, perhaps?" Megan and Jared laughed simultaneously.

"A lovely idea," explained Megan, "but we are both about to return to America: Jared this evening, and I with my friends and sister tomorrow. But thank you. So generous of you both. *However,* there is a greater, if temporary, gift you and Signor Finzi could accord us for a short period of time. Jared, why don't you explain to them?"

"Gladly. Signora and Signor Finzi, perhaps you remember how I introduced myself to you as a scholar of the Mendelssohn family in Germany. Explained more fully, I am the director of a unique cultural institution in New York City called the 'Mendelssohn Complex'—at once an archive, a library, a museum, and a musical performance venue for works by the two great Mendelssohn composers, Fanny and Felix. You may know Felix Mendelssohn from the famous and enchanting *Wedding March* recessional he composed." He hummed a few notes from it and was immediately joined by the other members of the Rome Quintet.

"How very nice," responded the Italian couple, who knew little of the German composers.

"Thank you," said Jared. "But what is even nicer is that, in a few weeks, an exhibition with daily musical performances will be held at my institution featuring the entire Mendelssohn clan, beginning with the overpowering grandfather Moses Mendelssohn, one of the greatest philosophers of the European Enlightenment. We would then progress by way of Fanny Mendelssohn and Wilhelm Hensel down to, *should you generously agree*, your Sebastian. What a climax for the exhibition if your portrait of the child were to be seen and admired in America and publicized by the American press and television! So might you consider. . ."

"*Sì, sì,* we do lend you Sebastian portrait for America!" interrupted an eager Devora. An equally excited Medad confirmed and echoed his wife's pronouncement, motioning Jared and Megan to sit down at the office conference table. He turned to the other three members of the group from America and apologized for not having more chairs.

"Not a problem at all," responded Mary for the group. We will leave you to your business and be awaiting our friends in the lobby. Good?"

"*Perfecto*," responded the Finzis with one voice.

After the trio had left the office, Jared got right down to business. He showed the Finzis photographs, newspaper articles, and documents concerning his Mendelssohn Complex to put them at ease concerning their loan. He also showed them the other three images from European loans he would be exhibiting along with their Sebastian portrait: the Nathan Bartholdy oil portrait of Fanny done around 1847, the small oil image of a youthful Felix from the Caffè Greco, and the one of a slightly older Felix from Hamburg's Fanny and Felix Mendelssohn Museum.

All this put the Finzis at ease and a loan contract was printed from an email attachment Jared immediately sent to Medad's office. The necessary signatures were attended to on the spot. Medad would see to it immediately that the local packing firm's employees come to the hotel as soon as possible to wrap up the framed Sebastian portrait on the spot, thus enabling Jared to drive it back to Rome with him later that afternoon and then on to the airport for his nine o'clock flight to America and New York. The professionally wrapped portrait should be ready within the next two hours.

“What is the latest time you could leave Terracina for your return to Rome?” Medad asked. Megan calculated the time it had taken to reach Terracina from Rome.

“It’s an hour-and-a-half drive back and Jared has to be at the airport by at least seven o’clock for his nine o’clock flight this evening So we should be leaving here at five, let’s say.”

“Fine, then,” said Devora. “It is only two o’clock now. So while my husband and I are waiting for the packers to arrive, might I make a suggestion concerning a wonderful way for you and your friends to spend the remainder of your time here?” Devora asked.

“Of course! What do you have in mind?” responded Megan.

“You may have noticed that Terracina is packed to the brim with cats and tourists right now. And that they are both eager, noisy, and pushy.”

Megan couldn’t help laughing in immediate agreement concerning the cats, which were as much in evidence around Terracina as they had been in Rome.

“So what I would recommend you do now is to allow our genial Gian Giorgio, captain of our hotel’s power yacht—it’s an Italian-made, one eighteen WallyPower—to ferry you out to the remarkable little island of Ponza, which you can see from the window behind Medad’s desk there. It’s just twenty-one miles south of us.”

Jared and Megan walked eagerly over to the window to focus on the dazzling, palm-tree-speckled ocean view which clearly showed the isand, the largest of its archipelago. Smiling at their enthusiasm, Devora continued speaking.

“Ponza is a volcanic outcrop, and it’s by far the most interesting of the several islands you can see. It has dolphins, it has blue grottoes, *and* it has Egyptian, Greek, Etruscan, and Roman ruins—actually the island has been inhabited since neolithic times. You can get a tremendous view of everything from the terrace of our rival there, the grand Hotel Chiaia di Luna. So! Our super-fast power yacht is at your ate disposal: it is a forty-five minute ride versus the hour and fifteen minutes the public ferries take, and our wonderful captain will dock in the small harbor from which it is literally just a few dozen steps up to the famous little red-domed, yellow-and-white church of Saints Silverio and Domitilla. It has a rich, image-laden interior, if that is of interest. You can stay as long as you like on Ponza; our yacht will be waiting for you at the same place where you have docked. What do you say? Spend an hour or even two hours there and when you return, our little Sebastian will be ready to travel with you."

It was difficult to determine whether Megan or Jared was the more excited by the island-visit offer and after saying a temporary goodbye to the kind-hearted Finzi couple, they immediately took the private elevator down to the noisy lobby to meet Tina, Mary, and Sire. They weren't anywhere to be seen at first, at least not relaxing on one of the upholstered chairs, all of which were taken, with sometimes two people to a chair. And then Megan spotted the trio. They were standing near the reception counter, eyeing the main elevators. And in fact they had seen and were already waving at Megan and Jared. Meeting in the middle of the lobby they exchanged hugs as though they had been separated for days, not minutes.

"It's so loud in here we couldn't hear ourselves talk," Tina told them.

"Wide-eyed tourists are swarming all over this place," added Mary.

"And most of them are American!" Sire exclaimed. Megan looked at Jared questioningly and he eagerly nodded. Megan announced the exciting news.

"All right, kiddos, what say we escape the terrible Terracina tourists and zip over to the island of Ponza in what the Finzis have offered us: their hotel's private power yacht. And the captain will wait for us until we decide to return to the mainland."

Elated yeses exploded and off they went. They crossed the hotel beach and hurried toward the sizable, slim, three-level power yacht tied up at its own pier. A wooden gangplank was in place and an obviously informed white-haired, grinning captain was gesticulating to them. Megan stopped to tell him that her first boyfriend when she was a student in Perugia was named Gian Giorgio—a piece of information that ignited a lively conversation between the two of them as to the beauty of that double first name. Minutes later the Rome Quintet was comfortably seated in a small, twelve-person, mid-level lounge with white leather couches and black glass housing through which the gentle heaving of the turquoise Tyrrhenian Sea could clearly be seen and scrutinized. What a change from the Via Appia!

The power yacht lounge had two large, blue-framed white

documents on one of the walls and a curious Mary sprang up to take a read. The first document's text was geared to fans of classic movies and aggrandizers of Ponza's fame: it presented a list of celebrities who had vacationed on the island and included both Kirk Douglas and his son Michael Douglas, Anthony Quinn, Burt Lancaster, Gina Lollobrigida, Elsa Martinelli, and Sophia Loren. Furthermore, Jacques Cousteau and his son Philippe Cousteau had filmed several documentaries in the Ponza area. Federico Fellini's *Satyricon* of 1969 was filmed on Ponza. Mary read the cast of stars out loud to her friends.

The second document offered a brief history of the four islands of the western part of the Pontine archipelago of which Ponza was the largest. After the Second World War, informed the document, the island was transformed from a place of confinement to a holiday destination. The final sentence read "Ponza's economy is based essentially on fishing and summer tourism."

Well, I'm certainly not going to tell my group that last bit! Mary told herself, as she returned to her seat. A further thought occurred to her: at least cats weren't mentioned!

In time Ponza, the entire area of which was only 4.2 square miles, appeared closer and closer until at last the 118 WallyPower yacht pulled up at the island's extended harbor, dotted with moored motorboats and yachts of all sizes. Two large ferries and two big hydrofoils were docked further out. Captain Gian Giorgio miraculously found a spot in the inner harbor opposite the long flight of stairs leading up to the right of the little yellow-and-white church of Saints Silverio and Domitilla. The small houses and low buildings rising up alongside the church were in many colors: pink, red, blue, yellow, gold, and white.

Mary, Sire, and Megan were gung-ho to see the church interior, which Signora Devora had recommended, whereas Tina and Jared stated their preference for exploring the streets and photographing views of what appealed to them on land and sea. Mainland Terracina appeared small on the horizon now but the other three islands of the archipelago were much closer and deserving of at least photographic attention. They agreed to meet again at the front of the church in half an hour. Then all would explore further together, perhaps climb up to the top, where the tightly packed residential houses and buildings line the upper town to the left of the cozy inner harbor. The view ought to be breathtaking.

The interior of the small church with its proud little dome was indeed enchanting. Against dazzlingly white walls and flat pillars were displayed life-size figures of saints in the round and painted images of all sorts of animals and birds. Behind a simple altar was a great arch with a black background against which a life-size painted crucified Christ sent streaks of gold down to the altar level. The multiplicity of lively interwoven animal and plant wall images and the compound presence of painted figures in the round added to the busy yet somehow serene atmosphere of the church interior. Megan was especially was surprised and delighted. She thought she had seen every type of church interior over her many years of travel, but no, this one was enchantingly different. The thirty-minute deadline came before any of the trio had stopped admiring the unique, diminutive church. But it was time to meet Tina and Jared and they exited the church just as the duo appeared. Both were smiling broadly.

"We were in a fascinating cemetery!" called Tina. Jared added his take.

"Yes. Hundreds of miniature gravestones compete for space; it's quite a sight!"

"Sounds creepy. Glad I didn't go with you," Mary said. "The church interior was a real treat. So inventive and comforting somehow."

"Shall we follow through on Megan's idea of exploring the streets and houses that wind up to that big white box of a building on top where we'll be able to spot Terracina?" asked Jared, the youngest and most vigorous of the group.

Upon seeing eager nods all around, he turned and led the way up the narrow, winding road. Mary and Sire followed, holding hands, with Tina and Megan bringing up the rear.

Almost all the little houses, painted in various bright colors, had earth-packed terraces devoted to crops like grapes, cactus pears, and even fig trees. Because, when they got higher, car traffic was non-existent as the "streets" were made of six-inch-high stone steps, children were everywhere with their chatting mothers close-by. Now and then snatches of song filled the air. Jared stopped briefly at an intersection to ask one of the women which was the better direction to take to get to the white building on top of the hill.

"The white gymnasium? Just continue going straight ahead; do not take the turn."

"'White gymnasium?' Is that what the building is?"

"Yes, It used to be a construction company but the town would not approve their building plans so they left. Now it is just used as a gym, and even that not very often."

Their cheerful expectancy ended all of a sudden when the Rome Quintet reached the rectangular white building atop the hill that had been their goal. Sitting on top of another white building of two floors, its exterior was cracked and what had seemed a commanding white from a distance was merely a thin, peeling overlay on an underlay of yellow. The walls of the building were hosts to cobwebs. And the front of the three-story building facing them had an off-center dilapidated entrance that looked unused as it sat atop the lower two-story edifice in which a door opened onto the narrow street where they stood. The only hint that the building was in use was a tall television antenna on the streetside top of the flat roof. On their climb upward the group had seen that a large terrace facing the sea was on the second level's opposite side.

So the building itself was a disappointment, but if they turned to their left they still had a view. And it was everything they had imagined it would be: spectacular. It seemed as if the whole southern coast, not just of Terracina, but of Italy was within sight. All five of the group fell silent as, fanning out a bit, each began photographing.

Their congenial silence was abruptly broken.

From within the white building complex a thundering series of shouts suddenly sounded. Men's voices were yelling a slogan over and over again: "*Va bene essere bianchi!*—It's all right to be white!"

"*What?*" asked an incredulous, disgusted Sire, recognizing the Italian neo-Nazi slogan designed to spark racial hatred. "Can such a thing be happening here in peaceful Ponza?"

Instinctively the five friends regrouped, staring at the white gymnasium. It was being used not for gymnastics but as a conference center for Italian neo-Nazis! The voices within burst into song and the five friends could not believe their ears. It was the official hymn of the Italian National Fascist Party—'*Giovinezza*'—'Youth.'

Giovinezza, giovinezza,
Per la vita, nell'asprezza
Il tuo canto squilla e va!

E per Benito Mussolini,
Eja eja alalà
E per la nostra Patria bella,
Eja eja alalà

Youth, youth,
For life,
In the harshness
Your song blasts and goes!
And for Benito Mussolini
Hooray, hooray, hoorah
And for our beautiful fatherland
Hooray, hooray, hoorah!

"My god," Mary hissed at the paralyzed group, "that's the Fascist national anthem Toscanini refused to conduct at Italian musical events during Mussolini's time and for which he was beaten up by a group of Blackshirts. That's why he fled to America!"

"I've got to get a better look at all this," said Sire, impetuously starting to walk toward the street level entrance door of the building. The intrepid photographer of Ukrainian destruction was certainly not going to lose a chance to document this Italian horror.

"Wait! I'm going with you!" Jared caught up with him. All of a sudden the three women were left on their own, shaking their heads in anger at the foolhardiness of their two male companions. A minute later Sire and Jared disappeared inside the gymnasium and two minutes after that the sound of a man's loud shouting could be heard coming from within. The gist of the angry words was understandable.

"That's the American man who helped attack me at Caffè Greco in Rome! Grab him! Throw him out of here and with a black eye he'll remember! And get that old man with him too!"

Minutes later a staggering and cursing Jared, one hand to his left eye, was flung onto the street by two men wearing Blackshirts. Limping behind him was a disheveled Sire. A third man appeared just behind him. It was Arlotto Zitto, the neo-Fascist who had attempted to throw coffee on the Felix portrait at the Caffè Greco! He and Megan recognized each other at the same moment.

"Grab that woman too!" he yelled to his companions, pointing to her: "She was also at Greco!"

A cursing Tina valiantly attempted to stop the men who were roughly forcing her sister to the ground, but to no avail. Instead they pushed her down as well. Then Mary tried to intervene with words.

"Stop! These people have done nothing against you! Let them go! Please!" There were no witnesses. No one would be coming to help. Now Mary was also attacked and pushed to the ground.

"Bring them all inside!" yelled Arlotto Zitto. "We know how to deal with types like these stupid foreigners. These *tourists*. We'll give them something to gape at!"

A sudden loud, whirring noise caught the attention of everyone. It was getting louder by the second and it came from above. Eight people—five hostages and three attackers—looked skywards. The increasingly deafening motor they all heard was that of a helicopter, the label *Polizia* on its side. It was setting down on the roof of the building just opposite the white gymnasium. The three neo-Fascists made a desperate dash back to the gym's entrance and disappeared inside as a unit of five policemen slid down their building's multi-balconied façade to the ground. They ran toward the entrance of the five-story structure facing them and moments later gunshots sounded from inside the white gymnasium. Then silence. Some seventy persons were being rounded up.

The sixth helicopter passenger walked to the five terrified tourists in front of him. He was a tall, noticeably thin man in police uniform.

"Everyone! Attention, please. I am Cesari Cacciatore, Rome's Chief of Police. You are safe now! You are all safe. The Terracina police called us after a power yacht captain docked here at Ponza alerted them when he noticed an unusual number of large vessels anchored in the outer harbor that had ferried crowds of neo-Fascists over to Ponza. He was worried on account of his five hotel passengers, afraid that as foreigners, they might be harassed by the swarm of troublemakers. His description of the five of you was certainly exact. Except for you, Signore. He did not mention a black eye. I presume that was a gift from one of the scoundrels my men are arresting."

Jared nodded weakly.

"Now if you will all kindly give me your names and cyber contact information, since you do not live in Italy, we will keep in touch with you. We may have to record testimony from you but that can be done via Zoom. So please do not worry. And these neo-Fascists animals will get what they deserve, never fear."

After the requested information had been noted down by the reassuring police chief, he stopped at one name.

"Megan Crespi. Aren't you the former professor of Alessandro Divitore?"

"Yes, I am," Megan gasped. "But how could you possibly know that?"

"Because he is a close friend of mine and he told me you were in Rome and that he had visited with you a couple of times."

"For heaven's sake! Please tell him what's happened and how we met, won't you?"

"But of course. He'll be frightened at first but then delighted, as he realizes this is an example of what he's always saying about you—that this is a typical Crespi adventure."

He turned to the other four people grouped around him.

"Now, you have all been through a frightening and fatiguing situation. I shall transport all of you down to the harbor where your worried Captain Gian Giorgio awaits you and will ferry you back to Terracina."

"*Terracina!*" gasped Jared and Megan at the same time. They had completely forgotten about the Sebastian portrait. And what was the time now? Both checked and uttered sighs of relief. It was only a little after three-thirty. Enough time to get back to Grand Hotel Palace, pick up the Finzis' packaged Sebastian portrait and then get back to Rome in time for Jared's flight. What a day!

All went exactly as planned: the Sebastian portrait was ready, they were in Rome by six, and had dropped a thankful, excited Jared off at Fiumicino airport well before seven. The exhausted, remaining Rome Quartet agreed to split up for dinner at their respective hotel rooftop restaurants. Conversation was the last thing all were up to and deep sleep was calling to them. But what a day! As with Kirk and Michael Douglas, Anthony Quinn, Burt Lancaster, Gina Lollobrigida, Elsa Martinelli, Sophia Loren, Jacques and Philippe Cousteau, and Federico Fellini, the island of Ponza would never be forgotten!

EPILOGUE

Exactly one month to the day after members of the Rome Quintet had returned from Italy to America, *The New York Times* published a short review of a remarkable event. It read:

> An unusual exhibition opened its doors today at the city's new Mendelssohn Complex. Entitled *Fanny and Felix Mendelssohn: How They Looked, How They Sounded*, it brings together the institution's sizable collection of the composers' music—much of it unknown—live concerts, and rare images, including three recently discovered portraits in Italy, where Fanny Mendelssohn Hensel spent a year from 1839 to 1840 with husband Wilhelm and their nine-year-old son Sebastian. Portraits of all three have been assembled along with important loans from Germany as well as images owned by the Complex.
>
> To top it all is the Mendelssohn Complex's very recently acquired remarkable oil portrait of Fanny at the age of forty-one, her last year of life. It clearly reveals the unfortunate physical heritage, never spoken of, that she received from her grandfather Moses Mendelssohn, famous philosopher of the Enlightenment and the first Jew received at Berlin's royal court. This spellbinding image equals, if not perhaps surpasses, New York's Jewish Museum's riveting 1832 oil portrait of Fanny in full fettle. A visit to both institutions is highly recommended. You will not be disappointed.

What the esteemed newspaper did not cover was mention of notable guests from abroad who were at the exhibition's opening night. They included Dr. Rachael Skylar, director of the Fanny and Felix Mendelssohn Museum in Hamburg; two direct descendants of Moses Mendelssohn, Salomon Mendelssohn of Hamburg and Nathan Bartholdy of Rome; Homer Capo, proprietor of the historic, portrait-lined Caffè Greco in Rome; and hotel owners Medad and Devora Finzi of Terracina. Involved in obtaining these European loans were Dr. Megan Crespi and her sister Tina Crespi, Dr. Mary Russell, and Richard Sire, all of Dallas. Introducing these prominent guests was the distinguished director of the Mendelssohn Complex, Jared Oppenheim.

It was an evening to remember.

READERS GUIDE

1. Retired professor Megan Crespi is on a flight from Dallas to Hamburg to research the nineteenth-century pianist/composer Fanny Mendelssohn Hensel for a forthcoming book she hopes will help establish Fanny's rightful place in music history. Who is Megan's travel companion and what is their itinerary?

2. Everyone Jared Oppenheim knows in New York tells him what a fabulous idea he has had to create a Mendelssohn Complex in The Big Apple. Who is Jared and has the realization of his plans turned out to be satisfying?

3. Enthusiastic neo-Nazi, Hamburg-based Michael Bormann comes to an important and possibly dangerous decision. What is it and what location does it involve?

4. Rachael Skylar, director of the recently founded Fanny and Felix Mendelssohn Museum in Hamburg-Neustadt, is especially proud of one of the institution's newest acquisitions. What is it and what is Skylar's background? With whom does she have an appointment on Wednesday?

5. On the second lap of their flight to Hamburg, Mary and Megan discuss Fanny Mendelssohn's works which number, without the latest discoveries, a good 466 compositions. Into what musical genres can they be divided? Once on the ground, where does the duo from Dallas go?

6. Michael Bormann is now planning three antisemitic demonstrations to take place on Wednesday. Where will these rallies take place and what "genius" idea has he had concerning the eye-catching image of the posters his followers will carry?

7. Megan and Mary visit the ninety-seven-year-old great-great-grandson of Fanny's younger sister, Rebecka. Where does Salomon Mendelssohn live and what does he look like? He tells them a fascinating fact about Fanny and her grandfather Moses of which they were totally unaware. What is it? And how does the visit conclude?

8. Jared's flight from New York to Hamburg arrives early Tuesday morning and he takes a cab to the outlying district of Altona where he checks into a hotel. Why has he chosen to stay in Altona rather than in Hamburg-Neustadt where the Fanny and Felix Mendelssohn Museum is located?

9. Rachael Skylar needs to find a way to explain to her anxious five-year-old son Davyd why his father—his Táto—has suddenly left them to return to the land of his birth, Ukraine. What is her inspired action?

10. Tuesday for Megan and Mary is without appointments but with plenty to do. Both want to see as much as they can at Hamburg's abundant museums. The choice is overwhelming, but they have narrowed their list down to three. What three institutions have they chosen and which do you find the most interesting?

11. Poster designs and images for Michael Bormann's three antisemitic demonstrations have mostly been finalized and are ready to be printed. What are the three museums that are targets for Bormann's hatred?

12. Visiting Hamburg's almost deserted Jewish Cemetery has affected Jared Oppenheim far more than he had anticipated. And for a very different reason from the heartrending one of paying respect to the dead. What horrible act does he witness?

13. Megan's old Hamburg friend Tönnies Helfer picks her and Mary up for dinner at a restaurant called Casa Mia. What are the three surprises he has in store for them?

14 Members of the Hamburg and Berlin neo-Nazi associations have gathered around their two leaders, Michael Bormann and Johannes von Bandtrop. Which composer's museum do the Brownshirts demonstrate in front of first?

15. What was the distraction Jared Oppenheim had sought in order to shake himself loose from the nightmare grip of his shocking experience at Hamburg's Jewish cemetery? What does he plan to visit on this new and better day, Wednesday? And what is another terrifying "distraction" awaiting him?

16. Richard Sire makes an abrupt and daring decision after his first full day in Berlin. Do we know what it is and what it affects?

17. Standing at his office window and looking down at the frothing scene below him, the director of the Mahler Museum is on the phone with the director of the Mendelssohn Museum. What terrible event is taking place? Two persons are detained by the police. One is released, the other is arrested. Who are they?

18. Early for their ten o'clock appointment with the director of the Fanny and Felix Mendelssohn Museum, Megan and Mary witness the end of a neo-Nazi demonstration in front of the museum. What do the two Americans talk about with Rachael Skylar and what particular exhibition pieces attract their attention? Why is a Richard Wagner document on display?

19. Arriving at Hamburg's Museum of History, Megan and Mary could see smashed menorahs on the ground testifying that the Brownshirts had carried out their demonstration before this museum as well. What specific exhibitions do the two Americans wish to visit and what happens as they read a plaque about the history of Jews in Hamburg?

20. Because of the arrest of their leader Michael Bormann, the inner circle of Hamburg's neo-Nazi organization chooses to replace him with someone suggested by Berlin's neo-Nazi chief Johannes von Bandtrop. Whom does he recommend?

21. After making each other's acquaintances at the Mendelssohn Museum, Jared suggests Megan and Mary have dinner with him at a nearby restaurant. After dinner what role does an adjacent park play, thanks to Jared's cellphone?

22. On Thursday morning a demoralized Hamburg group of neo-Nazis meet with and nominate Bandtrop's Berlin lieutenant as their proxy leader. Who is this new leader?

23. The bodies had been left in the middle of the highway. Heavy black tires had been dragged on top of them in an effort to conceal the dead from above. Someone is there photographing the corpses. Do we suspect who this is and where this is happening?

24. Aboard their morning flight from Hamburg to Berlin, Mary and Megan's conversation turns from Fanny Mendelssohn to Mary's worry over Richard Sire, whom she has not been able to contact by phone for the past three days. What interesting visit do the two women make after checking into their Berlin hotel and what do they learn?

25. Rachael Skylar is in tears in her museum office when Jared encounters her. What has upset her so and is Jared able to be of help?

26. As they eat lunch, Mary and Megan are still discussing Sire's bold, sudden decision to return to Ukraine. They have a Mendelssohn-related building to visit next and in the evening they will attend one of Berlin's most famous theaters. What are they going to see?

27. Barbara Badubrecht has set a Hamburg Zoom conference for nine o'clock Friday. What is her message to the many neo-Nazis of Hamburg?

28. On his flight to Berlin, what is Jared thinking about the emergency he participated in the night before? Does he like his Berlin Hotel Zoo and where does he go after checking in there? The Fanny and Felix Trio spend the morning in two different cemeteries. What do they visit there and what unusual restaurant do they have lunch at afterward? The afternoon is spent in Berlin's extraordinary new Jewish Museum. Who is the architect and what special exhibition has just opened? The museum visitors are taken aback by an announcement suddenly announced over the PA. What is it?

29. In Berlin an irate Johannes von Bandtrop, working from home, is on the phone with Barbara Badubrecht in Hamburg. What has upset him? Does Badubrecht have anything to do with this?

30. Still stunned by news of the desecration of Moses Mendelssohn's gravestone, the F & F Trio are at Jared's hotel rooftop bar. Their conversation moves from the phenomenon of yawning to Megan's former colleague, a composer and conductor. Who is he and what are his accomplishments? What new work by him will the Trio attend tomorrow evening?

31. Fifteen-year-old Helmut von Bandtrop, son of Berlin's neo-Nazi leader Johannes von Bandtrop, has done something he is sure will make his father happy and proud of him. Is he?

32. In Hamburg that evening an irritated Barbara Badubrecht sends a new directive to her neo-Nazi group. Why is she irritated and what is her message?

33. Berlin's Bandtrop is in need of something soothing and uplifting after learning that his own son vandalized the Moses Mendelssohn tombstone, thus alerting police and endangering the planned demonstrations for tomorrow. To soothe himself he turns to quotations he has written down from Richard Wagner's essay entitled "Jewishness in Music." What is Wagner's point of view concerning Jews? Is there validity to his critique?

34. Homer Wesselmann of Hamburg has certainly arrived in Berlin at the right time that Friday afternoon. Who is he, with whom has he been in contact, and why has he come to Berlin early?

35. Saturday morning finds the F & F Trio eager to execute Megan's carefully researched plan to visit the historic Mendelssohn home at Leipzigerstrasse 3, where Fanny's famous Sunday matinees and soirées were performed over a period of some twenty years. Is their visit successful?

36. Simon Saragon, Megan's composer colleague from Dallas, is on his way to Prenzlauer Berg to meet with conductor Nathaniel Darenborne for a private morning rehearsal of his *A Jewish Requiem* before its performance that evening at the historic Rykestrasse Synagogue. What at first hinders him from joining the maestro?

37. Both Bandtrop and Badubrecht will be at the Berlin demonstration site in person to witness what was going to be a potent and apropos act of condemnation this evening. Do we know where this site is?

38. Hamburg's Homer Wesselmann is spending his full day in Berlin as a tourist, visiting offbeat sites that interest him. What places does he visit and where and what does the culmination of his unusual touring offer?

39. At the Rykestrasse Synagogue Simon Saragon is in the midst of listening to the rehearsal of his *Requiem*. What are his reactions and thoughts?

40. Back at the Bristol Hotel the F & F Trio plan to play through Fanny's Rome-inspired piano piece. What is the name of the twelve-part piece and are they able to play it? What is the Museum Island and by what famous work of art is Jared completely overwhelmed?

41. Barbara Badubrecht has arrived in Berlin in time for dinner with the von Bandtrops at their home. What fascinating square does their apartment overlook and after whom was the square named?

42. In Hotel Zoo's fancy Grace Restaurant the F & F Trio are in jovial spirits and are entranced by the varied European-Asian menu. What else attracts their attention?

43. Simon Saragon and Nathaniel Darenborne are having dinner and a private preconcert discussion before the big performance this evening. What happens when Nathaniel's cellphone rings?

44. An emergency electrician arrives to check out the fuse box controlling the synagogue's ceiling lighting. Is it of interest for us to know the color of his eyes? What is taking place on the street in front of the synagogue and which concertgoers do we know enter the building?

45. We learn where in the Rykestrasse Synagogue certain characters we have met are seated. Who are they and in which parts of the building are they sitting? The *A Jewish Requiem* begins. How do some audience members receive the music texts? Which section in particular agitates one listener into action and what unthinkable thing happens next?

46. Amid the bedlam inside the synagogue with its horrible discoveries, Maestro Nathaniel Darenborne is given one piece of good news. What is it?

47. Sunday morning brings a bouquet of news, good and bad, to the F & F Trio. What do they learn?

48. One individual and one set of friends decide to take a cruise to Potsdam and Sanssouci. Who are they and which cruise do they all happen to take? Does anything occur on board because of this? What makes Sanssouci so different from other palaces? Two incidents take place, one on the steps toward it, the other within the building itself. What are they?

49. Richard Sire's attempt Saturday morning to reach Poland's Rzeszów Jasionka Airport had met with success because of his having having "tipped" two guards at the Ukraine border. Before his flight

to Berlin he makes two phone calls. To whom are they and what is discussed?

50. Back from their Sanssouci cruise the F & F Trio have a quick bite to eat at a nearby Burger King, then head back to their hotels. Will Jared remain in Germany and why is Mary in such a hurry?

51. Jared and Megan have agreed not to make any afternoon plans together after Mary leaves them to meet Sire at the airport. What does Megan do with her afternoon and why does the time pass so quickly?

52. That afternoon Jared needs to let off steam. But how? Where to go? The answer comes to him immediately: Berlin's Schöneberg district. What is this district famous for and what happens after Jared arrives there?

53. As Mary and Sire exit their Peking City restaurant, they pause to take in an unusual mini-exhibition in front of Galerie Gabor. What is the exhibition and what is its symbolism? Once they are inside the gallery, what treat awaits them?

54. Monday morning sees a breakfast gathering of Sire and the F & F Trio. Glancing at the caller ID when his phone suddenly rings, Jared answers immediately, turning away from his tablemates. When the call is over, what expression is on his face and what is his news? Good or bad?

55. By noon Megan, Mary, and Sire are sitting in a lounge of the Berlin Brandenburg International Airport waiting for their 2:55 p.m. Lufthansa flight via Munich to Rome's Leonardo da Vinci Fiumicino Airport with arrival at 6:25 p.m. What are the fascinating things they discuss? Who are some of the famous people who have visited the Caffè Greco and where is it? And what is the composition by Fanny that Megan describes at length?

56. New York-bound Jared arrives at the new Berlin International airport for his 5:30 overnight flight to JFK. He contemplates the

dreadful incident that occurred that afternoon in Berlin and is of two minds about it: a sense of disgust and a revengeful approval. What was the terrible incident?

57. On their flight to Rome the reunited couple Mary and Sire chat happily while Megan is glued to the two paperbacks she's brought with her. What are they and what does she find of such interest that she reads it aloud to them?

58. After their plane arrives in Rome Monday evening, what do Megan, Tina, Mary, and Sire decide to do?

59. Jared's flight arrives on time at JFK at 10:05 Tuesday morning. What is the first thing he does? And what is the mood of his staff when he arrives at the Mendelssohn Complex office? How does he end up feeling?

60. Early that same morning in Rome the reunited Crespi sisters are happily planning their day's itinerary over breakfast as they sit at a small table on the rooftop terrace of their hotel. What and where is their famous hotel and what historic site would Megan like to visit first?

61. Although Sire doesn't like doing touristy things in Rome, Mary persuades him to go with her to one specific, well-visited entity so they can reenact a famous movie scene. What is the object and what is the film?

62. Who is Nathan Bartholdy and why is he irritated at Megan whom he has never met?

63. As the Crespi sisters leave the Keats-Shelley Museum, Megan's phone rings incessantly. It is verbose Nathan Bartholdy of Rome, who uses every argument to persuade Megan to examine his so-called portrait of Fanny Mendelssohn in person. How does she react and how does a Maltese dog bring the sisters closer together?

64. When Mary asks Sire what he'd like to do that is "non-touristy"

in Rome, his immediate answer takes her by surprise. What is it and what do they do about it? And what, in their opinion, is the novel form of transportation available?

65. Nathan Bartholdy angrily dismisses his employee, painter Giorgio Complice, after asking him to describe what he sees in the framed painting above his desk. Do we have any idea why?

66. Tina and Megan visit Rome's Protestant Cemetery. What other names is it known by? Do they find the graves they're looking for and what is the "something rich and strange" they come upon? Mary and Sire are searching for the Crespi sisters in the cemetery. Do they find them?

67. "My third cousin, you say?" Who says this to whom, and how does this surprise telephone call from Hamburg to Rome conclude?

68. Chubby, genial, middle-aged Alessandro Divitore is the first to have arrived at Antico Caffè Greco. Who is he and by whom is he soon joined? What suddenly interrupts all conversation at the café?

69. The five friends are ready for something calming after the Caffè Greco catastrophe. They also wish somehow for a closeness to Jewish history in Rome. What is their solution? In what context does the 1956 film *The Ten Commandments* come up during dinner?

70. Nathan Bartholdy of Rome still cannot believe what he told his third cousin, Salomon Mendelssohn of Hamburg. What had he said and do we understand why he is upset?

71. That evening after simpatico Alessandro has taken his leave and the Quintet is a Quartet again, Mary has an unusual but welcome invitation for her friends. What is it and where does it take place?

72. It is August 15 in Italy. Why is this a special date? To where and why have Mary, Sire, and Tina departed Rome by car at eight o'clock this Wednesday morning? And what appointment does Megan have

at 11 a.m. in Rome? Where is it and what astounding discovery does she make?

73. Nathan's cleaning lady Signora Ursula Ladro complains about him to her husband Carlo. What does she propose they do and when?

74. The Naples battalion is back and meets up with Megan in Rome at eight o'clock. Where do they head for dinner and why? Catchup conversation about their day moves to Megan's activities and she describes her extraordinary discovery at Nathan Bartholdy's apartment. But Sire becomes worried and questions her relentlessly. What concerns Sire and how does Megan respond?

75. During the wee hours of the night Ursula and Carlo Ladro carry out their plan. What is the plan and are they successful?

76. In New York Jared is suddenly awakened by a telephone call at the ungodly hour of six in the morning. Who is it and what does he learn that causes him to make a reservation for the next flight to Rome?

77. Jared calls Megan back with disappointing news. What is it? What are the new logistics? What role will euros play?

78. The Rome Quartet reunite and visit the Villa Medici grounds in the afternoon. Why? Their big event for the evening is attending Giuseppe Verdi's early opera *Nabucco*. At what unusual venue will it be presented and for what reason has Megan chosen this particular opera?

79. Rome's chief of police still continues to keep Alessandro Divitore apprised of certain events. What do they discuss this time and what does the police chief's surname mean in English?

80. What inspiring event is the Rome Quartet attending at the Baths of Caracalla this evening? Does anything unusual occur?

81. A drugged Nathan Bartholdy does not wake up until ten that Friday morning. What are the horrifying two things he discovers?

82. Over a late, relaxed breakfast at their hotel roof restaurant the Crespi sisters are discussing the wild events of the previous evening. What happens when Megan answers her throbbing cellphone? Who is calling so urgently?

83. On his flight from New York to Rome, Jared is studying several high quality images of the two Oppenheim portraits of Fanny Mendelssohn Hensel for comparison purposes. How do the two images differ?

84. In their haste to carry out the theft of Signor Bartholdy's valuable painting, the Ladro couple have neglected to plan out what they would do next. What worries them now in particular?

85. Tina goes her separate way from Megan, Mary, and Sire today. Where is she off to with such pleasure and what concert do the other three attend at the Ottorino Respighi School of Music?

86. On his flight to Rome, Jared is excited about meeting the nonagenarian Nathan Bartholdy. Why?

87. What has so concerned Rome's Chief of Police Cesari Cacciatore that he needs to share it with his good friend Alessandro Divitore?

88. Jared has linked up with Megan and they visit Nathan Bartholdy in his apartment where Jared is able to examine and determine the authenticity of Oppenheim's portrait of the older Fanny. What is the extraordinary outcome of this meeting? Does Megan receive anything? And what has she brought along for the three of them?

89. When Carlo Ladro arrives home from work that evening, he is horrified by what Ursula has done, or rather tried to do. He corrects the situation but is taken by total surprise as to what his wife demands they do next. What is it?

90. After taking their leave of Nathan Bartholdy, Jared and Megan share the same worry concerning the old man. What is it and what do they do about it?

91. "'I should have been as frolicsome as a rabbit, if you had been there too,'" Megan reads aloud. Who has written this and what makes it such a treasure?

92. Vittorio Trovato is parked in his black, two-door Fiat 500 across the street from Via Portico d'Ottavia 72. What does he see that concerns him?

93. Ursula and Carlo Ladro have made their way into Nathan Bartholdy's apartment again. What do they plan to do there and are they successful?

94. Tina, Megan, and Jared are having a highly unusual conversation over breakfast. They discuss the small town on a cliff that Mary and Sire are off to visit, and Jared enjoys shocking the Crespi sisters with a description of what the unique and definitely surprising religious relic once hidden there was. What is it? After Tina leaves, Jared and Megan discuss two very different things. What are they? What do we learn about their plans for the day?

95. When Nathan Bartholdy calls Megan, what surprising thing does he learn from her? And what surprise does Jared have for her as they meet to go on their two tourist errands? They spend several hours at the first site. What is Rinascente and would we like to visit it as well?

96. Cesari Cacciatore, Rome's chief of police, calls his buddy Alessandro Divitore. What does he want to discuss with him and how does Alessandro's former professor in America, Megan Crespi, figure into the conversation?

97. What is the first thing Megan and Jared do upon entering the historic Caffè Greco after their very full morning at Rinascente? And why is the old café so famous? Who is the mustached man "reading" a newspaper nearby? Jared makes an extraordinary discovery

concerning one of the many portraits on the café's walls. What is it? And what is the final event Jared and Megan are involved in at the suddenly disrupted café?

98. Tullio Guido drives his enchanted guest Tina Crespi to the old Etruscan town of Cerveteri some thirty miles northwest of Rome. What does she see and admire there and at the nearby museum in the Ruspoli Castle?

99. Back at the Caffè Greco calm reigns again and the exciting agreement between the proprietor and Jared concerning his portrait discovery fills all involved parties with joy. What esoteric feature about it does Megan point out to her friends? And what is the name of their meeting point with the rest of the Rome Quintet? Is it very far away?

100. When Arlotto Zitto calls his commander at OAR to report the goings-on at Caffè Greco, he receives not praise but admonishment. What and where is the new assignment he is given?

101. Tina is the first to arrive at the Rome Quintet's meeting place. What is it and can you describe it? Three exciting accounts of their adventures follow: Tina's, Megan and Jared's, and Mary and Sire's. What are they?

102. Megan, Tina, Mary, and Sire decide to spend most of Sunday touring the Sistine Chapel and St. Peter's. They book a special "skip-the-line" tour and are guided by an informative, no-nonsense guide named Piacevole. Is she? The tour includes the papal grottoes, and afterward a "church opera concert" and dinner. How many women are buried in St. Peter's? Who and where are they? What aspect of the tour did you enjoy the most?

103. Jared's visit to Hamburg to see Rachael Skylar and her family on Sunday has proven successful and surprising. Why?

104. Next on the Rome Quartet's tour is a church opera concert in the Chiesa Evangelica Valdese. What sort of music was performed and where did the tour take them afterward?

105. It's Monday—their final day in Italy—and the reassembled Rome Quintet is driving down south to the town Fanny and her family stayed in, Terracina on the coast. When they have lunch there at the grand Hotel Palace, they make an extraordinary discovery. What is it? After they reveal what it is to the genial hotel owners, steps are taken to allow Jared to take it to America temporarily. Our Rome Quintet is then transported in the hotel's power yacht to the nearby and fascinating island of Ponza, inhabited since neolithic times. The last spot they visit is the "White Gymnasium" high above the harbor. What unlikely person spots them as they stand in front of it and why are their lives suddenly threatened? Does help come, and if so, in what form? Do we think we might ever like to visit Fanny Mendelssohn's Terracina?

www.ingramcontent.com/pod-product-compliance
Lightning Source LLC
Chambersburg PA
CBHW010747310726
48980CB00004B/396

* 9 7 8 1 6 3 2 9 3 6 5 9 2 *